How to Fake a Husband

A Small Town, Fake Marriage Romance

BELLA RIVERS

Copyright © 2025 by Bella Rivers

All rights reserved.

This book is a work of fiction. Names, characters, places and events are the product of the author's imagination. Any resemblance to actual persons, living or dead, events, or places, is purely coincidental.

No portion of this book may be reproduced in any form without written permission from the publisher or author, except for the use of brief quotations in a book review and as otherwise permitted by U.S. copyright law.

ISBN (digital): 978-1-962627-46-7

ISBN (illustrated cover): 978-1-962627-47-4

Developmental editing: Angela James

Copyediting/Proofreading: Grace Wynter, The Writer's Station

Final Review: Teresa Beeman, Next Chapter Editing

Cover design:

Illustrated cover: Camila Grivicich

Floral cover: Kari March

Contents

1. Noah   1
2. Willow   9
3. Noah   18
4. Willow   23
5. Willow   33
6. Willow   40
7. Noah   48
8. Willow   56
9. Noah   61
10. Willow   69
11. Noah   77
12. Willow   85
13. Willow   92
14. Willow   97

15.	Noah	108
16.	Willow	113
17.	Noah	123
18.	Willow	133
19.	Noah	138
20.	Willow	147
21.	Noah	160
22.	Willow	164
23.	Noah	172
24.	Willow	176
25.	Noah	180
26.	Willow	184
27.	Noah	191
28.	Willow	199
29.	Noah	207
30.	Willow	212
31.	Noah	220
32.	Noah	224
33.	Willow	232
34.	Noah	240
35.	Willow	243
36.	Willow	250
37.	Noah	260
38.	Willow	264

39.	Noah	269
40.	Willow	271
41.	Willow	278
42.	Noah	290
43.	Noah	299
44.	Willow	306
45.	Noah	316
46.	Willow	322
47.	Willow	327
48.	Willow	333
49.	Lilyvale	342
50.	Noah	345
51.	Willow	350
52.	Noah	354
53.	Willow	365
54.	Noah	375
55.	Willow	382
Epilogue		385
Acknowledgments		393
About the author		395

Chapter One

Noah

"I'm sorry, Noah. I didn't see it coming. Nobody did." My lawyer's voice is tinny in my earpiece, yet it sucker-punches me. "You've got four months left."

I take a deep breath and nudge my glasses back up, swallowing the expletives she doesn't deserve. Messenger and all that.

Although Tamberly's the lawyer who assured me we had a 99 percent chance of winning in court, so maybe she needs to feel the pain?

But that's not who I am. Instead, I keep it all in, my stomach twisting in agony, my head pounding, as I focus my gaze outside my bedroom window. On the gardens of Lilyvale, our family home, and on Emerald Creek, the town our ancestors founded—everything we're about to lose.

"They don't care that it violates my... rights? Or something?" I bite back. We've had this discussion countless times. The family trust requiring me to marry by a certain age is antiquated at best. It should be dismissed as the insulting remnant of a time when deeds were written with a pen dipped in ink.

We challenged it after Dad passed. Losing probate stung, but the appeal looked solid. I wasn't worried.

"I'm assuming none of your siblings are married or about to be?" Tamberly continues in a shaky voice. When I merely grunt, she adds, "I'm taking this to the Vermont Supreme Court, file a stay..." Her words blur into a buzzing in my ears.

My disbelief leaves place to something akin to panic. It's too late for more legal action. Four months from now, when I turn thirty-two unmarried, our home, the orchards, the plumbing business—everything the Callaways own—will be controlled by Dad's third wife. His gold-digging widow.

Knowing her, everything will be sold off to the highest bidder by Christmas, the cash financing her lavish lifestyle far away from Emerald Creek.

And the store I run, our family's pride, will belong to the town, which probably seemed like a good idea on paper decades ago, but not in the age of minimarts.

Because not a month goes by that a developer doesn't offer us a fortune for Lilyvale and its surrounding gardens, bulldozers at the ready to erase our childhood home and make place for cookie-cutter vacation rentals. Not a week ends that a chain hasn't approached us to turn the store into its umpteenth glass-and-metal, in-your-face ugliness stocked with mass-produced shit and self-checkout horror stations in the heart of our historic town.

I can almost see Gail's drool hitting the floor as the smell of our impending blood awakens her true instincts.

"Noah?" my younger sister, Lane, calls from the hallway.

I interrupt Tamberly. "Any publicity on this yet?" I ask in a hushed tone. I've managed to keep my siblings in the dark so they can live their lives without pressure. I don't need this to blow up now. Not until I've tried everything.

I'm the eldest by far. Griff was born when I was seven, Beck when I was nine, and Lane when I was ten. I've always been their protector—part nature, part the way life shaped me. When my birth mother walked out, it was just Dad and me, and I grew up faster than my years. Then Dad met the woman I came to call Mom, and life was sweet—until she died way too young, and Dad nearly lost his mind. By then, both parents had praised how protective I was, reminding me that with age came responsibility. So when it all fell apart, I stepped up and parented my siblings.

That shit that's about to hit us? It's mine alone to carry.

"A good chunk of the details were filed under seal, and so far, nobody seems interested," Tamberly answers, offering me a shred of reassurance.

She offers to discuss our options, but before I can lash out that these are insultingly narrow, the grandfather clock in the dining room starts striking. Slow yet inexorable, it reminds me that life goes on for others, and I need to show up. "I'm actually going to a wedding," I say as I button my shirt, the irony not lost on me. "Not mine," I add bitterly before ending the call.

I glance at my open door as impatient footsteps resonate down the hallway.

Lane barges into my bedroom. "Who was that?" she asks as she presses a deep red tie against my shirt.

"No one," I answer with a forced smile.

She rolls her eyes playfully. "Oooh... something you're not telling me?"

Where do I start? "Nothing like that, no." *I wish.* "It was the lawyer."

"Boring." Smoothing the tie with the back of her hand, she says, "This one was Dad's. He'd want you to wear it. Look good for the town."

Today is the wedding of the town's only mechanic and our pastry chef, with the whole town invited to celebrate Colton and Kiara. I'd been looking forward to it—until five minutes ago.

"What did she want? Her name's Tamberly, right?" Lane squints at me. "You seem worried."

I shrug for Lane's benefit. "Nothing. Just... some tax shit."

"Let that go for today," she tells me. "Stop grinding your teeth, and show your dimples."

I focus my gaze on my reflection in the mirror as I try to adjust the tie. "Show my what now?"

She snorts. "Put a smile on that handsome face of yours."

Oh, that. I stretch my mouth for my sister's benefit.

"You know what Dad used to say," Lane continues. She comes to my rescue as I struggle tying the knot around my neck. "Appearances might not be everything, but they're darn close."

"What's that supposed to mean?"

Lane tilts her head like I'm a little slow. "It means it's important how people perceive you. Also, you're in the wedding party, and I know they said no dress code, but that's bull. It's your job to look good up there with them. So you make *them* look good." She tugs on the tie, tightening the noose around my neck.

My tie adjusted, I walk to the open window and force a deep breath down my lungs.

Lane joins me. "Isn't it gorgeous?" she sighs. Our hometown shines in all its understated beauty today, a cruel reminder of everything my family is about to lose.

"Our ancestors knew what they were doing when they built Lilyvale right here," she continues, her words bruising me further. She whips out her phone, turns it to video mode, and starts narrating like the journalist she wants to become. "Situated at the edge of the Northeast Kingdom in Vermont, Emerald Creek is nestled in a bend of the eponymous river. Centered around a village of Federalist buildings, Georgian and Victorian homes, a white steeple church, a Green, and tree-lined streets, the town sprawls over acres and acres of farmland, pastures, and woodlands, all the way and including Emerald Lake and its upscale resort." She turns her phone off.

"What was that?" Another wave of panic hits me. If Lane is writing about Emerald Creek, her timing sucks.

"Nothing, just can't help myself." Taking a deep breath, she yells, "Beck! Time to go!"

Her Irish twin exits the barn he turned into his living quarters as I close the windows. How will I tell him that his whole universe is about to fall apart? He and I are the only ones to have stayed in Emerald Creek, and this town is our world. Just this morning, Beck was telling me about his ideas to start a landscaping business, the clients he's approached, the people he wants to hire. Like me, he breathes and lives this town.

Heartbroken for him, I follow Lane downstairs right in time to see a car I don't recognize pull up the driveway.

If this is another realtor, I might actually punch them.

But as I step out the door, Lane screeches, "Griiiiiff!" and throws herself into the arms of the bearded man who extricates himself from his car.

"Well look who decided to show up," Beck mumbles, fists on his hips as he settles next to me in a wide-legged stance. "Did you know about this?"

"Nuh-uh." Any other time, I would've been pissed that Griff didn't bother to call from the road. Today? I can hardly give anyone lessons in family etiquette.

Beck shrugs. "I guess it's his home too."

Not for long. I can't help but check the passenger seat. *Empty.* Shit.

Needing a mental breather, I glance at my youngest brother. "You clean up well."

He runs his gaze up and down me. "Runs in the family." He hops down a couple of steps, to Griff who's locking his car. "Yo! You'll unload later, it's time to go."

I have to give it to Griff. He does look happy to see us. Beck and I each get a warm hug, and his smile extends to his eyes.

"I can't stay the night," he informs us.

Beck visually deflates.

"Boo," Lane whines, then jumps. "Selfie!" She places herself in front of Griff, frames Lilyvale behind us, and snaps the first photo of the four of us since... maybe a decade?

"We should get going," she says after she's taken half a dozen shots.

We fall into step with her.

"Closed today?" Griff asks as we walk past the family store.

I nod. "Gave everyone the day off." I worked alone this morning in case someone had an emergency. From diapers to animal feed to our deli counter and greeting cards, we've been supplying the town with everything they might need for the past century and a half.

As we turn onto The Green, the four of us naturally line side by side. Lane links her arms with Griff and me. "I almost forgot the feeling of walking with some of the best-looking men around," she says as we return the smiles and greetings of the townspeople, all headed in the same direction.

"Nah, that's all me," Beck says, shoving his hands in his pockets.

I don't have the heart or energy to rib him for his customary arrogance. Or to point out that half the glances his way are wary, even if his troublemaker years are behind us.

By the time we reach the park where the wedding is set up, Griff, Beck, and Lane have scattered to meet up with their friends. I take this moment alone to wrangle the messed-up thoughts in my head, organize them in their little boxes, and let that shit go for today. There's guilt, for sure. But it's the powerlessness that's close to enraging.

Lane is right though, appearances are important, and supposedly there's something I can do about my dimples that's not a total fuck-up.

I'm drawn to a glint of blue-streaked hair lifting in the breeze. Cassandra, who used to babysit me before Dad married Mom, was always a calming presence in my life. Rumor is she's witchy, and that may be true. Right now she seems lost in contemplation of the whole town slowly gathering to celebrate the wedding she'll be officiating.

Sensing my arrival, she turns around and opens her arms to take me in an affectionate hug. "What are we going to do with you?" she asks in my neck.

Not what I expected, but hell.

She's right.

"You'll figure it out," she says when she lets me go.

I struggle to meet her gaze, but when I do, all I find is understanding. My glasses fog up a little.

I've never talked about the Callaway trust with her, but she's acting like she knows.

"On a lighter note, who let you walk out of your house wearing this?" She pulls on the tie Lane chose for me.

"What's wrong with it? It belonged to Dad."

She purses her lips in a sad smile. "Didn't mean it that way, honey. But..." Her swift fingers loosen the noose around my neck. "This isn't your look. Bend your head for me." Taking my tie off, she rolls it carefully into a purple canvas bag, next to her officiant guide.

A small strip of blue silk shimmers in her fingers as she pushes my jacket off my shoulders and lifts my shirt collar.

I trust Cassandra on a lot of things, but I'm kind of on the fence about this one. "A bow tie, seriously? Like the glasses aren't enough."

Her focus is now on my throat area, and she pushes my chin up. "Trust me." Cassandra owns a clothing shop in town. To be honest, I'm told it's mainly lingerie, not that I've ever been inside. Point is, it's possible she might be a little more knowledgeable about fashion than Lane. *Or not.* But I know better than to challenge her decision right now.

Once she's done, she folds my shirt collar down, pulls my jacket back in place, then takes a step back. "Much, much better," she says, reaching over to give the bow tie a perfunctory tug. "*Now* you're ready."

Ready?

I have four months to fix the mess we're in, and there's only one way I can think of.

I've never felt so *not* ready.

Chapter Two

Willow

"You're gorgeous," Kiara tells me as I enter her pastry delivery van turned bridal suite for the day. This was a stroke of genius from yours truly, delivering on my maid of honor duty to make the wedding as comfortable as possible for my best friend. The execution, though, was entirely Colton's, and he did a magnificent job of temporarily replacing the fridges and shelves with comfy chairs.

"Shut up," I joke, feeling myself blush. "It's from Goodwill," I lie.

"So? You're still gorgeous in it."

I laugh and do a little twirl in the small space. "I need to look good for you."

"Sexy too," she says. The light blue dress has a bare back, which was an immediate draw to me. It's not every day I get to dress up.

"But you're a bad liar," she adds, reaching under my arm to pull out the price tag.

"Oh shit." I thought I'd sewn the motherfucker securely inside. "Help me out, will you? There's stuff in the bride's kit I got you."

She pulls out a small pair of scissors.

"No!" I lower my arm and reach for a safety pin. "I'm not keeping the dress," I explain.

She snorts. "Seriously?"

There are so many things that can go wrong, from food, wine, or even grass stains on the dress to sweat marks on the price tag. "It's worth trying." I raise my arm. "Tuck it in and pin it in place, please?"

"I love your hair," she says as she secures the price tag inside the dress. Kiara is like that. She had her shitty times too, and she knows not to dwell on those. I don't want her pity and I don't need financial help. I just need her to pin the stupid tag inside the dress and talk to me about something else. "Did Fabrizio do it?" she continues, talking about my hair.

Why would I splurge on a hairdresser if I can't afford a dress? Kiara is just being nice, complimenting my updo. "Fabrizio gave me a tutorial a while back, but I did it myself," I answer. Six French braids gather at the nape of my neck in a loose bun, a few soft tendrils curling free to frame my face.

But enough about me. My eyes are now adjusted to the van's dim lighting. "Wow," I say as I take Kiara in. "Just wow." I saw her dress already, actually went with her to choose it, as well as for the fittings, but today, Kiara radiates with a glow that's just surreal. Her hair and makeup enhance her pixie cut and thin features in a way that's uniquely her but also more... subdued than her usual self. As if she didn't need the artifice anymore, the armor of over-the-top smoky eyes and excessively gelled hair.

The energy she emanates comes from within, and it's something so beautiful to witness, it brings tears to my eyes. "Marriage suits you," I say.

I place my bridesmaid's contribution on the small picnic table set in the middle of her van, between two large armchairs wrangled in here by her future husband just for the occasion. "Electrolytes, nuts, and a banana for you. Coke and chips for your uncle Bill, who'll be here any minute—I just saw him park. Napkins. Band-Aids. What else do you need?"

"I have everything I need," she says, lifting the blinds an inch to peek outside the van. Glancing over her shoulder, I smile at the sight of our small town gathered to celebrate the new couple. To the left, the closest covered bridge shimmers with fairy lights, still barely visible in the afternoon sun. To the right, party tents are lined with bistro lights, and the echoes of laughter, shrieking children, and barking dogs drift up to us. "Best place on earth," I murmur.

"Got that right," Kiara says. "You should go have fun," she adds. "I'm all set here, gonna just chill and wait for Uncle Bill to walk me down the aisle." She rummages through the bag of goodies and pulls out a bottle. "What's this?"

"Haley's bubbly. Wouldn't be a party without it."

"I'll keep it for later," she says, "or I'll yawn through the ceremony."

"I doubt you would," I say, laughing.

"D'you want some? We could totally open it now."

I shake my head. "I need to go pick up Mom."

Mom is battling cancer, and at her mention, Kiara's smile stretches downward. "How is she doing?"

I shrug. "She's got her ups and downs." Hopefully today's wedding will help her mood, although the fact that we're fighting the insurance company is weighing heavily on her. I keep telling her it's only money, but she's literally making herself sick with worry.

"Tell her to come sit in here if she needs to. It's comfy, and Uncle Bill will distract her."

"Thanks, that's sweet of you," I answer, knowing Mom won't want to impose like that.

"Hey, Willow," Kiara adds as I open the door to leave.

"Yeah?"

She winks at me. "Keep an open mind."

I shake my head and shut the door with a smile. Since I orchestrated Kiara and Colton finally getting together, Kiara decided it was her mission to find someone for me.

And she's not talking about an inconsequential fling. But although I believe with all my soul that Kiara and Colton were meant to be together, theirs is a rare story.

Growing up, I saw how marriage could be a trap, especially for women, and I vowed never to fall for it.

I find Mom reading a romance in what she calls her Lazy Girl, a pink recliner with frilly ruffles I got her for her birthday two years ago. The armrests and headrest are protected with crochet overlays she made herself and washes weekly. Mom is a neat freak, and I take after her.

I lean over her to kiss her cheek, then run a finger gently along her upper lip to wipe away a smudge of lipstick. If there's an upside to her illness, it's that our relationship has improved, and I'm making a conscious effort to create these small moments of deeper connection. "You look beautiful, Mom." She's wearing her prettiest dress and comfy platform shoes, and her head is wrapped in one of the silk scarves Cassandra gave her when she started chemo. "Are you ready?" I glance at the mail on the Formica table. Three envelopes, neatly sliced open, with soft blue logos in the upper left corner and angry red stamps across.

Hospital bills.

"As ready as I'll ever be," she says, righting the chair and standing. She's almost as tall as me, but she's gotten frail. I had to bring her dress down a size, and still it hangs loosely on her frame. She must have lost at least five pounds since I took the dress in for her last week. "Let me use the bathroom real quick." She pauses and turns to me, pointing to the bills with her chin. "Don't worry about these. Tonight is for fun. Monday will come soon enough."

I toy with the bills, knowing she just wants to protect me. She wasn't the best provider when I was little. But she did what she could. I know she did. The fact that life was a bitch to her isn't on her. She always loved me, even if she didn't always know how to show me, or protect me, or provide for me in the classic way of a mom.

I pretend to wait for her in the car, but really it's to hide the bills in the glove compartment. We'll argue about those for the sake of it on Monday when she finds out, or maybe tomorrow. But like she said, tonight is for fun.

"Kiara said you should go rest in her van if you need to. It's nice and comfy," I say as we drive away from her mobile home.

"The Barbie van?"

I laugh at her accurate description. "Her Uncle Bill is walking her down the aisle. He's fun. And really nice. Maybe I'll introduce you."

She grunts. Mom's history with men is a pain point in our relationship, but I'm trying to move us beyond that. "Why don't you focus on finding a nice man yourself. I wouldn't mind grandbabies, you know."

I nearly choke at her words. "Uh... Mom?"

"What? You're not getting any younger."

The smile and initial laughter of my surprise reaction die quickly in my throat as images of Mom's only husband flash in front of my eyes. I could never trust a man with my life the way she did.

And that's what marriage is: a complete abandonment of one's self, one's liberty, potentially one's life, to another person with more power.

I can't tell her this, but she's the reason I'll never marry, or even have a steady relationship.

"Ugh, of course *these* people are here. They're always everywhere, aren't they?" she mumbles, frowning in the direction of Noah Callaway, the only man who makes my heart skip a beat.

"Oh my, what a beautiful setting." As we reach the park, her mood swing is easy to follow: the setting is simply spectacular.

The river glistens under the sun, a flock of birds rises from a tree, twirling in the air before diving beyond the hill. All the town is slowly gathering on the chairs, and I spot several of Mom's friends.

"Why don't I drop you up here, and I'll go park behind town hall," I say.

"Oh, there's Aunt Angela. I'll walk with her," she says, pointing to my grandmother's sister.

Mom calls her Aunt Angela, but to everyone else including me, she's Ms. Angela, Emerald Creek's retired third-grade teacher, current owner of a bed-and-breakfast, secretary of the select board (our governing body), self-appointed unpaid employee of the stores she deems need her help, and most active member on ECHoes, our own social media (aka gossip central).

Among other things.

Oh and today, she's playing the part of wedding coordinator.

By the time I park and get back to the tent, she's dispensing the last instructions. Everyone seems to be here, from little Skye in an adorable light pink tutu dress all the way to... Noah Callaway, looking amazingly handsome in a suit and bow tie. My stomach does a little happy flip again, as it always does when it comes to Noah, but I quickly chastise myself.

Noah is way out of my league, which is probably the only reason I allowed myself to hold a torch for him for years. Nothing was ever going to happen between us, so fantasizing about him was safe. When he got engaged, I realized that crush I nurtured was hurting me, and it wasn't based on anything other than he's the embodiment of the perfect man, the exception to the rule. Noah Callaway is more than just a kind nerd in a jock's body.

He's the descendant of Emerald Creek's founding family, our local equivalent of royalty, but does he let that go to his head? No. No, he does not. He might live in a sixteen-bedroom (give or take a few) historic mansion significant enough to have a name (Lilyvale) and own half of Emerald Creek's real estate, but he still wakes up at the crack of dawn to open the shop so his employees don't have to. He still volunteers on our boards so the town is run right. He's still the high school coding club advisor because—*listen to this*—he gave up on his dream of studying at M.I.T. so he could take care of his siblings when Mrs. Callaway passed away way too young and their dad went berserk with grief.

He's perfect, okay?

But I digress. Just because he's single again doesn't mean anything.

Because Noah Callaway barely knows I exist, and I've decided that my days pining hopelessly for him are over.

O.V.E.R.

So thank god, after all, that I'm the maid of honor because this places me safely with the best man and not with Noah as we follow Ms. Angela's instructions and prepare for the procession.

The best man—Chris—owns the bakery where I work, which makes him my boss. His very pregnant wife, Alex, is also a bridesmaid.

The other couples all run their own places in town, leaving me the only one in the wedding party without my own business or badass job, and that's totally alright.

Because that's who I am.

Happiness to me is the smell of apple pie, beeswax, and the pages of a book. Happiness to me is when my friends and family are where they need to be in their life. Happiness is my whole town getting together to celebrate two amazing people.

I don't need, or want, anything else. Certainly not success, a stressful job, or god forbid, the weight of owning my own business.

The happiest I've ever been was when I trekked the Appalachian Trail alone. Not for the hardship, but for the beauty of the morning birdsong, the evening sunset, the dip and incline of a mountain, the soothing patter of rain despite the soaked shoes.

And for the people I met, like a woman who needed someone to listen, or the big dude I convinced to wear nylons under his hiking socks to ease his blisters.

I'm only cut for the simple stuff, and the Universe's plan for me is to be the grease on the squeaky wheel. Not the wheel. Absolutely not the vehicle.

Just a little droplet of grease, thank you very much.

"Alright, let's go," Ms. Angela says, and we file down the park to the sound of a soft electric guitar echoing through the hills and over the river. My heart swells at the sight of the whole town turning their faces to us, all genuinely happy to be here.

And when Kiara walks down the aisle, I start handing out the tissues I brought with her in mind.

But now Cassandra is talking about love and commitment, and I find myself struggling to not look at Noah. It breaks my heart to see the fine lines at the corner of his eyes, barely hidden by his glasses. Time is ticking and Noah is still alone, still sacrificing his own happiness for his family. It doesn't seem right.

I'm pulled from my thoughts by the faint sound of Alex stifling a groan. Glancing at her, I see her hide a grimace.

What was I thinking? I should have seen it coming. Whipping around, I run to grab an empty chair, slip in the grass and magically avoid face-planting, then slide the chair right behind Alex before anyone clues in to what's going on. She lets herself fall into it with a sigh of relief. "I'm fine," she mouths to Chris who's now frowning.

Next to him, Noah is narrowing his eyes on me like I'm some mystery.

I focus back on the wedding, the I dos, the tears of joy and suppressed sobs, my dwindling stock of tissues. Then Colton kisses Kiara and whisks her down the aisle.

Alex grabs my hand to lift herself up. "I'm gonna step ahead of you so Chris can help me, okay?"

"Yeah-yeah-yeah, sure." I step back, wondering if this baby is going to share a birthday with Kiara and Colton's anniversary.

"Ready?"

I whip my head to the deep voice way too close and see Noah offering his arm to me.

To the sound of "Best Day Of My Life."

Really? I need to do this? Walking down the aisle on a beautiful day on the arm of the one man I would want but won't ever have, sandwiched between two actual couples in front of us and two actual couples behind us?

Of course you can. You have *to.*
Squeaky wheel. Droplet of grease.

Chapter Three

Noah

Willow Fontaine doesn't even see my proffered arm, just looks straight ahead, lips pursed. Shouldn't she be happier about her friend getting married? She's who made this happen. Maybe she's worried about Alex, who's now leaning heavily on Chris? That would be like her.

I take her arm to avoid us both suffering the consequences of not following Ms. Angela's instructions, and she stiffens. "Everything okay?" I ask under my breath, leaning into her.

She wiggles and tucks something under her arm. "Yup," she quips, avoiding my gaze.

I adjust my glasses and scan the crowd. This wedding should be the perfect opportunity for me to meet the future Mrs. Callaway, yet the thought of why I'm even thinking that way revolts me. It's not like I can even think about flirting with someone. That'd be just plain... wrong.

We reach the end of the aisle, and Willow worms herself out of my hold to dash to the bar, leaving me standing stupidly, thinking I should just join her. Drown my worries for once.

But Lane interrupts my thoughts as she slides by my side. "What happened to your tie?" She frowns as she takes the bowtie between two fingers, examining it.

"Cass made me swap. Don't ask me why."

A small smile brightens her face. "Are you okay?"

"I'm great. Happy you're finally back." Even if it's only for the summer. *Even if it may be our last one here.*

She pecks my cheek. "Try to socialize for once. With women, you know—not your geeky friends. Get back in the game."

She needs to stop worrying about me. Especially over my fiancée. Water under the bridge and all that. "I'm not heartbroken." Probably the only reason I haven't been "back in the game" is that marriage clause. It was bound to taint any relationship. When I proposed to Anika, I didn't even know about the clause. Dad told me shortly after, and I'd thought of it as anecdotal. Then Dad passed away, Anika decided we weren't a good fit after all, and suddenly I was having Tamberly on speed dial.

Lane shrugs. "Just out of practice, I know." Leaning toward me, she says, "How about Willow? You guys looked cute together."

"She's alright," I pretend to agree. In all fairness, Willow is hot, and that's all my sister meant.

But Lane is only talking about casual dating, and I'm still holding on to a thread of hope that by some miracle, I'll find a wife over the summer. And for that, I'll need someone reliable, discreet, who'll understand the assignment and stick to it. Willow is a loose cannon, totally unpredictable, and she doesn't follow rules.

Besides, she clearly wants nothing to do with me.

Lane squeezes my elbow. "I'm gonna go hang out with her for a bit. We haven't caught up in a while."

"I don't remember you being close," I say, although in this small town, everyone is friends with everyone.

"She used to tutor me in middle school," Lane reminds me as she leaves my side.

I'd forgotten about that. It was after Mom passed away. Our lives were upside down, but the town rallied to help us the best way they could. Fuck it, I can't lose this. We can't lose this community.

I push my glasses up my nose. How do I walk up to a woman and ask her to *marry* me? It has got to be the most fucking awkward thing ever. Yet I'd do it if I thought there was any chance I could find someone who'd say yes.

How do I even broach the topic?

I might need to talk to Beck after all. He's always chasing one woman or the other. It wouldn't be hard for him, would it? Maybe he'd be happy. Maybe she would too, whoever *she* may be at the moment. Who knows? Maybe that's just the nudge he needs to settle down. After that, it's just a matter of appointing him trustee.

Here he comes, one beer in each hand. He hands me one and slaps my back. "Another one bites the dust. Looks like the Callaway brothers are the only smart ones standing."

Right. Beck will never be that guy.

I clink his bottle, hiding my bitterness behind words he expects. "Yeah... lucky us."

Later in the evening, while Willow is giving a speech, that I have to admit is funny, about how Kiara and Colton finally got together, her phone dings, catching my attention. She placed it on her chair when she left the table, and the screen now displays a low balance alert before going dark again.

Hmm.

Dude, this is none of your business.

Embarrassed that I'm now privy to something I shouldn't know, I push her chair under the table so I'm not tempted to look again.

But I can feel the thought forming from the depths of my desperation, and this time, with the help of a little bourbon, I'm going to let it blossom. See where that takes me.

I sit back in my chair, cross my arms, and focus my attention back on Willow, who now has the whole town laughing.

Let's see. For starters, she's not unpleasant to look at, which shouldn't even factor in, but I can't help where my mind goes when I look at her.

More importantly, she's no nonsense. She'll get the transactional and temporary part without needing loads of explanations. But she's also selfless, if her being a volunteer adaptive ski instructor is any indication. I don't see her pulling some blackmail or getting unreasonably greedy.

Even more importantly, she loves Emerald Creek. I wouldn't even consider this with someone who doesn't.

And… I should have started with that, but by all accounts she's single, which I'll admit is surprising, but plays in my favor.

It's actually the only hard prerequisite for what I have in mind.

If I'm honest, an unpredictable loose cannon who doesn't follow rules is who I need. And to continue with the honesty, the only reason I dismissed her earlier is because she can be a bit… intimidating.

I gulp my liquid courage and watch her walk back to the table.

She stands in front of me. "We don't need to do this if you don't want to," she says.

Chapter Four

Willow

Noah looks at me, seemingly lost.

Did he not hear Ms. Angela call us all to the dance floor or notice everyone leaving the table just now? I point my thumb behind my back to the wedding party dancing around Kiara and Colton.

His gaze moves beyond me, he adjusts his glasses, then he blushes slightly—so cute—and stands up.

"Um, no, this is actually... this is perfect."

Perfect? What does he mean? This man is a puzzle.

Good thing I'm over him.

O.V.E.R.

His hand grazes my lower back, bared thanks to this awesome dress. I'm already all gooey inside, when he takes me in a firm grip and sways us to some old-style tune.

Not complaining, though. Especially not now that Noah's hand is splayed confidently on my naked back, pulling me to within an inch of him while he places our joined hands over his heart.

Over him or not, I'm keeping this memory for my little spank bank. This is a nice change from guys who just wobble from foot to foot or worse, hold onto their beer while dancing because they don't know what to do with their hands.

I'll add that to the list of excellent reasons to have a crush on Noah.

Had.

Had a crush.

I don't anymore.

My gaze catches on Mom frowning at me, and I frown back. I know what she's thinking, and we start a silent argument yards from each other.

"Everything okay?" Noah asks, prompting me to look at him.

He caught me pulling a face, so I need to improvise, although as I look at him something deeply nostalgic stirs inside me. "My shoes are killing me."

Stopping us, he lets go of my back but keeps my hand in his. "Kick'em off."

"What?"

He shrugs and points downward. "Take your shoes off."

I toe them off while he watches, then he picks them up and sets them neatly to the side. "Better?" He smiles, dimples forming on his cheeks. I can't remember the last time I saw him smile, and *god* does it suit him.

"Much better."

"That was easy," he says as he turns me in a freaking underarm pass.

Total swoon.

My dress does a pretty little swirl, and he turns me again, making me just the right amount of dizzy and giddy. And what happens?

The stupid tag pops out.

Of course it does!

Acting as if this were perfectly normal, I tuck it back in. I swear the thing is cutting so badly into my flesh, I'm getting more worried about blood stains than sweat marks at this point.

"Let me cut if off for you," Noah says, *pulling the tag back out.*

I tuck it back in. "No-no-no!"

He frowns. "Is that actually part of the dress? Some trend I missed?" His lips twitch in the most irresistible smile.

Although it doesn't look like anyone else noticed, my giddiness turns into embarrassment. I shut my eyes briefly. "Can you keep a secret?"

He smirks. "I didn't think you knew the meaning of the word. Or does secret mean *high value gossip* to you?"

I fail to repress the laughter bubbling in my throat. "Very funny," I concede.

"I'm sorry," he says, surprising me. "I was out of line. Clearly, the reason you don't take the tag off your clothes is none of my business."

He really is clueless, isn't he? I settle safely back against his chest and say low enough only he can hear, "I'm returning the dress on Monday."

Then I try to hide my embarrassment by focusing on his bow tie. This shade of blue is a perfect choice as it brings out the color of his eyes. Did he choose it on purpose, to look even more attractive? And what are these little tone-on-tone shapes? I narrow my gaze, now intent on figuring out these... are these *ghosts*? Cute. And... what are these other...? Are these...? Ohmygod. I suppress my laughter.

"Why would you do that? It looks great on you," he says.

My throat tightens. "Wh—?" *Oh, the dress.* Noah just complimented my dress. He definitely *is* clueless. "I can't afford it. And no, it wasn't expensive. But seventy-three dollars is a week of food, so... yeah."

He frowns, and I expect either some questioning, a pity speech, or an offer to drive me to the food bank. Something demeaning that would fit the dynamic between the Callaways and the Fontaines. But instead he mumbles, "Knew it... Not ethical but not illegal either."

"I bought it online..." another underarm pass "from a chain store," I add, needing to be seen in a good light.

"Ooof. Online *and* chain store? Adding insult to injury." A discreet whiff of clean laundry and cedar emanates from him, weakening my knees. "I don't know if I can keep talking to you." His huge grin brings back the damn dimples.

"But I'm returning it," I add quickly.

"Good," he shoots back. Then with a quick frown he adds, "You do this often?"

"It's the first time," I confess.

He seems reassured, with a touch of concern. "Your mom?"

My breath catches in surprise, but then again, between the weight loss and the headscarf, anyone can see what's going on. "It's been tough," I admit. "But she'll get through it." I smile at him. There's something about being *seen* by Noah Callaway that brings the happy out in me.

"Good," he says, worry still marring his forehead.

"No, really. I mean it," I insist.

He takes a sharp inhale, as if he's about to ask me something, but stays quiet.

"What is it?" I prompt him.

"It's uh... this is going to sound weird."

I'm insanely curious now, and at the same time prepared to be disappointed. Weird in Noah Callaway's world is bound to be my ordinary boring. Maybe he doesn't know how to tell me that Wednesday before last, when he came to the bakery and I served him a Two Millers,

I chose a sightly under-baked one and he'd really prefer, in the future, the darker, crustier ones. It's got to be something along those lines.

He leans into me, his lips almost grazing my earlobe. "How would you feel about helping me out with... a project?"

His breath on my neck sends a ripple of desire down my spine. I try to suppress it as best as I can and jerk my head back. "Sure! What is it?"

He looks around and leans dangerously back into my space, his scent impressing itself on me like a childhood memory. "I can't tell you here."

Now I'm *really* curious. "Is it illegal?" I tease.

He raises an eyebrow. "Some people might object to it."

Noah is a color-inside-the-lines person. A rule stickler. Hell, he's a rule setter. He had me tickled curious. Now I'm hooked. "Then I'm your girl."

"You should wait until you know what it is," he says as the song ends and morphs into another.

"I trust you," I answer. *Besides, how bad can it be?*

We change dance partners and before long, all the girls are dancing together around Kiara. Then the parents' generation joins us, I dance with Uncle Bill, Mom dances with Ms. Angela, then Ms. Angela switches us so Mom and Uncle Bill are dancing together.

Finally a circle forms, someone inevitably spins a beer bottle, and we end up in a showdown of *How low can you go*. Lane wins, closely followed by Cassandra.

Sweaty and out of breath, I step out of the tent to cool down, my still-bare feet digging in the dewy grass as I walk down toward the river. Once at the shore, I raise my eyes to the starry sky and take a deep breath. *Best day of the year so far.*

A faint jingle has me turn my head. Noah is stepping out of the tent, nursing a bourbon. Against the brightness of the party behind him, I can't tell where he's looking, or if he even sees me.

"Willow?" he calls out.

Damn it—the sound of my name in his mouth… I shake my head, chuckling at my silly self. *Let it go, Willow. Jesus.*

"Over here!" When I've established he's heard and seen me and is coming down in order to, in all likelihood, tell me about this project of his, I turn around and sit on a bench to admire the river at my feet, gilded as it flows under the fairy-light covered bridge to my left, then on my right turning to a silver shimmer reflecting the moon.

Because frankly, I don't need to feast on Noah's rolled-up sleeves, his dangling bow tie, the messiness of his hair. Besides, I've decided it does nothing to me anymore.

Nothing.

"Hey," he says softly.

"Hey," I answer, not turning around.

"Brought you these," he says, standing in front of me, my shoes dangling off his fingers.

I can't help but giggle. "Careful, Prince Charming, they might actually fit."

He tilts his head. "Funny. Well, anyway," he starts, placing the shoes carefully at my feet, "about what I said earlier."

"Yeah?"

He takes a long draw on his drink, finishing his glass, and exhales loudly. "We should get married."

The desperation on his face cracks me up. I laugh out loud and look to the river. "I don't need to do anything like that. Just because all our friends are getting married doesn't mean we need to feel peer pressure. They're all happy now, but give 'em two, three years, and watch them all bitch about married life and sleepless nights as they 'start a family,'" I say, making air quotes.

"But you orchestrated Colton and Kiara's relationship." He sounds puzzled, maybe even a bit upset.

I sigh. He's right. "Look, except for our friends' rare cases, I don't believe in marriage. But I take back what I said. They're all great together, and they'll be happy until their tits and balls get in the way of their walking. But it doesn't mean you or I *have* to get married. There's nothing wrong with being single. And I'm *never* getting married."

He chuckles bitterly, and I wonder if he's heartbroken over his ex-fiancée.

"Wait. D'you need relationship advice?" That has to be it. He saw the magic I made happen with Kiara and Colton. He just mentioned it. "Who is it?" I sit taller, feeling a lot better about myself now. Since I'm O.V.E.R. Noah, I have no problem helping him out. There's something about feeling of value to others that just fuels me. My sight is adjusted to the night now, and I can clearly make out the crease between his eyebrows.

He takes the glass again, drinks what has to be melted ice cubes, then says, "I'm talking about getting married to each other."

"Sorry what?" I must have heard wrong.

He sighs. "I'll make it worth your while," he says, his gaze fleeting to the spot under my arm where the price tag digs into my flesh.

My brain freezes for a moment, then bile rises in my throat. He wants to *pay me* to *marry him*? "This is the twenty-first century. Things aren't done that way anymore." I want to add something biting, something that would betray how insulted I feel, but instead I ask, "Why would you even want to do that?"

He takes his glasses off, rubbing his eyes, but stays silent.

"I was serious when I said I'd give you dating advice. You can do this the right way, you know."

He looks a little hurt, and I feel guilty for it. His fiancée did break up with him, after all. But he doesn't show any animosity when he elaborates. "I'm required by the family trust to be married before my thirty-second birthday."

A *family trust*? I turn my gaze back to the river. "You're asking the wrong person." And here I was thinking Noah was different.

"I actually... I actually thought you'd be great for the role."

"The what now?"

"It's temporary. Just to meet a stupid condition. It's just that... so much depends on this. I thought you'd... you know. Like I said, I'll make it worth it." From the corner of my eye, I see him spread his hands as he continues, "We'll go to Vegas, to avoid questions here. And there'd be an end date, obviously, and... you know... whatever you need. Just ask for it."

My throat tightens at the sadness of it all. So much so that I can't look him in the eye and instead focus on the Emerald Creek flowing like a poetic reminder of time passing us by. When tears start prickling my eyes, I take a calming breath.

I doesn't matter how I feel about this. My hang-ups about marriage have nothing to do with Noah. He'd be a great husband, I know it. And he deserves better than a temporary Vegas sham.

My heart breaks for him. "You don't need to live your life the way a piece of paper tells you to. If you don't want to get married, then don't. Though I hope you do, someday," I add, my voice catching a little. *She'll be a lucky bitch.*

"But when you propose," I continue, "you need to have butterflies in your stomach and lose your appetite for days before and-and-and... your wedding day needs to be the most beautiful day of your life, and you need to marry your bride in your own garden, under the arch of roses your grandmother planted, overlooking the river."

I can just see it, touch it. Noah's wedding should be perfection. He deserves nothing less. "The whole town needs to be there, like today but even better, and everyone will be happy and your wife will be wearing some family heirloom jewel and you'll have plenty of babies wearing glasses and when they grow up they'll be driving Ms. Angela crazy and sneaking into Shy Rabit to read forbidden books and you and your wife and all your children will be on the store's carriage at Laskin and, by the way, you'll rename the store after her because truthfully that store needs a name."

Laying out Noah's married life the way it should play out, is a delicious pain. It's not like I was ever going to have that type of life. But he should.

So I turn to him to make sure he understands the magnitude of the error he's willing to make for some stupid reason. "None of this will ever happen if you married Willow-Fontaine-from-the-wrong-side-of-the-tracks in Vegas and divorced her months later. No woman in her right mind would want to marry someone who made such a poor decision! I mean think about it, Noah."

He takes his glasses off and rubs his eyes. He looks exhausted. "This isn't about love. It's... You're really telling me you're turning down my financial help because *I* should have some stupid fairytale wedding although *you* don't believe in marriage? None of this makes sense."

On the surface he's right, he's absolutely right. But we're way below the surface now. We're deep into emotions I can't allow myself to have.

How do I tell him the only reason I won't marry him is because I wouldn't be able to bear the fakeness of it all? If I live next to him for months, that crush I've been trying to tame will only blossom into something much more. I know it will. And what will be left of me when my time is up?

When just the sound of his voice turns me to mush. When I can feel the phantom brand of his hand on my back. When I know his scent from just a five-minute dance. When I won't ever hear the tune *I love you baby* and not think about him.

In what kind of state will I be after six months of daily exposure?

I can't subject myself to that kind of torture.

"Think of it as a piece of clothing, Willow. It's nothing. Doesn't define who you are. Temporary. Totally returnable. In fact, think of it as just another dress!"

I slip my feet in my shoes and stand, hollowness in my stomach. "You'll have to find someone else." Tears spring to my eyes, and I turn away and leave before he can see them.

Chapter Five

Willow

Five days later and the dress is still on its hanger, unstained, tag dangling to the side. It stares at me every time I go into my bedroom. It watches me sleep. It glistens in the morning, taunting its beauty at me, daring me to return it *today*, never to be mine again. So that someone else can look fabulous wearing it.

Every time I look at it, Noah's words ring in my memory. *"It's nothing. Doesn't define who you are. Temporary. Totally returnable."* As if marrying Noah, even on paper, could ever feel as shallow.

Enough.

I'll return it tomorrow.

Thankfully, tonight I have Game Night to change my mind, so I ditch my work clothes for yoga pants and an oversize T-shirt. Before driving the short distance that separates my apartment in Sunrise Farms from town, I go into Kiara and Colt's apartment one floor below to water their plants.

I took over Colt's apartment when he moved in with Kiara. We see each other a lot, and I gained a really cool space to call my own. As opposed to renting out the furnished studio apartment above Ms. Angela's garage, complete with doilies and cross-stitched artwork—which I love (being a stitcher myself), but in moderation. I promised to look after their place while they're away on their Parisian honeymoon.

Plants watered, I drive down to Cassandra's lingerie boutique, where the women in Emerald Creek meet on Thursday nights to play games or just gossip. With the sun setting, the sky is turning all hues of pink. The air is humid, and dark clouds on the horizon promise rain. If it's over by tomorrow, it'll be a beautiful weekend.

Cassandra's store is in a cape house in town, with Game Nights taking place in a large back room turned into some sort of modern-day parlor, both comfy and luxurious.

I'm greeted by Cassandra's warm hug, the hum of conversations, and the scent of vanilla wafting from soy candles. Some of the older women, including Ms. Angela, are sitting at small tables, playing cards and cackling, while my friends are mostly splayed on a white sectional.

"Still preggo?" I tease Alex. I honestly don't know how she does it.

She rolls her head on the back of the couch. "Still one month to go."

"Isn't it cooked at this point?" our friend Chloe jokes. "I hear the last month is just bonus time."

"Yeah, let's go on a hike this weekend," Grace chimes in. "Give the baby a hint. It could speed things up."

My friends' playful concern moves me. We even call ourselves the Bitch Brigade, because we help each other out.

Alex moans. "I don't think I can walk, to be honest."

I place my hand on Alex's belly, hoping to feel the baby kicking. "Might need to morph into the Witch Brigade to get things moving."

In the back, behind the mirrored bar, our friend Haley is pouring a light-colored wine in stem glasses while Cassandra now fusses over the charcuterie board Chloe brought. "Lemon wine?" Haley asks me, and I nod my assent. "Refills, anyone? Alex, I got your mocktail."

I help Haley with our drinks then squeeze on the couch between Chloe and Grace while Haley sits in front of us, cross-legged on the thick carpet.

"How's your mom? I heard she really enjoyed herself at the wedding." Going by her playful smile, she's not asking about the cancer.

"What's up with your mom?" Chloe asks.

I laugh. "Kiara's uncle Bill drove her home after the wedding, but I can't get anything from her other than 'it was just a ride.'" I shrug. "Guess we'll have to wait and see."

"Speaking of gossip," Ms. Angela says, leaning over from her card game and raising her voice so I can hear her, "I saw you and Noah have a long discussion at the wedding. Anything you'd like to share?"

Well, lay it out thick, why don't you?

Most of the side conversations die down, women lending an ear without being too obvious about it.

"The dancing was *hot*," Alex teases, her hands on her belly.

"You should have seen them at the river!" Haley says.

"You're blushing, Willow," Grace says.

"It's the wine," I answer a little too fast. "I don't even remember what we talked about. We were just getting some air. Why d'you ask?"

"He's been out of sorts at the store." Ever since she retired as a teacher, Ms. Angela has been making rounds at various shops around town, tidying shelves, helping customers out, and spreading information like wildfire.

It's obvious we share DNA, and I want to be her when I grow up. I can't think of a better way to spend my days than to be in everyone's business in a helpful way. In another life, I would have been a therapist. But this is the hand I've been dealt, and I'm quite content with it.

"What do you mean?" Grace asks. Noah is close friends with her husband, Ethan.

"Something's been eating at him since Mac passed away," Haley's mother, Lynn, says, referring to Noah's dad. "Such a shame about Mac. He really lost touch with reality when Amy died, didn't he? It was heartbreaking to see Noah take on so much when he was barely an adult himself."

Ms. Angela nods. "He started raising them."

"You all did a lot too," Cassandra says. "The whole town turned up for the Callaways, but they were just too proud to really let us in. At least Noah was."

I remember those days. Lane had started losing interest in class, and the guidance counselor asked me to help her with homework after school. He thought we'd be a good fit, and he was right. Despite our age difference of a few years, we clicked immediately. Lane even told me at Kiara's wedding that she believes my tutoring is what got her back on the right track, and ultimately, to where she's now. *Little droplet of grease.*

"But that was a while ago. There's something else," Ms. Angela insists, looking pointedly at me.

I give her my best poker face.

Haley throws a cheese puff in her mouth and leans over me. "I think he danshed with a hot chick and doeshn't know how to ashk her out." The way she looks at me leaves no doubt it's me she's talking about.

I give her a friendly shove. "Shut up."

Thankfully, someone pulls out tarot cards and the focus shifts away from me. The evening goes by real fast, and by the time we're ready to leave, fat raindrops are falling, with the promise of far more. "Drive me home, will you, sweetheart?" Ms. Angela orders me. "I walked."

"Of course. Wait right here." I dash to my car and pull up to the boutique. By the time she's inside the car, rain is pummeling the roof.

She's still fumbling with her seat belt when she says, "I heard Noah on the phone with his lawyer. He kept saying he'd meet the condition. You wouldn't happen to know anything about it, would you?"

I clench the wheel. So this *was* a trap. "I have no idea what you're talking about."

"M-hm. Your nose pinches when you're lying. Now tell me what you were talking about at the river."

Jesus F. Christ. "Absolutely not!"

"Okay then, I suppose it *was* all a bunch of boloney."

"What? What do you mean? What was a bunch of boloney?"

She lifts her shoulders. "Nothin'," she answers with the air of someone who has a lot to say but is miffed and waits to be begged.

"Aunt Angela," I threaten, reminding her I'm family. "What was it?" I slow down to let Chloe cross. She's running in the rain, but I'm not offering her a ride. I need to see this conversation through, and she's almost at her car anyway.

"Oh all right." Ms. Angela turns in her seat. "Did he tell you about the marriage clause? And don't lie to me."

How does she know? I sigh. "Yes, he did."

"Alright then. I assume he asked you?"

Why would she assume this? Low-key anger mixed with disbelief take hold of me. "I turned him down." Clenching the wheel, I make the turn on Winooski street, then slow down.

"And why would you do that?" Ms. Angela chirps as if I'd done the silliest thing possible.

I turn into her driveway, stop the car and look ahead, tears pooling.

"I'm not for hire," I snap.

From the corner of my eye, I see her head jerk back an inch as if I'd slapped her.

When I was young—very young—Mom had a string of so-called boyfriends, who'd spend an hour or two at our apartment in Burlington. Some were nice and had candy for me, some made her cry. Some made her scream. When social services took me away, the other kids quickly clued me into the fact that Mom was a sex worker.

Aunt Angela got custody of me, then Mom eventually got married and regained custody. Her husband was worse than her string of 'boyfriends.' Long story short, why do I even need to explain this to her?

Softer, I add, "You of all people should understand that."

She takes my hand. "I'm sorry, sweetheart. It was such a long time ago... I didn't think. I'm sorry," she repeats.

I turn to look at her. "Why do you even care?" She's always trying to be helpful to others, and I love her for it. I'm like her in this way. But there are limits.

She grunts. "He didn't tell you everything, then. That's so like him. If only he knew you better, he'd have explained," she says, almost to herself. Then, louder, she tells me, "It'll affect all of Emerald Creek. If none of the kids are married when one of them turns thirty-two, then Gail, Mac's widow, takes over as executor."

I blink, the words sinking in.

"She'll sell everything—the mansion, the buildings. Developers are already circling like vultures. There's even talk of knocking down Lilyvale for vacation cabins."

My heart pounds harder, while she adds, "As for the store, it automatically becomes the property of the town, and since they can't run it, they'll lease it out to a chain. A new manager will be shipped in, and they'll have to follow corporate orders. No more local sourcing. No more of Kiara's chocolates and Haley's wines and the Henderson's ice cream and the King's maple syrup."

My jaw hangs open and my heart beats harder. "What?" The store was my happy place growing up. Me and my friends from school would buy candy by the piece from big glass jars, and Mrs. Callaway would always add more, saying things like *"I heard you got an A on composition"* or *"great job scoring that goal"* or *"thank god for your beautiful smile."* Once, our Art teacher brought us to Lilyvale to teach us about perspective by drawing the mansion. I was instantly charmed, and I snuck back in several times after that, painting it in secret—my treasured escape.

"In the grand scheme of things, what's your signature on a marriage certificate?"

I take a deep breath, mulling over what Ms. Angela just said. "How do you know this?"

"I know a lot of things, honey. Believe me, this one is true." She lets it sink for a beat, then adds, "I know it rings awfully close to it, but no one's asking you to sleep with the man."

My cheeks burn at her words.

That's the worst part. That he'll never be mine.

Chapter Six

Willow

The rain stops, wind clearing the skies. It's a short drive to the Callaways' home, up through The Green, left on Elm, then right on Callaway Lane.

Bathed in pale moonlight, Lilyvale stands tall, secluded from the village, opening to the river. The main house is an austere three-story federalist brick framed by a pair of white columns and topped with a gabled roof. Beyond it, a white clapboard aisle with an oversized verandah overlooks the river and ends with a white turret.

Unkempt bushes grow too high, threatening to overtake the first-floor windows. Since Noah's father died, there's an air of sadness about Lilyvale that I hadn't fully realized.

It's entirely dark save for a rectangle of light pouring from a window near the front of the house. From the coffered ceiling and the top of a high bookshelf, I'll take a wild guess that this is an office. Feeling drawn to it, I push through the hedge. But the windowsill is higher than my eyes, and all I can see from where I'm standing is a ceiling, gleaming like a coffin. I jump up and catch a glimpse of Noah hunched over a massive desk, his head in his hands.

I pick up a couple of pebbles and throw one at the window.

Nothing.

I throw another.

Still nothing.

Is he wearing earbuds? I grab a handful now, swing my arm back, and throw with all my might—right as the window opens.

I gasp. Too late. Mortified and helpless, I watch as Noah rears back while I'm temporarily petrified, hiding in the darkness of the bushes.

"Jesus Fucking Christ!" Noah brushes his face and leans on the windowsill. "Show your face, you motherfucking coward!" he hisses.

I step in the light and look up. "I'm so sorry, I didn't think you—"

"Willow? Was that you?" he asks softer, astonishment in his tone.

I writhe. "I was trying to get your attention."

"You have it."

"I need to talk to you."

He pauses, his eyes narrowing. "I'll meet you at the front." He closes the window and disappears inside.

The massive front door opens with a creak, then closes on a thump after Noah lets me in. I'm familiar with Lilyvale's gardens, but it's the first time I'm inside the mansion. The faint scent of old wood and dust greets me like a favorite sweater. In the darkness of the night, the house seems even larger than I imagined. Noah guides us past a large staircase, its polished wood gleaming.

"Sorry about the pebble attack." My words echo up the walls.

He glances at me and lifts a shoulder. "It's fine; you throw like a girl."

"I do not!"

He chuckles. "Whatever you say." He pushes a side door and lets me into a massive kitchen. "I was going to have a glass of... something. You care to join?"

"Water is fine. I just came back from game nights."

"Late night house visits typically call for something stronger than water, but okay. Water it is," he says.

He pours two glasses from a pitcher in the fridge while I look around. The kitchen is almost as big as Mom's house. The length of one wall, there's a huge range with an overhang mantle, two ovens, a gigantic double stone sink, a microwave, and old-style wood cabinets. Off one side, a door leads to the garden, if I have my bearings right. On the other side, a double door fridge commands a large, empty space.

In the center of the room, eight chairs line one side of a massive island boasting a grill and a second sink. My gaze is drawn upward to the pots and pans hanging from the ceiling like this is a freaking cooking show. Except, of course, for a cooking show they'd get rid of the cobwebs, but hey—who cares?

This is the real deal.

I would hate—*hate*—to see this house bulldozed down in favor of vacation cottages or a motel.

Noah hands me a glass and is about to clink his to mine when Lane pads in.

She rubs her eyes, clearly blinded by the overhead lights. "Don't!" she whisper-screeches.

We halt mid-air. "Don't what?" Noah asks.

"Unless it's vodka. Don't clink with water. Hey, Willow."

"Hey, Lane."

Turning to her brother, she adds, "Clinking with water brings seven years of bad sex."

"How d'you know that?" I ask while Noah says, "You shouldn't talk about S-E-X. Or Vodka. Why are you up?" He asks this while Lane pours herself cereal, then adds milk a little too quickly, the white liquid swirling partly out of the shallow bowl.

She rolls her eyes behind her brother's back, winking at me.

I bite my lip to avoid giggling.

"Let's take this to the office," Noah tells me.

Lane laughs out loud. "Oooh, brotha."

He squeezes her nape playfully and smiles at her. "Go back to bed."

"Isn't she like... twenty-two now?" I ask as we walk down the dark hallway.

"Precisely," he answers as we enter the office he was occupying when I interrupted him.

He closes the door softly behind us, then gestures to a pair of deep leather armchairs, the kind that has little holes with push pins in the creases. He sets his glass of water on a table between the two chairs, then presses on a button and—voila! nice roaring fire in the fireplace. Just like in the movies.

"You don't like real fire?" I ask. "Or is it like—a hazard or something?"

"Look, Willow, I'm really tired," he says, stifling a yawn. His chest expands and trembles, his eyes water behind his glasses as he struggles to keep his mouth closed. The man isn't tired.

He's exhausted.

And I just threw a handful of pebbles right in his face, and not *like a girl*. There are a couple of red blotches on his cheekbones. Then I denied him the drink he clearly was craving.

He lifts his water to his lips.

"Sorry." I gather my hands on my knees and take a deep breath. "Okay, I'll do it. I'll marry you."

He full-on chokes on his water, liquid spurting from his mouth. "Sorry, sorry," he says, wiping his mouth and setting the glass down. "I—I just wasn't expecting that."

I frown. "Why d'you think I'm here?"

He shakes his head. "Y-yeah. Nothing. I wasn't thinking anything. It's been a long day."

Clearly. "Okay," I say, standing. "So we're good? You wanna hash out the details later?"

He removes his glasses slowly. "Sit down," he orders me. I'm taken by the seriousness of his tone. By how it's contrasted with the vulnerability I see every time he's not hiding behind his glasses. "Why the change of mind?" he asks when I'm back in my seat.

"It's the right thing to do," I blurt.

"Was that the hot topic at Gossip Night? What, did they send you here as some kind of sacrifice?" The bitterness in his tone is hard to miss. "Let me guess, they're worried about the store?"

What's with him? "Get over yourself, will you. We're all in this mess together. No one wants the general store sold to some chain, or this house turned into god knows what. The Callaways are part of Emerald Creek. Why didn't you tell me the other night what was at stake? I would have said yes right away. So yeah, thank god for Ms. Angela. And she spoke to me privately, if gossip is what you're worried about."

He rubs his eyes. "After you left the wedding, I realized how messed up it was to ask what I asked from you. It feels wrong, and I'm sorry."

I sit up straight in my armchair. "What's wrong is that stupid, antiquated will... or trust—whatever. What's wrong is that you're left fending for yourself, this whole estate, your siblings, the Callaway name and influence, and yet your stepmother is going to swipe it all from you from the comfort of her tropical island." Heated by my own arguments, I stand and start pacing the room, the oriental rug muffling my steps.

"What's wrong is that since your dad passed away, you've done a great job at keeping it all together, and now it's going to be taken away from you *because you're not married*. That's insanely absurd, and I just can't stand there and do nothing about it."

Noah rubs his face again, then his gaze falls on me. He should stop doing that, because each time he does, there's a flutter in my stomach that feels an awful lot like the crush I *used* to have for him. And if I'm doing the fake marriage thing with Noah, I absolutely cannot have a crush on him.

I have my limits, and here they are.

"The man who will have you as his wife will be a lucky bastard, and I hate to be doing that to you."

That stupid stomach flutters again from the compliment. "Doing what?"

"You said it the other day. The being divorced."

"I'm never getting married for real, remember? Besides, that's something that matters in your world, Noah. Not in mine." I'll be lucky if I find a guy decent enough to stick around if he knocks me up. Not that I plan on letting that happen to me, but just as a figure of speech.

"Now how's that for antiquated talk? We all live in the same world, Willow. There's no right or wrong side of the tracks anymore. No family where divorce is more or less frowned upon."

I snort, stop my pacing, and plant myself in front of him, arms crossed, shaking my head. We do live in different worlds.

He studies me, a question in his eyes, then defiance flickers in his gaze. "How much?"

I turn to face him. "How much what?"

"You must have a number in mind."

My skin goes numb. Surely I heard him wrong.

"Fifty thousand? A hundred? I'll need a little time to free up more than a hundred K if your price is higher."

My stomach bottoms. I didn't hear him wrong. For a heartbeat, I'm a kid again discovering the ugliness of adult life. "I'm not for sale." My words come out wooden.

He pales and stands, moving to a darker corner of the room, where a glass-and-brass cart holds several expensive-looking bottles. He pours himself a generous amount of amber liquid in his now empty glass of water. "That's not how I meant it. But we're entering an agreement. Unless we both benefit from it, it's not a contract."

"I'm not gonna walk away from it." Voice shaky, I add, "You think money will tie me down?"

The shadow of a smile plays on his face. *God* he's handsome, even if I feel like slapping him right now. "Clearly not. I was wrong again when it comes to you. Guilty as charged."

His words settle me down, but I'm still rattled. This is exactly what I didn't want, but it's too late to back away.

He swirls the alcohol in his glass. "Then what's in it for you, Willow? Besides all this nonsense about saving Emerald Creek. What do you want?"

"It's *not* nonsense! I don't do things because I want something in return. I do them because they're the right thing to do in that moment. Is everything in your world transactional?" If I can't bring myself to ask for money, how do I convince this hot nerd to fake marry me in order to save my hometown, if he doesn't think that's a valid enough argument?

He's quiet. Not a good sign.

I change tactics. "Oh all right, then. Truthfully? I just want the vampire room."

He takes a deep breath and narrows his gaze on me. I expect him to laugh me out of here. Or to tell me that his family is sick and tired of all the rumors; that he should have seen me coming.

I expect to have to report back to Ms. Angela that my mission aborted.

"And what makes you think that's not where I sleep?" he asks.

Chapter Seven

Noah

Vegas is the exact opposite of Emerald Creek.

    Hot.

Dry.

Crowded.

Neon lights everywhere.

Concrete, steel, and glass structures.

Artificial grass, real palm trees.

Casinos, restaurants, concerts, shows, both on the street and in every recess of every building.

I hate it.

"Ohmygod I love it!" Willow shrieks gleefully as we pass street artists adding to the ambient heat by blowing flames out of their mouths. "Look! Dragon men!" They're pretty much naked, too, which I can't blame them for. I speed up while Willow stays behind. We're on our way back from the courthouse, marriage license in hand.

We could have darted into the first wedding chapel we encountered, but back in Emerald Creek, Willow made me pack a suit "so no one can say we didn't plan this." She sent me links to hotels with all-included wedding packages with a bunch of over-excited emojis, signed off "can't wait, xoxo," then promptly called to say this was "just in case someone wanted to see proof."

Proof that we're a real couple, marrying for love even if no one saw it coming.

My plan once in Vegas was to get married and get out. But now I have Willow to take into account, and she seems to have other ideas.

Giving in to these is the least I can do.

She catches up to me. "Did you see those tats?"

"Uh, yeah, pretty cool," I lie. I didn't notice tattoos. I was too busy getting out of the heat while evaluating the likelihood that one of them might screw up and inhale flames. Would their insides burn? What would be the life-saving gesture a random passer-by—me—would need to administer to save their life?

She falls in step with me. "You must have seen this a million times."

"Me? No. Why d'you say that? It's my first time in Vegas."

She stops in her tracks, mouth agape. "Noah Callaway!"

I stop and turn to face her. She's got her fists on her hips, fire in her eyes hotter than any flamethrower could summon, and a sheen of sweat on her forehead that I wouldn't mind—

"You little poser. You can drop the cool nerd act with me!" She beams a smile brighter than the brutal desert sun.

I raise my hands in protest but can't help the burst of laughter coming from my chest. "I'm not *posing*. I uh..." My laughter gets caught in my throat. I drop my head and mirror her fist-on-hip pose. "I've had a lot on my mind. I'm sorry. I'm gonna make an effort."

She nods. "Good. Now come here." She whips her phone out and pulls me against her. "Smile! Pretend you're about to marry the love of your life." Our joined faces are staring back at us in the rectangle of her phone, smiles plastered on, and Willow's eyes light up. She takes the picture then lets me go, the sweet scent of her skin lingering around me. "I'll post it on ECHoes later," she says, referring to Emerald Creek's own social media, one I created to keep everyone safe yet constantly in touch.

As she looks at the screen, a shadow mars her face, quickly replaced by another beaming smile. "I bet you'd like the casino." She pockets her phone as we cross the street in front of our hotel. "D'you want to go real quick?"

"What makes you think I'd like it?"

"It's... math. You like math, don't you?"

Math? "Would *you* like to go to the casino?"

She shrugs. "Nah. Besides I should get ready for the wedding." She says it like this is a major ceremony, when it's only a formality.

"Our reservation is in two hours. Plenty of time to go gambling if you'd like." I point to the slot machines in the darkened lobby, a sea of them, and to the blackjack tables beyond. I've been grumpy, and I want to make it up to her. If gambling is what she wants right now, gambling is what she'll get.

"Two hours? Oooh, I need to hurry." She dashes to the bank of elevators.

I chuckle. I didn't take Willow for a woman who needed two hours to get ready. I need to seriously revise all my assumptions when it comes to her.

"I'll go get us some water," I say as she walks away from me.

I picked one of Vegas's top hotels and booked us the *lavish wedding* package, which includes two suites, flowers, champagne, thirty minutes at the wedding chapel and T-shirts. Yes, fucking T-shirts.

What it does *not* come with, is enough water to keep us alive. We're both parched, and Willow mentioned that whatever comes out of the tap makes her feel queasy, so I go back into the heat to a convenience store I noticed on the way and get us several gallons of water.

"Is your suite as cool as mine?" she asks when she opens her door for me half an hour later. "Come in for a minute." She's wrapped in a plush robe, her hair falling in wet waves on her shoulders, her scent of vanilla dangerously enticing.

I was going to haul her water in anyway, so I follow her inside. Her suite is a little nicer than mine. Set in a corner of the building, its floor to ceiling windows offer views on the brightly lit city at our feet and on the mountains in the distance, their tops snow-capped.

She nods. "Did you see this?" she adds without missing a beat, grabbing a remote. One press of a button, and a large TV screen slides up from the foot of her king-size bed. Another press, and what I thought was a vanity revolves to reveal a minibar to the tinny sound of "Here Comes The Bride." "This suite is dreamy. I just want to live here forever."

Her pink-painted toes dig into the plush carpet, matching fingernails playing in the wisps of her wet hair. Her robe opens slightly, revealing the milky swell of her breast. Turning my back to her, I grab two glasses from the minibar and pour us water.

"Thanks so much," she says again and gulps her water, her throat bobbing up and down as she swallows.

Noticing all the details in which Willow is beautiful is all kinds of wrong, so I avert my gaze and skim the rest of her suite, my eyes trailing inadvertently to the open door leading to her bedroom.

Fuck. There's a freaking *wedding gown* on the bed. After her advice that I pack a suit, I did expect a pretty dress, maybe white if she had one.

I did not expect a wedding dress.

The knot of guilt in my stomach tightens. Is this really the only wedding Willow thinks she'll ever get? Because judging by her excitement, by the dress, by the fact she's painted her nails—it's a huge deal for her.

"What's wrong?" she asks.

I set my glass down, close the distance between us and give her a brief hug. "Thank you." What I want to say is *I'm sorry*, but that would unravel the tangled threads of my guilt, and I need to go through with this wedding. I didn't bring us all the way to Vegas to back off because of some bullshit that belongs in a therapist's notebook.

She shakes slightly under my touch and her breath catches. "It's fine," she says, turning away from me and gulping the rest of her water.

I step back quickly. Something's off with Willow, but I can't quite put my finger on it.

First she doesn't believe in marriage, but she has very set ideas on how my wedding should go. Then she says that I should find someone else, but barges in my home in the middle of night and declares we shouldn't waste any more time. Following that, she's offended about me wanting to compensate her financially. Finally when I say a simple thank you, she looks about to cry.

"Come knock on my door when you're ready," I say, giving the view from her window one last glance.

Right then, the Sphere lights up with the logo of my favorite group, Phish. *Live at the Sphere*, the moving display announces. I haven't heard them live in so long, seeing their name sprawled here is a reminder of everything I gave up to hold it together in Emerald Creek. Bitterness fills my mouth.

Willow gasps, clutching at her chest. "Ohmy*gaaawd*! Phish is in town!" She turns to me, eyes rounded. Then her face falls a little and she adds, "They're probably sold out."

I frown and smile at the same time. "You like Phish?"

"Who doesn't?" she shrieks.

"You'd be surprised," I answer as she says, "They're my favorite band."

Turning back to the Sphere where their name sprawls on an off-purple background, she coos, "awww," and starts humming.

I pull out my phone. "Farmhouse? Really?"

"Don't judge. You wouldn't understand," she says with a mock pout.

"Try me. Let's see. Your mom played it while cleaning the house before you could even walk?"

Another of those fucking clouds passes through her gaze, but she quickly smiles. "Close enough. What's your favorite piece? Wait, let me guess..." The Sphere's display changes to a smiley, and she focuses her gaze on me, one finger on her lips.

"I don't have a favorite," I volunteer.

"Right. It all depends on your—"

"Mood," we both say with a quick laugh.

Fuck. I haven't felt so light in... a long, long time. My thumbs fly on the screen of my phone.

"Okay, but what would you say is their most iconic?" she pushes.

"Ah, I'm a classic guy—"

"Bathtub gin," we say at the same time.

"Solid," she says and what can I say? Her approval means something to me. Here's one thing I'm not fucking up with her.

"How 'bout you? Most iconic?" I ask back.

"Take a guess."

"Harry Hood?"

She tilts her head. "Truth?"

I frown. "Come on. Always."

"Blaze."

"Ah, yeah. I can see that. Uplifting." I nod. That kind of suits the idea I have of Willow. Shucking a hard childhood to make something out of herself, or at least, live life on her own terms.

"It's a good sign, right?" She turns to face the Sphere again, now displaying abstract mobile shapes, and sets her hands on her hips. "I think it's a good sign."

"What d'you mean, a good sign?"

"They're from Vermont. We're from Vermont. What are the odds?"

"That's one way to look at it."

"What are you doing?" she asks, narrowing her gaze on my phone.

"Trying to get us tickets."

She stays silent for a beat. Two. "For Phish?" she asks in a whisper.

I run my thumbs on the screen and glance at her. "Yeah," I say, smiling.

"For real?"

I laugh. "Yes." A feeling of careless happiness bubbles up, stretching my lips in a big smile.

"Are you sure?"

I turn my phone to her, showing her our tickets.

She throws herself in my arms. This is not the awkward, polite thank-you hug I gave her earlier. This is a full-on display of gratefulness.

Willow, I'm discovering, is generous in her displays of affection.

I pat her awkwardly on the back. If I were to hug her back, it could get... not what she meant it to be. Hers is a real thank-you hug.

As for me, the excitement about seeing Phish later tonight doesn't erase my lingering emotion about Willow. It only exacerbates it. The curve of her breast, now pressed against me, remains burned in my sensory memory. Forcing myself to pretend stone indifference is a necessity.

I clear my throat. "Knock on my door when you're ready?"

She lets go of me and says, "You should go first. I'll meet you at the chapel."

I raise an eyebrow, but she continues with a smile. "It's bad luck to see the bride in her dress before the wedding."

The vision of Willow walking alone through a Vegas hotel in a wedding gown makes me sad. "You know it's a fake wedding, right? Bad luck is sort of built in."

"See, that's where you're wrong. People get married for a bunch of different reasons. It might be fake in our hearts, but it's a real wedding. The rules still apply."

She has a point. This wedding better be airtight real if it's to accomplish its purpose.

But how the fuck is me seeing her in her dress prior to the ceremony jeopardizing that? "I'll see you down there, then."

"Don't forget your boutonniere," she says, pointing to the console. Next to a simple pink bouquet, there's a matching rosebud in a plastic tube. My heartbeat increases. These were Mom's favorite flowers.

Chapter Eight

Willow

Phish! I can't believe Noah got us tickets to *Phish*! It feels kind of surreal. I've only seen them live once. Now, if anyone tells you you haven't experienced Phish unless you saw them live—there is *some* truth to that. But I'm not letting that negate my own experience.

Having their music in my earbuds carried me through some stuff. No one gets to tell me that wasn't real. It's my life, and it's real to me.

Just like this wedding. Sure, I know there are a lot of things about it that aren't real. It has an end date. It's not founded on romantic love. We won't be intimate with each other. We won't be starting a family.

But as I stare at myself in the mirror, hair now done in an artful updo courtesy of YouTube, discreet makeup on point, I feel proud of myself. I'm living *my* life, doing what *I* believe is right, and in exchange the Universe is gifting me with tickets to Phish, a wedding dress from Goodwill that looks freaking awesome on me, and if I may say so, a promising friendship with Noah.

I always knew the man had a heart of gold. Now I get to experience it firsthand. And no, I'm not letting that go to my head. Or to my heart. We're past that now.

I don't know how to properly thank him for how well he's treating me. Not only did he give me a credit card (which I've yet to use), but he put me up in the most luxurious place I've ever seen. Marble bathroom with jets in the shower. A jacuzzi bath in an alcove off the bedroom, overlooking the scenery of desert and high peaks and glitz right beneath us—not least of which is the Sphere with its constantly changing colorful display.

I get that he's benefiting from the wedding, but come on. All I can say is, the man has class.

Which—I always knew that.

My heartbeat picks up when I notice the time. *Fifteen minutes left.* There's more traffic here at the elevators than I've ever seen in Emerald Creek, so I'd better get going.

I freeze as I enter the small chapel where Noah is chatting with the officiant. Suddenly the wedding gown, the bouquet of button roses matching his boutonniere, all this seems superfluous and... unnecessary. I feel self-conscious, silly even for putting so much effort into a fake wedding. Would I have been a bridezilla in real life?

Christ.

But Noah straightens, and his gaze on me instantly puts me at ease. "There she is," he says with a big smile right as some canned music blares from hidden speakers.

I'm not sure how to walk down the small aisle between rows of empty seats. The Bitch Brigade isn't here to ground me, guide me. To tell me I'm beautiful, and powerful, and he's lucky to have me. Of course they're not; I haven't told them a thing. I keep telling myself it's because Kiara's on her honeymoon, and Alex is too pregnant, and Chloe, Grace, and the others are dealing with an influx of tourists in each of their businesses.

But the reality is, I'm alone in this one. I have to be.

And it sucks.

So I just get up there as quickly as I can, my knuckles white around the small bouquet.

Noah must be sensing my nervousness, because he winks at me. "Nice touch," he says, pointing to the flowers. "She would have liked that," he adds, his voice catching a bit.

I gaze down at the bouquet, and the need for being back in Emerald Creek intensifies as the officiant goes through this shortcut of a wedding. But a smile tugs at my lips as I realize that all of this is perfection. This was meant to be.

Because just as Emerald Creek saved me, I'm here to save Emerald Creek.

"I do," I answer the ritual question right after Noah.

Noah takes my hand and slips a ring on my finger. "Does it fit?" he whispers. "I took a guess when I had it sized."

I glance down at the vintage ring, instantly recognizing the emerald and gold ring as a Callaway family heirloom. My eyes blur, my heart clenches. This part of it isn't fake.

"You may kiss the bride," the officiant says.

Noah lifts my hand and kisses it, winking at me again. "We did it," he whispers.

My left hand is burning with the feeling of the ring and his kiss, while my right is clenching my dress. "Pictures! We need pictures," I say, needing something to do.

"Plenty of those already," Noah says, pointing to a photographer I hadn't noticed. "You alright?" he asks me as he takes me under one arm and turns us for a posed picture.

"Look at each other!" the photographer instructs.

Noah gives my shoulder a squeeze. "We did it," he repeats as our gazes lock, and I exhale, joining him in a freeing laugh.

We did it.

I honestly don't know how Noah managed to get us seats just a few hours ago—and really good ones too. The Sphere is packed but the atmosphere is chill and electric at the same time. The three-sixty screens are beyond awesome, and I'm gaping during the whole opening act. But when Phish comes on scene and the haptics go into overdrive, we jump to our feet.

"Ohmygod it's so cool!" I can't help but yell in Noah's ear.

He smiles at me then tilts his head back, eyes half closed, and I too get lost in the music and visual of the dome above our heads and all around us, going from a night sky as starry as Vermont's, to psychedelic flowers, animals, landscapes and abstract shapes designing intertwining paths in rhythm with the music. All while the vocals, drums, and guitars reverberate deeply into my core. I am one with the music, letting it cradle me, jumping—and singing along when I can.

When they perform "Character Zero," Noah and I belt it out together, looking at each other, wagging our fingers. Noah lifts his shoulders in a "whatever" gesture and laughs. His glasses are long gone, his gaze vulnerable and free. It's the happiest I've ever seen him.

It's the happiest I've been in a long time too.

After that piece, our section starts swaying together, and we're pushed together. I trip, and Noah takes me under his arm to stabilize me. He keeps his arm around my shoulders as we sway together. "Ohmygod it's your song!" I shriek when Phish starts on "Bathtub Gin." I'm a little drunk on the music—and the margaritas we've gotten from the bar in memorabilia containers.

And yes, I kinda like that Noah keeps me under his arm for just a little longer.

To, you know, keep me from tripping over people.

Chapter Nine

Noah

"Woop!" Willow cries as we make our way out of the Sphere, carried by the crowd. "Ohmygod best day of my life," she continues. She takes her phone out of her back pocket and leans against me to bring us to an empty spot. Then she turns us into selfie mode. "Awww look at that smile on you!" Her eyes are dancing, locking with mine on the screen of her phone. She angles the phone so that the Phish logo is in the frame, then takes several shots. Tucking her phone back in her pocket, she turns serious. "We should probably post on ECHoes," she drops as we walk toward the rideshare line.

"It's the middle of the night over there."

"Pushing this off won't make it any easier."

"True. But this was a good day. Best day in a long time. No need to ruin it yet." My phone buzzes, telling me our ride is already here. I hold the door open for her.

"Good concert?" the driver asks us once we've confirmed our destination.

"Epic," we both answer.

"Newlyweds?" he says, glancing at us in the rearview mirror.

"Um... y-n..."

He doesn't catch onto our hesitation, just beams at us and wiggles his fingers in the air. "I can tell. You have that uh..." He swerves to avoid another car, muttering under his breath. Then he glances at us again with a larger smile. "You have that *glow*. Congratulations, huh?"

"Thank you," we both answer, looking at each other uneasily.

The atmosphere becomes heavy between us as we grasp the depth of what we just did. Of how this is going to make one big problem go away for me, but create a myriad of others for the both of us.

Willow stares at her phone, as if it has any answers for her. "If I post now, they'll see it when they wake up, and by the time *we're* up they'll have calmed down. And we can deal with all the comments in one shot, on our way to the airport."

I groan. She's right, I know she is. I was just hoping for a few more hours of peace. Once I text my siblings, chances are they'll blow up my phone with stupid jokes. I don't know that I have the patience right now. "Shouldn't you talk to your mom first?"

She bites on her lip. "Shit. Yeah, you're right." She sighs and shuts down her phone. "Tomorrow, then."

The next morning, she answers my knock with a tight smile. Her phone is squeezed between her shoulder and her ear as she zips up her travel bag and sets it next to the door. "Well this *is* me telling you, Mom. I'm sorry it didn't happen the way you were hoping but..."

That familiar feeling of guilt squeezes my stomach, and I clench my jaw. Willow's mother is upset, rightfully so, and it's creating a rift with her daughter—all because of me. *Fuck.*

Willow rolls her eyes at me while she's being interrupted. Setting the phone on the bed, she does a check of the room—crouching under the bed, opening the closet and each and every drawer. Her mother's voice is still coming out of the phone, her tone upset bordering on angry, her words unintelligible. Willow's gestures grow snappier, the last closet door banging shut. She storms past me, goes into the bathroom and lets out a muffled growl.

Should I go in there and see what's wrong?

Maybe not. Better to sit this one out. Her mom is still going on, and I have the feeling this isn't the first time it's happened. Willow seems to know her mother's rant isn't anywhere near done.

When Willow finally marches out of the bathroom, she picks up her phone. "Mom, I gotta hang up now. I'll see you at home. We land tomorrow." Without any more warning, she stabs the phone off and slides it in her back pocket. "How'd it go with your family?" she asks in a casual voice. As if all this was nothing. As if I couldn't see the blotches on her neck, the cold fire in her eyes, the set of her jaw.

"What were your mother's concerns?"

She frowns, pretending to be confused as if she just hadn't been yelled at for five minutes straight by her mother. "What?" She picks up her bag.

I press on it to force her to set it back on the floor. "What were your mother's concerns about us getting married?"

Willow swallows. "It doesn't matter."

"It matters to me."

She looks up at me, a little shock in her eyes and what looks like... maybe the shadow of a smile? She bites her lip. "She thinks I should have told her before." She blinks tears away, but she doesn't look exactly sad. It's a storm of emotions I can't quite figure out. "She's wrong. I don't owe her that," she adds in a whisper. "I know she's my mom and all, but even though it's gotten better recently, we don't really have that type of relationship." She looks at me with defiance, and I know better than to ask more. She's opened up to me way more than a fake marriage would ever warrant, and I'm grateful to her for that.

I jump on what she said. "About that. I'll be taking care of her medical bills."

Willow opens her mouth to protest, but I interrupt her. "There's no discussion," I say, keeping my voice firm but soft. I know how she feels about this, but she needs to benefit from this arrangement as well.

Her pupils widen, and I get that surge of warmth that I always do when I take care of my family. Except now, it twists lower, settling down in my dick. "When we're back in Emerald Creek, I'll expect to see medical charges on the credit card I gave you." Willow doesn't understand how much she's helping my family out. The least I can do is to help hers out. What I don't understand is why this is giving me a hard-on.

"Maybe this'll win her over," I add.

"I doubt it," Willow mumbles. She takes a deep breath. "But thanks." She doesn't sound convinced.

"So you'll do it," I state.

"Do what?"

"Pay her medical bills with the credit card I gave you."

Her gaze is full of challenge. "I'm in discussions with her insurance."

I knew it. She wasn't going to do it. "Until her situation is sorted out with the insurance, you'll pay the bills with the card I gave you."

She shakes her head, goes to pick up her bag again. "It's really not necess—"

"Fine then. I'll go see your mom, ask her for her bills, and pay them off myself. Will she object to her son-in-law helping out?" I fucking swear to god, I will do this if I don't see pending charges on Willow's credit card when we get home. No way in hell am I going to be the only one benefiting from this fake marriage.

Willow's gaze snaps up to me, and there's something that looks close to fear in her eyes. "Don't, please."

I feel shitty for scaring her, and I'm not sure what to make of it. But at least we're getting somewhere. "Great. Then take care of it yourself."

She shuts her eyes for a brief moment. "Fine," she concedes. Then she puts her hands on her hips. "Are you going to call your siblings now?"

"I thought I'd text them from the airport."

She huffs. "Coward. Come on, rip off that Band-Aid," she adds with a tilt of her chin. "Who are you going to tell first?" She sets her handbag on top of her travel bag and crosses her arms.

If she can handle the wrath of a mother whose only child seems to have committed the ultimate betrayal, I can face whatever reaction my siblings have for me. I remember changing diapers, wiping noses, putting Band-Aids *on*.

Taking out my phone, I click on our group chat. "Send me that selfie of us in front of the Sphere, please?" I ask Willow while I type a factual update. *Went to Vegas. Married Willow Fontaine. Saw Phish. Back late tomorrow night. Don't wait up for us.*

The whooshing sound of an outgoing text fills the room, then I forward the picture that just landed on my phone. Our faces are slightly distorted by the angle, but we look happy. Carefree. Might be the slight margarita-induced buzz. Might be the aftermath of that concert. Narrowing my gaze on Willow's expression in that picture, I can't quite figure it out. She looks... at peace.

Hours later we're on the plane, and it's still crickets from my siblings. Do they not care at all? Did something happen in Emerald Creek and they're waiting until I'm home to break the news to me?

I suddenly feel old. So old. So fucking lonesome too. No one to talk to about this shit. I'm tired of all this. My jaw clenches just at the idea of going back to Emerald Creek, and the back of my neck pinches. The wedding part of the getting fake-married turned out fun, and that's clearly over.

Seeing Phish in concert was epic and not something I would have done on my own. Probably not something I'll ever do again. I glance at Willow, wanting to thank her for the idea. It was her enthusiasm that made me get us tickets.

But she's already sleeping, eyebrows furrowed, hands in balled fists like she's about to fight someone. *Yeah, I get it.* Mom's wedding band gleams on her finger. Am I an asshole for giving her this band instead of buying a brand new one without any charged history?

It's just a fucking old ring, even if I like seeing it on *someone's* hand.

Lane doesn't want it.

Griff and Beck certainly don't give a shit.

Besides, this marriage is fake. It's not like the ring can do anything more to curse it. If questions are raised about the reality of our marriage, surely giving her this ring would prove my feelings were real?

And when the time comes to break the marriage, I'll simply let the gossips accuse the ring again and call me a fool. Who cares?

"Can you check your wife's seatbelt, please?" the flight attendant asks me, pulling me out of my thoughts. It takes me a beat or two to realize she's talking about Willow. *My wife.* The thought makes me nervous as I tighten her seatbelt around her hips. My fingers brush hers—cool and tense. I grab the airline blanket and spread it over her, reassured to see her immediately relax. She was only cold, nothing else.

She shifts in her seat, and her head rolls against my shoulder right as I'm settling in to watch a movie.

Her warmth is comforting, making me drift in and out of consciousness, the surreal last two days replaying in my head. The concert, especially, starts taking up a disproportionate amount of my headspace. What possessed me to wrap her under my arm as if she were my real wife? I was expecting her to swat me away. Instead, she fit under me like the missing piece of a puzzle, her heat and delicate female scent bringing my dick alive, my fingers barely managing to avoid the swell of her breast as she jumped up and down with the music.

I have no right to think about that moment in this way, because I know that for her, she was just enjoying the scene. I was only there to keep her from falling over the people next to us who were invading her space.

But after a few minutes I had a raging boner, and I didn't even realize my hand was kneading her shoulder, drawing her closer to me, while I imagined what her skin might feel like without the tight T-shirt.

Needless to say, I didn't touch her after she had to peel herself from me to use the bathroom. Too fucking dangerous for my sanity.

It was all kinds of wrong but I've been too damn long without a woman.

And now—fuck.

Now, I can't even *have* a woman given that I'm fucking *married*.

The irony.

She shifts and burrows deeper against me, digging my arm up with her head until she's wrapped under it. Then she gives a huge sigh of contentment, all while sleeping deeply. I lower the back of my seat and drift off to the warm rhythm of her breathing against my chest. I know it's wrong, but she feels… right.

Chapter Ten

Willow

I take a deep breath of cool air as we walk to Noah's truck. There's a conversation we've carefully avoided but it's not like we can push it back much longer.

"So...What are we going to tell everyone? About why we got married?" By everyone, I mean our friends.

Noah takes my bag from my hands and opens the passenger door for me, sets our luggage in the back seat, rounds the truck, climbs in, starts the engine. "Whaddaya mean?"

"Noah," I semi-snap. "You don't even really like me." Before he can argue to the opposite (because he's a nice guy), I proactively counter. "You think I make rash decisions, have little consideration for propriety, am an airhead, have no education. Which is all true, by the way, but mostly—*mostly*—you like thin blondes. Which I am most definitely not."

"What makes you think I like thin blondes?"

"Anika?" The name slides coldly out of my lips. It wasn't her fault, but she's who crushed my stupid hopes.

"Maybe I don't like them anymore."

My belly does a little something funny, but I shut that shit down right away. "Okay, you're not superficial like that, but—"

"We fell madly in love, couldn't wait to get married, so we eloped."

What? My jaw slackens, my tongue trying to form words. Clearly, it isn't working.

"It happened during Colton and Kiara's wedding," he continues. "We realized we'd had feelings for each other for a long time, just like them. Except we weren't as clumsy, irrational, or immature as they were. Once we realized we were it for each other, we didn't want to wait any longer."

He takes my hand and brings it briefly to his lips, the gesture meant as part of the play but still making me all woozy. "You are now my wife, for better or worse. Of course the worse will come soon enough."

I nod while he continues. "We'll both realize we made a huge mistake and we should have waited for an eternity like Colton and Kiara before entering the sacred vows of marriage. Fortunately nothing is sacred anymore and we'll get a speedy divorce. I'll be too grumpy, you'll cheat on me, and—"

"I am not a cheater!" I can't believe this would cross his mind. "And no, I will not cheat to create a reason for us to divorce."

He glances at me, his brow furrowed but his mouth twitching. "Okay, okay, chill. Nobody needs to cheat. We'll just... realize we were better off as friends."

"We were never really friends, but sure." Why did I need to say that? It's not a nice thing to say. "I didn't mean it that way—I'm sorry. I guess I'm just rattled that you would think I could cheat on someone." We stay silent for a while.

I try to picture us as a married couple in Emerald Creek. There's lots we avoided talking about. Pushing the conversation out isn't going to help. "We need to practice looking totally in love."

He quirks an eyebrow, seeming amused. *Funny, I used to think he was so serious and borderline stuck-up.* "You're really relieved you're married, aren't you?" I ask him. He does seem to have a huge weight off his shoulders, even if his worry frown seems to be deepening as we approach our hometown.

His grin broadens. "Honestly? I'm thinking I was pretty inspired when I chose you as my wife. You're very resourceful. You're making this whole fake marriage thing seem... doable."

He keeps going on and on about stuff, but my brain is stuck on just a few words. *When I chose you as my wife.* And I know he didn't choose me in the sense that he didn't spend days and months thinking this over. No, he saw desperate Willow and figured he could turn that to his advantage while offering to help her out. And kudos to him. I'm not complaining. Him taking care of Mom's medical bills is going to be a huge help while I wait for the insurance to get their act together. Regardless of how hard I tried to push back on that, I'm grateful.

But it's nice to hear, "*when I chose you as my wife.*" I'm firmly rooted in the twenty-first century and I consider myself a strong woman, but who doesn't want to hear those words, especially coming from the most eligible bachelor on whom I *used to* crush hard?

"So, what were you thinking in terms of looking totally in love?" he asks casually, although his voice catches on the last words.

I look out the passenger window. "Um, you know, holding hands and stuff."

He clears his throat. "Right. You're right. That seems important." He clears his throat again. "And by 'and stuff' you mean...?" His voice ends in a question mark, inviting me to go further.

Oh, you know, you could throw your arm on my shoulders on the regular, letting your hand graze my breast. Or French kiss me in the morning in front of the whole town as we casually stroll to Chris's bakery for croissants. "Just, whatever." *Like give me a shoulder rub at Lazy's and bring my back to your front when all our friends show up and we need to huddle in a booth, or even have me on your lap and, like, let your hands casually glide up and down my thighs as we have a beer.* "Natural, you know. Everyday stuff newlyweds do."

This time he full-on coughs.

I huff. "I mean in public. Jesus, Noah, your mind is in the gutter!" Oh that was nasty—Willow the prude. But I had to do something to offset what I'd just said. Because now we're both thinking about the same thing. And it's mortifying.

"Speaking of which," Noah says, and his jaw clenches as he thinks through his next words. "Lane is staying at Lilyvale for the summer. And Beck technically lives above the barn, but he's in and out. The place is large, but still..."

"I'm aware," I say, my voice strangling a bit. I'm going to let him make suggestions about that situation. *We probably need to share a bedroom.*

"We'll just move to the crypt," he drops casually.

"The what now?" I didn't know the mansion had... a crypt. I thought those were under churches.

"The crypt. Where the vampire is buried."

I laugh. "Nice try. Lilyvale doesn't have a crypt. The vampire is buried under The Green."

He looks at me sideways. "You don't believe that shit, do you?"

"Course I do. It's the truth. My gramps was there when the high schoolers tried to unearth him and The Green *froze over in the month of June*. So don't tell me it's a bunch of crap just because he was your ancestor."

"He was not our ancestor."

"Was too."

"Willow! He died at the age of thirteen! He was not our ancestor."

Ha! Got him. "Oh. So you know exactly who I'm talking about."

"Of course I know who you're talking about. He's just not our direct ancestor."

"Don't get all technical on me. He was in your family, therefore he lived at the mansion, and, by the way, we never finished that conversation but I would very much like to have his bedroom if that's at all feasible. Since we both know Lilyvale doesn't have a *crypt*."

He shakes his head but his mouth twitches right as his gaze slides to me, then back to the road. I wonder what he sees when he looks at me. Beyond the curvy brunette who doesn't give much of a fuck about what people think about her.

"My wife sleeps in my bedroom."

Lust zings through me, a sharp stab in my center, warmth all around me making me temporarily unable to speak.

"Don't worry, there's a couch there. Or two," he adds after a too-long pause.

Two couches in a bedroom? How big is this room? I cross my arms to hide the confused state of my body. "Were you planning on having a lot of arguments with the previous future Mrs. Callaway?" Somehow the mention of *his wife* summoned Anika in my mind.

He pulls abruptly over to the side, stopping the truck and facing me. "One thing I won't allow, is my wife to be disrespected by anyone—including you. I won't tolerate any of my exes names to be brought up in front of you, or by you."

Why so upset? I soften my tone. "This is a fake marriage, Noah. There's no need to be so protective." Although I can't say it's not making me all hot and bothered. Whoever becomes the real Mrs. Callaway is in for a treat. For the millionth time, I wonder what happened with Anika. "She really did a number on you, didn't she?"

"Who?" he frowns.

"She who shall not be named."

Surprisingly, he laughs lightly at that, and not even in a bitter way. "Nah. She was okay," he says, looking away from me and getting us back on the road.

I nod tightly, trying to let my whole being relax. After a few beats, I can't hold it anymore. "She *dumped* you. Right after your dad passed away." Everyone in Emerald Creek was shocked at the news.

He shrugs. "She realized we weren't meant to be together. She was right."

I breathe easier. "You believe in soul mates?"

He glances my way. "No."

That was a stupid question to ask, because now he's going to ask me if I believe in soul mates. And what am I going to answer? That I had an inkling there might be such a thing when he helped me tie my shoelace at school, my first day living with Aunt Angela? That I started really believing in soul mates when he helped me pick up my books when he was in high school and I was in middle school and for some reason he was right there the only time all my books slid out of my grasp?

That besides the time he appeared out of nowhere to help me haul bags of topsoil at the school greenhouse, what really cemented my belief was when he let me use his phone—his cellphone—to call Ms. Angela and let her know I'd be late because a bunch of us were at the river and we were going to start a bonfire and who knows when that was going to end. I'd been twenty-one at the time, and I had run out of minutes on the cheapo plan I had for my cheapo phone, and Noah had—

"You don't understand," Noah interrupts my dangerous train of thought, bringing me back to the present where reality is a bitch that can still hold a certain appeal. "Things are going to get nasty. People are going to question our marriage."

I try to backpedal from memory lane. "How do you know that?'

He huffs. "Tell me again how your mother reacted?"

"I handled her," I say.

"That's not what I asked."

"Pissed and hurt with a generous sprinkling of judgmental." I understand she feels hurt and left out, but for some reason she got bent out of shape over me marrying a Callaway. I don't know what her problem is with this family, and I don't care. She gets no say in how I live my romantic life—because as far as she knows, this *is* my romantic life.

"Pissed and hurt comes from the heart, and judgmental can come from being a mother, I suppose," Noah volunteers, and my anger at my mom vanishes with his words. "What I'm worried about is greed. Most people will do way worse things to protect their wallets than their hearts."

"We're talking about Gail?"

"Yes."

What could she possibly do? She doesn't even live in Emerald Creek. "What did Lane say about us getting married?" I'm more concerned about her. Will she be angry at us? At me? She was a cool kid. I'd like to stay friends with her.

Noah raises his eyebrows. "None of those little shits answered my messages," he says as a huge grin spreads on his face. "They might be planning a prank."

But it doesn't seem that they did. As we pull into Emerald Creek, it's already night and the mansion is dark. We enter through the kitchen door and Noah shouts, "Anybody home?"

But only the grandfather clock answers us, and we make it upstairs.

"So this is the bridal suite," I chirp, sounding way more happy-go-lucky than I feel. And the minute I walk in, I can tell Noah has no idea what to do now.

Chapter Eleven

Noah

This whole getting married is messing with me. I thought it was just going to be a transaction. It's so much more than that.

It's Willow's underwear in my dresser, her dresses next to my jeans, our toothbrushes in the same glass. "If we're going to make this look real," she whispers to me as we're unpacking in my bedroom, "we have to do it right."

Later that night, our first in Emerald Creek, it's sleeping on a too-small couch and having to argue with *my wife* about it. "I fit right on it. Look," she says, nudging herself on my pillow, under the blanket, showing me how her feet don't stick out because she likes to sleep in a fetal position.

"Absolutely not," I growl. Usually that tone gets me whatever I want in this house. Not this time.

"Make me go," she says, closing her eyes and crossing her arms.

I'm tired. My nerves are shot.

I have blue balls from the past days in close proximity to Willow's soft curves and sweet scent and singing voice and overall bubbly personality that is such a contrast to my own at times it feels like I am drowning in her—and the last thing I want, is to come up for air.

I pick her up, which makes her shriek in the most feminine way while bringing her whole body right against mine, her hair tickling my face, her feet kicking the air, pink toes dancing up and down, the full underside of her breast against my chest. I drop her on the bed, letting her bounce up and down, because if I'm going to let her go easy I might end up... not letting her go at all.

She shrieks again, then laughs out loud.

"Gross!" my sister shouts from across the hallway.

Willow rounds her eyes, whispers, "When did she get home?" then laughs harder before putting a hand in front of her mouth, hiding under the covers.

I settle myself on the couch and spend all night with the scent of her on my pillowcase and the sound of her breathing shooting straight to my dick.

I don't get any sleep.

"I slept like a baby," Willow declares the next morning as she stretches in bed, dark hair splayed on my pillow, small hands grabbing onto the headboard, full breasts pushing up. "Is that coffee?" she asks in disbelief, her sleepy eyes narrowing on the mug I just set on the nightstand.

Her tongue darts out from between her puffy lips.

I turn my back to her, pulling the drapes open. "Rise and shine."

"Man it's laaaate," she says, not looking at her phone or any clock, just widening her eyes at the morning light spilling into the bedroom. "This house has such good vibes."

It's the first time I've heard anyone say Lilyvale has "good vibes." Wanting to ask her what she means, I turn around to see her bending over to fluff the pillow over the freshly made bed. She frowns as she picks up her coffee mug, taking a long sip. Her dark hair falls over her naked shoulders, leading my gaze where it shouldn't stray, to the curve of her generous breasts testing the resistance of the too-thin fabric of her sleepwear. "Ohmygod. You know, I would have done it just for that," she says, her voice deep and sultry.

I turn back to look out the window. "Done what?" The hell is she even talking about?

"This whole getting married thing. Coffee in bed is enough to make it worthwhile. Are you going to do that every morning?" She chuckles. "For the sake of keeping appearances and stuff."

My breath fogs the window. I need to get out of here.

"Don't turn around!" she whisper-shrieks. "I'm getting dressed."

Holy hell. Note to self: from now on, no morning chat with my fake wife. I'm setting the coffee on her nightstand and rushing out while I still can.

The door to the bathroom creaks. "I'll meet you downstairs in a minute," she says, the door clicking shut behind her.

I guess that means it's safe to turn around. I do stay stuck in place for a beat, looking toward my bed that has to be still full of her warmth and smell, then to the bathroom where she disappeared.

Get a grip.

I get to the kitchen and find my siblings in various states of undress, hair sticking out, rumpled pajamas, Beck eating straight from a box of Froot Loops and Lane slurping Diet Coke.

"Morning!" I say, glancing at them for any sign of... something.

"Mornin'," Lane mumbles.

"Hey, guys!" Willow singsongs as she waltzes into the kitchen.

"Um... hi?" Beck says. He runs a hand in his hair and straightens his posture. "I didn't know Lane was having a sleepover. You could have told us," he adds, turning to Lane.

Lane is coughing into her drink and laughing at the same time.

"What's so funny?" Beck says, looking between me and Lane, then settling his gaze on Willow. "Good morning, Willow," he says with his most charming smile as he stands. "How do you like your coffee?"

"She likes her coffee the way her husband brought it to her this morning," I answer.

His jaw falls open. "You got *married*?" he asks Willow. "To who? Is he here?" He genuinely looks around.

I can't help but roll my eyes while Lane laughs harder and Willow joins in the giggling.

"She married Noah, you dumbass. Might wanna read your text messages," Lane finally says.

"Oh, so you read them?" I ask her.

She shrugs. "Duh."

"Why didn't you answer?"

"I didn't find anything nice to say," she answers.

I feel Willow tense next to me and automatically get closer to her.

"I mean, you guys go to Vegas and see Phish at the Sphere and you don't think to ask if we wanted to go?"

"You saw Phish at the Sphere?!" Beck exclaims, clearly offended.

Lane waves her phone at him. "Dude."

"I can't believe this shit!"

"Join the club."

Lane goes to Willow and wraps her in a hug, which Willow reciprocates. "I'm low-key pissed that I didn't get to wear a pretty dress and go to a bachelorette party, but I'm happy to have a sister," she says, putting my anxiety to rest.

"Awww," Willow coos. "I'm happy too. And I'm sure they have something like Thunder From Down Under in Montreal. Why don't you look it up for us?"

Lane glances at me, a question in her eyes.

Good to know I still have some authority around here. "Whatever Willow wants," I tell her.

Willow tilts her head. "I like how you trust me," she says, smiling funny at me.

Beck hands his phone to me, a line of half naked, overly muscled men occupying his whole screen. "Your wife and our sister are going to go see *that*."

"Cool," I say, feeling my jaw clench and my heartbeat pick up.

Willow taps my chest, then pecks my cheek. "You did good. Don't worry, we're not going to that. It's overrated." She stays tucked against me, her hand lingering where it has no business being, then turns her back to my front to talk with Lane, clasping my hand so it wraps on her shoulder and ends dangerously close to her breast. "We'll go on a shopping spree. We can have fun with all the money we saved on a wedding."

Beck snorts. "And... another reason never to get married."

"Dude, I don't see a line out the door to marry you," Lane says as she sits back at the counter.

"I didn't see a line for No-no either. Matter of fact—"

Lane swats him behind the head.

"No-no?" Willow asks, turning her face at me, playing the loving wife a little too much to a *T*. She has my arm clasped so tight around her I wonder if she's using it as a shield.

"It's what I used to call him when I was little," Lane says.

"Uh-nope," Beck says. "It's because he always says no to everything."

If I didn't say no to their crazy ideas, we'd probably all be dead by now.

"Like what?" Willow asks.

I free myself enough from her to refill my coffee, and give it three more minutes before heading out.

"Like hiking Mount Mansfield in the winter—"

"No! You were twelve."

Willow looks at me weirdly, and I know she's doing the math in her head.

"Having hot air balloons on The Green."

"That was your idea?" Willow laughs, looking at Beck.

"No, are you nuts? You need open fields."

"Or reopening the underground passage between the house and the shop," Lane says.

Willow gasps. "Shut up! There's an underground passage?

I have to say something before she falls for that. "No! No, that's a myth."

"No-no! No no no no," they both repeat.

"Alright, assholes, I got work to do."

"After breakfast," Willow says.

Heat hits my cheekbones. "I'm good." I try to round her, but she blocks my exit and sets her hand on my chest *again*, making it feel warm and tingly.

"No one goes out until they've had a hot breakfast in them. It'll just be a minute." She pushes me firmly back to a stool next to Beck. "Sit." She opens the fridge, pulls out milk, bangs cupboards open and closed, then sets a saucepan on the stove. "Anyone have any allergies?"

Beck raises his hand. "I'm allergic to orders," he says, standing.

"Beck, sit your ass down," I growl. "It's Willow's first morning here, give her a break."

"A break from what?" Willow asks, stirring oatmeal on the stove. Somehow she managed to find cinnamon and walnuts, which she sets on the table. "Where d'you keep your maple syrup?"

Lane pulls it out from the cupboard.

Willow frowns. "Maple syrup goes in the fridge," she says, and I'm bracing for Beck to lose it.

"That doesn't have time to go bad here. Be gone in two days," he says of the quarter gallon bottle.

Willow frowns. "Really? What d'you do with it?"

"Glaze vegetables."

"Marinate ribs."

"Marinate salmon."

Willow's eyes dance between Beck and Lane while they continue to show off.

"Rice pudding."

"Brownies."

"Skin mask."

"Pre-workout energy drink."

"Yogurt."

Now they're pushing it. "Really, when was the last time you made yogurt?" I ask.

"You make your own yogurt?" Willow marvels.

Lane shrugs. "Used to," she says while Beck continues, "Lemonade. Ice cream. Maple taffy."

"What happened to breakfast?" Willow asks, hands on her hips as if she's about to scold them.

I suppress a chuckle, but at the same time... "You seem disappointed," I say, realizing it's me who's disappointed. I guess I wanted to impress Willow.

"Not at all. I'm gonna slide right into my role of breakfast maker. And cleaner," she adds, looking around.

But we won't give her time to do that. If there's one thing growing up without parents really present for the last ten years taught us, it's to not be pigs.

"Here," she says, setting piping hot bowls of oatmeal in front of each of us and sliding next to me. "You like it?" she whispers just for me, while Beck and Lane bicker loudly about maple syrup grade. I'm still not quite over the fact that they had virtually nothing to say about our getting married. I don't know what reaction I was expecting but... something.

Instead, it looks like Willow is... sliding right in, like she said.

And I'm already getting uncomfortably attached to my wife. First it was all this sexiness driving me crazy, but I could rationalize that. Attribute it to hormones and proximity.

But now? She's taking care of me—of us—and I don't know that I can rationalize exactly what that does to me.

I dig into my oatmeal, which she's sprinkled with nuts without asking me. And yes, I like it. I like it a little too much.

A day away from Willow should help me gain perspective.

Chapter Twelve

Willow

"You drive to work?" Lane asks me with a frown when I come back from the bedroom with my handbag, car keys in hand, after Noah leaves for the store. The bakery is on The Green, a two-minute walk from Lilyvale.

Beck is jiggling one leg off the footrest, his eyes bouncing between the two of us, a tint of amusement in his eyes.

"Going to see my mom. Time to face the music." It's morning, she'll be cranky, but it needs to happen. I don't like how we left things on the phone, and my usual text message check-ins aren't going to cut it.

Lane's eyebrows shoot to her hairline. "You didn't tell her directly?"

"On the phone. She wasn't happy."

Beck hisses air between his teeth. "Damn." Then, frowning, he adds, "So... now that No-no's gone, you can tell us. You preggo?"

"Beckett Rowan Callaway!" Lane cries.

"What? It'd be cool to be an uncle. Just sayin'. It's not like we can count on Griff for that."

"Why not?" I ask.

Beck shrugs. "Eh, he's messed up."

"What the fuck, Beck. Griff is not messed up," Lane snaps. I feel in my bones Lane's protectiveness—I've been called messed up a few times, and it hurts.

"Okay then, why did he leave Emerald Creek? Why don't we ever see him? He came up for Colt's wedding but didn't even spend the night." I stand corrected: Beck isn't dismissive of Griff. He's in pain—misses his brother.

"He's living his life."

"Is he, though?" Beck's bitterness slices through me. I want to know more, but it's not my place to ask.

Lane sighs. "Not everyone believes the world revolves around Emerald Creek. Far as Griff is concerned, you and Noah might be the messed-up ones."

I'd have a lot to say about that, but I keep it in. These are not my real in-laws, even if they're treating me as such.

"I guess," he says. Turning to me, he beams, mischief in his eye. "Hey, you want a tour of the house? Like, the grand tour. With everything. I'm sure No-no hasn't done that yet."

No, he has not. And for a reason. Imposter syndrome taints the warmth of being included in the family. "Sure, that'd be fun."

I ignore the look Beck and Lane give each other. "It's my day off, so as soon's I get back from my mom's, if you're still up for it?" I leave from the kitchen door that leads outside. On our way back from the airport last night, we swung by my place so I could pick up my car. There's a path that meanders through the garden to the carriage house, where the cars are parked along with some equipment.

It feels awkward pulling my Subaru out of Lilyvale, using the small driveway in the back that leads to Main Street. I take a deep breath. After I visit Mom and sort things out with her, and once Lane and Beck show me around, I'll go on a long hike. It'll clear my head. I'll take Hunger Path, up the mountain, with a heart-stopping view of the valley down below and the surrounding peaks. I'll sit for a bit with my sketchpad and draw. It always helps me to put things into perspective.

When I pull up to Mom's, her car isn't there. Could it be at the shop? She would have said something, right? I knock on the door and let myself in without expecting an answer. The house is empty. One mug is on the drying rack. Her bed is made, the window cracked open just enough to air the bedroom out.

8:03

Me:
> Where are you?

I get in my car. On the way back, I stop by my apartment to gather a few more clothes, my hiking gear, plus my shampoo. Colton and Kiara's cars are both in the parking lot, and my guilt feeling tingles uneasily. I didn't check or notice that last night, but now I can't ignore it. They're back from their honeymoon, and I'm due a visit to them as well.

Maybe later? It's too early to knock on newlyweds' door, right?

God, I'm such a wimp. I know the longer I wait, the harder it'll be. Kiara and I became very close friends over the past few years. She taught me how to bake. I was her confidante. I helped her and Colton get together. She should have been the first to know about my marriage. Heck, she should have known *before* I got married to Noah.

In a nutshell, I broke the trust we had.

Can I break this trust even further by lying to her about the circumstances of my marriage?

What am I going to tell Kiara? Will she buy my lie? *Can* I even lie to her? What's more important? That everyone believes we're married? Or that my friend understands and supports me—and that I don't lie to her?

My stomach in knots, with no answers to my questions other than I feel shitty about myself. I drive away.

8:40

Me:
Hello?

8:41

Mom:
Went shopping with Cheryl! Why?

That's kinda early for a shopping trip, but sure.

Me:
Oh, great!

I expect her to ask me *why* again, but she doesn't. She must be distracted. Having fun. That has to be good, right? Then why do I think she's giving me the cold shoulder?

Because Mom doesn't go shopping at eight in the morning. Not in her state.

"Back already?" Beck asks as I pull back into the carriage house. "Hey, Lane!" he shouts at the top of his lungs while I haul my travel bag out the car. "Willie's back! Get your ass here!"

She opens her bedroom window and shouts back, "In a minute!"

"I'm starting without you!" he yells. Turning his attention to me, he spreads his arms. "Da carriage house, cos it used to be for horses and carriages, and now it's for cars and shit. Not much difference." Pointing to the barn across a wide-open space, he adds, "My digs. Stay out of there."

I frown. "Why?" I can never resist a little ribbing, and I know Beck from the adaptive sports program on the mountain. He still carries around a tinge of bad reputation from his teenage years, but now he really is just a prankster—and a player. "You have to know the moment you tell someone to stay out of someplace, they're gonna want to go in. I mean, you've seen the movies, right?"

"You mean the ones where the stupid girl runs to the barn when someone's chasing her?"

"Ha-ha." Switching my bag to my other shoulder and heading toward the mansion, I add, "Note to self: sneak into Beck's digs when he's not around."

"Don't you dare!"

"Afraid I might find your conquests chained to the bed?"

"Ugh," he growls, but drops the topic.

Ten minutes later, we're in the basement of the main house, facing a brick wall, a bare light bulb projecting our distorted shadows.

"You see it?" Beck asks. His finger traces the contours of the brick.

There's clearly a difference in the color of the bricks. And there's a straight line where the bricks aren't staggered. As if a door had been walled in. "Nope."

"You're fucking shitting me."

"What do you think it is?"

"People have been known to disappear in the past. Visitors to Lilyvale. I think this is where they were buried. Walled in."

So much bullshit, I can't help but laugh out loud.

Lane sighs. "I think this is a passage to the store."

Now that makes more sense. "Why would you think that?"

"Cos' there's the same one in the store's basement."

I shrug. "Why don't you open them up?"

"Noah would have a heart attack."

I consider this for a second. "Do you need his permission?"

"I like her thinking," Lane says.

Beck shrugs. "Or we might find bodies."

"Or we might find bodies," I agree, an unexpected giddiness spreading through me as our easy banter carries on.

"Which would explain the weird noises at night," Beck says as we retreat upstairs.

"I didn't hear anything last night."

"Oh, you will. Eventually."

Jesus. Are they trying to scare me? We're a little old for this, but I'm still having more fun than I expected. No wonder Noah is so protective of them.

I didn't grow up with siblings, and with the way I ping-ponged in and out of Emerald Creek, I never could create a steady group of childhood friends. Besides the Bitch Brigade, which Kiara consolidated to help save Grace's spa last summer, this is the closest I'm getting to having my group. I'll take it and enjoy it, and hope it continues once the marriage with Noah is over.

"So this is where she hanged herself," Beck says when we're in the powder room of the main house. He's referring to a local legend, presenting it like it's this morning's front-page story.

"Uh-huh."

"So... like, if you hear your name at night, just don't get up," Lane says, looking dead serious.

An eerie shadow floats about two feet above and behind Beck for a fleeting second, and warmth envelops me. "Gotcha," I say, my gaze pulled upward, a smile forming on my lips. It's got to be the way the sun hits the old glass panel at this time of day, and they knew it would happen.

And yet.

They're trying to spook me, but instead, it's the unfamiliar feeling of *coming home* that seizes me.

It has to be because Lane and Beck are sharing their family lore with me.

Beck jumps, looking up. "Fucking shit," he curses, slapping his nape as if a mosquito was biting him.

I laugh out loud, feeling part of something. Even if it's pretend, to me it feels real. And after Mom's brush-off this morning and the dread of facing Kiara, I needed this more than I want to admit.

Chapter Thirteen

Willow

"I can't believe Noah never gave you the grand tour," Lane says once Beck is gone and she proceeds to show me each room, one after the other, starting at the front. She huffs. "It's not a secret I didn't like Anika," she says, which is actually news to me, "but you... you're one of us. You need to know this place inside and out.

"Big picture, this wing is the oldest, built in the 1820s on the ruins of the original house built in the 1790s. That one burned to the ground..." She stops herself, then adds, "but you know that, right?"

Why would I know that? "Uh... no."

Setting her hands on her hips, she says, "A *Fontaine* set it on fire."

"Pfff," I laugh. "They did not."

"Did too."

"You're kidding."

"Am not." She doesn't seem to care that much, just stating the facts.

Some old stories resurface in my memory. "My Gramps' used to say that the Callaways stole our land." It looks like each family had their own reasons to dislike the other. Aunt Angela never mentioned any of these stories, but they could explain Mom's hangups with the Callaways.

She shrugs. "Wouldn't be surprised. Ancient history," she says as we take two steps up and turn at an angle, which places us in the white aisle of the mansion. "This part was added in the 1850s or '60s."

The rooms are larger, airier, and a wide wraparound porch offers stunning views of the river. White columns still give this aisle a stately feel, but it's so much brighter and relaxed than the older aisle, with its smaller windows and dark wood paneling.

"What's your plan now?" I ask Lane as she shows me bedrooms that once were probably cute with their paisley bedspreads and maple furniture, but now are in dire need of TLC.

"I'm sending my resume to newspapers, online outlets, magazines." She pushes the door to a music room, revealing the baby grand covered by a sheet. "Twenty a day."

"You always had a knack with words. You'll find something." Lane majored in journalism, and when we chatted at Kiara's wedding, she was hoping to find a job in New York.

"Used to have the best parties in here," she murmurs to herself with a little melancholy as she shows me a game room at garden level. "Yeah, journalism isn't dead. I just need to keep trying."

"Maybe expand beyond New York?" I suggest as we circle back to the main aisle through the third-floor hallway, peeking into another set of adorable yet dusty bedrooms under the eaves.

She shrugs. "I always dreamed of the big city. Cliché for a small-town girl, I know."

I can see that. We always dream of what we think we can't have.

I go back into the bedroom I'll be sharing with Noah for the next few months and pause at its entrance, the conflicting feelings of excitement, dread, familiarity, and newness heightening. The room is large enough to have three windows facing the village, with heavy drapes providing darkness against those four a.m. sunrises in the summer. Two navy blue couches are at an angle, one a loveseat against the hallway wall, the longer one—where Noah slept last night and with its back to the bed—facing a small fireplace. Leaning down, I verify that it's not a pull-out couch and feel guilty that he feels he's the one who needs to pretzel-fit onto it at night.

Maybe we should swap nights? I'm not giving up the fight.

His scent floats in the room, discreet but very present, sending butterflies in my stomach as I walk around.

He must have tucked his pillow under the bedspread at some point, because it's no longer on the couch. Yep. It's right there. No pajamas under it, though.

Hmm.

I open his nightstand's drawer (mine was empty last night). A notebook, a pen, a flashlight, batteries, a phone charger, another phone charger, a Swiss army knife.

Boring.

I flip the notebook open, expecting to find random to-do lists. Or maybe doodles. Possibly phone numbers?

Instead, there's a recent date, then some neatly written text that ends with,

I didn't expect this from being married.

Shit. I shut the notebook. Is this... is this a diary? I open it halfway, taking a brief peek.

It's totally a diary.

Ohmygod.

Noah has a diary and I almost read it.

Heartbeat significantly higher, I set the notebook back where it was and swiftly retreat from the now-forbidden nightstand.

I unpack the extra stuff I brought from home, sliding Noah's shirts a bit down the rod in the closet so I can fit a few more dresses, fighting the urge to read... whatever he has to say about being married.

Then I bring the rest of my toiletries to the en-suite bathroom we share. It's so large, it might have been a bedroom in another era. There's a clawfoot tub and a separate walk-in shower, a whole linen closet with antique doors painted off-white. The walls are covered in white subway tile, the floor in a black-and-white mosaic. An oval mirror and chrome sconces top the large pedestal sink. No vanity, but a whole pine chest under the window with four drawers.

One is full of Noah's things.

Three are empty—he made space for me last night. And I know it's normal (anyone would do that), but still it gives me a sense of belonging, just like Beck and Lane giving me a tour made me feel welcome even if they were trying to spook me.

I take possession of the empty drawers, all the time dying to know what's in his diary.

Sharing such intimacy with Noah is a sweet torture. From showering this morning, I know where his forest scent comes from—his body wash. But that earthy tone is different. It's *him*. Or maybe it's his deodorant? Does he wear aftershave? I don't think I ever noticed that.

A wife should know these things.

Like, she-I should not read her husband's diary (very generally speaking. I'm sure there are some valid exceptions to that) but she-I should definitely at least know what products he uses. What painkillers he prefers.

A real wife might even buy them for him.

Right?

And isn't it better to go through someone's drawers than read their diary? If that someone is your husband.

And shouldn't I know what's in the drawers of the room I shower in?

Noah has three different electric razors, a pack of twelve toothbrushes, toothpaste for sensitive gums, whitening toothpaste, two humongous bottles of mouthwash, Q-Tips, a manual razor like the one on the side of the sink in a little holder thingamajig, extra blades, shaving cream, tiny Band-Aids, some foot spray, a pack of deodorant sticks, and... bear repellent? Why does he have bear repellent in the bathroom? What else is in there?

A nail clipper, three combs still wrapped in plastic, a shoe brush.

In the very back, massage oil. Covered in a vaguely greasy dust, the bottle looks a little old, and there's hardly any oil missing.

Hmm.

Moving the stuff around, I keep looking.

No condoms.

Absolutely none.

Chapter Fourteen

Willow

That afternoon, my hike up Hunger Path doesn't bring me the peace I expect. The threat of a storm makes the air tense and insects nervous. I came to clear my mind, think things through, but it doesn't do that. Not today. I make it to the summit, watch the minuscule human activity down below, and jog back down wondering about the meaning of... everything. Of Mom pouting. Of ancient stories. Of my curiosity about a diary. Even the absence of condoms in a certain drawer seems like something I should be able to make sense of, but cannot.

Halfway down the trail, I'm nearly toppled over by a big dog running loose. "Moose!" I call out. The Saint Bernard is Justin's dog. He usually never leaves Lazy's, Justin's pub, and he's always down for a scratch behind the ears. But today he barely slows down before galloping to the village. Even the dogs are acting weird. Must be the weather.

Back at Lilyvale, I bring some wood from the neat stack outside into a room at the front where earlier I noticed ashes in the fireplace. Feeling semi-useful, I take a shower then settle down with a mystery novel.

That evening, as heavy clouds roll in, Noah and I have dinner alone, sitting catty-corner at the kitchen counter. "You didn't have to wait for me," Noah says with an apology in his voice.

The truth is, I don't know what the etiquette is for fake newlyweds. Do we keep tabs on each other, *I'm-on-my-way* type of thing, or do we just ignore each other when no one is present?

Somewhere along the middle of that seems about right. "Wild guess, newlyweds wait on each other for dinner," I counter. "At least in the beginning?"

Lane is out on a date, Beck is god knows where—but he left heating instructions taped to the fridge for a chicken casserole, which I took as an invitation to have for dinner.

Truth is, I didn't feel like eating alone.

Noah is quiet, and the silence irks me. "I can't wait to go back to work tomorrow," I confess, breaking the soft sounds of metal on china. "Get back to normal." I need to talk to someone.

Noah grunts. "Not sure what normal is going to look like."

It occurs to me that Noah didn't have the luxury of hiding today, and his day might have been tough on the social side. "Did... were people... annoying?" For lack of a better word.

"Surprisingly, Ms. Angela didn't come over to find out what was what."

She wouldn't, since she's who put me up to this. I stay quiet on that topic.

"Grace and Alex came looking for you," he continues, "which... okay. Didn't quite know what to say to that."

Alex is my boss's soon-to-be-wife, and Grace is his cousin. They know I work at the bakery. "That's weird."

"The whole day has been weird. They'll get used to it." He clears both our plates, declares he has work to do, and goes into his office.

On the first rumble of thunder, I go upstairs, brush my teeth, wash my face, put my pajamas on, grab a pillow and a throw blanket, and cuddle on the couch, windows wide open, to the sound of the rain and the bursts of lightning, not really worried about the wind pushing water inside. I'm in need of some weather tonight. Something loud and soothing.

I barely feel him carrying me to bed, strong arms and his manly scent awakening my core before my brain has time to catch up, but it all goes by way too fast. After that, I sleep like a baby, waking up to the smell of coffee on my nightstand. *Sweet.*

But no Noah.

He slips out of the house before me, and it's just as well. As newlyweds, if we were to walk to work together—me to the bakery and Noah to the store—we'd have to hold hands, which I'm sure Noah could manage. But wouldn't we be expected to at least peck when we part ways? That would be awkward, yet if we aren't good enough at pretending, people will start talking.

The rain is still falling steadily, and I pull on the hood on my raincoat, keeping my head down if only to avoid having to talk to anyone.

On my way to work, I can't help but glance at the store. Although the sign on the door is turned to Open, it looks dark inside. And why didn't they put any umbrellas in the display windows? It seems like an easy, natural thing. It rains, you show that you sell umbrellas.

At least the gutters aren't overflowing, and the rain is already receding.

Continuing on my way to work, I send a quick text message to Mom. It's the same message every day since she's been diagnosed. We might have had a poor relationship in the past, but like Noah said, it can be fixed. Things between us seem to constantly ebb and flow, and at this point it's on me to get us to a peaceful stage.

> How's it going today?

And every day, generally within a couple of hours, she answers with either a thumbs up or a poop emoji. The one time she didn't answer, I stormed her double-wide over lunch break and found her asleep at the kitchen table, face on her arms, tea spilled. That day, something shifted in our relationship.

I didn't see a sick woman too weak to care for herself. Beyond the filter of illness that blurred the reality, I saw the reality of my mother who didn't have in her bones the will to fight for herself. Who never had someone look out for her when she was weak. A woman who'd been taken advantage of, and either failed to see it or didn't know the first thing to do about it.

That day, seeing her balding head sprawled on her spindly arms, bony shoulders barely lifting with her shallow breaths, it was as if I'd bottled all the love I couldn't give her growing up, and it was now spilling out of me. I carried her to bed, made her take her meds, spoon-fed her oatmeal. It didn't matter that she was trying to shoo me away, trying to convince me she'd been taking a cat nap and I should try it someday.

I told her I loved her, and her answer was, "I'm sorry."

I keep my eyes on the screen of my phone, hoping she won't give me the silent treatment. I know I've changed when it comes to our relationship. I'm not sure she has yet.

> **Mom:**
> <Thumbs up emoji>

> **Me:**
> I'll come over after work.

> **Mom:**
> You and Noah come over for dinner.

That stops me in my tracks. So many things bounce in my head, from Mom being too tired, to why does she even—*but of course she does*. There could be genuine reasons, such as she now has a son-in-law and not only that, but he's a Callaway, to she-saw-straight-through-our-lie-and-what-in-the-world. The thing that sticks, though, is that Mom shouldn't get tired.

> **Mom:**
> Cleaned the house little by little with Aunt Angela over the last few days. Shannon dropped off lasagna and Cassandra a salad.

I don't ask her more about yesterday morning. She'll tell me if she wants to.

> **Me:**
> That's really nice. What time do you want us there?

> **Mom:**
> Whenever you kids can get here. Not going anywhere.

Huh. *You kids.* Okay.

I heart her message and send a quick text to Noah to let him know.

I'm already at Chris's bakery, a large Victorian that stands on The Green.

I'm early and on rainy days, business is quiet. I'll have time to get "the conversation" with my boss out of the way. I haven't told him we got married, only that I urgently needed PTO, and I don't know that Noah told him either. We relied on ECHoes, and that was sort of a dick move.

Kiara's cute pink vintage delivery van (the one she used as a bridal suite) is outside the bakery, doubling my nervousness. She must be making her daily delivery, and I'm in for not one, but two hard conversations. But somehow, I'm almost relieved to have these soon be over.

The scent of fresh croissants greets me as I push the door open, easing my tension with its familiarity and pure yumminess. Chris has already loaded the shelves with a variety of breads.

"Here comes the bride!" Kiara says as she sets a tray of colorful macarons on a display shelf, then walks to me with a tight smile.

"Hey," I answer, giving her a side hug. "How was Paris?" Lame attempt to change the topic.

We walk in silence to the back of the bakery, where I shuck my coat off, toe off my rain boots, and don my work shoes. "I'm sorry," I say, finally finding the courage to look her in the eye. "I don't know what else to say." I'm clutching my boots and my coat, and even I can tell it's to feel protected.

"Put your stuff away," she says. "I'm not going to bite you."

I shove my things in the closet then turn to her. My gaze flickers to her left hand, where Colton's solitaire is shining next to the simple white gold band he slipped on her finger just days before Noah and I eloped. My heart clenches at my betrayal. "I'm sorry I hurt you."

Her eyes mist. "You did hurt me." Blinking tears away, she pulls me in for a hug and holds me against her, her arms clenched around me. "What happened?" she whispers.

I shut my eyes. Can I go with the lie Noah and I agreed on? Or do I owe my best friend the truth? Who comes first? My fake husband and real-life crush, or my best friend?

Remembering that the interests of the whole town hang on this fake marriage, I make my choice as she releases her hug. Unable to quite look her in the eye, I busy myself making coffee—the first task of my workday. "Noah... Noah opened up to me during the wedding and I... you know how I've always felt about him. So..." I look at her, hoping she'll fill in the rest.

She crosses her arms, her eyes dancing. "So you did the big nasty. And...?" she quips.

I gape at her, not knowing where to go with that. This is a direction I didn't see coming, and now I can't remember... What did Noah and I agree to say again? I swallow with difficulty. "We decided we didn't want to waste more time and-and-and we didn't want a big wedding and—"

"You're so full of shit," Kiara interrupts me. Narrowing her eyes on me, she adds, "On a scale of one to ten, how worried should I be?"

"W-what do you mean?"

"People are asking questions."

"People?" I repeat stupidly. What people? What questions? Ohmygod are *people* already saying the wedding is fake?

"Look, I don't know what's going on, but out-of-staters have been asking Colt—as chair of the select board—about development opportunities in town in the near future... specifically, revolving around the store. And other out-of-staters are checking zoning in the Lilyvale area. It's... weird. We didn't think much about it, but then you go and get married and it's just... the timing, you know?"

My mouth is dry. "What did Colton answer?" I might be showing our hand to Kiara, but I need to know.

Kiara gives me a long look. Nods slowly. "Obviously... to go fuck themselves."

My heart gives a thump at the show of support. Before I can say anything, she raises her hand and adds, "Don't tell me anything. I'm a terrible liar."

Solitude weighs heavily on me. But she's right; this is not something we should talk about at the moment. Or ever.

"Whatever this is, I got your back. We're the Bitch Brigade," she reminds me.

Before I can answer, Chris's voice booms, startling us. "Congratulations!" He comes out of the bakehouse in his stiff chef's apron and crosses his arms on his chest, seizing me with his gaze.

I tuck a strand of hair behind my ear. "Thanks," I say and clear my throat. "Would you like some coffee? It looks like it's going to be a quiet morning." I pour him a mug before he can answer.

"What are you doing?" Chris asks with barely a glance at the coffee.

"What do you mean? Are-are we closed because of the storm?" Stupid question. In addition to the fully stocked shelves, the heavenly smell of freshly baked bread is making my stomach rumble.

He shrugs. "Course not. Isn't the store open?"

"The store?" Where's he going with that?

"Your husband's store. *Your* store now."

It's definitely *not* my store. Before getting married, in addition to the contract drawn by Noah to look after my interests (he gave me no other choice), we signed an airtight prenup drawn up by his lawyer. But I can't tell them that. "What about it?"

"Aren't you open today?" Kiara asks. *Why does she need to repeat Chris's question?*

"You should start learning the ropes. There's more to that business than meets the eye," Chris adds, then takes a sip of coffee.

I breathe easier. "Oh no! I'm not going to work there. No way." It hasn't even crossed my mind. "I love it too much here," I say. Which isn't exactly a lie but isn't the honest truth either. It's a job, in a place I like, with people I like. I enjoy it. Saying that I love it is a bit of a stretch. But at any rate, I need to make it up to Chris and Kiara—on account of getting married without telling them—so the least I can say is that I love working here.

"I'm sorry to hear that," Chris says.

"What do you mean?" I glance at Kiara, but she only has a small smile for Chris. *There's something she knows that I don't.*

"I can't keep you away from Noah."

What? Even if we were in love, we wouldn't be pawing at each other at the store. It makes no sense. I smile and blow on my coffee. "I appreciate the thought, but we'll be fine." I even manage to giggle despite my growing feeling of unease.

Chris shakes his head. "Can't do it, Willow. You marry into the Callaway family, you have to go all in."

Oh... no-no-no. "Wh-what if I don't want to?"

"What do you mean? You're married, right?"

Kiara looks at me. "Right?" she echoes.

I nod. "And?"

"And Mrs. Callaway does not work at the bakery," Chris answers. "She works on any one or all of the Callaway businesses. There's enough to keep you busy your whole life. Take your pick: the store, the land management foundation, the orchards, the real estate business, the plumbing business. I'm probably forgetting one or ten." His gaze drops to my left hand. "This was Noah's mom's wedding band. You need to honor that."

My heart skips a beat as I fidget with the ring. The emerald gleams subtly, the smaller stones shining around the band just like the river hugging our town.

This ring? It means something to the Callaways. It means something to the town.

I blink emotion away, refusing to hope that it might have meant something for Noah to slip it on my finger. "I didn't see it that way, I suppose."

They glance at each other, then look back at me, both with their arms crossed. "Well I'm glad we got that squared away. Would have hated for Noah to resent me," Chris drops. "I'll advertise the opening on ECHoes, and meantime maybe Alex will have fun helping out here."

I clutch my coffee mug with sweaty palms. "Oh don't be silly! Alex is way too pregnant for this, and Noah hasn't mentioned anything. I'm sure it's fine that I stay here." I really can't work there. It'll be tough enough playing the role of loving couple at Lilyvale; it'd be way too awkward if I worked with Noah.

Chris sets his empty cup in the sink. "You're a great salesperson, Willow. You have a sense for business. I always knew you could do better than the bakery. I'm not really giving you a choice here."

Tears prickle my eyes and my hands start shaking. "You're *firing* me?" I croak. When I signed up for the fake marriage, I didn't agree to ditch the rest of my life.

He gives me a friendly pat on the shoulder. "I'll see you around, Mrs. Callaway."

Once he's gone, Kiara's facial expression darkens as she pulls me into another hug. "Don't you go fucking falling in love with him, you hear me? It's one thing to... help him out—or whatever it is you're doing. But you *cannot* fall for him." She strokes my back as if she's already picking up the pieces of my broken heart.

"Kiara—"

"Shh, don't answer that," she interrupts me. "Just promise me." She steps back and holds my shoulders, looking up from her five foot one to meet my eyes. "I said, promise me."

My gaze falters.

"Shit." Her eyes shine with anger and concern. "You idiot! You fucking idiot." Then she grabs me again in a full bear hug. "I *hate* that for you. Why did you have to go and do that?"

Her question hangs between us as I step back into the storm.

Because no one else can fake being Noah's wife as well as I can. Pretending to love Noah comes easy to me—because I'm not pretending at all.

Chapter Fifteen

Noah

I start the day holed up in the small office tucked under the staircase, the quarterly report spread in front of me. I try to focus on my task, but thoughts of Willow keep interrupting me, even though I managed to avoid her this morning.

When my father told me about the marriage clause, he explained it originated with the store: according to Noah The First, you couldn't run a general store on your own. You needed a partner you could trust. More than a business partner: a life partner. Someone with complementary skills and a different sensitivity.

A wife.

"It's a load of shit, son," Dad had said, "but there's no way around it. Thankfully nowhere does it say that your wife needs to work in the business, so you just let her do her thing while you do yours and you'll live a happy life."

Dad didn't always have a happy life in the romance department, but I knew what he meant, and I planned to follow his advice. Ironically,

Mom would often be at the store and seemed happy here. But she never made it sound like she was necessary to the smooth running of the operation.

I've been operating the store on my own for years now, and I couldn't see myself sharing the work. I'm set in my ways. I have my processes. I know what sells and what doesn't. I know how to sell it: just like we always have.

My employees, Dean on the floor and register and Elaine at the deli, have been working here for decades, and they have their routine perfected to a science. When it's tourist season, they call in their family members to help, and that's enough. Having a partner would mean discussing changes, options, putting everything I do in question.

Talk about a nightmare.

Adjusting my glasses, I savor the solitude, until it's interrupted by the front door chiming before Dean's start time. Against all odds considering the weather, we have a customer. They have to be regulars. With a few lights on, they'll be able to find their way.

"Let me know if you need anything!" I holler.

I chuckle at an email from a vendor insisting I stock their vacuum cleaning robots, then finish the analysis of the quarterly report. Sales are slipping, but I don't want to worry about it. It'll pick up in the summer, when tourists flock into town. Although, I tell myself that each year. It'd be nice to have a solution against seasonal dips in sales, but I suppose that's the nature of the beast. It's always been that way, and generations of Callaways have dealt with it.

I will too.

"There you are!" Willow's voice sounds right next to me.

I jump, taking her in. Her raincoat is open on a summer dress, a splattering of raindrops making it cling to her thighs. Her hair is lightly matted with water, and her eyes are shiny.

I stand from my desk and take my glasses off. She's quite a sight, and I need to blur the whole picture for a minute. "Hey! On your way to work?" I hope she doesn't make it a habit to spring on me like that. I could get addicted to it.

She spreads her hands in the pockets of her coat, her floral perfume hitting me in a wave. "Nope. What can I do to help?"

Maybe the bakery had a power outage. Or Chris decided to just stay in bed with Alex, customers be damned. The recent memory of Willow in my own bed overpowers me, and I avert my eyes from her. "Literal rain check?" I ask.

"Something like that." She takes her coat off, looking for a place to hang it.

"What are you doing?"

She takes a deep breath. "We have a problem," she says and closes the door to my office. After a slight hesitation, she hangs her coat behind the door, on top of my windbreaker.

I slump on my chair, gesturing to the seat across from my desk.

She chooses to sit one butt cheek on my desk, her foot dangling. It's too comfortable. Too easygoing. Too natural. Like we've been doing this for years. "I'm going to have to work here," she says.

Absolutely not. I chuckle. "And why is that?" I wipe my glasses and put them back on.

She starts telling me about people asking weird questions at town hall, how Kiara seems to think that the timing of our wedding is a tell there's more to it, and finally Chris having some theories about what the Callaway women should and shouldn't do in town. "For what it's worth, he did say I was a great salesperson, with a sense for business, so…" She looks at me with hope in her eyes, and it nearly kills me.

"He let you go?" I bark and reach for my phone.

Her eyes widen. "What are you doing?"

I scroll through my contacts list. "Telling Chris this is no way to treat my wife. The fuck is wrong with him?" It's all my fault. First, she gets into a fight with her mom. Now this.

"Noah, no." She takes a shaky breath. "Please don't do this. It's... embarrassing. He meant well. The Callaway image and all that."

Jaw clenched, I set my phone down. "Alright. You can just pick a spot and read a book... or whatever."

She narrows her eyes on me. "Excuse-me-what? Did you hear the part where he said I was a great salesperson?"

Oh hell no. "I'm not... I don't... this was never the plan." It's hard enough to have her at home.

I'm not a big enough man to subject myself to the temptation of her 24/7.

She leans over to look me in the eye, giving me a prime view on her cleavage, and suddenly my mood is elevated to heights previously unknown. I try to keep my gaze focused on her eyes.

It's hard.

"I am not risking the very generous arrangement I have with you because you don't know how to delegate," she says in a tone she might think is threatening.

I don't know *what*? "Excuse me?" I ask, trying to sound way more irritated than I feel. Her answer is lost to me. Only the sound of her voice makes it to my consciousness, the message irrelevant. The vision of my wife all mussed up from the rain, perched on my desk, with her boobs close enough that I could lose myself in them just by tilting my head is enough to dissipate any kind of annoyance life might throw at me.

Willow is rarely upset, but when she is—full-on fire. Her skin gets a sort of inner glow, her eyes brighten, her lips are redder and fuller, and there's an overall energy radiating from her... it just makes me wonder what she's like in bed.

"Got me?" she asks.

I have no fucking clue what she said, but her delivery was chef's kiss. "Sure," I answer, shaking my head, hoping I can rile her up on the regular.

She hops off the desk, a great big smile on her face. "Great! I'll get right on it." She turns on her heel and *bends over*, the damp dress clinging to her ass.

I clear my throat and shift in my chair, my hard-on uncomfortable. "What are you doing?"

She looks at me over her shoulder, still partly bent, one foot up, unsteady on the other. "Putting on my house shoes."

Ah, hell.

That must mean she's staying.

Chapter Sixteen

Willow

Well that was easy. All I needed to do was put my foot down and the man just... caved. Who knew marriage could be so easy peasy?

So maybe Kiara's right. Maybe my heart will end up being collateral damage. But so what? My goal is to be the most believable wife to Noah Callaway, and looking around me, I see I have my work cut out. Chris is right, all the Callaway ladies always worked at the store—I remember from old pictures on a projector during social studies, and Mrs. Callaway was here most of the time, keeping a gentle eye on the candy aisle when we came by after school.

With a renewed sense of purpose, I turn most of the lights on and get the coffee machine started. It might make horrible lattes, but there's nothing like the smell of coffee in the morning. It just wakes people up, and it's at the intersection of home and workday—that perfect moment when your whole life is in balance, and everything seems possible. It seems to me the store should smell like coffee in the morning and cinnamon in the afternoon.

Next, I go to the very back, where all the outdoor gear is sold. And frankly, what's up with that? It makes no sense. I personally hate it when stores change the layout on you constantly, but frankly, now that I'm on the other side of it, I can relate. It's not to annoy and confuse your customer, but to present to her what she is going to absolutely want in this moment.

Today? Umbrellas.

I grab an assortment of various colors. Thank god they're wrapped in plastic sleeves, because there's a lot of dust there. I unwrap them and step into the window display, moving aside dusty board games and crockpots. *That was fine for winter—maybe. But now it's almost summer. Please.* Rummaging under the register, I find a microfiber rag and cleaning product and get to work. Then I dart to the hardware rack at the very back of the store.

"Why, if it isn't little Mrs. Callaway!" Dean, the store's main employee, says as I return with a hammer, nails, hooks, and nylon string. "Can I help?" He's standing in front of the greeting cards rack, a notebook and pencil in hand. It's refreshing and surprising at the same time how natural he seems to think that I'm here.

"I'm all set, thank you!"

Elaine comes out of the prep room wiping her hands on her apron and takes me in a warm hug. "I told you she'd be here! Congratulations, dear," she says before turning to her colleague. "See? Our Willow understands what it means to be a Callaway." She pats my cheek. "You know where to find me if you need a snack."

Forty-five minutes later, I duck into Noah's office to grab my boots. He barely lifts his gaze from his computer. "How long have we had these umbrellas?" I ask.

"No one buys umbrellas here."

"So—a long time?"

"I could check," he says, not looking at all like someone who wants to check.

"Nope, all good." I step outside, and staying under the awning, look at my display. Two umbrellas hang from the ceiling of the window at an angle, five more rest on the bottom of the display, large splashes of color facing the street. Three or four are still folded and neatly tucked in a vintage metal bin. The whole thing looks playful... and necessary. I'll just switch the yellow and the red so the whole composition is both more balanced and more contrasted.

Nathaniel, the old man in charge of flower baskets, mowing, snow removal, and trashcans around town, comes up to me. "How much for these?"

We never sell umbrellas, so I make the price up. "Fifteen apiece, two for twenty-five, three for thirty."

He raises an eyebrow. "Three for thirty, huh? I'll take the pink, the blue, and the yellow. For the grandkids and the wife." I grab the umbrellas from inside, and he hands me rumpled bills.

"What was that about?" Noah asks, frowning. He's holding a paper cup of coffee in his hand, making a face as he sips from it.

"Sold three umbrellas," I say, feeling very proud.

"To Nathaniel?"

I nod. "For his family." I give him the bills.

Noah huffs and shakes his head like that's the weirdest thing ever. He gets behind the register, sets his coffee on the wooden counter, and starts typing a whole lot of stuff.

"Wait, show me," I say, sliding right next to him.

He pushes his glasses up. "I have to do a little finagling for the tax," he explains. "Lemme show you."

We spend the next ten minutes going over the operation of the register. Noah's fingers grazing against mine don't exactly help in the focus department, but overall I stay on task.

"I could take the second register, you know. This way people would see my face and—"

"One register's enough. If there's a line, I go. You can... just keep doing what you're doing."

"Oh. Cool." *That's good, right?* He's happy I sold something. I think.

Once we're done, I drag the whole container of umbrellas right next to the entrance. Then I put a sign with the pricing I came up with and Noah didn't seem to have a problem with.

Sensing I'm onto something, I grab a large wicker basket and go around the store gathering items for a rainy day: Foldable ponchos, rain boots, coloring books and crayons, yarn and knitting needles, playing cards and other small games. Then I put them right next to the umbrellas and make a pretty sign indicating where they can all be found.

When that's done, I tackle the endcap shelf that's most visible from the entrance, clearing it of all the maple syrup products and filling it with Father's Day gift ideas for any budget. Pocket knives, engraved mugs, fishing lures, beer sleeves, rolled T-shirts. The display is both attractive and affordable. But there's so much more in the store that could go on that shelf. So I add a sign: *Ask us for ideas for Father's Day!*

I'm just done tacking the sign at eye level when Haley comes in. "Oh cool!" She wraps me in a hug. "Look at you, going all Mrs. Callaway on us! I couldn't believe it—had to come check it out for myself. You sneaky little bee-atch. I love you, you know." She takes stock of me visually. "How are you doing?" she asks. "I mean, really," she adds in a whisper.

I blink, not knowing how to answer that. This isn't the place for open-heart confessions. "Hanging in there," I answer. "Doing my best."

"Awww, babe. You *are* the best," she says, taking me in a hug again.

Noah comes out of his office, walking up to us. "Haley. I thought I heard voices. Anything I can help you with?"

Haley wraps her arm around my shoulders. "Nope! I came to say hi to Willow. Maybe shop for Dad, and Willow can help me with that," she says, pointing to the display I just put together.

Noah's gaze falls on me and... is that *tenderness*? He smiles and says, "You're in good hands with her. I'll leave you to it." He walks away, and I can't help but admire his broad shoulders, and the way his khakis mold his butt. He turns around and catches me staring. "Babe?"

Babe? Did he call me Babe? How does that make me all hot and bothered?

"Yep?" I quip. This is totally off script. We only talked about PDA in a general fashion. I don't know how to act right now.

"Lemme know if you need anything, 'kay, sweetheart?"

Sweetheart? I give him a thumbs up, unable to say anything.

"Ohmygod you two are soooo sweet together. Like, I *never, ever*, saw it coming." Haley squeezes my arm. "Okay, show me your Father's Day stuff."

I take her to the different areas of the store—the wine cellar with its rare vintages and select whiskeys, as well as some of Haley's own production, then to the clothing with super comfortable outdoor gear, the back area with gardening, animal feed, barbecue paraphernalia, and heavy equipment. Finally, I take her upstairs to show her the larger furniture pieces that her dad, Craig, would enjoy.

"Let me recap," she says, opening the notes app on her phone. "Leather gloves and matching tool belt."

I nod. "Made in Vermont, and we can have them custom engraved."

"Rocking chair."

"Same. Local makers, and you could have the family name engraved. Top it with a nice wool blanket."

"'Kay," she says, focusing on her screen. "Timberland American Craft boots. A smoker—I think his is getting pretty old. A fishing rod. A heating wool jacket. Um... wow. Okay. Lemme text the gang, and I'll let you know what we settle for."

I walk her back to the entrance. "Cards and wrapping paper will be on us," I say, pointing to our gift-wrapping display.

She pulls me close to her as we walk back in front of the Father's Day display. "Selfie!" she says! "Remember Alex's lessons!" Alex was, and still is, all over the small businesses in town using social media to promote themselves and Emerald Creek for free.

She taps her screen, possibly posting the photo already, then says, "I'll tag you, Noah, and the store. And I'll text you about Dad's gift."

"You do that," I say, smiling at her.

Right after she leaves, Lane comes in. "Oh, I'm happy to see you," she says. "I saw Chris is hiring... I didn't know... Noah didn't say..." She takes me in a hug without a warning. "I'm glad you're here," she says, rubbing my back.

Her support is unexpected but also so genuine, I wish I could have this bond with her for real and forever. "I'm good. Your brother is going to have to put up with me."

She tilts her head back dramatically. "Ohmygod, yessss." Letting go of me, she motions toward the display window and checks to make sure Dean is out of earshot. "I sort of figured you were here, when I saw that. It's the little things, you know? It matters to people. Noah is always locked up in his office." She rolls her eyes. "You gotta be on the floor, selling. You'll be great, and you make him so happy."

Surely what she's seeing is Noah's peace of mind now that he's met the condition of the trust, yet I can't help the strange warmth spreading through me at her words.

I'm saved from my spiraling thoughts by an incoming text message.

Haley: Rocking chair, blanket, and smoker. Rocking chair should be engraved, *The King*.

I answer with a thumbs up and raise my eyebrows. "Looks like I just sold a few hundred dollars' worth of Father's Day gifts to the King family," I announce rather proudly.

"Look at you!"

"By the way, how do we get the rocking chairs engraved?" I ask Dean, who's now settling at the register.

He raises a bushy eyebrow. "Gotta ask the boss."

"Oh, so he is sometimes useful," I say, smiling.

"Eh, every now and then. That's why we keep him around," he answers with a wink.

Lane links our arms. "Gives you an excuse to go into his office. Not that you need one." She blushes slightly and adds under her breath, "By the way, I moved my stuff to the tower. Give you your privacy and all that."

For a beat I'm unsure what she's talking about, but the deepening crimson of her cheeks clues me in. Last night she heard me laugh loudly in Noah's bedroom and drew her own conclusions.

Having nothing to say to that, I turn around and dash to Noah's office as Lane goes to the prep room to chat with Elaine. "Hey so, how do we go about engraving a rocking chair?"

"What for?" he asks, not even looking up from his computer.

"Haley, and I guess Hunter and Logan—and maybe Justin and Ethan—are getting that for Craig for Father's Day. They want the chair to be engraved *The King*."

He takes his glasses off and narrows his eyes on me. "They're buying a rocking chair?"

What's the big deal? "Yeah. And a blanket and a smoker."

He looks stunned and mutters, "I don't think they ever bought anything here for Father's Day other than a stupid plastic mug years ago." Then he shakes himself up and says, "Uh, lemme call the maker. They're in Middlebury."

I plop into the seat in front of him while he places the custom order. "Well that was nice and easy," I say.

He quirks an eyebrow at me. "Not even ten o'clock and my wife has sold more than we sometimes do in a whole day. Very impressive... Mrs. Callaway." He adds the last part after a beat, giving me a half smile that twists my solar plexus.

This is exactly what I shouldn't want.

I stand from my chair. "Surprised Ms. Angela isn't here to check out the attraction," I drop. I might feel great about what I'm doing, but I know everyone in Emerald Creek has their own opinion and will be sharing it. "Oh," I say, realizing, "they're all at Millie's, aren't they?" Millie owns the best coffee shop in town, aptly called Easy Monday. A stop there just sets the day right. It comes with free romance books and more gossip than you will ever need.

"That would be my guess, yes. Does that bother you?" His gaze unsettles me in the best way possible.

I shrug. "Nah."

"Let's go out to dinner tonight," he blurts. "Just me and you..." His gaze drifts away then narrows sharply back on me as if he's made a decision. "At Chloe's Nook, not Lazy's. Make it look special, you know. Holding hands and stuff. Shut them up and be done with it."

That sounds terribly like a date. I shouldn't think about it this way, because Noah is my husband, but the fact that I do tells me one thing:

I'm still seeing him as my crush. That little flutter in my stomach? My hands clamming up? That's not from going to dinner with my fake husband.

That's from going on a date with Noah.

Kiara is right: I'm screwed.

"We can't," I blurt.

He pushes his glasses up his nose, a question painted on his face. "Willow…" he starts, his words trailing as if he's trying to break some hard news.

"We're having dinner at my mom's," I remind him.

"So—tomorrow."

I massage the kink building in my neck. I can't picture myself on a date with Noah. I'm going to start getting ideas, and if I drink a little too much, I might forget all this is fake. "It's community dinner at Lazy's," I conveniently remember. No one would want to miss that. The whole town gets together for a potluck dinner, and the less fortunate leave with food, cash if they need it, and more importantly, a sense of belonging.

"Shit, I forgot about that."

I raise a finger, trying to make a point. "Opportunity for PDA," I whisper. We'll be among our friends, which, as far as I'm concerned, is way safer than face-to-face in a romantic setting. "Everyone will see us. More bang for our buck than just the two of us at a restaurant."

His cheekbones color adorably and he clears his throat. "What did you have in mind? Feels like we should discuss this."

My gaze drifts over his chest to his rolled-up sleeves, my brain giving me an endless supply of ideas. "Let's just wing it," I whisper, frowning like this is nothing. Nothing at all. "Anything feels uncomfortable to you, just let me know…"

He pretends to clean his glasses. "Should we choose a safe word?"

Right then, Lane barges into the office and turns crimson as she hears Noah's last words. Her mouth drops open. "Oopsie, I did not hear that," she mumbles as she retreats.

"Might wanna knock next time!" Noah bellows.

CHAPTER SEVENTEEN

Noah

"What should I call her?" I ask Willow. We're on our way to her mom's, and we're going through the story of why we got married, how I proposed, things like that. Things that Willow thinks her mom might ask. Willow is faking a relaxed confidence that this will go well, but the set in her jaw, the way she clenches the wheel tell a different story.

I'm trying—really trying—to stay open and nonjudgmental. To give her mom the benefit of the doubt. I remember when Willow used to bounce in and out of Emerald Creek. In a town like ours, that kind of thing stands out. I never knew the whole story, just enough to guess it had to do with her mom. If she'd been sick, we'd have known. And I don't ever remember a father in the picture. That must have been hard, raising a kid on your own, outside the safety net of Emerald Creek. Still... there was always something about Willow going back and forth that didn't sit right with me.

"Her friends call her Marcy. I mean, what else could you call her?"

"Marcy it is."

I need to tamp down my protective streak when it comes to Willow and remember that she's only my wife on paper.

But that counts for something, too, doesn't it?

Willow pulls onto the piece of land where her mom's mobile home sits. It's been here for as long as I can remember, back when Willow's grandfather lived in it. What used to be a cute house is now slightly sagging on one side like a sinking ship, probably from the ground underneath it being soaked. Paint is peeling off. Two planters on either side of the front door add a pop of color but aren't enough to fend off the sense of hopelessness that permeates the whole place.

Willow parks the car to the side, where some gravel might have been spread a year or two ago.

"Come on, let's get this over with." She's already almost at the door, while I'm barely out of the car.

I grab the flowers I set on the back seat and reach her right in time to place my hand on the small of her back as she enters her mother's house.

"Mom! We're here!" she calls out.

While Willow goes to find Marcy, I hang back a bit and look at the pictures on the wall.

Willow with a gap-toothed smile, skinny legs poking out of her shorts and a Patriots T-shirt hanging too big on her frame. She's holding Ms. Angela's hand, and they're both at a little league football game here in Emerald Creek.

Willow eating a hot dog at the King's Farm, mustard on the tip of her nose, a dog sitting at her feet, looking up at her with a lolling tongue.

Willow on a bicycle zipping down a grass-covered hill, long hair floating behind her, hands in the air, mouth wide open as if she's screaming her joy.

"I wasn't there, or she would have worn a helmet." I turn to see the two women walking toward me.

Willow's lips are pursed at her mother's words, but she doesn't respond.

Marcy extends her hand and gives me a small smile. "Welp, welcome to the family," she says and snickers, a dried out, bitter version of Willow's generous, wholehearted laughter. "Bet you didn't see that one coming," she adds.

I'm not sure what she's referring to. Our marriage? The being welcomed into the family? I take her frail, cold hand in mine. "Thank you. These are for you," I add, handing her the flowers, which she takes without looking at them.

"Take care of these, will ya," Marcy tells Willow, handing her the bouquet as if it might bite her.

"Smells delicious in here," I add, not knowing what else to say.

Marcy answers with a gesture toward the table set for three. A cupboard slaps shut as Willow pulls a vase and unwraps the flowers I brought.

"Anything I can do?" I ask while Marcy sinks onto her chair.

"Nope," the two women answer at the same time. Willow places the bouquet on the coffee table in the living room, then pulls a carton of juice out of the fridge. The oven beeps and I stand, but Willow stares me back into my seat.

After some agonizingly long silent moments where a piping hot lasagna and a salad appear on the table, my wife sits down. But when she reaches for the serving spoon, I take it from her, needing to do something about the icy atmosphere before we all freeze over. "Marcy. Big or small appetite?"

"No appetite at all," she sighs.

I scoop a small serving and set it on her plate. "If I'm not mistaken, this looks like Shannon's lasagna," I answer, referring to Colton's mom's signature dish. "Should do wonders to your appetite."

"I could never cook to save my life. Raised Weeping here on Chef Boyardee."

"Weeping?" I ask.

"Weeping Willow," Willow volunteers, and my heart clenches. That's the only nickname her mother could come up with? Suddenly memories of the scared kid who moved in with Ms. Angela, holding her books tight against her in the school hallways, come haunting me. It's no wonder Emerald Creek felt like home to her. No one here gave her demeaning nicknames or made her feel unwelcome.

I make a noncommittal grunt as I scoop lasagna onto Willow's and my plate.

"Do you know Chef Boyardee?" Marcy asks.

"Not personally, no," I answer with a smile.

"Funny one," Marcy answers with a straight face.

Well shit. Now I've insulted her with my sense of humor. "I've had it," I lie. Mom had the luxury of time to cook for us from scratch, and it's something I've continued. "Pretty good, if I recall."

"The salad is from Cassandra," Marcy says.

"Ah, with basil and parsley?"

She shrugs. "We'll find out."

Once Willow and Marcy have food in them, the tension releases partially. The bout of bad weather is an easy topic of conversation. Once we've milked it until there's nothing more to add, Marcy says, "So, when are you due?"

I nearly spit out my food.

Willow is ashen. "We're not pregnant."

Marcy snorts. "Then why would you go and get married like that? And to a Callaway?"

I ignore the jab at my family, focusing my gaze on my wife.

"Mom," she hisses.

"What?" Marcy takes a sip of apple cider, her hands shaking slightly, and I can't help but wonder if it's due to her condition or to something else.

I set my fork down and clear my throat.

Willow glances nervously at me. "Don't. Just don't."

In a last-ditch effort to save the evening, I motion to the table. "Shannon's lasagna, babe. You should have more."

"You can take it home, big man," Marcy says.

I take a sip of apple cider, load another forkful, and say, "Is this about the Callaway who didn't want to marry you guys's great-grandmother?" There'd been some scandal in the past century, the kind that gets passed down from generation to generation with no one ever caring about fact-checking, because where would the fun be in that?

The horrible realization finally strikes me. With gritted teeth, I ask, "Are you suggesting we might be related? Because now would be a good time to bring it up."

She fakes a smile at her daughter. "See, that's why decent people get married the good ol'-fashioned way, with advance notice, and a couple of minutes for folk to come forward during the ceremony and share their information."

Willow makes a face. "Yeah, they don't do that anymore."

"Do you have any reason to believe we're related?" I ask again.

Willow rounds her eyes at me, lifts her shoulder in a how-is-this-even-relevant way.

And she's right. It's not. There's no law that says I can't marry a distant cousin, and even if that would be icky, it doesn't matter at all in this marriage.

It's not like we're going to get pregnant.

Or have sex.

Or even kiss. Although...

"No great-grandmother of ours ever considered marrying a Callaway. Are you nuts?" Marcy bites back.

"Maybe I am. What's so terrible about us anyway?"

Marcy lifts her chin, and Willow rolls her eyes. With a deep sigh, she says, "Supposedly you guys stole from us a long, long time ago."

Not this again. "Stole... what?" Better to play stupid than to explain how this is not relevant.

"Land," Marcy drops. "Like you didn't know that's why you're so rich."

I want to tell her we're not rich. At least not in the way she thinks—the way Gail does, where money can be spent without counting. We are land rich and asset rich. But some years that means we are cash poor, trying to cover all the associated expenses. "I—I don't know that anyone can actually steal land that easily. I mean there would be a trace of that... I'm not sure what you're referring to, Mrs.—Marcy."

"That's enough," Willow snaps before her mother can answer. She pushes her chair back and stands, makes quick work of removing our unfinished plates, clears the rest of the table, loads the dishwasher, and wipes the table in no time.

I risk a glance at Marcy, but she's looking at her daughter with something like sadness and envy. There are a dozen things a normal son-in-law could say right now, including a promise I can't hold ("I promise to make your daughter happy"), a minefield of a question

("What can I do to make this right?"), and the cowardly and untrue, "It was her idea to fly to Vegas."

I settle for the innocent, blanket, "Can I see Willow's baby photos?" accompanied with my best impression of an enamored smile toward my wife. Surely bringing back happy memories will salvage this evening.

Marcy exhales an exhausted sigh, and I regret the question. Who knows where she needs to dig them out of? "Didn't have time for no photos. But lemme ask you a question, Noah Callaway. What's in it for you?" Her eyes are narrowed on me. "'Cause she's always sworn she'd never get married. To anyone. Now, I can see how you might turn her head, but what could you possibly see in her?"

"Gee, thanks, Mom," Willow says before I can come up with an answer. She barely glances down at us from where she stands, arms crossed, leaning against the sink.

"Don't get all high and mighty, Weeping," Marcy retorts. "It's not like you bring anything to the table, like they say."

As Willow's eyes blur with unshed tears that she swiftly blinks away, a cold wave descends on me as I battle shame mixed with a dose of anger. "I'm not sure where to start, Marcy. Maybe with her generosity? She spends her winter weekends as a volunteer teacher of adaptive skiing, after all. Or her courage? Talking here about her being a thru-hiker. But if you're insisting on something she 'brings to the table,' let's see. She makes me laugh, her beauty makes me look good just by being by her side, her magic touch is already turning the store around, and she makes a mean oatmeal. I could go on all day."

Marcy grunts, seeming unsatisfied, then stands, fists on the table to stand up.

My wife's cheekbones are red, and she struggles to keep her voice soft. "Let me help you," she tells her mother. She avoids my gaze as she helps her mother down the hall.

"Thank you for dinner, Marcy!" I holler.

"Yeah, yeah," she says, waving back as she disappears in the dark hallway.

My heartbeat is still out of whack, and I hope my anger didn't show. When Willow comes back minutes later, I feel her shake as I set a hand on her arm.

Marcy's illness is taking a toll on her, physically and emotionally, and she seems to have her reasons to be upset at us. At me. But I hate how it's affecting Willow.

We dash under the rain to her car. "Why don't you let me drive," I offer, expecting her to say she's fine.

But she hands me her keys, and I open her door, watching her ball onto her seat.

I quickly round the car and get in. "Hey," I say softly.

She looks up at me.

"I'm sorry," we both say.

"Come here," I add, taking her into the most PG hug.

She leans into me, letting me rub her back, burrowing her face deeper in my chest. I drop a kiss on the top of her head and she lifts her face to me. "You give really good hugs."

"So I've been told," I say smiling.

"Can we go home now?" she whispers, rubbing her arms and staring out the windshield.

I drive us in silence, desperate to make her feel better. But sweeping this under the rug won't do it. Willow is embarrassed, and she needs to know she has no reason to be. "We should talk about what happened," I say as we both walk into the kitchen.

She shrugs, the look of defeat in her eyes undoing me. "As long as you don't try to fix it," she says.

"What do you mean?" Of course I want to fix it. I'm responsible for this, dammit. Without this marriage, none of this would have happened. *I need a drink.* "D'you like bourbon?"

"Not really." She frowns. "You go ahead. I'll meet you in the... what's the name of the room at the front?"

"The parlor."

She giggles and leaves with a finger wave, sashaying with exaggeration. "I'll meet you in the parlor, *dahling*."

My gaze goes to her ass—where else?— and my mood improves incrementally. When I join her, there's a fire roaring and little lamps lit here and there. I haven't been in this room in forever—I'm glad chimney sweeps are scheduled on the regular. "Where'd you find the firewood?" I ask as I set both our drinks on a side table.

"Oh, there was an old chair that worked out just fine," she answers, making me startle. But my gaze darts to a neat woodpile on the side of the fireplace.

"I brought this in this morning. That's okay, right?"

"You're the lady of the house," I say, my dick slightly twitching at the words—and what the fuck is that about? I hand her the whiskey sour I made for her. "Let me know what you think." I hope she likes it. Bourbon has a way of mellowing you; it's a shame for her to miss out on that.

She takes a sip. "It's really good, thank you." Then she lets out an airy laugh. "Look at us, all proper, sipping whiskey in front of a fire in the—the what now? The *parlor*?"

I nod, liking the way the flames dance on her skin and make her hair look ablaze. "We look like we've been married fifteen years."

"Dahling, Nanny said Noah the third threw a tantrum. Whatever shall we do?" she says in a mock British accent.

I nearly choke on my drink. "Noah the third?"

"Obviously," she says, swinging her foot, looking at the fire. "Your father was Noah, right, although everyone called him Mac?" Her voice is soft, as if she needs to be careful.

I take a long gulp of bourbon. "How d'you know that?"

She lifts an eyebrow. "We're married, remember? I did my homework."

Shit. I should do mine.

"That's not true. It was in his obituary," she says even softer. "D'you miss him a lot?"

A vise tightens around my stomach, memories flashing, bitter snippets in my soul. Dad becoming a different person after Mom died. Dad losing interest in us, in his businesses, in Emerald Creek. And then meeting Gail. "I missed him a lot after our mother died. He... he checked out. His passing was a shock but... we'd already lost him. He wasn't even living here anymore, in the end."

"That must have been so tough," she says softly. A ball forms in my throat. How nice would it be, to have someone to share the burden with?

Eager to change the conversation, I ask, "So—what happened back there?"

Chapter Eighteen

Willow

I raise my gaze to Noah, suddenly feeling overwhelmed by his concern. This should not be happening right now. I shouldn't be opening up to him.

Not if I'm to protect my heart. Keep myself from falling harder.

"Willow," he insists softly, his hand reaching for mine, then quickly retracting as if he remembers at the last minute that this marriage is fake.

His concern for me isn't.

The heat of the drink he made for me fills my lungs as I take a sip. "We don't see eye to eye on a lot of things and she needs…" I take a deep breath. Understanding of what's going on with Mom is crystallizing as I talk to Noah. "She can't help the way she is. Sometimes it seems that she just needs to bring me down. And other times, it's like she's trying to replace all the times we didn't have together, but…" I turn my eyes to him and find his gaze on me, deep and understanding "…it's too late now."

He frowns. "It's never too late to repair a relationship," he says quickly. "She's sick and..." His words hang in the air as he struggles to finish his sentence. I know what he means. That he wishes he had more time with both his parents.

"Mom was not... she was not a model parent like yours." Understatement of the year. I still remember hoping she'd never visit me in Emerald Creek, so I didn't have to face the other kids' curious stares.

"It doesn't mean it wouldn't hurt just as much to lose her."

"I suppose not," I whisper. A mother is a mother.

He takes a sharp inhale as if he's about to speak but stays silent.

"What?" Somehow, now that I've opened that door, I'm craving this heart-to-heart. I've hardly shared with anyone the shame and trouble of my early years. But Noah's gentle understanding makes it easy to unburden on him.

The earlier compliments at Mom's didn't exactly hurt either. How does he know all this about me?

"No... I..." He takes another quick inhale.

His hesitancy is endearing. "Go on. You can ask me anything," I say. Truthfully, it feels good to unload on someone who actually cares.

"What's with the nickname?" he asks. I noticed his frown when Mom called me Weeping, but I never thought anything of it. "I used to cry a lot as a baby. I guess it stuck." At least *she* never called me Pillow. I chase *that* bitter memory away by smiling encouragingly at Noah. Another question right about now would work out just fine.

"Your father...?" He narrows his eyes on me, his concern clear.

I shake my head, a small smile spreading on my lips. "Never knew him. I don't think she did either."

He doesn't even flinch. Just raises his chin, his stare on the fire. "She probably didn't have an easy life."

"No, she didn't," I whisper. Did she have a choice? Or was she just too weak to fight for a better life for us? "I can't believe she brought up the stolen land thing. I thought that stupid story died with Gramps. He was always complaining about everything and blaming everyone for the way his life turned out." And yes, he was jealous to the point of obsession of the Callaways, and clearly Mom retained some of the toxicity on that topic.

Noah grunts, his gaze still on the fire.

"I don't know if she takes advantage of being ill or if she genuinely is more abrasive because of what she's going through. But just so you know, it's not normally like this." I realize it's unimportant how bad it is or isn't. He didn't genuinely *meet the parents*. It was a matter of necessity for me, of appearances for him.

"I didn't ask her about her health tonight," he says, looking at me. "It felt too personal, for a first time. And now I realize I haven't asked you either, and that's really shitty of me. I'm sorry I've been so self-centered. How... how is she... is she going to be okay?"

It was not self-centered. We've talked about it, if briefly. And I started using his credit card to pay for medical bills. "She was diagnosed with stage III ovarian cancer late last year. She had chemo and surgery, and she was stable for a while. Last month, they found it had returned. But it's small, and slow growing. So for now she's staying home, on daily meds."

"How does she manage that?"

I shrug. "She tires easily, can get a little confused. Her hair is growing back slowly, so that makes her happy. Gives her hope." She still wears a scarf when she's not alone, as her hair is growing back in uneven wisps.

"She's lucky to have you," he says, his gravelly voice making me all kinds of funny inside.

"You know what, I think you're right."

He laughs. "You know your worth, and I love that about you."

My heart stumbles at his unfortunate word choice. *Don't dwell on it. He didn't mean it that way. You know he didn't.* "I'll take that as a compliment."

"Well aren't you two cute!" Lane calls out.

I jump in my chair as if I'd been caught kissing in the janitor's closet. "Hey, what's up?" I ask, my gaze snapping briefly to the handsome man at her side.

"This is Jake," she says with a wink for me. "He's just visiting Emerald Creek, you're forbidden to ask awkward questions, and I'm just grabbing my ID," she says as she runs up the stairs.

Noah sizes the guy up and down but doesn't get up. "Jake. Noah. Where are you guys going?"

"The Grumbler? The Howler? The Grunter. I think she said the Grunter."

"The Growler," I offer. It's an event space up in the hills with several bars, live music, pool tables. Trouble will find you there if you're looking for it, or you can just have a really good time. "That's awesome. You'll have fun. D'you know who's playing tonight?"

"I didn't even know they had live music."

Noah takes my hand. "Maybe we should go?" He squeezes it spasmodically as if he's trying to pass along a message in Morse.

"Babe, I don't think that's what Lane wants."

"What? Like a double date." He stands. "Come on, it'll be fun."

Jake stretches a smile and stuffs his hands in his pockets. "Sure," he says.

"Sure what?" Lane asks, materializing at his side. She touched up her makeup and is holding the cutest sparkling clutch that matches a bedazzled jacket.

I stand next to Noah and tug on his hand, leaning my body against his, feeling his tension. "Babe, next time. It's their first time going out together." I can feel him relax against me, and it brings me a tiny little bit of joy. Then I pull out my phone and snap Jake's picture before anyone has a chance of knowing what's happening.

"You can never be too safe," I say with a wink for Lane.

She pulls on Jake's hand and rolls her eyes at me.

"You kids have fun," Noah says, and I stifle my laughter. As the door starts closing on them, he adds, "Don't—" at a high volume, but he doesn't have time to finish. Whatever he was going to say? *Don't do anything I wouldn't do. Don't come back past midnight. Don't sleep with*—scratch that, I sure hope he wouldn't go there. Point is, anything he was going to say starting with *Don't* is a bad idea.

So before I can think about it, I implement *my* terrible idea, which is to shut him up with my hand on his mouth right as the door closes, leaving us both alone and way too close.

Time seems to stop as his lips touch the palm of my hand and his glasses slightly fog. I drop my hand as if nothing happened, eyes widening on him. But it's too late. Heat spreads from my fingertips to my whole body, and I have to step back to keep myself in check.

"I got his picture," I croak to shift his attention from my inappropriate touching.

"I saw that," he answers in a perfectly normal voice. As if he hadn't felt it too. As if the tension in his body, the light flickering in his eyes, his briefly erratic breathing, weren't a tell of anything. "You're actually worse than me."

"I can be sneaky," I admit, "but only for a good cause."

"I think we've established that already," he answers, his gaze dropping to my mouth.

Chapter Nineteen

Noah

Fuck but her lips are tempting.

I take a step back, scolding myself. She was only trying to be a good friend to Lane. Her hand on my mouth didn't mean anything to her. She wasn't flirting or taunting me. She didn't feel anything, not the way I did. She was just laser-focused on protecting Lane, even reminding me about the picture she took.

"I have work to do," I say, which is an awkward thing to say. It's not like we're a real married couple, needing to keep each other in the loop of our nightly activities. I just don't know how else to tell her that I can't be in her presence anymore without a serious danger to my sanity.

I was prepared to be forever indebted to this woman for helping our family out. In Vegas, I became aware that she would probably turn into the closest female friend I'd have, one that was off-limits.

But tonight I'm down another infuriating level of intimacy. Tonight, I've seen up close her tiny family, the thin threads of belonging she's trying to pull together to weave her life, and I understand now how our small town is so important to her. For all intents and purposes, *we* are her family. And this endears her to me in ways she will never understand. It's as if our DNAs were rooted together by the same primal need for Emerald Creek to always be there.

If that weren't enough, she has a level of patience and understanding of others that leaves me in awe, while being fun and lighthearted.

To top it off, I'm becoming intimately familiar with the pattern of her breathing, the scent of her skin, the fragrance of her shampoo, the silkiness of her hair, the clarity of her laughter, and the register of her voice, although I still need to figure out why sometimes it comes out breathy and uncertain.

I'm falling in love with my wife.

And there's nothing I can do about it, because no way in hell am I even going to suggest I feel anything for her.

Because that would be a real dick move.

"Take your time, I won't be up there for at least a couple of hours," I add. Since that first morning when she started getting dressed in front of me, we've been trying to protect each other's intimacy in a way that doesn't raise suspicion from Lane or Beck.

Getting the hint, Willow walks away. "Ladida, dahling," she sing-songs in her fake British accent, wiggling her hand at me, tripping a bit.

That whiskey sour sure relaxed her. "You gonna be okay getting up the stairs?" I ask, trying not to laugh.

"Yup! Yup-yup-yup." She disappears up the dark staircase. I listen to make sure she doesn't need help, then go to my office.

I open my emails and type a message to my lawyer, attaching my marriage certificate and asking for next steps.

Then I review our numbers until my eyes cross on the lines of the spreadsheet. I check the time.

She's got to be asleep by now. No risk of late-night chatter in the room we're sharing.

Now that Lane has moved to the tower, I suppose Willow and I could spread out if we wanted to. We'd maintain the appearance of sharing a bedroom, but with no one to snoop around at night, I could crash in a guest room and get a decent night's sleep in a real bed. *And not hear her breathe? Not feel her stir with the first ray of sunlight?*

I'll take the couch any time.

When I get upstairs, I find Willow curled up on the couch again. *Stubborn.*

Bathed in moonlight, her silver shape moves to the rhythm of her soft breathing.

I take a moment to admire her lips puffed up from sleep, the lock of dark hair curling on her cheek, her eyelids fluttering as she dreams. She's absolute perfection, asleep just as much as when she's awake.

Sliding my hands carefully under her frame, I carry her where she belongs. In my large, fluffy bed. Then I tuck her in, leaving quickly for the bathroom. She stirs but doesn't wake up. *Good.*

Because for the next... how many months this needs to go on for, no way in hell is she sleeping on the couch.

I slide under the light blanket still warm from her body and try to fall asleep, but her smell and the sound of her breathing just paces from me give me a raging hard-on that's not conducive to even dozing off. I fight it by thinking about my endless to-do list, then my thoughts drift to Griff, a mix of longing, resentment, and envy taking hold.

Griff made his life in Boston long before Dad died, for no reason I could understand other than he liked a big city better than our small town. It still stung when after Dad's funeral, over maybe too much whiskey, he said that he'd understand and even support me if I wanted to sell everything. I might have said things I now regret. He might have told me to get lost. It's all a little blurry now. All I know is I miss him, and I hardly saw him at Colt's wedding.

I should call him.

And Lane. Shouldn't she be back by now? Who is this guy she went out with? We only have a first name, which may or may not be real, and a picture. Thank god for Willow's quick thinking.

Lane wants to go live in New York City. A dozen scenarios of how bad that could end runs through my mind. But at least if Lane is away, I won't see her going out. I won't need to worry in real time, like I used to with Beck.

Beck. He's turned his life around. No more calls to pick him up at the police station. No more mandated community service. Doesn't mean I don't worry about him. I always will. I need to talk to him about the landscaping business. See how many new clients we could get with a couple more guys and equipment. I start running the numbers in my head, until sleep seizes me at dawn.

"It's community dinner tonight," I tell Beck when he barges into the kitchen the next morning, his hair a riot, wearing nothing but low-hanging jeans.

"Cool," he answers.

He's irritating me. I'm running on two hours of sleep, three at best; I can't deal with him this morning. "Would you mind wearing a shirt?"

He snaps his head up, eyelids heavy, looking utterly relaxed. He gives me his lazy smile. Is there a girl in his studio apartment above the barn? "Sure," he says as he exits through the kitchen door.

There's totally a girl in his bed right fucking now. I know I'm in the wrong, but I totally hate him for the sex look on his face. It's just unfair.

He comes right back wearing a jean jacket with shiny things on it. The thing is so small it constricts his shoulders, stops above his belly button, and there's no chance in hell he can close it.

I know this is a redirection on his part, and it's a job well done. Now I need to be the big fucking brother again. This trap is so old. "Is this Lane's?" I ask in my inquisitive pseudo-parent voice.

He shrugs. "Think so. Found it outside. There was a guy's jacket, too, but eh... didn't wanna wear some random dude's shit." Oh yeah, total redirection. Beck knows I'll always fall for protecting his Irish twin, aka being on her case rather than on his.

He busies himself making two coffees. Which means he'll be gone in thirty seconds. Which reminds me, I need to bring Willow a coffee.

The left side of my skull starts pounding. "Are you telling me..." I'm having trouble processing that Lane might have had someone overnight. Should I put this into words? If I don't say it out loud, did it really happen?

Beck takes the two coffees and hands me one. "You look like you could use this."

I take the hot cup absentmindedly and resume my train of thought. Did my sister bring a random stranger in our house to...? How did I not hear a thing? What would I have done if I'd heard anything? Holy shit. At least when they were teenagers I could have rules. Now? Forget it.

I decide to turn my attention back to Beck. Easier. Nursing his coffee, he's looking out the kitchen window, toward the garden and the barn. Why is he still here?

"Is there someone in the barn I should know about?" Proud of myself for not letting him off the hook.

"Not that you should know about, and not for long." He cranes his neck. "Yep, there she goes."

"That's disgusting."

He turns around and laughs at me, coffee splashing out of his mug. Then something must catch his eye, because he turns his attention back to the garden. "What the fuck?" he mutters.

I close the distance and peer out the window. Beyond the rhododendrons, Jake is tiptoeing to retrieve the jacket he was wearing last night. He picks it up then casts a hopeful glance to the upper levels, before backing up excruciatingly slowly.

"Huh," Beck says. "Not sure what happened there."

Whatever happened was not in the house. Not sure if I feel better about it.

"Are you wearing my jacket?" Lane screeches, startling us both into turning around. We puff ourselves up and stay shoulder-to-shoulder to hide the view from the window. Some sort of weird fraternal instinct makes us want to keep this guy outside of Lane's line of sight, in case she decides he should have coffee with us. She's wearing her pajamas; her makeup is gone. All signs pointing to a restful night alone. No reason to muddy the waters.

"Finders keepers," Beck deadpans.

"Fuck finders," Lane lashes out, lunging at Beck.

"Ah-ah-ah," Beck says, lifting his cup of coffee. "Already had a close call."

"Take it off!" she says, pulling at the jacket, so focused on her mission, there's no chance she's looking outside.

He moves away from the window, leading her to the other side of the kitchen. "No-no said I should wear something. He can't stand how sexy I am."

"Ugh," Lane growls, giving up the fight. "Fine. I don't want to see your nipples at breakfast."

"Speaking of breakfast, where's Willow?" Beck asks. "She makes a mean oatmeal."

"You can make your oatmeal yourself," I grunt as my eye is drawn to the kitchen entrance.

Willow is standing there, a smile spreading on her morning-soft face. She walks to me, *places a kiss on the corner of my mouth*, and turns around to Beck and Lane. "Is Halloween early this year?"

My whole body feels live wired. Her lips barely grazed me, yet I can't breathe, can't think, can't move.

"Man, No-no doesn't do well with PDA," Beck drops. "Look at him. Flaming up."

Willow swings back to me and sets her hand on my chest. *What is she doing?* I know we're supposed to make this look real, but does she need to...

"Aww... is that right?" she coos.

I guess she does.

Winking at me, she runs her hand on my cheek. "Or are you too prudish, Becky?"

This time, Lane snorts.

"I'll make oatmeal for everyone," Willow says, turning her back to my front, still dangerously close to me. "How many of us this morning?"

Lane turns red, Beck laughs, and I try to avoid stroking the spots her lips and hands touched.

"I only see four of us," I finally say, catching up to the fact that my wife is up to speed on last night's developments.

"You snooze, you lose. Noted," Willow answers.

The implications of that answer are too complex for me to handle this morning, so I... redirect *again*.

"It's community dinner tonight at Lazy's. I expect both of you to be there and bring food. And cash."

"Just us? Not Willow?" Beck grunts.

Willow quirks an eyebrow. "I'm his wife. I go where he goes," she says, stirring the oatmeal while my inner caveman is pounding his chest.

"That's incredibly patriarchal," Lane objects.

Willow shrugs. "I wouldn't miss community dinner. That was just an easy cop-out to please hubby. Give me some grace, I haven't had my coffee yet," she adds with a glance my way and a small smile.

"Ooof... not even married a week and already he lets things slide," Beck says, an arrogant smile on his face. "I'll make you your coffee."

I sit at the counter. Might as well own up that I messed up this morning and won't be good for shit. "Make me another one, too, will you?"

Willow serves the oatmeal in little bowls, then picks up a sheet of paper from the counter. "What's this?"

Beck looks over her shoulder. "Ah. That's your husband's house duties schedule. Guess his OCD is acting up again. Want me to tack it on the fridge, like the good old days?"

Lane frowns. "He still does that? When's my turn? Who's on vacuuming duty this week? Please tell me it isn't me. I can't stand the vacuuming."

"And that's why we need this," I manage to interject.

"I don't see my name," Willow says.

Lane and Beck look at me. Like I'm going to put Willow's name on our stupid chore table.

Willow turns around and dramatically tears the schedule apart, dropping it in the recycling pail and swiping her gaze across us. "You guys need to grow up."

My heart swells. "That's a tall order."

Lane and Beck look from Willow to me with their mouths hanging open.

"Now everyone eat their oatmeal while it's warm," Willow says as she slides onto the stool right next to me.

"So... you guys ready to face the mob?" Lane asks after a decent enough time has gone by.

"What mob?" What did I miss now?

"Um... *the whole town*? At Lazy's? Tonight?"

"I'm bracing myself for the Bitch Brigade for sure," Willow answers.

Chapter Twenty

Willow

This fake marriage does a lot of things to me. And making me nervous about going to the community dinner is at the top of the list right now.

I'll be facing the whole town as Noah's wife, Willow-from-the-wrong-side-of-the-tracks. I try to shake the imposter syndrome that's deeper than just from this marriage being fake. I can't help but still see Noah as someone I shouldn't have.

I know Emerald Creek isn't judgmental the way other small towns can be. We're in a hardscrabble part of the country, relying on each other to make it through. Rich or poor doesn't matter when you're stuck in a snowstorm or a barn fire threatens your house. Everyone's help counts.

And yet here I am. A nervous wreck.

Probably more so because I lied to my friends, and that was strategically stupid on my part. I should have made up a proposal and a decision to elope. They would have bought it. *I think*. Now it's going to be a repeat of the other day at the bakery, times ten.

"We have to really put on a good show," I remind Noah as I'm applying makeup, looking at myself in the bathroom mirror while he gets ready in the bedroom.

I washed my hair and let it hang loose so it finishes drying naturally. I chose my bell bottom jeans with the stitched flowers in all sorts of colors, and the short-sleeved ruffled shirt in a light yellow that looks awesome with my tan. I'll throw a shawl on my shoulders just in case.

"Really make them believe we're together-together," I add, not wanting to pronounce the words "in love" but wanting to make sure Noah understands that his mission tonight is to put his hands on me, whether he likes it or not.

Noah's changing the shirt he wore all day for a fresh one, and I catch a glimpse of his torso and abs as I glance at him while talking. *Oops*. Didn't mean to, but *damn*. He's *ripped*. Hides it well too. I avert my eyes and swallow with difficulty.

"I know," he says, tension radiating from him.

"I called the robot vacuum people today," I say to change the topic as I lean closer to the mirror to attach my hoop earrings. After he placed the order for the Kings' rocking chair, Noah showed me how to contact our vendors and gave me free rein as long as I follow the tracking process he has in place. There's no chance in hell I'm placing real orders anytime soon, but this one company I saw on his online POS tickled me.

"Uh-huh?" Shirt buttoned, he leans against the bathroom door and looks at my reflection, rolling his sleeves up while he listens to me. I try not to look at his corded forearms, at the way his veins bulge along the side of his wrists, at the glimmer of the wedding band I slipped on his finger.

"They're gonna send us some samples so we can try them."

"Samples?"

Ready, I turn around and find him pushing his glasses up his nose as if he needs to examine me closer. "Yeah."

His gaze flicks ever so slightly to my lips. "How do you get *samples* of vacuum cleaners?"

"Oh no. We're getting actual vacuum cleaners. So we can sample them."

He's half-blocking my exit from the bathroom, so I brush past him to go into the bedroom, trying not to be obvious as I inhale his subtle scent.

"They're sending us robot vacuum cleaners," he repeats.

"Three of them," I confirm as I pull my platform shoes from the closet. "One for each floor. They think it's to let people try them at home. Which is sorta what we're doing."

"Uh-huh," he says, this time with admiration in his tone.

"You can say it, you know," I tease him.

"Say what?"

I sit on the edge of the bed to buckle my platforms. "That you're proud of your wife." I give him an exaggerated wink that's meant to say I'm joking.

"I'm very proud of my wife," he answers seriously. If I didn't know better, I'd think his vibe is more smoulder than playful, but that's just my wishful thinking.

I zip around to the nightstand so he can't catch how good those words make me feel.

"Hey," I tell him as I slide my wedding band on. "It'll be fine. Just treat me as your girlfriend or something." I glance at him, catching him with his hands on his hips, looking at me top to bottom as if he's not sure what to do with me.

"You mean as my *wife*."

The sharpness of hopeless longing carves its way to my heart. *Don't be silly, Willow. He's just practicing. It's just this whole getting-ready-together-in-the-bedroom that's getting to your head.* I force a laugh. "Right—good point." I take my leather cross-body bag and turn on my heels, eager to leave the bedroom and join Beck and Lane downstairs. Away from Noah for a minute while I collect myself.

"You're not taking this?" he asks, and I turn around. He's spreading my shawl open.

"Oh, thanks."

I extend my hand, but he wraps it around my shoulders instead and lifts my hair out from under it. "Just getting the hang of this wife thing," he murmurs.

Someone please make him stop.

"Course," I answer, my voice stranded.

But he doesn't stop.

Because he understands the assignment perfectly.

When the four of us get to Lazy's, he leads me inside with a hand on the small of my back. The din of conversation dips a bit as we make our entrance, all of Emerald Creek taking in our presence. Then the noise level increases again, confirming we're the hot new topic of gossip.

"Let's get this over with," Noah says, teeth clenched, his hand going from my lower back to my shoulders.

Beck and Lane set the Callaway mac'n cheese on the bar counter while Noah and I make our way to the booth occupied by our friends. We're stopped on our way by Owen. He was a few grades above me in school, but his reputation as a bully was known to all. Now he's a lawyer and still gives me the ick, so I leave Noah's side and latch onto Cassandra who just came in.

She takes me in a warm hug and pulls a small bundle wrapped in a purple muslin out of her bag. "Sage," she says. "You know how to use it, right?" Cassandra's witchy reputation is well-deserved.

I smile as I place the thoughtful gift in my bag. "I sure do. Thank you."

She squeezes my shoulder as we walk farther inside the room. "You'll need it."

Will I, though? Haven't done this since I was a preteen. "I'm sure I will," I answer as she leaves to greet other people.

Alone in the loud room, there's no going back now. My friends are gathered at our usual table. I take a deep breath and join them.

All eyes are on me.

"Show us," Alex says, pointing to my ring finger, not giving me a chance to sit down as my friends crowd me.

"Oh darn it, he's wasn't joking when he married you. That *is* the Callaway ring," Grace says.

"Um—yeah," I say, feeling really self-conscious about wearing a family heirloom I definitely don't deserve. *But it makes the marriage look real.* Alex takes my hand, and my friends fawn over the wedding band.

"That is just so totally Emerald Creek in the form of a ring," Grace whispers. "I've never seen it up close like that." She glances at me with a soft smile. Grace knows about my seemingly life-long infatuation with Noah. There's no way she's not wondering what happened, but she's too sweet to ask or even imply anything.

Her seven-year-old cousin and Alex's adopted daughter wiggles her way within the circle of women and gasps in awe. With a dramatic eye flutter, Skye says, "I think I'll get married after all."

She's met with a concert of awwws, then Alex's comment, "It's not about the ring, sweetie."

"Isn't it, though?" Grace muses, then to Skye, she says, "Your mom is right. You can get your own ring, you know, if that's what you really want."

"But I think it'd be better if someone I looooove gave it to me," Skye answers. Then she turns around and gives her mom's belly a hug before running to join a group of kids.

"How's married life?" Kiara asks, winking at me. "Where's hubby?"

I motion in the general direction of where I left Noah and pointedly focus on Alex. I can't lie to Kiara, neither can I answer truthfully in public. "You feeling okay?" I ask Alex. She looks miserable, sprawled on a chair, both hands on her lower belly.

"I probably won't stay long," she says. "Hey, I have a favor to ask. Would you guys be cool looking after Skye in case no one else is available when the baby comes? I figured you're the closest. When we made our birth plan, we thought of Grace and Ethan, with Kiara and Colton as contingency, but—"

"We're around the corner. Of course we're cool with that," I answer right as Noah joins us, holding a heaping plate of food but looking a little upset. *Owen, for sure.* I slip my hand around his waist and bring him up to speed.

His free arm curves around my shoulders, his fingers stroking the naked skin under my shawl. *Good.* He remembered we're supposed to be married.

And he's damn good at faking it. "We'd love to look after Skye. Right, babe?" He skims my temple with his mouth, inhaling softly. "I got you Shane's shepherd's pie," he says as he sets the plate on the table. "Be right back." He dashes to the back of the room, no doubt to fill up the cash collection box.

Kiara narrows her eyes at Noah's back, then squints at me, a thousand words in the turbulence of her gray eyes. She has her we-have-to-talk look, but I can't go there.

A wave of sadness takes hold of me as I fully grasp the implications of my commitment. I'm truly alone, unable to confide in my friends, to lean into their friendship, to count on their support for however long this lasts. Meanwhile, I'm fast becoming desperately accustomed to my fake husband's displays of physical attraction in public and friendship in private. I feel fucking alone and desperate, and as if that weren't enough, more than just horny.

I'm not going to fall in love with my husband, but it doesn't mean I can't love the way he treats his siblings. The way he shows up every day. At work. At home. For everyone. The way he deals with the loss of his parents, and the responsibilities too-soon bestowed on him. I used to crush on him because he was the real nice guy with a nerd vibe and an outdoorsy body. I didn't know everything else hiding under this yumminess. And I can love all that without being *in love* with him.

Right?

"Babe?" Noah nudges me when he comes back. "Gotta slide in there," he grumbles in my ear. There's ten of us milling around the booth, more coming, and that means we're sitting in pairs. Women on their men's laps. Pregnant woman at the head of the table.

Noah slides in and pulls me onto him as if this were the most natural thing. As if we did this all the time. I have to say, our movements are natural. There's no awkwardness. His palm scoops me up, his hand lands on my hip, nudging me against him. I feel a brief tremor coming from him, some understandable tension. But what are we going to do? We're newlyweds; we're supposed to not be able to keep our hands off each other.

His hand that was on my hip slides down my thigh while the other twirls my hair, moving it to the side. "You okay?" I ask, suddenly self-conscious of my weight.

The rumble of his voice comes right back. "Never been better."

I lean into his ear, getting a whiff of his scent. "You're sure I'm not too heavy?" I whisper.

His hand clenches on my thigh. "What did you say?"

"I said—" I start, but he interrupts me with a spasmodic clench on my thigh.

"Don't ever say that again," he growls. "You're perfect," he says loud enough for everyone to hear, but not in an ostentatious way. Then he turns me sideways on his lap, my back to the wall so we can see each other. Picks up a potato chip, homemade by Chloe, from a bowl in the center of the table and... brings it to my lips.

"They're the best," he says. "Come on, open wide."

Across the table, Kiara averts her gaze from us, her cheeks tinting. I open my mouth, letting Noah drop the chip on the tip of my tongue, briefly feeling the rough pad of his finger.

"You like it?" he asks.

I clench my thighs and try not to choke as air rushes inside my lungs.

He takes another chip and pops it in his mouth. "Go ahead," he says, pointing to the overflowing shared plate he made for the two of us.

There's no way I can push anything down right now. Everything in me is clenching. Belly. Lungs. Thighs.

"Willow, when are you giving up your apartment?" Grace asks.

"Yeah, the new bartender at the restaurant was hoping to rent it," Chloe chimes in, "but he found another place."

Water. I need water. "I'm locked into my lease for a little bit," I lie. "I was gonna take my time sorting through things."

Kiara leans in, clearly enjoying this moment. "Let us know, and we'll help with the move. Colt will take some of his stuff back. He's been missing his big ass TV." Colton left a lot of his furniture to me when he moved in with Kiara, and now I feel totally selfish for not moving out faster. *First my job, now my apartment. Everything that made my life seems to be taken from me.*

"I have not," Colton counters. "I have you," he says as he kisses her neck. To me, he says, "Take all the time you need."

His reassurance isn't enough to lift my anxiety. I wasn't going to give my apartment up. I was going to keep it so I could go back to my home when all this is over, but clearly I didn't think this through! Because of course people would notice.

Stupid, horny me for thinking about the PDA—right—and not the most obvious: not just moving into Lilyvale but officially moving out of my apartment.

Noah wraps his arm around my waist, pulls my side to his front, and nuzzles my ear lobe. "Stop worrying," he whispers in my ear.

My spine arches in delight before I can stop myself. Then Chloe says, "So, Willow, when did you know Noah was the one?" and the whole table quiets down.

Chloe is fairly new to town. She's been here what—a year? She loves the caring tapestry that this whole town weaves; she doesn't know the history of each strand.

She doesn't know about my long-standing crush on Noah, and how my childhood friends kept warning me against it. I suppose this means they didn't tell her about it either, which in a sense is super respectful but also puts me in a pickle.

Especially now that Owen has wandered to our table, plate in hand as he makes the rounds like the politician he is.

I open my mouth to answer, but Noah answers instead, "Willow believes in soul mates."

"Ooh," Chloe coos. "And you don't?"

I feel more than see him shrug. "I believe in Willow."

Suddenly that shepherd's pie is a fascinating object to study.

The whole table awwws, except for Kiara who, I find out when I finally raise my gaze, is throwing daggers at me.

Thankfully that closes the chapter of questions people have for me. For the rest of the evening, I'm snuggled on Noah's hard thighs, listening to Chloe go on about how their dog Moose keeps running away, Chris explaining to the guys what it means when a baby drops, and Kiara talking wedding cakes with Grace and Alex.

When we leave, Noah walks me out with an arm around my shoulders. "Owen is onto something," he whispers under his breath, and I instinctively tug myself closer to him.

"Little weasel," I say into Noah's neck, and push my hand in his back pocket. "I hope he's watching."

He doesn't answer, just runs his lips on my temple as we head for the wide-open doors, onto The Green.

I almost trip on Moose, Justin's massive dog, as he sneaks inside, his fur matted with mud. "Hey buddy," Noah and I say at the same time, but the dog just continues on.

A cool breeze coming from the river envelops us, and I instinctively wrap my shawl tighter around my shoulders, while Noah runs his warm hand up and down my upper arm, like a proper husband.

"What did Owen say?" I ask once we're at a safe distance.

Noah glances behind us. Lowering his voice to a whisper, he says, "That he doesn't believe our marriage is real."

"So?" I whisper back. "Why do we care about Owen?"

"He represents developers, and I've turned down offers that came through him in the past. When he said he was warning me about our marriage, he made it sound like a threat. I can't even talk to my lawyer about this."

"I never liked Owen."

"I should hope not."

We reach the end of The Green and make the left onto Elm street, nearing the store. The awning is rolled back. In the dim inside lighting, the display windows have the potential of showing soft coziness—if the accumulation of stuff there didn't look so haphazard. I removed the umbrellas and placed the board games back where they were, which made me extremely unhappy. "Who normally does the windows?" I ask Noah.

His voice is clipped when he answers. It's something I've noticed whenever he talks about the store. He seems stressed. "Whoever has time. Honestly, I can't remember the last time we did anything to it." *Yes, the layer of dust attests to that.*

"Maybe I could take a stab at it?" I could see thematic displays by season or occasion. Cute kitchen items displayed at varying heights. A pine shelf with bath products and fluffy towels artfully arranged. Toys piling out of a painted chest. Clothing is trickier—but I'm sure I can figure it out.

"Knock yourself out," he says, turning his gaze straight ahead as he takes us at a fast clip away from the store and toward Lilyvale.

Glancing behind us, he removes his arm from around my shoulders. "Coast is clear," he announces with a grin. My hand slips out of his pocket as he sidesteps to a respectable distance.

"Phew," I joke, wrapping the shawl tighter around my shoulders, unable to repress a shiver as a gust of wind penetrates through the thin wool layer.

Noah moves closer to me, as if to warm me up, and shoves his hands in his pockets, looking up to the star-filled sky. "Can't believe we have this cold spell now."

Then as we reach the house, he holds the door open for me, and I brush against him as I make my way in, bracing myself against the feeling of safety he gives me. Against the feeling of being cared for. Reminding myself that I can't fall too deep for Noah.

I kick my shoes off while Noah turns some lights on. Beck and Lane were still at Lazy's when we left. "Chloe almost busted us. I can't believe I didn't think about the lease on my apartment." Where am I even going to live after this is over? "How long... how long d'you think we need to stay married?"

His gaze registers something like pain, and yeah, I get it. It must be a real pain in the ass for him. He sleeps on a couch each night, for fucks' sakes.

"Would be great if we could stretch it until after my birthday. If it's okay with you." His voice is low, like he doesn't dare ask me, and his vulnerability slices through me.

"Of course," I say. I'll think about the rest of my life later. "But we have a problem. We don't know each other well enough. Something's bound to come out between now and then."

Noah takes his glasses off and rubs the bridge of his nose. "Nah." He sets his gaze on me, effectively rooting me to where I'm standing, while a sad smile softens his expression. "I'd say we gave them a good show tonight."

A pang of desire mixed with sadness stabs me. It was all a show and yet... I let myself believe it was real. And it felt so good.

Idiot.

"You don't understand," I counter, my outer self insisting on being all fiery, when inside I just want to curl up in a sad little ball. "What if... what if someone contests our marriage and-and-and we're asked to testify or something? You know how they ask parents going through a divorce the name of their kids' best friend or favorite stuffed animal?"

"They do that?"

Pretty sure I saw that in a movie, but that's beside the point. "What if they did that for us? You know how Owen can get. Always looking to create trouble. It's like he can't stand to see other people happy."

He huffs "What do you suggest?"

"We need to study each other."

Chapter Twenty-One

Noah

I do enough of studying Willow. In my mind at the store. The eternal hour she spent on my lap during dinner, chatting with our friends, her hair caressing my cheek, her perfect ass on my crotch, her laughter ringing deep inside my being. The three minutes' walk from Lazy's to the store where she fit so perfectly under my arm it was like I was made to hold her. The fraction of a second where I held the door for her and memorized the moment as an example of the perfect life I'll likely never have. The four seconds it takes me to carry her from the couch to the bed, each night. The one-point-two seconds when she's still sleeping and I set her coffee on her nightstand and softly say, "Rise and shine," because she's my wife and that's how I talk to my wife—fake or not. She *is* the sunshine. That's what wives always are for men. Their sunshine.

For some strange reason we both walk into the kitchen when we get home. "What kind of studying are you suggesting?" I ask as I busy myself pouring a whiskey and purposefully don't offer her a drink.

This whole evening is dangerous enough as it is without the implied connotation of me offering her a drink.

Her question is open for interpretation. With my back to Willow, my eyes won't wander where they're not supposed to and risk giving a lewd connotation to my words.

The last thing I want is for Willow to feel uncomfortable. She's going through great lengths of sacrifice for me.

But she's attractive. She can't help it. I certainly can't help it. She's *very* attractive. And even though I can keep my attraction in check for the most part, there are things I can't help. Like the way I look at her. Ms. Angela said it just yesterday when Willow was out of earshot, rummaging in the back. "The way you look at her just makes my little heart melt."

"I'm sure we could do this your way—spreadsheets and stuff—"

Spreadsheets sound like a great idea. I can already see it. A column for each of us and rows of topics. Date of birth, middle name, favorite sports, favorite team, favorite athlete, GPA, SAT scores, make and model of your first bike, make and model of your first car, favorite food, first movie you remember seeing, first video game you played, favorite mountain...

"—but I kinda liked sitting in the parlor and drinking a whiskey sour."

Now, that sounds extremely unproductive. Time-consuming. Haphazard.

Dangerous.

I clear my throat, preparing my argument in favor of spreadsheets.

She doesn't let me. "Or any other whiskey-based drink. I don't think I'm ready for straight-up whiskey, though that's pretty badass, for one, and for two, I have to say it does make me all mellow, so I wouldn't mind growing a taste for it while we talk. You could teach me. What do you think?"

No. No-no-no. I teach my group of high schoolers the fun and beauty of coding. I don't teach my fake wife how to appreciate whiskey. It's too... personal.

She must be reading my face, because she takes half a breath and goes on. "It might be too much work? I'm a lost cause, right? We can just talk."

Just talk? Jesus. I don't think that I can.

She puts a red nail on her plump mouth. "I mean, we could do spreadsheets. Let's see. First kiss. First time all the way. And for both, age, name of the other person, place, time, weather, what you were wearing. Next, name of your college roommates—I didn't go to college. Favorite color. Favorite song. One dish you love. One dish you hate. Allergies! Do you have any allergies? We definitely need a spreadsheet. The first time you heard Phish—your first Phish concert. Three memories from childhood—two happy and one sad. Politics. We need to know each other's politics. And religion. Ohmygod we didn't even talk about that and we're *married*. What is *wrong* with us?"

"We're not really married, remember?"

Her mouth gapes open. "But, Noah, they're gonna *come* for us."

"Nobody's coming for us, Willow." *They're definitely coming for us.*

"I can feel it," she whispers, looking around conspiratorially. Then she laughs. "Seriously though, Owen would have a field day with us."

He would. "How about we draft a spreadsheet and fill it each on our own time?"

"Okay, let's draft the questions together, though. Pour your wifey one of your magic drinks and let's get to work in the off—the *study*." She waves her fingers at me and sashays away, making me chuckle. "I'll light the fire!" she shouts from the hallway.

"It's gas!" I shout back.

"Okey dokey! No loggies! Easy peasy!"

When I join her in the office—the study—in addition to the gas fireplace going at a good pace, she's got some candles lit and has switched on little side lamps I'd totally forgotten about. She's standing in the middle of the room, hands on her hips. "I can't wait for the robot vacuum cleaners."

"I vacuum it at least once a month," I say, feeling very on top of things.

"I can tell." *Is that sarcasm in her tone?* "I turned your antique PC on. Does it run on electric or gas?" she asks, snorting. Definitely sarcasm this time, but I can't help the smile spreading on my face.

I set our drinks down and take a seat behind the desk. "Okay, first things first, when did we get married again?"

"Wow-wow-wow. Wait for me," Willow says, lifting a chair.

I spring from mine and carry the heavy piece of furniture next to me. "I'm just changing the password. Our wedding date seems like the right thing to put in."

"That makes sense," she says.

I put in the six digits, officially changing the password to one a man in love with his wife would use. Then I open a spreadsheet.

Chapter Twenty-Two

Willow

Of course he went for the spreadsheet. I'm impressed, though, that he would change his computer password to our wedding date. "Sounds like a hack. You know, for men to remember their anniversary."

"Smart one at that," he replies, "if you need a hack."

"Why can't more men remember their wedding anniversary?" I might as well have asked, *Why can't more men be more like you,* but he doesn't seem to get my cryptic compliment.

"Seems to me the wedding is more the woman's thing? I wouldn't know."

My heart sinks a little. "See? That's why I don't want to get married *for real*."

"And why is that?!"

"Men don't care," I say, looking at the empty spreadsheet, my stupid little Noah fantasy about to be crushed. *It's about time, Willow. Wake up.*

I sense Noah's gaze on me, and his voice deepens when he answers. "They don't care about the party. About the drama. About the weird speeches. About having to pose for pictures when everyone else is having a drink."

I hate to admit that I wouldn't care much about that if I'd ever consider getting married. "My point exactly."

"What they do care about is to *be* married." His gaze drops to my left hand. "To put a ring that was their mother's on her finger. To call her mine. To know there will always be someone strong and soft at the same time to go home to. To go through life with." My mouth is dry, my throat tight as he finishes. "Men care about the *marriage*, not the wedding."

I take a sharp inhale as despair and reassurance take fifty-fifty control of my heart. I knew Noah would be the perfect husband. I also always knew he'd never see me that way.

"We should add a row for first argument," I say, needing to get back on track. "Let's just put '*Wedding*.'"

Peeling his eyes off me, he focuses back on the computer screen. "I'm not going to remember our first argument. Or the second. Or the third. It's petty."

"Ok, so I'm petty," I snap. *Fuck me. Why do I need to be mean now? Where did that come from?*

"I didn't say that," he replies patiently, not picking up on my tone. "I said *remembering* the argument was petty. And you know what? Maybe that's how you function. Maybe you log in every argument you've had with everyone so they don't screw you over again. It's a perfectly valid mechanism."

That cuts deep, because I'm not like that. Not at all. Ashamed of how I just talked to him, I take a long sip before quietly answering. "No one ever fucked me over."

He takes a deep breath, and his leg starts bouncing up and down. "People screw people over all the time, Willow. It's the way of the world. Maybe that should be one of the entries on the spreadsheet." He types in *People Who Screwed Us Over*, then moves the cursor to the column under his name.

"See?" I say. "No one fucked you over either."

"I'm just trying to remember how to put several entries in the same cell," he bites back.

A little dagger twists right below my ribcage. Who would want to fuck over Noah? I'd like to have a word with them.

Before I can say anything that will betray my feelings, I snap, "Alt+enter, smartass."

He glances at me, his glasses fogging as he shakes with silent laughter. Then he goes to a new row, types *First Argument*, merges our two columns and types *Willow called Noah a smart ass*.

I snort, then laugh so hard, droplets of my drink make it through my nose. It hurts like hell. While I cough my way out of this, he types: *Outcome*.

I put a hand on his forearm. "You don't need to type anything there."

"No? I was going to say 'Willow drowned her embarrassment in a Manhattan.'" His eyes dance with mischief up and down my face, pure gold. There's a tiny wrinkle at the corner of his eye, and I allow myself to imagine what can't be there: a deeper connection.

He's waiting for my retort, so I say the first thing that comes to mind. "That'd be a tell that our relationship is fake. Any normal couple settles an argument with sex." An unexpected flash of heat creeps up my neck as Noah kills our eye connection, straightening and turning to the spreadsheet.

Clearing his throat, he promptly erases the Outcome cell.

Is it his body or mine that's vibrating? There's a tension between us that's hard to ignore. "Here," I say, handing him his glass of whiskey.

"Thanks," he says then takes a long gulp. The man doesn't like talking about sex. Maybe he should add *that* to the spreadsheet.

The slight guilt I feel at embarrassing him is nothing compared to the glee of making him lose his composure. "Better?" I ask.

"Much better." Setting the glass down, he types *DOB* in the left-hand column.

This is going to take forever, and we'll never even scratch the surface. "I have an idea."

"No shit," he says as he fills in his answer.

Birthday in September. I should be counting the days until I'm free of this "project," but instead I find myself picturing a large get-together at Lilyvale, with a birthday cake to replace the wedding cake, the smell of a barbecue, the ringing laughter of people spilling from the patio to the porch to the river to the rose garden, a bonfire and marshmallows after sunset, fire crackling into the cool autumn air, and all the bedrooms occupied by people happy to stay over.

"Don't be snarky," I retort.

"I'm trying." A semi-smile dances in his eyes.

"Are you, though?" He types in my date of birth, getting it right. "Okay, I guess you are trying." *Why is my voice so... unsteady?*

"It's a thing I have with numbers. I always memorize them," he says. This time his mouth twitches. Is he full-on pulling my leg, or am I just delusional?

"Oh, you know how to make a girl feel special."

He stays quiet, giving me nothing to interpret how he remembers my date of birth, but his leg resumes its bouncing as he creates new rows: major illnesses or accidents. Allergies? Food dislikes? First bike (how old were you). First car (make and model).

"Color of the first car," I chime in, wanting to feel useful.

He types it in and continues, row after row, his long, strong fingers flying on the keyboard, his veined forearms flexing subtly. Sitting close to him, I tune into his breathing, inhale his scent.

God, what am I *doing*?

I go sit next to the fireplace, taking a deep, calming breath as I look up to the ceiling where shadows are dancing.

"What did you say after allergies?" he asks. Our gazes lock for a fraction of a second. I've never opened up to anyone the way I'm about to with him. What is it about Noah Callaway that makes me feel safe?

"Politics and religion," I answer.

He glances at the screen. "Got that. There was something else." He pushes his glasses up and turns his gaze to me, squinting as if the answer is written on my face. "Oh right. Memories. Childhood memories. There. That should settle it."

There's something extremely sad about the way he types the final entry in the spreadsheet. "Don't you think there's something concerning about how a husband and wife can reduce their knowledge of each other to a spreadsheet?"

He pushes his glasses up his nose, a telltale sign of moderate nervousness. "That's one way to look at it." His voice falters, like he's about to say something.

Silence stretches between us. "What's another way?" I push him. So what if my feelings are on the line? I still want to know everything about Noah Callaway.

His voice is so low that when he answers it's almost as if he's talking to himself. But his gaze in unmistakably on me. It's confession time. "People should start with that, would avoid heartache."

This is the part where he opens up about how he's not over his ex-fiancée, and my stupid little heart will cry silently while my face stretches into a comforting kind of smile. "How so?" I ask. This is going to hurt so good.

He comes to sit next to me in the other chair facing the fireplace, but instead of talking, he just twirls his drink, looking straight through it at something on the faded oriental carpet.

For some twisted reason I'm craving the heartache, because I push. "How was she—Anika?" My strangled voice barely comes out, protesting the pain my words are sure to bring me. Now I'm going to hear all about how she hopelessly owns his heart

He glances up at me, a flash of surprise in his eyes. Was she not the heartache he was talking about? He shrugs and takes a sip of whiskey. "She was your all-American woman, the girl next door."

"That doesn't really define a person. So she likes the Patriots like you do—

He stands. "I forgot that. Favorite sport, favorite team, favorite athlete. Let me add it."

I ignore him and continue with my train of thought. "And she wears her ponytail through the strap of her cap and her Chuck Taylors are always as white as her teeth and she makes the best chili on the block. So what? Does that mean she knows how to comfort you when you had a bad day? Does that make her more understanding of your child's night terrors? Or was she going to make Noah The Third a perfect, all-American boy who'll be too neurotic to even talk to a therapist?" I can't help but let my frustration seep through. *What did he see in her?*

He manages to chuckle. "For all your speeches about not wanting to get married, you seem to have some pretty set ideas on marriage and children." He comes back to sit in front of the fire.

Taking a steadying breath, I answer, "The upside of being single. You have time to observe others. How they mess up their life when they're trying to make it complete." I make air quotes around the last word, realizing what a hypocrite I am. I've never felt so *complete* as in this moment, talking about life with Noah.

"I didn't take you for such a cynic," he says, squinting again as he seems to try and pierce my soul with his gaze. There's a chance he might succeed, so I look away. "I see lots of alt plus enter for you in that column about people who effed you over," he says.

Damn him.

"*Effed* me over?" I laugh. "You don't do curse words?" *Atta girl, Willow, bring this convo back to surface-level and take a breath.*

"Oh, I do curse words alright, though not in daily conversation." His gaze grows darker, in a way that makes me feel deliciously dirty.

"Really," I say on a breath. Did the all-American girl with her ponytail and her cap like his dirty talk? *I bet she did. I know I would.* I clear my throat. "What do you mean by not in daily…?" Damn, that drink is making me more than chatty. It's making me brash. Even I can tell.

"I don't think anyone will ask you…" There's fire in his eyes, and it's not just the reflection of the flames three feet from us.

"Will ask me what?" I'll stop at nothing to make Noah, master of Lilyvale, Emerald Creek royalty, and nerd extraordinaire in the body of a mountain man, squirm under my indecent questions.

"You like playing with fire, don't you," he states—not a question.

My heartbeat picks up wildly. "You always knew that."

"True. It's what… attracted me to you." He takes a long sip. What is he saying? Is this for real or for the spreadsheet?

He's definitely not squirming—I am. Under his stare, under his confidence. He breaks the silence. "We're going to be living here, together, for the next few months. Playing house. Sleeping in the same bedroom. I'm not sure opening up to each other about our sexual habits is the safe way to go about it. And it certainly won't be brought up in whatever legal inquiry your curious little mind dreamed up we might get entangled into."

My heart hammers in my chest. "I'm sorry," I say, not feeling sorry at all. I'd do anything to hear him say again that for the next few months, we'll be living together, playing house, sleeping in the same bedroom. "You're right," I concede. He's *absolutely* right that no one will ask us about S.E.X.

He twirls his whiskey in his glass, the quickly melting cubes clinking softly. "There's one thing my wife should know. Something that never comes up in conversation, so you might have missed it." He tips his head back and downs the rest of his drink, then adds, "My birth mother left me and Dad when I was four years old."

A cold shiver takes hold of me as I stay speechless. I didn't know there was a *birth* mother. "I... I thought..." I only ever thought of Amy as his mother, and it's bad enough that she died years ago. "Noah, I'm so sorry. I didn't know." Sitting up in my chair, I place a comforting hand on his forearm—such a meager attempt to compensate for the unthinkable.

He shrugs. "I just didn't know under what category to put that on the spreadsheet. Childhood memory?"

I take a beat to process that, then harp on his self-deprecation. "That would be perfect under the People Who Fucked Us Over."

Chapter Twenty-Three

Noah

Willow seems positively horrified. The way she looks at me right now is not what I was going for. It's not pity, thank god. It's worse than that. It's compassion, and a connection. Willingness to know more. To understand me. I can shrug off pity. But this? This is dangerous—way more than trading sex secrets. This might actually endear her to me on a deeper level. I should resist this at all cost.

Yet I crave it. Need it. Need to talk to someone who might actually understand it. She removes her cool hand from my forearm as I start talking, and suddenly I wish I'd stayed quiet. I'd take her touch over the sound of my voice any day. "I'm not sure she really screwed me over, at the time. After that, Dad met Mom, married her, and they gave me three siblings I adore. Mom always treated me as her child." For the most part, but Willow doesn't need to know that.

And it was nothing Mom did, really. It was just that I knew I was not hers. Seeing her cradle my infant siblings, I told myself the bond between a mother and child were formed during those precious months. I would never have this with Mom. And at times it made me wonder, what had I done to my birth mother for her to leave me?

"What is it?" Willow asks me.

"Hmm?"

"Where did you go?" She sits back in her chair, crossing her legs. "You don't need to tell me," she says, looking away, toward the fire. "I can be really nosy." Then her gaze comes back on me, and I want to tell her. I really do. I just don't know what or how, exactly.

"I sought her out, years later. When I was in college. I found her."

Willow takes a sharp breath. "And?"

"And she wanted nothing to do with me."

Willow sets her hand back on my forearm. She seems ready to cry. "Noah, I'm so sorry. That's terrible."

"Nah, I was an idiot. What was I thinking? That she would welcome me with open arms? Course not." I'd felt a little lost, at the time. I was away, and meanwhile, life was going on without me at home. Thinking about who I wanted to become, I'd naturally been reflecting on my origins. I'd looked her up. Turned out, she wasn't that hard to find. And she was living right there, in Boston, where I was attending college. "It's a good thing I went. It set me straight. I was ashamed of myself, really."

"For what?"

"For seeking her out. Mom... it felt like a betrayal of her love. She'd never done anything to make me feel less than her birth children. It served me right, to be rejected—"

"Wow—hold it. Served you right?" Willow's hand clamps on my forearm again, but now she's rubbing her hand up and down. "You were looking for answers. You'd lived with the trauma of rejection for years and now you were rejected again. Don't ever blame yourself for what you did. Your... birth mother owed you answers as to why she left you. Even if—good riddance. She's a horrible person."

I glance at her right as she wipes a tear off her cheek. I didn't mean to make her feel sorry for me. That wasn't the point. I just thought, as my wife, this is the type of information she should know. I'm about to tell her that, but she continues.

"Your Mom made you into this beautiful, caring man. I'm sure she never blamed you or felt hurt that you tried to rekindle... some sort of relationship with your birth mother. Any mother would understand that—"

I shake my head. "I never told her, or anyone."

"Oh, honey," she says, the word barely a whisper. She clears her throat. "Well, now you told me. How does it feel?" She stands and picks up my glass, going to the small bar.

"Scary," I admit. "I'm a little relieved too."

The sound of a drink being poured fills the room. She brings the glass to her nose and sniffs it, then grimaces.

"Not used to opening up?" she asks as she hands me my refill.

"You won't tell anyone, will you?" Suddenly I have a vision of Griff, Beck, and Lane looking at me like I'd betrayed them. Like I wasn't one of them after all.

Willow messes with her hair and rubs her face. "What kind of wife would do that?" she says, her voice a little broken.

"Right, I'm sorry." I take a sip of the whiskey.

"I don't know how you can drink that stuff," she says, and I know it's to lighten the mood. I'm thankful to her for that.

I smile. "That's not the good stuff. The good stuff I keep in the kitchen. This is just for when I need to take the edge off while I'm working. If I kept the good stuff here, I'd be plastered every night."

She squints. "Take the edge off? Hmm. Maybe we should try yoga."

We? There's so much packed in this tiny word, I can't imagine even going there. "Sorry—what? Is that some kind of drink that's better than whiskey?"

"If you're drinking to take the edge off, that could become a problem. Second class alcohol isn't your answer. Something else might be."

My heart pounds. Who's shown me this kind of concern—apart from Ms. Angela—in years?

Willow quickly adds, "Since sex is off the table, I'm suggesting yoga."

"I'm not doing yoga. And not... the other thing either, obviously."

Her gaze lingers on me, soft and inscrutable, until her giggle lightens the room. "The other thing? That's what we're calling it—okay."

Did I just disappoint her? I wish I could take back what I said, tell her I'll do yoga every day with her. "I'm afraid you're stuck with a husband on the verge of alcoholism. Hey! That could be a good excuse for the divorce. You didn't know how bad it was until—"

"I don't think so." She crosses her arms with a cute, stubborn frown. "We already agreed we'd say we found out we were better off as friends."

I nod. "Yes. Should we shake on that so I don't bring it up again?" I hate that it's the second time I mention the divorce by trying to make it her fault.

With a smile that goes straight to my heart, she extends her hand. "I want your word, Callaway."

There's no one around us. This isn't fake. The way her eyes dance. The way she touched my forearm to console me moments earlier. The way my chest expands right now, at her touch. The way my hand closes on hers, wanting to protect her. To give her everything she needs. "I promise I'll be the jerk."

Chapter Twenty-Four

Willow

After we shake on it, I'm a little off-kilter. The more I know Noah, the more I want to know him at a deeper level.

And the way he looks at me? The way he doesn't let go of my hand? Am I making it up or...?

Jeez, Willow. He needs a friend. Don't go and ruin it now.

The front door slams shut and we promptly let go of each other as if we were doing something wrong.

Beck barges in seconds later. "Gotta talk to you," he tells his brother.

Noah rubs his eyes, setting his glasses in his shirt pocket. "We were going to bed," he answers. Warmth pools in my center, even if it's not what he meant. At all.

Beck drops on a sofa. "You're such a party pooper since you got married."

Noah's mouth twitches, but his tone is stern when he replies. "Don't disrespect my wife."

"I'll just..." I trail, indicating the door.

"I'll be right up," Noah says.

"No he won't," Beck says with a crooked smile. "Sorry, Willow."

I don't take my time. I rush it. I rush it so I can fall asleep on the sofa again and get carried to bed by my husband.

I brush my teeth, slip into the short lace nightgown Kiara brought me back from France, and slide under the duvet, making a deep cocoon for myself as I dip as deep as I can. Inhaling Noah's scent and falling asleep to it.

I wake up with a start when I hear a muttered, "Fuck me." Noah opens and closes the bathroom door, not trying to be quiet. I open my eyes briefly, then tuck back under the duvet, dozing back asleep to the sound of the shower.

I'm awakened by his strong arms lifting me effortlessly and carrying me to the bed. I let my head roll onto his chest, feeling his breath catch and nearly jumping as I realize he's bare-chested and this is his skin under my lips.

That's new.

Two long strides and he's setting me on top of the sheet and pillow, then folding the blankets back on me, tucking me in snuggly. I extend my legs, sighing deeply. That seems like a natural reaction, right? I don't think he's ever caught onto the fact I'm awake the whole time.

But then the feather-like touch of his fingers on my forehead startles me, and my eyes fly open, meeting his gaze. "My wife sleeps in my bed," he says under his breath, cupping my cheek in his warm hand. I can't find anything to say to that. It seems like an eternity passes where we just look at each other, then he adds, "Okay?"

"Yeah, okay," I whisper.

And then he's gone, the sofa creaks, and for a while his deep breathing is all I hear with the occasional ruffling of the wind in the trees.

Too wound up to fall asleep, I slowly become attuned to all the other noises in the house. The faint scuffle of a mouse in the wall. A branch scraping against the roof as the wind picks up. Lane's footsteps as she tiptoes to her bedroom in the middle of the night.

The furnace kicking in (Lane taking a shower?). A pipe banging. This house never seems to sleep. It breathes and creaks just like we toss and turn. It's huge and complex, with additions over the decades, rooms that are never used, memories asleep. It feels like a person welcoming me in its warm embrace. Complicated and loving.

It soothes me.

And yet, right as I'm about to fall asleep, I'm startled by someone calling my name. I push myself up on my elbow. Nothing. Thinking it's my imagination, I fall back on the soft pillow, pulling the covers tighter over me.

"Willooooow!"

This time it was clear. Lane? Not wanting to wake Noah, I slip out of the bedroom and take a few steps down the dark hallway, toward the tower. But I hear my name again, behind me. Retracing my steps toward the top of the staircase, I continue downstairs.

On the last step, a young boy is looking up at me with a strange smile. "Hi?" I whisper, continuing down. He seems vaguely familiar, but I can't say I know who he is. He's dressed a little formally, too, like he just attended a funeral or something. Maybe he's lost? Maybe we left the door unlocked. "Can I help you?"

He shrugs. "I don't think so."

Curious, I continue to his level, shivering under a sudden cold draft. "Are you hungry?" I try. Surely he's here for a reason.

"Not anymore," he says, and holy shit.... He *disappears*.

Poof.

Gone.

And the staircase gets warmer.

I knew it! I chuckle and mentally pat myself on the back. Lilyvale is haunted and I have proof.

That being said, I can't keep ghost hours. I need to sleep at night. So I run quietly back up to the bedroom, grab the sage Cassandra gave me (smart woman, that one), and go get some matches from the parlor. Two young women, barely dressed in translucent white dresses, look at me with envy in their eyes. "This is crazy," I mutter. "You better not wake me up again," I say as I light the sage and start fumigating the parlor. The women—girls, really—let out a giggle and disappear before my eyes.

"Willow!" A loud whisper almost makes me jump. These ghosts are getting on my nerves.

"And who might you be?" I hiss at the dark shape beyond the doorframe, waving my smoky sage at it.

"It's me," Noah says, taking one step closer. He reaches up for the door frame, a question in his eyes, moonlight now kissing his naked torso.

Damn, the man is *fine*.

Chapter Twenty-Five

Noah

Willow looks a tad insane and a lot desirable with her hair falling on her naked shoulders, spaghetti straps barely holding together the fabric tensing on her breasts, waving a smoldering bundle in a house mainly comprised of wood. "Go back to bed, I got it," she says as she turns on her heels and moves the thing three times in the air in one corner of the parlor, billows of smoke in her wake, before she goes to another corner and repeats the process.

"Got what?"

She shrugs. "The spirits. I'm showing them who's boss. They need to go back into the netherlands."

"The Netherlands is a country."

She rolls her eyes. "Not *those* Netherlands."

"You're going to set the place on fire."

She snorts. "I'm sageing. Don't worry, I know what I'm doing." She comes toward me, glancing at my bare chest as I move aside to let her out. "Aren't you cold? You should put a shirt on if you're going to stay here. Or a sweater." She licks her bottom lip, then turns her back to me as she slides to the hallway, then into the dining room.

Holding my smirk, I follow her. "I'm not cold." When Willow is around me, it could be freezing—I wouldn't know.

She's already in one corner of the dining room, then she runs to another. "I need more sage," she mumbles. Then she turns to me, and her eyes slide down to my abs before hopping back up to my eyes. "Well, you're distracting me. And you need some sleep. You have a big day tomorrow." She's still sageing the place, three strokes in each corner of the room, the smoking herbs leaving a sweet scent in their wake.

I follow her into the study. "What ghosts are you trying to chase, exactly?"

"I'll let you know if they tell me their names. Although I'm told that stuff from Cass is pretty effective. Used it on my great-grandfather when he wouldn't stop tickling Ms. Angela's toes at night because her grandmother had refused to marry him. Said he'd haunt her whole family tree—and he held to his promise."

"Please tell me you don't believe that shit."

She stops, her jaw dropping. "No wonder they live here! You're giving them free rein."

I don't know if she's insane, or if she's messing with me. Because no one—no one—outside my family knows how to deal with our ghosts. We don't talk about them, not amongst ourselves, and certainly not to others.

The last time someone brought them up, I lost a fiancée. Not that I regret it—it was a baptism by fire. She didn't pass the test.

The thing is, Willow wasn't supposed to pass the test. At all. Now that I think about it, this was probably my guess all along, when it came to why our marriage would end. She'd tire of hearing her name called in the night when everyone else was asleep.

I mean, what woman could stand that? Only Mom did.

All the other reasons I came up with were only to give her acceptable excuses. Seeing her now creates an even deeper longing for her. She's so close, yet so unattainable. So perfect for me, yet so not mine.

Willow is done with the study, and she goes to the kitchen. "You have a meeting with Zach from Coding Club tomorrow. Seven in the morning. If you want to get a run in before, and a shower, and a healthy breakfast, that leaves you—maybe five hours of sleep." She puts a fist on her hips. "You need to go back to bed. Chipitty-chop."

My chuckle stays strangled in my mouth. Mom used to say that, but never to me. When she came into my life, I was already older, or acting like it. No one ever babied me, and although it's not something I want, it moves me deeply.

She'll be a great mom some day.

Unable to deal with the feelings overtaking me, I follow my wife's orders and turn to go back to bed.

"You again?" Willow exclaims, frustration in her tone. Is she actually talking to the ghosts? I stop on the first step and listen. "All that hotness he parades around," she mumbles barely loudly enough for me to hear. "No wonder you don't want to leave."

So she thinks I'm hot.

I teeter on the staircase. Should I go back down and... and what?

Hmm. Any other woman, I'd go back down there and just... watch her, knowing what she thinks. Try some light banter. Offer to sit on the porch and watch the stars and if she says yes, read her body language. Slide my arm around her shoulders.

Kiss her.

Read how she kisses me back.

See where the night takes us.

But this is Willow. Who's doing me and my family a solid. Going out of her way to save our small town.

Just because she thinks I'm hot doesn't mean anything.

She only agreed to be my wife.

Okay, and to sleep in my bed.

And maybe I've told her my intimate secrets.

But that doesn't mean I should get carried away.

I'm reading this wrong, I know I am. I'm losing sight of the reason for all this. And I can't afford to lose everything simply because I now have feelings.

Because if Beck is right, Gail is back in town, stirring up trouble.

Chapter Twenty-Six

Willow

Once I take care of the ghosts, I sleep like a baby and wake up refreshed to a hot cup of coffee—but no husband. Good. I don't need the reminder of how good he looked last night, bare-chested in the dark hallway.

Encouraged by my success with the other residents of Lilyvale, I'm ready to tackle my next task: making the store's display windows more appealing. Beyond being the placeholder wife, I want to add tangible value. Create something that would make *me* proud.

Because honestly, the store looks sad. It used to be a fun place to shop or just browse around. It's become... utilitarian. For obvious reasons, I've always had butterflies in my stomach when I came here, but it had nothing to do with the store and everything to do with its owner.

Now that I'm looking at it with a more critical eye... Yeah, I'm totally going to have fun with it.

This time, instead of stripping the windows bare of their current displays and working in front of the entire town for hours, I'll paper the windows with something more interesting to gape at than my ass up in the air while I work inside.

I pop into Noah's office. "Where can I find old photos of the store?" I ask him.

His gaze seems to take inventory of me, and suddenly it gets very hot in this small space. "The attic at Lilyvale." He removes his glasses. "I could show you. What's this for?"

I wet my lips. Images of Noah and me in yet another dark and secluded area dance in front of my eyes. I know what's under his T-shirt. I know how strong his arms are and how his bare skin smells.

"The windows?" I answer.

He leans back in his chair, arms crossed, amusement in his eyes. "What about the windows?" His lips twitch, and the heat pooling in my center becomes untenable.

I pull myself together. "Just wanted to ask if it was okay to cover them with photos?" Something in his body language makes me lose my composure, and I continue in a mumble. "I'll just go to the library. I'm sure their local history section will have all I need. And they can print... and... I'll see you later."

What am I—a teenager? Jesus, Willow.

Get.

A.

Grip.

I rush out of the store, struggling to tame the visions of Noah in a dark attic.

Once at the library I skim through history books, snapping photos of the general store through the years with my cellphone.

"I just want something fun, nothing artistic," I explain to Sophie, the librarian, as we figure out a way for me to transfer all the photos to her for printing.

"Let me check the newspaper archives," she says, typing quickly on her desktop. "There. Look at all that!"

Joining her behind her desk, I look at historical photos of the store that I've never seen. Dozens of them. "Awesome."

"I'll print all of those as well, and in A3 format," Sophie suggests.

"Would you? That would look great. Hopefully my displays turn out okay. The store has so much to offer. It just needs a little magic to make it happen."

"It can't look worse than it already does, honey," Sophie tells me with an eye roll while my pictures download to her printer app. "You're a godsend."

"Thanks," I say, unsure if I really am until I see the result.

"There. Ooh, you have some good ones," Sophie says. "It'll take me about half an hour. This thing sometimes jams."

"Can I help?"

"Nah, I'm good. We have some really good new books that just came in."

That sounds really tempting, but I'd like to do something nice for Sophie instead, as a thank-you. "I'll head over to Easy Monday. What can I get you?"

***

As I exit the library, my attention is drawn to a sleek red car parked on the other side of The Green. A driver is inside—I can't make out who—engine idling as if they're waiting for someone. Who could it be? I wonder how long it will take for someone to post about that on ECHoes, and smile inwardly at my town's nosiness as I hasten my steps.

Easy Monday is Emerald Creek's coffee shop. Set right in a sturdy stone building overlooking the river, it's everyone's favorite hangout place from morning until it's time to head to Lazy's. The owner, Millie, has a romance book lending system there that guarantees high occupancy of her comfy couches and reading nooks. She also displays local artists. And of course, she crafts ah-mazing coffees (as stated on her sign).

"Two Roads to Heaven please," I ask.

"Willow! One for you and one for the lucky groom?" Millie asks.

I feel myself blush. "No, actually the other one is for Sophie."

"Oh—good to know. She likes oat milk in hers," Millie says as she writes Sophie's name on a to-go mug. "Why don't you choose a mug for yourself, sweetie." She points to her display shelf of travel mugs. "My little wedding gift," she adds with a wink.

"That's so sweet of you." I settle for the deep-blue mug with a sprinkling of stars. Millie takes her permanent gold marker and writes my name on it with a flourish, *Willow Callaway*.

It's the first time I see my married name written down. It gives me a little shock. Like the earth has moved or something shifted and will never be quite the same.

"We could talk about making those for the store, you know," she says, mistaking my emotion for something entirely different. She's been partnering with businesses around town to create their own signature mugs, promoting herself and the business at the same time.

"That's a great idea," I say. "Though to be honest, the coffee we have at the store is an insult. I think Noah doesn't want to change it because of you. Like, the only good coffee should be here."

Millie laughs. "I have a better idea. Why don't I sell you the coffee, wholesale, don't make a profit, but you package it in Easy Monday cups and have a list of the offerings we have here in store?"

I can see it and smell it already, and I gasp. "That sounds perfect! I'll talk to Noah about it."

"You don't need to talk to Noah about it," Cassandra says, startling me.

I turn to face her, wondering how to thank her for the sage without revealing too much. But she continues. "It's your shop, too, now. And he *needs you* to bring in these ideas and implement them."

"Oh! I've been telling him so many times that the store needs a little something-something," Ms. Angela calls out from the back of the line. "But does he listen?"

I give my aunt a warm smile. I've occasionally been a witness to her loud opinion-sharing in the middle of the store and can see where a lighter touch might have worked better on Noah. "Speaking of which, I should go," I say as I pay for Sophie's coffee—mine is on the house, Millie says as she hands it to me in my gorgeous new travel mug.

"Yup, Sophie's all ready for you," Ms. Angela says. "Just came from there. Love what you're doing."

"What are you doing?" Millie and Cassandra ask.

Ms. Angela waves me away. "You go on, I'll fill them in. You got your work cut out for yourself."

I can't help but laugh at that as I thank her. I dash out of Easy Monday, hearing Ms. Angela explaining my whole plan to everyone who wants to hear.

As I pull the bright yellow door shut behind me, the rear lights of a red Mercedes flash as the car pulls out of the parking lot. An uneasy feeling spreads through me, but I shrug off the goosebumps. It's a small town. Bumping into the same people comes with the territory.

When I get back to the library, the stack of photographs is ready. Sophie also printed a bunch of little stars with the words, "Willow Callaway is working her magic".

She thanks me for the coffee. "I wish I could take a break with you, but it's story time," she says, pointing to a group of toddlers sitting cross-legged in the mezzanine, quietly waiting for her—the poster image of adorableness.

I hurry to the store with a smile on my lips, eager to get to work. But first, I go straight to Noah's office to run my plan by him.

"Close the door," he says once I'm done talking, his tone stern.

"What's wrong?" I ask, taking a sip from my coffee for countenance.

He frowns. "What's that?" His gaze is narrowed on the mug. More specifically, on the words Willow Callaway.

I feel myself blush. Well, this is embarrassing. "I-it's a gift from Millie. Obviously, I couldn't say no..."

"Why would you say no? It's..." His words trail off. "Did you choose it?"

Why is he asking me that? "Well, yes, but then she wrote my name on it... well, that name and uh..."

"It's *your* name. You don't like it?" he asks.

Willow Callaway. Of course I like it. I love it. It runs over my tongue like a brook in spring. It's-it's-it's... But I don't know what to say to him. Damned if I do, damned if I don't. There will be a real Mrs. Noah Callaway, someday, and in all likelihood her first name will not be Willow. So in a sense, this feels like a fraud.

But I like it.

"You like it," he states, as if I'd spoken out loud, which I definitely did not. "Now, onto the other thing."

What other thing?

"You do not ask me for permission to do anything, Willow. *My wife* doesn't need my permission. If *my wife* thinks the window displays need to be changed, then they do. If *my wife* decides she's doing it, then she is." I'm pretty sure half the store heard this, on account of the wooden walls that enclose his office space. His voice softens when he adds, "Are we good?"

I'm burning up right now with all his "my wife" statements. It's hot. It's possessive. Even when he's telling me I don't need his permission, it feels like I belong to him in a way I can't explain. But of course, that's just what's going on in *my* mind right now. Because what *he's* doing is making sure we project the image of the perfect couple, and in what perfect couple in this century does the wife ask her husband for permission to do anything?

"Are we good?" he repeats even softer, and I swear I feel something hot going from his gaze straight through my center.

I lower my voice so only he can hear me. "What if your wife wants to sleep on the couch?"

Chapter Twenty-Seven

Noah

I can't take my eyes off her plump lips as she leans into me. "What if your wife wants to sleep on the couch?" she breathes.

The couch is fucking uncomfortable—I know from experience. There's no way anyone would actually want to sleep on it. I suspect what she wants is for me to carry her to bed.

I can do that—anytime.

I force my gaze to her eyes. "If my wife is more comfortable falling asleep watching the stars from the couch, then I'm more than happy to carry her to bed." There. That should settle it.

Willow's eyes widen, irises ablaze—a beautiful spectacle. The tip of her nose twitches almost imperceptibly, but I catch it. Her neck turns rosy.

She straightens. "I'll get to work," she says, clamping the stack of prints in one hand and clutching her coffee mug in the other.

I jump off my chair to get the door for her. Our bodies are close, too close and yet not close enough. She doesn't take a step back, although there's ample place to. She doesn't look away. I expect her to say something snarky, but she softens.

"What?" she asks, her voice barely above a whisper. Her gaze glides down to my lips. I want to kiss her so bad, it's painful.

The irony is, if she weren't my wife—my fake wife—I probably would. Her body language tells me she wants this. Hell, what she said last night when we were half naked surrounded by ghosts told the same story.

"You're even more beautiful when you're all flustered," I whisper back. "I'd add it to the spreadsheet, but it's not something I can ever forget." Then I step back, open the door wide for her, and say in a voice as normal as I can, "Call if you need help."

She all but runs away.

I spend the next hour fighting my erection by doing all sorts of unnecessary tasks that fill my time while keeping me off the shop floor. I'm opening and closing my email for the millionth time when our mail lady comes in. "You didn't have to come all the way here," I say as I stand to greet her.

"Just need a signature, Mr. Callaway."

I scribble my name on the card attached to an envelope. "Noah." I correct her. She's my father's age—they went to school together. You'd think she'd drop the Mister.

She hands me a thick envelope. "Thanks, Mr. Callaway."

I chuckle and smile. *Old habits die hard.* I just wish people didn't treat me like I was better than. Because I'm not.

The top-left corner of the envelope indicates this comes from Mrs. Gail Callaway. I tense up, though I'm not surprised. Last night, Beck told me she'd been spotted in town, and he was asking if there was anything to worry about.

I reassured him there wasn't, but this letter can't be good news. I slice through the envelope, unfold the document, and reach for my phone.

"Hey, Noah, I only have a minute." Tamberly's out of breath and there are voices in the background. "Going into a hearing. What's up?"

I read the title of the document, Notice of Concern Regarding Trust Execution, then sum it up for her as I skim through it. "She's claiming the marriage is false." My stomach sinks. I should have seen it coming.

"Not surprised," Tamberly says. "Scan me a copy, will ya?"

"What's our next step?"

"Nothing. She's trying to scare you, wants you to engage. We just wait it out."

"How worried should I be?"

"Nothin' to worry about. You married Willow for love. How's she gonna prove you didn't? Very hard to prove a negative, especially if it's not there."

I can think of fifteen thousand, six hundred and twenty-two reasons on Willow's side (give or take a few cents), and a few millions on mine. But I can't tell Tamberly that. I'd disappoint her as a person. And I'd make her life as a lawyer much harder than it needs to be.

I wonder if she senses my hesitation, because she says, "Right?"

"Correct," I say. *Gail can't find anything to prove my marriage isn't real.* "Anything I can do at this point?"

"Stop worrying. Though I would say, if you and Willow were planning on starting a family anytime soon, now would be a good time. There's nothing like a pregnancy to kill the rumor of a fake marriage."

Right. Perfect. Excellent. On it, Tamberly. A vision of Willow manifests in my mind's eye, her belly rounding with my child. I suddenly feel very hot. "Thanks. Talk to you soon." I hang up and stare into nothingness for a while. Then I go get a cup of awful coffee, just to give the next five minutes a purpose. From the corner of my eye, I can see Willow crouched on all fours, her ass pointed at me like a tease. She's papered the windows almost to the ceiling with what from here looks like... I'm not sure. I left my glasses on my desk somewhere in the middle of my phone conversation.

I turn my gaze away from her and get back into my office, thinking about all the clues we've left that our marriage isn't real.

The fact that we were never engaged before the wedding, were never seen together alone, never a date, not even a coffee.

The fact that we got married in *Vegas*, of all places.

Fuck. This isn't looking good.

At noon Willow pokes her head in the office. "Hungry?" she asks.

Thank god there's no trace in her demeanor of where we last left things. I made it awkward earlier, but here she is, acting all normal. Saving the day, just as she's saving so much more just by being in my life.

"No, but I could use a break."

"Why don't we take the trail up the hill toward Kiara's pastry shop?" she asks. "I'll just run home to change my shoes."

As we leave the store, I notice what the display windows are entirely papered in... "Are these old photographs?" She did ask about photos earlier, but I had no clue why. I just had this vision of her and me in the attic, and after that I stopped listening to what she was saying.

She nods. "Copies. Look! This is your great-great-grandfather. You should wear one of these aprons! Look at this one," she says, pointing to a photograph with horses and carriages waiting where cars now line our sidewalk. Each one of these photos is of the store, and she has them arranged in chronological order, with the older ones to the left and the more recent ones to the right. There are even reproductions of newspapers advertisements.

"That's awesome." I let go of her hand to pull her into a side hug, my cheeks hurting from the big smile she's put on my face as I peer over each photograph. I lean over to give her a friendly kiss on the head. "Thank you." For the first time in a long time, the store and the family name don't feel like a burden. Instead, Willow has made me proud of where I've come from.

Minutes later we're on the trail that runs from the river up the hill. While Willow swapped her sandals for walking shoes, I filled two water bottles. "Welcome gift," I joke, handing her the bottle I took from the store.

She examines it, then takes a sip. "We should brand those to the store," she says. "But then again, the store needs a better name than just *the store*. It needs a logo and colors. You should talk to Alex about this."

"Why don't you talk to Alex?"

She halts briefly to turn toward me, maybe to check if I'm joking. When she sees I'm not, a smile plays on her face. "Might as well make myself useful while I'm here."

I don't like the way she says it, or even the words themselves. But she's right. She's only here for a while, a few months at least—maybe we'll make it a year, to be on the safe side. If she'll consider it.

Point is, just because I like her presence in my life doesn't mean I should get used to it.

"Is this something you'd like to do?" I ask.

"Are you kidding? Of course I would."

She must miss the bakery. And making cakes. "You miss working with Kiara?" I don't know how long she worked for her (something I should add to the spreadsheet), but I know they're tight.

Willow shrugs. "Yes and no. I miss her company, but I didn't like being cooped up inside, seeing the same two-three people every day. I preferred when I was at the register."

We get to a fork in the trail, and we leave the path hugging the riverbank to climb up the hill. Willow's breath doesn't show any sign of fatigue. "I miss hanging out with her. But for now, working at the store fills my well. I feel like this morning I got to see half the town!" she says, giggling.

"How is your little project coming along?" When we left, the inside of the windows were, as far as I could tell, a mess of various objects.

"My little project, huh?" she says. "Probably needs one more day."

"Wow, that's more than a little project." I feel shitty about what I said. I stop on the trail. What follows is going to be more than just casual conversation. "Look, I didn't mean to brush it off like that."

"I know," she says, turning to me. "You coming?"

"The truth is, I got some shitty news this morning." I look her straight in the eye. I need to talk to someone, and she's the only one I can talk to about that.

"What's going on?"

"Gail is contesting the authenticity of our marriage." I give her a summary of the paperwork I received this morning, and of my conversation with our lawyer, leaving out the baby part, of course. I don't think she was even serious about that.

"Fuck. Well, we kinda saw it coming. That's why we're sleeping in the same bedroom, and faking the PDA, and I'm working at the store. We got this." She turns around, takes a few steps up the trail, then turns back toward me. "Sorry, you said you needed to talk and I did all the talking. What's got you worried?" She walks to a flat boulder and sits on it, giving me her full attention.

Now I feel like an idiot, because in a few words, Willow managed to alleviate my concerns. I'm no longer worried. Tough luck trying to prove our marriage isn't real. I sit next to her, but not too close, my elbows on my knees. "We might need to stay married a little longer than anticipated." If Gail starts legal proceedings, these are going to take months. A divorce right in the middle of it all would help her case tremendously.

"I'm sorry," Willow says. "I know it must suck for you to have a stranger living in your house, sleeping in your bed."

I shake my head and look away, trying to hide the embarrassment that must be painted all over my face. Finally, I man up and turn my head to look her in the eye. "You're not a stranger. And it doesn't suck. At all." I look away again, fearing my face will tell too much. "In fact, I've... very much appreciated getting to know you."

Her voice small, she says, "Well, the feeling is mutual."

I don't think she knows what feelings I have, or she wouldn't be saying that. "Do you miss living on your own?"

She shrugs. "I was going to move back home to help Mom by paying rent. And then you came along," she adds with a smile, looking me straight in the eye and making me squirm.

"We should move your stuff from your apartment to my—*our* place." Since the close call at community dinner, we haven't talked about her lease, but there's something I should have thought about sooner.

That of course she'd want her shit—not saying this in a demeaning way. But she's a woman. She needs her stuff. Is it sexist of me to think that women want to make a home out of any house? "You should change things around at Lilyvale. Make it feel like your home."

Her eyes widen. "Really? No, no, I couldn't. Why would I?"

"So you *feel* more at home." *And because I want you to. It's stuffy, and full of memories I'd sometimes rather forget, and for some reason I can't explain I'm certain the changes you'll bring will make me feel better.*

"It doesn't sound right. Maybe if we were married for real, and even then, I think I'd tiptoe around it."

Inspiration strikes me. "It'd help make our case that our marriage is real." Her smile flattens a little, and I'm not sure why. She's always the one coming up with ideas to make our marriage look real. The PDA at community dinner. The studying each other.

There's something that I can't quite put my finger on. Something that seems to have clicked in my brain when I saw her with our ghosts last night.

As crazy as it seems, it was as if she belonged there. In this house. In our family.

The only *rational* explanation I can come up with is that the ghosts know she's the one who can save us.

Lips pursed downward, she nods. "Okay." Then her attention turns to the side of the trail. A big smile replaces the signs of her puzzling disappointment as she cries, "Ohmygod! What are you doing here?"

Chapter Twenty-Eight

Willow

Moose drops something on the ground, then gives me his goofy grin. After a beat of hesitation, he runs to me, gives me a lick, then turns to Noah and does the same. His belly is covered in mud, his tongue hanging low.

"What you got here?" I ask. But before I can cuddle him more, he dashes away from my reach, picks up what he dropped off, and runs up the trail, away from the village.

I turn to Noah. "What's he doing?"

Noah jumps to his feet. "Let's find out."

We sprint uphill, trying to keep up with Moose. Halfway up, he darts off trail, leading us through thickening underbrush. Trampling ferns and ducking under low branches, we follow him until we hear little cries.

Under a hollow boulder, a big brown and white dog is nursing three puppies, Moose whining in frustration. He pushes his offering closer to her then trots to us.

"He brought her meat!" I whisper.

"Hey, big boy," Noah says, petting Moose. "What do we have here? A little secret family?"

We take a few steps closer, and the mamma dog growls.

Noah and I crouch next to Moose to make ourselves look as harmless as possible, but the mother still seems anxious.

"Let's back up," I say.

We backtrack to a safe distance. "I can't believe he's bringing her food," Noah whispers as we crouch and observe the dogs from afar.

"I wonder where he found it. Justin would never let him into Lazy's kitchen, and even then..."

"I hope he doesn't go through people's garbage. Who knows what he could find there."

Oh shit. Yes. Feeling both worried and proud of Moose, I watch as the mamma dog shakes her puppies off her. Standing on wobbly feet, she wolfs down what Moose set next to her.

"Wonder how rotten that meat was," I say as she lies back down with a satisfied grunt, letting her puppies crawl hungrily over her.

Moose turns toward us and whines, then turns back to the litter, running half circles from one side of the boulder to the other, defining a perimeter he seems to protect for his little family.

Noah smiles. "Never seen a dog in love before."

"So sweet. How are we gonna do this?" I ask.

"No idea."

Something passes between us. We don't need words as we decide to take this dog family under our protection.

"Mom is going to be worried, might even get aggressive, if we try to take her puppies. Let me see how close to her I can get."

"Careful, though," Noah says, strain in his voice.

"Hey," I whisper, getting on all fours and crawling gently to her.

She raises her head for a beat, then drops it, panting.

"How you feelin'? Not great, huh?"

"I'm calling Justin," Noah says softly.

"Hey, sweetie," I coo while Moose continues his semi circles in front of the hollow cave, now encompassing me. That has to be good, right? I'm in the protected zone. Part of them. Surely she understands that.

When I'm close enough that I could touch her, I lie down on the soft moss of the forest floor, still alert. Just because Moose trusts me doesn't mean she will. The three puppies' eyes are closed. They aren't walking yet and barely crawling. They're only a few days old, if that. Their pink tongues dart out in the most adorable way, and their chests lift with rapid breaths.

My attention quickly shifts to the mom. Under the deceitfully ample fur, she's extremely thin, bones poking, ribcage showing. Her back leg bulges at an unnatural angle—likely a poorly-healed break.

"We need to get her to the vet," I say softly to Noah, who relays the information to Justin.

Then, purposely ignoring the puppies so I don't worry her, I stroke her paws, then scratch her side. When she's groaning in contentment with eyes half closed, I risk sitting up.

Her eyes dart open.

"Hey," I whisper and move my hand up her back to scratch between her shoulder blades. She gives me satisfied grunts.

Moose lies down three feet from us, head on his paws. The puppies fall asleep, two right next to me, tucked against her belly, and one hiding between her front paws.

"This is good," Noah whispers. "Let her get used to your scent so she trusts you."

Less than an hour later, Justin and Chloe arrive with a crate, a wheelbarrow, and blankets in both. "Trail is too narrow for anything else," Justin explains in a low voice. "Think she'll let us fit her in there?"

The mamma dog barely lifts her head at their voices. My eyes fill with tears. "We gotta hurry. Bring the crate."

Chloe hands me the crate, spreading the blanket. "Hey, mom," I coo, "we're going on a little family trip, okay?"

She lifts her head as I softly pick up each puppy. She half grunts, but there's no fight in her gaze.

"Let's go," I snap. There's no time to lose.

Noah grabs the crate while Justin positions the wheelbarrow next to me. I lift momma dog in my arms—as I suspected, she's much lighter than she looks—and place her as comfortably as I can. "I'll walk next to her," I say.

Noah goes first with the puppies. Momma dog hangs her head out the wheelbarrow to look at them. I scratch her between the shoulders and she relaxes. Moose runs in front and around us, and Chloe is right behind, on the phone with the vet.

"He said to drive everyone right over," she says when she ends the call. "We left the truck at the trailhead."

Good. That'll be quicker than going all the way back into town.

"You really should get Moose neutered," I scold Justin.

"Oh, he's fixed alright," Justin says. We maneuver in silence through a narrow part of the trail, and he adds, "Not sure what happened there, but those aren't his puppies."

"Aww that's double the sweet," I can't help but coo, giving Moose another pet as he reaches my spot before running to the front again.

"It's the Emerald Creek bug," Chloe says.

Noah glances over his shoulder. "The what now?"

"You know. The found family thing," Chloe answers.

I chuckle at my friend's accurate description. So many people have found their tribe here, why not the dogs?

That evening, the four of us share dinner at the kitchen counter—tomato soup from Clover's Nook, cheese, and a hearty country bread. Mamma is snoring in the mansion's kitchen, rehydrated and her belly full. The puppies got a clean bill of health and are tucked against her and each other, the furry group lying on thick blankets, making cute little squeaky noises. Moose goes to lick her, but she growls at him.

"Nice to see you have your bite back," I say, smiling.

"She's tired, Moose," Noah says.

"Leave her be," Justin adds, pulling gently on his collar. "You did good."

Moose grunts and ambles to Chloe, poking her hand up. She gives him a head scratch "Yes, you did great."

"You sure you're okay with that?" Justin asks, his chin pointing at the four canines sleeping in the kitchen.

Noah beams. "Are you kidding? Best thing ever." Blushing, he pulls me into a side hug. "Second best thing ever." I feel his heart boom as I lay my hand on his chest in the public gesture of affection that I've perfected.

I look up at him, telling myself I'm playing the loving wife for Justin and Chloe's benefit, but our eyes lock for a beat, and Noah sets his glasses on the kitchen counter.

Two. His gaze drops to my lips.

Three. My knees weaken.

"Alright, well, we'll be on our way," Justin says, wrapping Chloe under his arm and giving Moose a quick whistle.

Their footsteps recede, and the only sound is our heavy breathing—and a few squeaks from the furry balls in the corner.

Familiar voices sound in the foyer, but we ignore them.

When the door slams shut, Noah's hand glides down my arm, and he pulls me from a side hug to a full-on embrace. My gaze drops to his lips, my body tensing for him to lower his mouth to mine.

Footsteps sound outside the kitchen, but we ignore them.

He takes a deep breath, like he's in pain or something, his eyelids heavy. His free hand lifts my chin just so, his thumb grazing the side of my face.

My tongue lazily wets my bottom lip.

The kitchen door bangs open, but we ignore it. "Ohmygod what is this?!" Lane runs to the dogs.

Noah closes his eyes and grunts.

Mamma dog growls.

Lane yaps, scared.

The puppies yap, happy.

Mamma dog snaps at Lane, who cries, looking down at her finger.

"Yeah, you kinda provoked her," Noah says, not looking at Lane.

"I know! She scared me. The skin didn't even break," Lane says. "Who is this?"

Noah turns me around so my back is at his front, his arms wrapped around my collarbone while we give her an account of the situation. Before long, Lane has the puppies on her lap.

"We should go to bed," Noah murmurs loud enough for Lane to hear.

Panic strikes me at the implication of his words. I want this, yet it scares me.

Lane stands, carefully setting the puppies next to the mamma dog.

Noah tenses, letting go of me. "Where's pretty boy?" he asks, shifting the awkwardness from our situation to hers.

"You mean Jake?" she responds icily. "He had to go back to work."

I feel her sadness hit me in a wave. "Are you okay?"

"Goodnight," Noah says to no one in particular as he leaves the kitchen.

"'Night," Lane answers, not cluing in to the fact that she's interrupted something, and her brother is *pissed*.

Me? I'm confused by what just happened, and I think Noah is as well. We got carried away by an overload of puppy cuteness, and one thing leading to another.... To be honest, I'm relieved we were interrupted. There's no reason to make things more awkward than they already are, and I have no interest in being a temporary fling for Noah.

Because if he felt something for me, surely he'd tell me.

"Can you tell my brother not to be such a dick to me?" Lane grumbles once he's gone.

"What do you mean?" I ask as I refill Mamma's bowl of water.

"He's not the only one who has a right to happiness," she quips as she straightens the blankets pooling under and around the dogs. "He's not the boss of us, you know. I thought he'd cool it now that he got married, but it doesn't look like it."

I turn the lights off, the glow from the fridge's ice dispenser bathing the kitchen in soft blue. "Is this about Jake?"

She leans against the counter. "It's about whoever. I'm twenty-two, Willow. I think I can sleep with whoever I want. And just so you know, this house isn't just his. He can't tell me 'my house, my rules.'"

I haven't heard Noah say that, but I bite my tongue. There's history there, one I don't know. And she's clearly wanting to talk to me. "You care about him—Jake?"

Even in the dim lighting, I can make out the tears shining in her eyes. "Yes," she whispers.

"Then... what's the problem?" One of the puppies crawls away from the blanket, and the mamma drags it back by the scruff of its neck.

Lane wipes her tears with the back of her hand. "I... he... I want to make my life in New York. I have interviews lined up and he... he says he'll be settling here, in Emerald Creek."

I frown, curious. "Really? What... does he work from home?" Didn't she just say he had to go back to work?

"That's not really the point, but no. He's in land management or something. The point is, I'm falling for him and I hate myself for that. I don't want to change my plans for *some guy*." She pushes herself from the counter.

I wrap my arm around her shoulders. "Then don't."

"But he's not *some guy* to me. I know it's new but it feels so right. You know what I mean," she says as we leave the kitchen, closing the door carefully behind us.

My voice catches when I answer, "Yes, honey, I know what you mean."

Chapter Twenty-Nine

Noah

"I broke my lease," Willow says one morning two weeks later, eyes a little shiny.

We're having a cup of extremely satisfying coffee, thanks to my ingenious wife's new partnership with Millie, and our mid-morning breaks around the new dispenser are becoming a routine. I never attempted to kiss her again, after that night with the rescues, and I'm glad I didn't. It was the puppy love making her act all emotional with me that night, I know it. She doesn't feel anything for me, and I'm not interested in empty sex anymore. Or so I keep telling myself.

But today she's distraught, and I hate it.

"You..." Fuck this is hard. I know she needs to hear this. "We'll find you another place when..." *When we divorce? When you move out? When I don't get to see your lovely face every morning, witness your magic all day long?* How do I even put this into words? "When the time comes. Maybe there'll be another opening at Sunrise Farms. Who knows?"

"Totally," she says, gaze focused on her coffee. "I don't have much personal stuff. Most of the furniture was Colton's. I can store the rest in the basement."

"Absolutely not."

I can't wait to be surrounded by Willow's stuff.

"How did today's coding meeting with Zach go?" she asks.

I don't call her out for changing the topic. I get it. Rehashing hard stuff doesn't make it go away. "He needs a summer project, something a little complex that will look good on his college applications. We were talking about his options."

She gives me a small laugh. "He could come and set up the vacuum cleaners at Lilyvale when we receive them. If he doesn't mind."

It's a small, menial task, but Zach won't mind. He kept going on and on about what a great woman Willow was. How she taught him to ski independently. Listening to him, you'd think we're the power couple in town. *Fuck, the kid is going to be disappointed.* "Sure, I'll let him know. He'll be happy to see you."

At the end of the day, we take the truck to Sunrise Farms and pull up next to the entrance. We grab Willow's skiing and hiking gear from the downstairs lockers, then go upstairs to her apartment.

When I walk inside, I'm taken by how homey it feels. Sure, there's Colt's dark couch and his oversize TV (which he's switching with Kiara's), but there are so many feminine touches that scream Willow.

The plants. The decorative pillows in hues of pink and green. The scarves hanging from sconces. Even the stack of trail maps and the local plant guides have her stamp.

But mostly, her drawings and watercolors—serene mountains, colorful flowers, joyous waterfalls. As she removes them one by one from the walls to place them in a large box, the place loses its appeal.

Colton worked it out with the landlord that he can leave his furniture there and the apartment will be rented furnished. So while Willow sorts through her things, I help him carry his TV down to the apartment he now shares with Kiara, and we bring her smaller one upstairs, Kiara in tow carrying the cables.

Willow comes out of the bedroom holding a pile of clothes on hangers. "I'm going to set these on the back seat," she says, calling my attention to a very familiar dress.

I close the distance between us. "Didn't end up returning it," I state, something like happiness at this trivial detail warming my chest. Unable to hide how I feel, I give her my biggest smile.

"I..." A million emotions show on her face, seemingly warring to take over as she focuses her gaze on my chest, the cutest pink tinting her neck, making its way up her face. Finally, she looks up at me. "No."

"Good." I take a step forward, grab the tag, and tear it off. "There. Even better."

Her eyes widen and she steps to the side. "Hey, Kiara," she says in a funny voice as she scampers away.

"What was that?" Kiara hisses as Willow disappears on the staircase. She pushes me inside the bedroom and shuts the door so Colton, currently hooking up her TV, doesn't hear us.

"What was what?" The fuck does she want with me?

"Don't hurt her."

"What?!"

She actually pokes my chest. "Don't play mind games with her."

I take a step back but don't answer. She has me very confused, and her anger with me is puzzling.

"Don't make her believe what's not there, Callaway."

Ah hell. Willow must have told her about our arrangement. I play stupid to buy some time. "What's not there?"

She points to the door. "What was that, right now?"

Me smiling at Willow like a goof? "I care about her, okay?"

"That's all?"

Oh, she means the way I look at her? I saw her notice. So what? "She's my wife."

"Cut the crap. I know what this marriage is."

My throat tightens and my eyes blur a bit. Not because she knows about the marriage. But because someone else can tell how far gone I am. What do I have to lose? I might as well be honest, especially with myself. "I'm in love with her. Didn't see it coming. These things happen." Saying it out loud, it feels so obvious, and so natural, and at the same time so vulnerable. The pit in my stomach deepens under the weight of this reality. There's nothing about Willow I don't love, and when she moves on from me, I'll be a shadow of myself.

Kiara's mouth gapes, but for once she has nothing to say, so I continue. "I'll do anything for her. Anything. I'm so fucking sorry she has to lose this apartment, and when the time comes," I say, using that stupid expression, "I'll make it right. I'll be sure she gets something just as nice, and hopefully nicer. And in the meantime, yeah, she gets to keep all the dresses she wants, if that makes her happy. You got a problem with that?"

"You love her."

I nod. "Now get out of my way, I got shit to do," I bark. I hate it when I get unhinged, but she pissed me off big time.

"You need to tell her."

I whip back, and this time I'm the one almost (almost) poking her chest. "Absolutely not, and you better keep your mouth shut."

The bedroom door swings open on my last words. "Wooooow, man," Colton says, jaw set, eyes dark. "What the fuck?" He stands right next to Kiara, dwarfing her.

Her eyes are shiny. "I deserved that. Totally deserved."

"Deserved what?" Willow asks as the bedroom becomes more crowded with her presence.

"Nothing," Kiara and I both answer.

Chapter Thirty

Willow

What happened back there between Noah and Kiara? One minute we're a happy group, the next the two of them are having a secret argument. I need to find out from Kiara.

"You guys should come over for dinner," I declare when the apartment is emptied of my stuff and clean, keys in the super's mailbox. It took the four of us less than an hour, and that's including setting up the smaller TV.

"You sure?" Colton asks, eyes darting between Noah and Kiara.

"Damn right I am." I have every intention of sneaking a conversation with my bestie. We're both too busy with tourist season to catch a coffee just the two of us.

"I'd say it's about time," Kiara drops with a smile. "I'll bring a strawberry shortcake."

Noah clears his throat. "Perfect." He wraps me under his arm and gives me a shoulder squeeze. "Come by whenever you want. I'll fire up the grill."

Two hours later I'm slightly relaxed thanks to some breathing exercises and the Gold Rush Noah placed in my hand when I came down from my shower. Kiara and Colton are playing with the puppies, Beck took over the barbecue, and Lane texted me she was out and not to expect her for dinner.

Noah is tucked against me on the patio sofa, his arm around my shoulders, stroking my bare arm and holding me close enough that I can feel his heartbeat.

"Ribs'll be done in fifteen minutes," Beck announces.

I lean into Noah, enjoying the PDA. We should have friends over more often. Then I remember why I wanted Colton and Kiara over to begin with. "Kiara, let me give you a quick tour," I sort of order, reluctantly leaving Noah's arm and stretching my hand to her as if she were a little girl.

I know how these things go with our friends. We end up talking for hours, then suddenly someone decides it's time to break and everyone scatters.

If I don't manufacture an alone moment now, I'll never have it.

"You need to tell Noah how you feel," she states the minute we're alone in the library, an imposing room right next to the parlor.

"How I feel about what?" I ask, guiding her upstairs.

She stays quiet while we're on the staircase, her footsteps and breathing enough to convey she's... annoyed? angry? upset? It's hard to tell.

"How you feel about him," she hisses, catching up with me as I swing bedroom doors open on our way to the end of the house.

I stop abruptly. "How I *feel* about him?" I repeat.

She crosses her arms, legs slightly apart, and declares, "He needs to know you love him."

Ab-so-lu-tely not. Why is she bringing this up? Is this to distract me from the reason we're having this evening together? I frown at her. "What happened back there, between you and Noah?"

She shakes her head in weird little jerks. "Nothing. What are you talking about?"

"You're not gonna tell me?"

"Nothing happened."

I cross my arms. "I'll ask him. You better spill. Now."

Amusement twinkles in her eye. "Sure, ask him," she answers with a shrug. "See what he says."

Why is she so smug? I'm about to lash out at her, call her out for keeping something from me. But I know what she'll say. That I'm the bigger liar.

"I'm getting hungry," I say, trying to hide my frustration. Damn right I'll ask Noah. This isn't the end of it.

I pivot to take us back downstairs, then stop abruptly and take her in a hug, emotion overtaking me. "I can't be in a fight with you."

"We're not in a fight," she answers.

"Okay-good," I say, exhaling. "I—I need my friend back."

"Been right here all the time, believe me." There's that smugness again, but I'm not pushing my luck and asking her what *that's* about.

"Okay-good."

She pushes me away, a big smile on her face. "Okay." She nods. "Good."

As we go down the stairs, the front door opens. "Anybody home?"

"Puppies!" Skye yells as she rushes down the hallway.

Chris drops a small pink bag, and we don't need to see his face to know that the baby is coming. "Gotta go, Grace and Ethan are out, and Alex is—"

"Ohmygod yes! Go-go-go." Kiara and I push him out, tell him to drive slow but make it fast, to call, to tell Alex we love her, to—

"The car just left," Skye says, giggling over us. She's holding a puppy—from the white spot on the front paw, I know it's the shy one. "He's so sweet," she says, petting the dog who's licking her face.

"I think she's a girl," I offer.

"Awww."

We've barely sat down on the patio to eat when Moose jumps over the fence, and he and mamma dog greet each other. She lets him sniff the puppies, and before long he starts playing with them, letting them crawl all over him.

"Ribs are delish," I tell Beck, and a chorus of thank yous echo my words. Between the baby coming tonight and the dogs, our attention's been everywhere except on the food.

Then Noah's phone rings, and he confirms Moose is here, so within minutes Justin and Chloe join us.

Then it's pure, utter chaos. At some point someone decides we should take a swim. Beck appoints himself puppy guardian, Kiara and Colton hold Skye's hand as they dip their feet in the river, Noah brings a ball out, and I swim across.

"Careful!" Noah calls out.

I reach the opposite shore and give him a wave, then pause for a minute to take in the picture of this evening. The mansion's windows cast an inviting glow against the darkening sky, the bistro lights on the patio bringing a smile to my face. My friends' laughter. Puppy barks echoing. Shreds of conversation drifting my way. All this speaks of a simple and glorious life I want to preserve.

And so far, I have. So no matter what Kiara thinks, I'm not going to ruin it all by spilling my stupid heart.

As I'm about to swim back across, car headlights sweep slowly across Lilyvale's façade, making me instantly feel uneasy.

Sure, it could be curious tourists. Or someone making a U-turn. But it looks vaguely familiar.

It's too dark to make out the color, but I'm ready to bet it's red.

Shaking the unease, I swim quickly back to our group.

As Noah wraps me in a towel and gently squeezes the water out of my hair, I think back to Kiara's words and dismiss them. I do the same when we end the night roasting marshmallows and he takes me onto his lap because that's what the other couples are doing. Then again as he lets his hand roam on my naked thigh. And as he whispers in my neck, "I think it's time for Skye to go to bed," and that makes me shiver and he says "are you cold" and I answer "no" and I feel his body tense and I wonder if he's got an erection and that's why he's pushing me away from his warmth and toward his knees.

But I'm too chicken to risk what I have for something more.

Skye falls deeply asleep two pages into the story she asked me to read. She's wiped out from the excitement of the day and from staying up past her bedtime. I leave a nightlight in her bathroom and close her door softly, then pad to our bedroom.

From the couch, Noah mumbles, "Beat you," with a smile in his voice, then stirs and settles. I stay still, memorizing this moment. So what if I'm not his real wife? I'd give anything for this. Our race to the couch. Our fake PDA. Our moments together at the store. This can be enough for me. More than enough.

The next morning, Grace picks up Skye and convinces her to go to school. "You can skip school when the baby comes home," she says, and this wins her the argument.

Skye's still holding a puppy when she's about to leave, after breakfast. "Can I come and visit her?" she asks timidly, hope in her large eyes.

"Of course you can," I say as I hug her goodbye.

Noah smiles once they're gone. "I see a puppy request in the near future. Chris is going to have his hands full with a baby and a dog."

"Ohmygod yes," I snort. "Good luck trying to tell that little one no. Skye is the best kid."

"Plus they have the space," Noah says.

"They are so totally getting a dog."

"A real big dog."

For some reason the idea of our friends getting one of our puppies makes us laugh like crazy.

That night, I stay up late in the parlor talking with Lane on the phone. Her happiness seeps through, all giddy laughter and soft sighs. Her dinner with Jake went better than she'd hoped, and now they're headed out of town for a few days. "Would you mind telling Noah?" she asks me, hesitation in her voice.

"Of course," I tell her. After I hang up, I stay still for a moment. Lane's trust lingers like a gift, warming my chest. It's something I didn't know I needed, but it's there now, soft and powerful. A sister's confidence.

But now this means Noah and I will have the place to ourselves, and this sends a confusing shiver through me. We're getting better and better at acting as a real couple in public, and I don't trust myself alone with him. What if I mistakenly sit on his lap when we're alone in the kitchen? Kiss him good morning when there's no one around? It's not like I have to remind myself to do that. It's scary how naturally it comes to me. This man is a magnet to me, always has been. What if I ruin everything just by being myself?

Its dark inside the bedroom when I enter. No shape on the couch. Disappointingly, not in the bed either.

The bathroom door creaks, partly open, light spilling onto the floor. I reach for the lamp, ready to say something. But no one comes out.

And the shower starts running.

Steam curls upward, blurring the glass partition.

My pulse quickens as Noah steps into view. Naked. The sight of his body pierces me with want.

I shouldn't be looking.

I shouldn't even be here.

I should tiptoe out of the room before he senses my presence.

That's what any decent human being would do.

But he steps into the shower, tilts his head back, the water pelting his face. Heat ripples through me. I can almost feel the warmth of the shower hitting him rhythmically.

Soap suds slide down his back and I track them shamelessly, pulse thudding in my throat. His shoulders roll as he scrubs. His thighs tense and relax. It's impossible to keep my gaze from lowering, and I stay transfixed.

Then he turns.

I've imagined him plenty of times. Filled in the blanks.

But nothing, nothing prepared me for the vibration I feel as my eyes follow the V carved low on his abdomen, the trail of hair leading down to his magnificent, half-hard cock.

Oh. God.

His erection grows. "Ah, fuck," he mutters, the curse vibrating through me.

He wraps his fist around his cock, and my hand slides under my panties.

Everything about this is wrong, and yet the craving takes over. My body responds to his.

Head thrown back, bracing against the wall with one hand, he increases his pace. The crease between his brow deepens as he opens his eyes partway. It feels like he's looking at me, even though he can't possibly see me in the dark room.

Still, I fantasize as the air between us seems to hum.

What would it feel like to have him hover over me, come inside me, kiss me, whisper my name as he made me his? If I were brave enough, I'd take my clothes off right this minute and slide into the shower, get on my knees, and finish him off. There's no way he'd say no to that. No rejection possible.

Turns out, I'm a wimp because I stay hidden and come on my fingers, which is absolutely frustrating and does nothing to quiet my ache for him. It's been brewing for a while; it was going somewhere with that almost kiss the day we found the puppies.

As he steps out of the shower and towels off, I dash to the couch and duck under the duvet he laid out, burying myself in his scent. I try to calm my heartbeat, but it's still wild in my chest when Noah comes out of the bathroom and flicks the light off. By the sound of it, he's turning down the sheets. All senses alert, I wait for him.

Chapter Thirty-One

Noah

She was watching me. I know she was. I could feel it. I almost, *almost* called her out on it.

I considered asking if she wanted to join me.

I considered bringing her to bed like I normally do, then sliding in with her. She'd be under me right now, or maybe on top of me, or maybe her mouth would be wrapped around my cock.

But it didn't seem like the right thing to do.

Too impulsive. Because I don't trust myself not to change my mind, I don't go even near the couch. I spend the night in what I've come to think of as her bed. The next morning, I set her coffee on a side table near the couch and dash out.

I'm crouched next to our rescues when she comes into the kitchen. "Awww," she coos. Without a hint at what happened last night, she sets her cup in the sink.

Maybe she didn't see me.

"Thanks for the coffee," she says with a sweet smile as she sits next to me on the floor, close enough that our knees are touching.

Maybe she wasn't there at all.

Two of the three puppies climb on her, their mother greeting her with a tail wag. One of the puppies licks her face when she lifts it and kisses it on the nose. "Aren't they cute?" she whispers.

The little guy lets a stream of pee hit her horizontally. "Oh you little devil you," she says, laughing. Doesn't put him down, certainly doesn't seem to mind. She just nuzzles him closer. "You peeing because you scared or you peeing because you comfy? Hmm? Which is it?" Then she cradles him against her, the wetness on her sweatshirt smearing on his fur as she pets him like a perfectly clean stuffed animal.

I stand and put warm water on a clean kitchen towel, then sit back cross-legged next to her. "Here," I say, awkwardly patting the puppy's fur.

"Awww look what Daddy brought," she says, moving the puppy my way while I clean him. Our fingers keep touching, and I try to avoid it but I can't. "What should we call them?" I ask.

Because the vet established the mom was in bad shape, was not tagged, and had signs of abuse, we're not looking to reunite her with her previous owners. The vet said once momma dog was spayed, she could help finding her and the puppies good families *when the time comes*. Her exact words, and I've come to hate them.

"I don't know, what do you think?" she says.

"Maybe we should let their future owners decide." *When the fucking time comes.*

"Oh... Oh right." Are her eyes welling up? She kisses the puppy's nose and gently puts him down. He sneezes, then follows his brother wandering around the kitchen on wobbly paws. Willow gets on her knees to fetch the third puppy—the shy one. "Hi," she says. The little creature is shaking. "You poor little thing. You have the right idea. Better not get attached to us, if we're going to give you away."

My throat tightens as she sets the puppy between her mother's paws. I feel like shit.

"Obviously, I mean maybe, we could keep 'em." They're big dogs, but this house is large, and there's the barn and meadows where they could live happily in the summer. "What do you think?" I ask her as she stands.

Her gaze meets mine. "We don't need to decide that right now. I just thought..."

I stand and brush my hands together. "Yes?"

"While they're with us, it'd be nicer if they had names. When you decide to give them away, they can always take a different name. It's not forever." She says all this while she prepares her second cup of coffee of the day and pours it in the to-go cup that Millie gave her, with her name, Willow Callaway, written all around it.

She sees me look at the mug, and the air suddenly gets heavy. "They could also end up staying here forever," I say, looking her straight in the eyes. "I find myself getting attached." This time, for sure, she's going to tell me off. When she doesn't, I push her. "Don't you?"

"I've been attached since the second I saw them. It's the falling in love and having to say goodbye part that sucks. But that's part of life, isn't it?"

My heart threatens to escape from my ribcage. "It doesn't have to be."

Her lips part, she takes a short inhale as if she's about to say something heavy, but then her alarm rings. "Almost time to go open the store," she says, and god—god!—I've never felt so happy about going to the store. "We still have time for granola and yogurt, but first let me change into a clean clothes."

After a quick breakfast, we let momma dog out, refill her water, and lay newspapers on the floor for the little ones' business.

Then Willow takes her pretty travel mug of coffee and we step outside. In a practiced movement, I take her free hand in mine, and she twines our fingers together as we cross onto busy Elm Street. She's warm under my touch, her fingers strong. Her shoulder rubs against mine, our forearms linked, her floral scent wafting to me. I tilt my head to the sky and close my eyes for a brief second.

"Everything okay?" There's real concern in her tone.

I give her hand a squeeze. "Just saying a quick thank-you to the guy upstairs."

She tilts her head to me. "For what?" she asks sweetly.

I take a moment to admire the way the sun plays with her irises, gold speckles dancing in the hues of chestnut. "For you." Her gaze turns darker, telling me so much more than her silence.

And her lips are very close to mine, and if we weren't standing on the street right now I'm pretty sure I'd be kissing her. "Can I finally take my wife out to dinner?"

I need us to stop with the innuendos. I need an open conversation, and for that I need time off from the store, from Lilyvale, from our obligations.

I need to romance my wife.

Chapter Thirty-Two

Noah

Chloe seats us at a very private table, "the nook of The Nook," and I look into Willow's eyes as we clink our glasses of expensive Bordeaux. Her discreet floral fragrance (rose? lilac?) spirals around me, drawing me closer. No matter what happens next, this will forever be the scent of happiness. She spent an hour in the bathroom getting ready, and although she'll never be more beautiful than all messed up from sleep in the morning, I have to admit the shine of her lush brown locks, the glow of her skin, the sparkle of her jewelry, all make her heart-stoppingly, head-spinningly gorgeous.

All I want is to cup her nape in my hand and pull her in for a kiss.

I almost do, but then she breaks the connection, eyes blinking, a tremor on the surface of her wine betraying she's unsettled and struggling to keep it together.

Chill, Noah. You have all dinner to get your point across. This is about romancing her, not jumping her bones.

"You look beautiful," I say. *So lame.*

She murmurs "Thank you," with a small smile and maybe even a slight blush.

I thought I had a plan. I've been turning this evening over in my head the whole day at the store. While she was unpacking flannel shirts, humming along to "Down With Disease." Then singing the whole lyrics to "If I Could" while rearranging our different grades of maple syrup in hay-filled wooden cases, sprinkling individually wrapped maple candies around.

"Any idea when and where Phish are playing next?" *Nice. Make it seem casual but bring it back to a moment when we shared a connection.*

Looking at the menu, she answers right away, "Down south for now, Upstate New York in a couple of months." Her eyebrows narrow, as if she's hesitating between the cod with braised bok choi and the gnocchi with locally foraged mushrooms.

Me? I'm stricken. By how she knows about all of Phish's upcoming concerts. By our familiarity—how she answers without looking at me. It's almost as if we're an old couple already, in tune with each other. I'm not sure I like it this early in what I'm determined to make a relationship.

Lowering her menu with one finger, I force her to look at me.

"What?" she asks, an adorable smile on her face. "This menu is... awesome." She takes my finger in hers to halt my interruption, and all I can think about is how soft her skin is and how I want this moment to last forever. How I want my whole fucking life to be like this. Easy, playful, sexy.

"Listen to this: 'Sustainably farmed in Vermont and humanely harvested locally, these chops melt in your mouth. Served with a generous side of Cortland apples sauteed in ghee and lightly deglazed in apple cider vinegar. Suggested pairing: Make it classic with a Finger Lakes

Riesling or keep it focused and hyperlocal with a Stillpoint hard cider.' I think I'll have that."

She finally looks up at me, then looks down at our clasped fingers, hardly blushes, then clears her throat and sets her menu down.

Then, instead of letting go of my finger, she intertwines our hands, her silk touch keeping me captive. "How about you?" she asks. "I think you'd like the flank steak. It's marinated in olive oil and..." She continues, but only her melodic voice makes it to my consciousness—the lyrics are lost to me. I don't need to know what the menu says. If my wife thinks I'll like it, then I most certainly will.

I'm hooked on the fact that our hands are now rested on the table, although we're secluded enough that no PDA is warranted—not that it ever was the point of this outing. Further, I'm drawing circles inside her palm *and she's letting me*, and not only that but are those tiny goose bumps on her arm?

"Right?" she says, startling me. Then, "What's wrong?"

"Nothing. Sounds great."

She removes her hand, folds our menus together, and rattles out our order to Chloe.

"So Phish..." I start once we're alone again. "We'll go, obviously." I want to tell her we'll make a weekend out of it. Maybe a weekend date. One room or two?

Maybe reading my mind, she picks up her glass of wine, leaving the other hand on the table—a temptation too hard to resist.

I place a finger on the inside of her wrist, marveling at the soft beat of her pulse.

I'm not going to talk about last night. Of course I'm not. But we should address the cupid in the room. I'm going to retrace our steps a bit, do what I should have done days ago.

"Remember that first evening, the day we got the puppies?" Her pulse accelerates under my fingers. I didn't mean to do this evaluation of her feelings by reading her pulse, I swear I didn't, but it's brilliant. She definitely remembers.

I hesitate only briefly. "Was it my imagination or did you... did we..." Fuck. Why is it so hard for me to tell Willow that I wish we hadn't been interrupted? That I want to know if she feels the same way I do? "When Lane came in, were we about to—"

"Oh my god aren't you two just a-do-ra-ble," Cassandra coos as she walks to us, beaming. "Our love birds..." She leans toward us and grabs our hands. "I am *so* happy that you are finally together." She turns to Willow. "Did you tell him how long it's been?" Willow turns crimson, her gaze darting between Cass and me.

Ignoring Willow's embarrassment, Cass turns to me. "This woman has been crushing on you for...everrrrr..." she says, dragging the word out.

My eyes must be bugging out of their sockets because she continues, "I know, right? It's like... how? How did you not see that? What took you so long?"

Well... what does she mean, *forever*? And *crushing*? What is *crushing*, specifically?

Cass laughs and turns to Willow. "I'm glad you didn't follow your friends' advice and move on, sweetie." She grabs our hands and lays them on each other, the way they were just a minute ago. "Tenacious, this one," she says and leaves.

"She was kidding, right?" I ask under my breath. Because if she wasn't, what kind of a fucking moron am I?

Adorable guilt is painted all over my wife's features.

Well now, this changes everything.

I'll think about what kind of a fucking stupid idiot I've been later. Now's not the time for introspection.

Willow goes to pull her hand from under mine but I clasp her wrist, feeling her fast pulse under my fingers. "How long has it been?" Maybe it's recent. That would make it... passable. "Since Colt and Kiara's wedding?" I'm a pretty good dancer. Maybe that did it.

She chuckles sadly. That would be a hell no.

Way longer than that.

Fuck! Her wrist beats like a trapped animal under my grasp. I let her go, vaguely ashamed, and steeple my fingers. "Please look at me. And please tell me. How long?"

She shakes her head. "Umm..." She shrugs, stifles a chuckle, looks everywhere except at me.

"When did it start?" And how could I have missed this?

"You weren't supposed to find out—ever."

"What the actual fuck, Willow."

"I know—I'm sorry," she stammers.

I am, officially, the biggest dick ever. "That's not what I'm talking about. Why the fuck wouldn't you tell me?"

She smiles softly.

"What?"

"You're cursing," she explains, and she looks positively entertained by the fact. "Remember, you said—"

"Oh I remember all right." The memory of us in the study, going over that stupid spreadsheet, her teasing me because I wouldn't use the F word, me telling her I cursed in the right circumstances—sex might have been hinted at. "Consider this foreplay, then."

Her chest rises and falls, breath coming in shallow pants.

I flag a server and hand her my credit card. "Abby, something came up. Bag our order, take my card. I'll pick everything up later tonight."

Then I take Willow's hand, and when she twines her fingers with mine I almost roar.

Once outside, I pull her to my side as she sets a hurried pace toward Lilyvale. "You have some explaining to do."

"No-I-don't," she quips, wrapping her arm around my hips like she's done a dozen times now—and now I know why she was *so good* at it. She wasn't faking.

Neither was I. "What did Cassandra mean by crushing on me?"

"Noah, please," she breathes.

"Careful. You're even sexier when you beg."

She looks around as if someone could hear us. As if I wasn't growling right against her ear.

I give her earlobe a nibble as we turn from Elm street onto Callaway Drive.

She hisses, throwing her neck back. "Ah," she coos, wrapping her hand tighter around me.

"How long has it been? Tell me."

She hastens her steps. "No."

Okay. I'll pick this up later. "Are you in a hurry to get somewhere?" I murmur against her neck. She almost trips, would have if she weren't so glued to me.

"Home," she says, and I love the way it sounds in her mouth. I love that home is the same place for her and for me. "There's too much happening right now."

I open the front door. "I disagree. There's not enough happening." Then before she can step inside, I scoop her up and carry her over the threshold. She twines her hands behind my nape, and we pause for a moment. Eye to eye, no talking.

I'm carrying my bride into my family home. Lilyvale is eerily silent for several beats. Willow's irises darken, my heart threatens to escape from my ribcage, and we're in a time warp—what seems like an eternity stretches, lasting forever yet way too short.

The grandfather clock starts its seemingly endless striking, and I kick the front door shut.

The puppies start on their puppy barking but that doesn't stop me. I carry my wife up to our bedroom.

Setting her on her feet, I lock our door. She backs up a few paces, and says, "What is happening right now?" Darts her tongue out, the little tease.

Closing the distance, I cup her nape in my hand. "Let's find out." I skim her lips with mine, my dick straining in my pants. "You don't want to tell me how long you've been crushing on me—fine. Would you like to hear how hard I've been fantasizing about you since you became my wife?"

She takes a quick breath, then gently removes my glasses and drops them on top of her bag, at our feet.

"Just for the record... because I'm not one to keep secrets... I know you looked at me last night... when I was in the shower."

She bites her lip, drops her gaze. *Good girl*. "I shouldn't have—"

"Yeah you should've," I whisper. Feeling her bristle, I grab a fistful of her hair and gently force her to look at me. "You're my *wife*, Willow. I've been fantasizing about you since that Phish concert, maybe before. It was driving me crazy... never spent so much time in my office here, trying to make sure you were asleep before coming upstairs."

She brings her body flush against mine, hands tugging at my shirt.

"And it's not just lust, it's so much deeper than that—"

She shuts me up with her lips on mine, full and greedy and taking.

I pull her tighter to me, explore her mouth, relishing her taste, loving how she darts her tongue around mine. When I hoist her on my hips she deepens the kiss.

I didn't expect that. Not at all. The force of her... it incenses me. Sets me alive. She's soft and so strong at the same time, everything I was afraid she'd be. Everything I love her for. Getting lost in her, I know I'm in for an ocean of pain if I ever lose her.

Breaking the kiss for a beat, she chuckles nervously. "What if the judge asks us our favorite position, or if you snore after sex, or if I drool in my sleep? We *have* to know, right?"

Chapter Thirty-Three

Willow

"That judge better not ask those kinds of questions if he cares about his life," he says, skimming my chin with the ridge of his nose, dipping down to furrow my neck. "I think you're who wants to know, and my question is, if Cass hadn't said anything, when were you going to tell me?" He unclasps the top of my dress, and the delicious sound of the zipper tears over our heavy breathing while his fingers barely skim my back. "Answer me."

Damn Cassandra. But also, maybe not. "You weren't supposed to know," I admit.

He rears back and I miss the feel of his skin already. "Why not?"

"I'm-It's embarrassing."

He laughs. "You, embarrassed?" His laughter dies down, his gaze turning soft. "Must be true, then." He takes my mouth in a soft kiss, then deepens our embrace, pulling me flush against him again, his heartbeat as fast as mine.

I run my hands in his hair, and he hoists my legs up on him, taking us to the couch. He sets me on the back of it and pulls his shirt off in one movement. My eyes fall to his flat stomach, the muscles rippling under a dusting of hair, then to the bulge in his pants.

"It's yours, Willow. Take it." He strokes himself through his pants, then unbuckles his belt and opens up.

Swallowing with difficulty, I pull myself up and stroke him through his boxer shorts. "I'm on the Pill," I whisper, "and I haven't been with anyone in... I don't know how long."

"Fuck," he grunts. "Same. But I can still..." he hisses "try and find a condom if you prefer."

I free his cock, wetness instantly pooling between my legs. "No." Pulling him to me with one hand behind his ass, I take him in my mouth.

"Jeeeesus," he hisses. "I thought I said I haven't been with anyone in a very long time."

I look up at him, taking him deeper, my tongue relishing the salty bead of precum. I just want to make Noah Callaway come, and I don't know what that says about me.

"The first time I come is going to be inside my wife."

I nod, sucking him harder.

He pulls himself off of me. "Fucking hell. Inside my wife's *pussy*." Then he flips me on my stomach. "You should know, you have the most perfect, erotic ass." He slaps my butt cheek, making me shriek in surprise but also... that was hot.

I glance at him over my shoulder.

"You like that, don't you?" Another slap on the other cheek, just enough to give me a tingle and a clench of my middle.

"Aaaah, my wife likes a light spanking. What an interesting discovery." Another slap, and the zing of pleasure shoots straight to my nipples. "I shouldn't be surprised. Your ass should be X-rated," he says as his hand roughly kneads my butt cheeks. I'm pulsating, hoping for more, arching my back. "No one should see it molded in jeans," he continues, "or that fucking little summer dress you wore at the store and you had the gall to get on your knees and lift your butt and ahhhhh." He pulls my hair in his fist. "Just so you know, I'm going to ride your sweet little cunt while looking at your perfect butthole."

He runs a finger alongside my clit and I moan. "Fucking hell, Willow. You. Are. Soaked." He enters me with two fingers, and I clench around him. "That's what I'm talking about. Fucking pulsating for me and I did nothing at all. You waiting for me, wifey? You want your husband to fuck you properly, don't you?"

I want to tell him to just shut up and fuck me already, but the only sound that comes out of my mouth is a needy whine.

"What was that?" he growls.

"Fuck me, please."

"Atta girl." Another slap, and his cock drives into me, making me buck and clench the fabric of the couch. "You said a lot of things about how my marriage should go." His fingers dig deep into my hips, possessive. "But you never said how I was supposed to feel when I fucked *my wife*," he drops as he pulls out to better plunge into me again.

I arch my back under the pleasure of his cock filling me, jutting my hips to him so he hits the hilt. I let out a moan when I feel his balls.

"Willow," he grunts.

"Harder," I answer.

He gives me a few agonizingly slow movements, and leans over my back, wrapping me closer into him, one hand reaching for my breast, massaging it until two fingers narrow on my nipple and he worries them. I almost come.

"Oh, Noah, keep going, keep going."

He lets go of my breast, nibbles on my shoulder, stroking in and out of me, and his left hand runs down my arm until our wedding bands are aligned. He takes a ragged breath, then kisses the crux of my neck.

Pulling out, he carries me to the bed. "I want to see your gorgeous face when you come," he explains. "But we need to talk a little."

Talk? I mean sure, if he's doing the talking.

Noah Callaway married me *and* is making love to me, when not so long ago I was still a nobody to him. There is no way in hell I am able to *talk*. But of course he doesn't know the magnitude of the earthquake that's been going on in my heart from the moment Cassandra outed me, up to the surreal moment when *he carried me over the threshold*.

Returning to the moment, I try to focus on only enjoying the sight of his pecs flexing over me, his biceps framing me, his six-pack clenching as his cock enters me. I could do this all night. Probably will. I can think on the big picture later.

Setting himself up on his forearms, he pulls back again, then enters me at an agonizingly slow pace. "You never said," he says.

My inside clenches around him, and I loop one leg higher on him to pull him closer to me.

"Na-na-na-na-na," he says, resisting my pull. He pushes a strand of hair behind my ear. His cock pulses inside me, but heck if that shows on his face. I know that expression. He frowns like he wants to *talk*.

"Babe—"

"Babe?" He looks amused. "I like that." He looks somewhere above my head then repeats, "Babe." Then he huffs, "Never been called babe before."

I drop my hips to the mattress, my pussy drying up. "Really."

"Really, what?"

"You're bringing your exes right in the middle of our first time having sex?"

His cock pulses inside me, and god dammit, just the feel of that and I get wet again. That and the way he looks at me, feral, hungry, possessive as fuck.

"Jealous?" he dips his mouth to my breast, sucking on my nipple.

"Noah," I plead.

He runs his hand down the length of me, until he finds my clit with the pad of his thumb. He sucks and teases and finally moves his hips again, helping me chase an orgasm I deeply need, if only to erase the frustration. I get into a promising rhythm, then he lets go of my nipple with a pop and says, "So, about my ideal wife..."

What the hell is he talking about? The guy needs to *shut up*. "Almost there, babe," I whine, pushing his head down toward my breast.

He stops moving inside me. "You in a hurry to go somewhere?" He's frowning at me, like I'm this mystery he's trying to figure out.

I close my eyes in frustration. "Alright, let's just... What's going through your mind right now?" It can't be that bad, because he's hard as a rock inside me.

A slow smile spreads across his face. "I thought you'd never ask."

For real? I'd laugh at that, but the way his biceps are bulging right next to my breasts, the way his neck is tense right above me, the way the vein is bulging on his forehead... I don't understand how he wants to talk when clearly all signs indicate he wants to fuck me.

"Is this... is this some kind of weird sex game nerds like to play? Cos I wouldn't know."

His cock deflates a tad. Guess that must have hurt. "See how it feels when we bring exes into the bedroom?" Keep frustrating me sexually, and the sass comes right out.

"I'm sorry you've only known inarticulate bedmates," he says. "Must have been boring as hell." He withdraws and starts a slow descent of his mouth down my torso. Laving the breast that didn't get any attention yet, he uses his teeth just to the limit of pain, cupping my pussy with his hand. He slides a finger down my center, all the way to my butthole, his thumb pad barely skimming my clit.

Leaving my breast, he lowers himself slowly, peppering kisses on my stomach while he continues teasing both my entrances with one hand. "Remember when you gave me that whole speech about how I should feel when I propose to my wife?" He lifts his head, gaze locked on mine, awaiting an answer.

"Yeah?" I'm not sure what he's talking about, if I'm being honest.

"You had all these ideas about the wedding and the babies wearing glasses."

Oh, that. Right.

He presses two fingers on my butthole while his thumb enters me, the feeling new and scary and *so good*. "You forgot something."

Oh god. What now?

He lifts his gaze to me, spearing me with his darkened irises. "Well like I said, you forgot something. You forgot to say that the first time I'd make love to her, I should feel reborn."

My heart swells at his words. *The sass has left the building.*

With his free hand, he cups my throat. "Like Superman. Yet humbled."

I blink out the tears of overwhelm that threaten to spill. *Noah. This is how Noah thinks about me.*

He flips us over so I straddle him. "You forgot to say I'd feel like a god and a slave at the same time," he says, palming my breasts. "Like her master and her servant."

I move on his cock, and we stay that way for a little bit, the weight of his words engulfing me.

He slaps the side of my butt cheek. "Now ride your husband like a good little housewife," he orders, circling my waist with his strong hands and spearing me on his cock, "before I fuck you properly."

He keeps his promise. After I come undone on him, he sets me on my knees against the headboard and takes me from behind, one flexed arm against the wall, the other holding me, fingers teasing my nipple. He sucks on my neck. "I was thinking about you in the shower, Willow, I hope you know that. But, fuck, your cunt is so much better than I ever thought it could be. You forgot to say my wife's pussy should feel like it was custom-made for me. The exes can come in the bedroom and take a lesson. You're the best I've ever had. And I want to be the best for you."

He rams into me harder, his words morphing into grunts, his hands gripping my waist. I feel another orgasm build, weeks of suppressed need finding their release, and let it roll out as he empties himself inside me, clenching me close to him.

We collapse on the bed, and he pulls me against his chest as we catch our breaths.

He kisses my forehead, the most tender look in his eyes. Then his gaze moves to the window, where the moon is rising, shining bright, the tall trees casting shadows on the bedroom walls.

"When I asked you to marry me, by the lake at the wedding, and you turned me down... You also said something about butterflies in my stomach and losing my appetite. That the woman I marry should do that to me."

That sounds like something I would say, so I nod.

"You do that to me, Willow. And a lot more." A sad smile plays on his face. "I don't understand why I never looked at you in this way before."

My heart falters a bit. "It's because I'm not the right match for you, Noah," I croak. "Your family—"

"That's BS and you know it," he interrupts me, his voice snapping. "The truth is, you scared me. Still do. You fly through life while I trudge." *But when I fly, it's from fear.* "Where I stay put out of fear or duty, you trailblaze" *Wrong again. I try new things because I don't like the present me.* "I mistook our difference for incompatibility. I was wrong." His breath stutters. "I was awestruck."

Chapter Thirty-Four

Noah

Okay, so maybe I went overboard with all the talking during sex. I don't know. I just wanted Willow to know how much she means to me. If she weren't already my wife, I'd be on one knee right now, begging her to be mine 'til death do us part.

I don't know what tonight means to her. She's not saying much. I can tell she likes the sex though, but that's not enough to build a life on.

I bring her a warm, wet cloth to clean up, then take a quick shower before picking up our food at Clover's Nook. When I return, she's wrapped in a robe, descending the staircase. I set the bag of food on the console and wrap her in my arms. She smells of sex, and I take a large inhale, getting instantly hard.

Without missing a beat, she runs a hand over my cock. "Not tired yet?"

I skim her lips with mine. "Just getting warmed up."

She raises an eyebrow, clearly impressed, but doesn't say anything.

"Just say the word, and I'm at your service."

"So chivalrous."

"You have no idea. My sword belongs to you."

"Okay—you're making me horny again."

I smirk. "Good."

She moves inside my embrace, the robe parting to reveal her breast. I dip my head down and give it a lick, my cock pulsing, begging for release.

"Noah," Willow breathes.

"Yes?"

Her fingers fumble with my jeans zipper, and she falls to her knees on the first step of the oak staircase, freeing my cock and taking it in her mouth.

I place my hands on her head, my fingers playing through her silky-soft mane while she licks my shaft. Throwing her head back, she looks at me with adoring eyes as she takes the tip in her mouth. With a soft growl that intensifies my erection, she closes her eyes and takes my length in, bobbing her head, sucking and licking.

My knees start giving out. This woman is pure heaven, and the fact she's giving me head under the stern watch of the portraits of my ancestors doesn't turn me off at all.

She takes my hands and places them firmly on her head, then lets go of my cock only to say, "Fuck my mouth, Callaway."

"You're doing just fine," I croak.

She looks me in the eye, one hand stroking my cock, the tip against her mouth, the other digging into my ass. "I'm not going for just fine. I want you to fuck my mouth like you never thought you could."

My dick strains painfully, trying to enter her against my better judgment. Willow's plump mouth, deep throat, and willingness to please me could be a dangerous cocktail for her.

"I'll let you know if it's too much," she says, her whispers echoing against the walls. "Please. I want you to. I'm begging you." She pulls me in, and I almost teeter when I hit the back of her throat.

With both hands on her head, I set a rhythm, encouraged by her moans. She pulls me to her as she lies down on the staircase, making me straddle her. Her hands pulls my hips, encouraging me to keep going.

"I'm gonna come." My dick is enraged, my vision blurred. "Let me go, Willow." I can't hold it in anymore, but she has an iron grip on me, whimpering and sucking. Her half-closed eyes seem to be begging me. "Willow, did you hear me?"

She nods and sucks harder, until I empty myself in her.

Minutes later, I'm still sprawled on the staircase, catching my breath, when Willow says, "So, two things. First, this was the best dinner delivery *ever*. Second, we need to baptize every room at Lilyvale this way."

I roll over to kiss her, then start laughing uncontrollably.

Chapter Thirty-Five

Willow

Minutes later, we hear whining from the kitchen. "Stay right there," Noah says. "I'll let Momma out."

When he comes back, he sits on the steps, uncorks the bottle of expensive Bordeaux we'd ordered at Chloe's Nook, and hands it to me. I take a gulp straight from the bottle. "That's sacrilege, you know," Noah says.

"I know. But it's still good." A drop of wine slides down the corner of my mouth, and he leans over to lick it. "Good boy. Don't let it go to waste."

"I'd say that's... fifty cents right there."

Horrified, I hold the bottle away from me.

"Just kidding, I wanted a reason to lick your neck." He goes for seconds, suckling on the base of my neck.

"Are you trying to give me a hickey, Callaway?"

He growls, his mouth still against my skin. "I wasn't, but fuck yeah," he says as he nibbles hard enough on me to make me cry out in surprise and low-grade pain. "Oh shit," he says. "You mark easily."

I laugh hysterically, the wine and the release from sex and the overall easiness of this surreal setting and of what's happening right now hitting me.

Me sipping expensive wine on the grand staircase of the Callaway mansion, having given head to Noah Callaway after he'd made me come twice in the master bedroom.

Me bearing the last name Callaway.

Me being Noah's wife, when months ago crushing on him was just hurting me.

Me seeing the way Noah looks at me, with want and hunger but also more than just lust.

He leans and nibbles again. "That's what happens when you marry into a vampire family."

Right then, the grandfather clock strikes midnight, and I laugh again, the timing of the endless peals amplifying my deep happiness.

Noah reaches inside the paper bag and pulls out the appetizer—goat cheese puffs with a honey-base dipping sauce. I take a bite. "Man. All this sex made me hungry. You?"

His gaze glances down my length. "Made me hungry for more of you, Mrs. Callaway." He drops his puff in the container, running his hand through his hair. "Ah fuck."

"What?"

"I just... want you again." He looks genuinely pained.

I giggle. "Eat something first. We have all the time in the world."

He looks at me with a question in his eyes.

It's a weird situation we're in. Married and lusting after each other, getting to know and appreciate each other. But we have it all backward. The steps are reversed. We're already at the end-game stage. I'm not ready to push the tough conversation.

Momma dog makes her way to us, followed by her three puppies. They're steadier on their feet, but they struggle following her up the steps and keep tumbling down. "How was it, growing up here?" I ask.

"Depends. Before Mom got here, it was kinda dark and sad, I guess? I don't have a lot of memories of that time. But mainly, it was a happy place to grow up in. Especially in the summer."

"Why the summer?"

"We were always outside, running around. Going up to the orchards, helping with the vegetable garden."

I look around, at the hallway with the doors closed, the high ceilings. "It is kinda gloomy in here," I finally say.

"I told you to make it yours. Make any changes you want. Mom never did—I don't know why. This stuff around here is... it's been here for over a century."

"Maybe that's why. She wanted to respect the history," I venture.

He takes my hand. "And I'd love for *you* to make history here." The pad of his thumb strokes the inside of my wrist, and he brings it to his lips.

My heart hammers inside my chest. What is he really talking about—the house, or us? I'm too scared to ask and see my illusions shattered. Because how permanent are we, really? What happens to us, to me, once his inheritance is secured? He said he feels more than lust, but how deep do his feelings really go?

It's all so new to him.

I clench my jaw, not knowing what to answer.

"You have an eye for things," he says, misreading my anxiety. "I don't. Griff seems to have given up on us and Emerald Creek. Beck is too busy spending all his energy outdoors to care about Lilyvale. And Lane... she wants a bigger life away from here."

Noah's voice betrays his distress.

I already have so much I never expected; so what if my feelings get bruised in the end?

"Sure, I'll do it," I say, focusing my thoughts on the heavy drapes gone, airy spotlights shedding light on contemporary art pieces, comfortable sectionals replacing the stiff settees, wicker baskets full of throws and local pottery vases with wildflowers bringing simplicity inside.

Mamma dog whines and nudges my hand, bringing me back to the present. "You tired of always giving your attention to your babies, aren't you?" I dig my fingers into her thick fur, feeling how she's filled up. "You need attention too. Yes you do."

"We need to find her a name," Noah says, reaching over my lap to pet her as well.

"I was thinking Calla, like the lilies? and like Callaway."

Noah turns his face to me, grazing my mouth with his lips. "Oh, you were thinking about her name, huh?" He smiles and nibbles on my earlobe, making me want him again.

I whisper the lie. "Only a little. Randomly, you know." I like her and hate that I can't call her... anything.

Noah chuckles and boops my nose. "Moose and Calla. That sounds good. Two names drawn from nature. I like it."

"What do you think?" I ask Calla. She answers me by licking my cheek, then nips gently at one of her puppies who's managed to climb the steps and is now biting at her nipple.

The two other puppies yap in frustration, wanting in yet bumping against the first step cluelessly.

"Almost there," Noah says, chuckling. Grazing my cheek with the back of his hand, he adds, "And did you officially change *your* name yet?"

My cheeks burn. I wasn't planning on it. It's a pain in the neck. Why would I do that? Yet something warm coils inside of me. "Right," I say. "Let's not give Gail more ammo than she already has. I'm sorry, I should have—"

Noah's gaze darkens. "Fuck Gail. That's not why I was asking." He shakes his head. "I'm sorry."

"No, I'll do it. You're right."

He switches positions so he's kneeling in front and below me on the steps, moving the puppy gently to the side. "Willow. You're my wife. I want for you what you want for yourself. If you don't think it's right that a woman changes her name when she gets married, it's fine by me." He stands. "We should definitely add that to the spreadsheet."

I grab his hand before he can go anywhere. "What did you say?"

"I'm gonna add it to the spreadsheet."

"Before that." *The thing about being your wife.* "About..." I lick my lips, unsure how to phrase this. He dropped a bomb on me, not even realizing it. "You wanting for me what I want for myself."

He pulls me up, and being above him on the staircase, our eyes are level. "Absolutely. My wife calls the shots in this household. Anybody who doesn't like it can go to hell." His mouth closes on mine, his kiss giving me the strength I need to process what he just said.

Noah Callaway sees me and treats me as his real wife.

"Come on, let's finish this dinner in style," he says, grabbing the takeout bag in one hand and pulling me against him.

The adventurous puppy tumbles down the steps as Calla jumps down, and we all snuggle in the parlor in front of a real fire. "They get a pass for today," Noah declares as he pulls out a couple of china plates and crystal glasses that we set on a small bench in front of us.

"Fire dinner! Much better than a TV dinner," I say, leaning over to press a kiss on my husband's cheek. Calla settles at my feet while the little ones go and explore. "Don't get lost!" I tell them.

From the corner of my eye, I detect movement. "I can't believe you guys!" I hiss. The two young women in white are in a corner, whispering to each other. Noah glances at them. "Oh, they're harmless," he says. "The one you want to watch out for is Elsbeth."

I lean closer to him and whisper, "The one who hanged herself?"

Giggles sound from the corner of the room, while Noah takes a healthy bite from his flank steak. He moves the food in his mouth and answers, circling his fork around to make the point. "That's the thing. That's what she wants people to believe. In reality, Elsbeth died of pneumonia—still sad."

"Okay," I say, relieved that the story of the hanging bride isn't true, but a little disappointed at the same time that the most gruesome ghost story in Emerald Creek turned out to be fake.

"However," he says, "Elsbeth's widower remarried. And Elsbeth turned out to be the jealous kind."

"Okay?"

"She appeared to each of his new wives as... you guessed it, hanging from the bathroom ceiling on the night of their nuptials. Before the wedding could be consummated."

"You said wives? As in several?"

He nods, forks another healthy serving of food into his mouth, and continues. "First wife ran straight back to her parents' home. Got the marriage annulled. The next two, ditto. That was the end of the wedding adventures of the first Noah."

"Wait—his name was Noah?"

"Yeah, we're all called Noah. Every first born."

"Holy shit. So Elsbeth is—"

"My great-great-great grandmother. Seven generations back."

Seven generations? Wow. "Why don't you guys set the record straight? Tell the true story?"

He laughs. "Yeah, like people are going to believe we're perfectly okay people if we come out and explain it was just a ghost playing a prank?"

I shrug. "I guess. People are silly." I glance to the corner of the room, now empty.

"Who were those two?" I ask.

"No idea. We sort of have an agreement. We let them be, they let us be. We start asking them questions, they might get social with us. I don't mind them, but I prefer live people."

"Depends which live people," I answer.

"Fair enough." He drops a kiss on my head. "Mmm... Fuck," he says, a slow smile spreading on his face.

"What?"

He twirls a strand of my hair between his fingers. "We're gonna be sleeping in the same bed." He leans in for a soft kiss, then pulls me tighter to him with one hand on my nape. A low growl comes from deep inside him. "You get the puppies, I'll get the food?'

"Uh-huh."

Chapter Thirty-Six

Willow

We don't get much sleep, and it's the best night of my life. Noah wraps me in his fold, holding me against his chest, peppering kisses on my forehead until we doze off.

The next day, he wakes me with a coffee on my nightstand, but this time, instead of scampering out of the bedroom, he sits on the bed, nursing his own cup. He's quite a sight with his messy hair, his glasses on, his morning stubble, and his ripped bare chest with just the right amount of hair. "What you got going today?" he asks, dimples forming on his cheeks as his eyes dance on me.

My center tingles alarmingly, so I pull the sheet up to cover my breasts and take a grounding sip of coffee. "New window displays. I'm switching out the Father's Day stuff and going full summer mode."

He pulls the sheet off my breasts, runs the pad of his thumb on my perk nipples. "You're going to paper the windows again first?" A crease appears between his eyebrows.

I bristle under his touch and his gaze. "Didn't you like it last time?"

His gaze goes back up to my face, stopping on my mouth. "Loved it."

"Oh! This time I'm adding *Magic in progress* at the very top. Is that too much?"

"No, that's good. That's great." He takes my cup from my hands and sets it down. "There's no rush," he whispers against my bare skin. He shucks his sweatpants, revealing that he was going commando *and* has a massive erection—how did I miss that? "Now say a proper good morning to your husband."

He clasps my nape in his hand, pulling me possessively in for a kiss. Soon the sheet is gone and his other hand is between my thighs.

Before I can process, he flips me around, demanding—just the right amount of rough and impatient. "You like it like that, don't you?" he groans against my ear when he has me on my knees, against the headboard. "Gotta tell you som'thin'," he says as his cock fills me, and I barely register; my knees are already giving in. "Got all the time in the world to figure out what you like. Yeah?"

Does he think I can talk with his cock hitting just the right spot, his fingers playing with my nipples? Even his breath down my neck makes me wet. As he sucks on my shoulder, the roughness of his stubble against my bare skin might be what takes me over the edge.

"But right now I gotta say, this is how I wanna take my wife, and I'm not gonna last long with that tight wet pussy o'yours and those boobs and your ass, fucking hell your ass—"

I come undone under him, his corded arms flexing around my middle to hold me up. "Noah," I exhale, and he follows in powerful strokes, kneading my breasts. "Your fucking tits, babe," he groans. "And your ass. Ah, fucking hell, your ass."

We collapse on the bed, catching our breaths, then he shakes softly with quiet laughter.

"What?" I ask.

"Nothing. Happy. Come here." He pulls me to his chest, and I wrap my leg across his thigh. "I need to shower and shave," he grumbles.

I run a hand on his jawline. "I kinda like it like that. Keep it for a couple of days?"

He looks down at me. "Anything for my wife."

We shower together and get to the store on the late side but in the best mood. I text Mom on the way, and she answers with a thumbs up emoji.

Swing by the store today? I offer, not getting my hopes up.

I get straight to work, first papering the windows. I have the system down from last time, so it doesn't take me long. Then, crouched inside the windows, I focus on creating a display of summer essentials.

In one window, two beach chairs anchor the decor, with heart-shaped sunglasses, sunscreen, and striped beach towels in tones of lime, orange, and white. Neon colored frisbees lean on sleek coolers on each side of the chairs.

I haul wicker shelves from upstairs, nudge them in, and add colorful tumblers, different brands of sunscreen, and battery-operated fans. A straw hat with flowery fabric tied around it goes in the upper corner of the bookcase, giving the whole display a feminine charm.

I open a deck of playing cards and set it on the floor as if four players had just left their game, cards face down, and were returning any minute. Paddle board sets complete the fun vibe. I pin colorful T-shirts to the side wall facing the bookcase and declare myself satisfied. For now.

Pulling out the notes app on my phone, I type.

Emerald Creek T-shirts

T Shirts with fun stuff: too hot to handle, stay cool at the Creek, etc. (Ask N.)

Branded tumblers

Dog things

Next, I tackle the other window. This one's theme is porch nightlife. A rocking chair and a side table with a citronella candle and a romance book. Different size lanterns on the floor. A light flannel throw in blue and pink plaid for those cool nights. An old-fashioned cookie box and Mason jar tumblers. A shaker.

All I need now are the final touches—string lights and a trio of electric candles flickering.

I'm ready for my coffee break with Noah when a familiar voice sounds through the store.

"Ms. Willow!" I look up to see my favorite adaptive ski student wheel himself at high speed through the narrow alleys of the store.

"Hey, Zach! What's up?"

"Mister C said the vacuum cleaners were delivered?"

"Right over here," Noah says, exiting his office. He pecks my lips and places his hand on the small of my back as we go to the delivery dock. Three white boxes are neatly stacked next to a pallet of leaf blowers.

Zach examines a box, leaning over on his wheelchair, then his fingers fly across his phone screen. "You sure that's what you want?" he asks Noah as he shows him his phone.

Noah ignores the phone and scratches the back of his neck. "You know me, Zach. Don't have to repeat myself to you. But uh… Mrs. Callaway thought it'd be a good idea. Lilyvale isn't exactly a two-minute job."

"Setting up the vacuum cleaners could be my project," he tells Noah.

"Any twelve-year old can do that."

Zach nods. "Oh, hundred percent. Now, hear me out..." he says as Noah shakes his head.

I chuckle quietly. I don't know what Zach has in mind, but I know his tells. I saw him convince the program director at the adaptive sports school to let him try his self-made contraption at the park—and by park, I mean the ski slope equipped with ramps and jumps for daredevils—using valid arguments such as his lower center of gravity and four points of friction on the surface. What we failed to notice was the thing had hydraulic springs that propelled him higher than anyone had ever been. Of course Zach being Zach had equipped his machine with a camera streaming in real time, so when he face-planted, the entire world went through it live with him.

And when I say the entire world, I mean his parents enjoying a quiet day at the office, who'd gotten a notification on their respective phones, and went through the stomach-churning experience of increasing speed, multiple sightings of the sky, his "fuck-fuck-fuck" mutters, and then a light-gray screen and nothing for agonizingly long seconds.

Then, "I'm aliiiiiive," something that sounded like laughter and crying, a gloved finger scraping snow off the screen, and Zach's distorted face saying into the camera, "That was epic. Dad, did you see that? Mom?"

His mom deleted the app from her phone for a little while, and his dad thanked the program director.

So that's Zach.

"Come on, Mister C. You know what I'm talking about. These can—and when I say can, that means they absolutely do—send mapping information to the cloud. Servers that anyone can break into." He glances at me, hoping I'm as terrified as he makes it out to be. "Plus the information of other connected household objects. Like, when you turn off your coffee machine and remote-start your car to warm it up from the app on your phone—it can definitely make sense of the information that you're getting ready to leave the house and it sends it to the cloud which is a very shady place. And don't get me started on baby monitors."

Noah pushes his glasses up. "I know all that. Now tell me what you have in mind. With all the details this time, please." Something passes between the two that tells me Zach is just as rogue at the computer as he is on the slopes. I can't wait to see what he makes of his life.

"We replace the firmware and chips with our own code. I can talk to Mister K about getting their discarded Raspberry Pis or ESP32 boards." Mister K, aka Ethan, started a cybersecurity firm with some of his fellow ex-Air Force friends and other computer geeks. He helped with a breach at the high school last year and has been helping mentor the coding club along with Noah.

Noah slaps Zach's shoulder to signify his agreement. "I'll need a full project description by tonight. And not just the technical details. But cost and timeline, too, as well as who'll be on your team."

Zach starts to protest, but Noah cuts him off. "This isn't a one-person job, even though you could probably do it on your own. But I need this quick, and you have to build your leadership skills if you want to move onto larger projects. Ask Ethan—Mister K. He'll tell you all about it. Actually, see if he'd be your advisor for this project."

Zach extends his hand, shaking Noah's profusely. "Thanks." Then he turns to me. "You guys are the coolest. We'll get you the best vacuum cleaners there is."

We watch him leave, then I say, "Thank you. For Zach, I mean. This is great."

"He's a good kid. Gonna drive Ethan crazy," he says, laughing.

Footsteps on the floorboards bring our attention back to the store.

"Oh hey, Marcy," Noah says, his tone softer with a hint of hesitation.

"Mom! You came." Somehow I'm insanely happy about it. Reading my mood, Noah says, "Coffee for you ladies? It's actually good now."

Noah pours us fresh coffee and helps Mom with creamers and sweeteners.

Then we take our mugs with us as we walk through the store. "Little bird told me you do the window displays now?" Mom asks. "You were always so neat and tidy and cutesy as a kid. I can see you doing that."

Noah wraps me under his arm. "She's still neat and tidy and cutesy. Matter of fact, she ordered us some automatic vacuum cleaners. We should get you one," he says before excusing himself.

"That's an idea!" I tell Mom as I admire Noah's broad shoulders, the new energy he seems to radiate today.

"I don't know about that." She chuckles dryly for my benefit once Noah is in his office. "Don't wanna get lazy."

I link our arms. "Wait til you see how ours work, and then you can decide?" I insist as I walk her toward the staircase leading to the upper level. I'm sure she'll like to look at the furniture.

A heady perfume lingers in the air—too heavy for the cedar and beeswax polish Dean uses. Probably just some customer passing through, but an uneasy feeling settles in my stomach.

"Sorry I didn't get here earlier," Mom says, pausing to catch her breath. "You could have introduced me to your new mother-in-law."

My blood goes cold. Why would Gail be here, even in passing? Maybe Mom is confused? I pretend I didn't hear what she just said and force brightness into my voice as I point out the maple tables. Mom runs her hand on the soft surface, then moves onto a display of woven baskets.

Before she can double down about Gail, I'm struck by inspiration. "D'you want to help me put together something for Alex and Chris? I thought it'd be nice to have a little welcome home basket. I think she and baby Ivy are coming home tomorrow." I grab a round wheatgrass basket and line it with a muslin shawl in tones of greens. "That will look great on Alex." Next I grab a small jar of organic beeswax salve and an incredibly nourishing hair mask. "Pretty sure Grace will come do her nails, so I'm gonna skip the mini-manicure set."

"I thought you were putting together a basket for the baby?" Mom asks.

"Oh no," I say, snorting. "I was at the baby shower, and that kiddo is *set*. Alex, however, is gonna need some pampering." I add a natural candle, local honey, dry shampoo, three bars of chocolate and chocolate-covered wafers. "I guess she can't have booze yet."

"How about tea?"

"Ohmygod yes, and we have these adorable teapots that keep tea warm for hours."

Mom helps me load the basket and arrange it prettily, then I ring everything up and put it on our house account.

"I'm off to Justin's," Noah says as we wrap up. "Some business about the fair." He kisses my temple and admires the basket. "I can drop this off at the bakery." He holds the door for a group of three schoolteachers, and we chat with them for a bit.

"Why don't you walk home with me," I tell Mom when Noah's gone and Dean and Elaine are taking care of the teachers. "I need to let the dogs out."

She gasps. "I saw pictures on ECHoes and thought it was a joke!"

We're interrupted by Chloe, who's on her way back from a run alongside the river, then by Sophie, delivering library books to someone who broke their leg.

"They're rescues," I continue where we left off once we're alone—for now. "Remember, I told you we found them in the woods?"

"I didn't know you'd kept 'em." She takes my arm as we walk to Lilyvale, leaning on me. "I'm sorry about the other night," she says. "I... I'm just worried about you. I don't want these people to—"

"Mom," I say under my breath. I can't believe she's starting this again, and on the street, where everyone can hear us.

"Okay, okay," she says. "I mean, he seems nice enough, I suppose."

Gee, thanks.

I breathe better once we get home. Whatever she says now won't be overheard. "Who's a good dog?" I coo as I let Calla out. Now fully recovered, she seems to be enjoying her time without her puppies. Mom stays at a distance. She's never had a dog, and Calla is impressive.

One of the puppies takes advantage and slips out, tumbling down the steps, straightening himself, then running around. His sister follows, and I whip my phone out to video her rolling down the two shallow steps. I'm so happy to see her gain confidence.

"Here." I pick up the third one and hand him to Mom. "Set him on the grass. He needs a little help." His more adventurous brother is already exploring the rose bushes. Before long they'll be rolling down to the river. "Calla, get your puppy back here!" I holler.

The dog looks at me, tongue lolling, then drops to the grass to scratch her back. Coming to an abrupt stop, she stands and trots to the wayward pup, grabs him by the scruff of his neck, and drops him back inside.

"That's the spirit," I say, laughing as I place the shy one and his sister inside the kitchen. The pups teeter in, then crawl over their mother for another feed.

"Tough being a mother," Mom says, looking at the dogs. She sits on a stool, elbows on the kitchen counter. "Never a quiet moment." The bitter set of her mouth hits me in the solar plexus, but I refuse to let it hurt me. This is her lived experience, not mine.

"They grow up so fast," I say, pouring two glasses of lemonade. "Gotta enjoy it while it lasts."

Mom's expression sours. Does she really think I'm passing judgment on her maternal qualities? It's so hard for me to get across to her. "They couldn't even walk properly a couple of weeks ago," I say, hoping she'll get I'm only talking about the dogs.

"You know, I'm only looking out for you," she declares. *Not this again.* "People like the Callaways, they're not like us." *I suppose if I let her say her piece when it's just the two of us, we can get this over with?* She looks around the kitchen, envy painted on her face—not a trace of appreciation for the beautiful surroundings. "They have different rules. And if they cross over to people like us, it's never a good thing. They use us, and then they throw us away like yesterday's trash."

Bile fills my mouth as doubt seeps in, ugly, destructive. "Noah loves me." She doesn't know what she's talking about, yet tears fill my eyes.

It's so, so early in whatever strange relationship Noah and I are building. What do I know about his feelings? "He does." Maybe if I repeat this three times, it will make it true. "He *loves me*."

Chapter Thirty-Seven

Noah

My steps freeze in the hallway as I hear Marcy going on a rant about our family, *again.* Ignoring what she has to say about us, I turn silently away from the kitchen to slip into the office, where I'll get some work done until she's gone.

But Willow's voice breaks through. Teary. Angry. Desperate.

I've never seen or heard her so undone. "Noah loves me," she chokes.

I turn around. Whatever is going on, she's not fighting this alone. Of course I love her, even if I haven't told her yet in as many words. Hearing her say it out loud—it's obvious.

"He does. He loves me," she cries with desperate rage.

I struggle to stay calm as I sneak up behind my wife. "Damn right I love her." I wrap her in my arms from behind and kiss her neck. Startled, she gasps, and her uneven breathing tears me apart.

Is she crying? Fucking shit. "Babe? What's going on?" I turn her in my arms. I know what's going on, but going all feral on Marcy right now isn't the right move.

Willow gives me a poor excuse for a smile. "How was your meeting?" Her gaze holds mine, pleading not to ask questions. "Mom was just leaving."

Marcy pushes herself from the stool and sighs but offers no explanation and no apology.

They say a quick goodbye, and Marcy sees herself out.

"Wanna talk about it?" I ask.

Lips tight, Willow forces a smile. "Nope." Her anguish is visible, nearly killing me.

"Too bad." I sit on a stool and pull her between my legs. "We're still gonna talk about it."

Her shoulders slump. "Same old, but with a twist."

"Let's hear it."

She rolls her eyes, sighs. "This time, I'm gonna be taken out like yesterday's trash when you don't need me anymore."

Yesterday's trash? White rage boils inside me. "She said that?"

Willow shrugs. "It's alright. She—she really thinks she's looking out for me. Trying to save me from becoming her." She's bitter and I fucking hate—*hate*—the way she's holding in her tears.

I pull her tight against my chest. "You're not her."

She nods but stays silent.

"You're right about something else, though."

She squeaks, a question without words.

"I do love you."

I think she's about to say something that'll rock my world, something really fucking awesome, something I was afraid to tell her first because I didn't want her to feel pressured. But it's out there now, and I get it. There's an abyss between having a crush for someone and what I feel for Willow. Even the greatest sex can't bridge that gap. There needs to be more and so far I don't know if this is how she feels for me.

Maybe not, because the next thing she says is, "Mind you, she doesn't know that our marriage is fake, or—"

I cup her head in my hands. "Our marriage isn't fake. It might have been for a minute. It's not anymore." Panic suddenly seizes me. What if I'm just a fling to her? "At least for me it's not." My voice is raspy, my throat tightening. Was she putting on a show for her mother?

"Okay," she says softly.

I'll go with *okay*. For now.

The next day, I decide it's time for me to pay my mother-in-law a visit and hash it out. I find her sitting outside on a plastic chair, stubbing out a cigarette which she tries to hide under some dirt. She tightens the scarf around her head.

"I brought you some coffee." I hand her one of Easy Monday's summer specials. "I think Millie calls it Turn Down the Heat. It's got hazelnut and honey."

She takes the cup with a nod. If she notices that I remembered her preferences, she doesn't say anything. She doesn't offer for us to go inside either. Not wanting to crowd her, I flip an empty flowerpot upside down and sit on it. "I'm gonna cut straight to the chase," I say. "I want Willow to be happy. I know you do too," I venture. "She's hurt by your insinuations. Since they have to do with me, I'd like to give you the opportunity to tell me what you're concerned about." Somehow I don't think Marcy will mind me being forward.

She narrows her gaze on me, and it strikes me again how she's like a dried up, bitter version of her daughter. "Willow set you up to this?"

Why would Willow do that? Sending her husband to fix her problems is not her style. "She doesn't know I'm here."

She takes a sip of coffee, then sets the cup on her lap, both hands around it as if this wasn't a hot summer morning. "You lie to her already?"

My laughter is bitter. It's hard to stay cool around Marcy. I don't know how Willow does it. "I'm hoping to surprise her. Tell her I had a nice talk with you and we understand each other. That she doesn't need to be concerned about... whatever was going on between the two of you."

She looks me up and down, shakes her head. "Men," she drops, then reaches down for the cigarette stub, flicks it clear of dirt, lights it again, then takes a long drag.

I wait for the rest of her answer. When it doesn't come, I chuckle. "That's it?"

She shrugs. "She's a big girl. She'll figure it out soon enough. Thought she knew better. God knows she used to tell anybody who cared to listen that she'd never marry, but... you come along and she thinks you're different."

My coffee is still hot but already my patience is wearing thin. When she's with Willow, her snark is directed at me. But when she's with me? It's Willow who's in her line of sight. I stand and give her shoulder an affectionate squeeze. "I'm different, Marcy. You got that right." At least that part of Marcy's anger didn't rub me the wrong way.

Her fingers tremble when she brings the cigarette to her lips.

"I hope you'll see that, with time." I hesitate, then add, "Come by Lilyvale whenever you want. Just don't make my wife sad, please. She loves you, and I love her. It's that simple."

Chapter Thirty-Eight

Willow

"Zach was at the store again today?" I ask Noah. On a whim we decided to walk Calla around town after dinner, and we plopped the puppies in a wagon, dragging them along.

Lazy's and Chloe's Nook are open, shining bright on The Green. Maybe we'll go later, once the puppies are back home. For now, there's nothing else I'd rather do than walk under the early evening's silver sky with our little rescue family.

Noah nods. "He came to have me sign off on his project."

Something in his tone sets off alarm bells. "It wasn't good?"

He shrugs. "It was great. Why?"

"You look... preoccupied." He's been off all day. I wish he'd just tell me what's going on. Lowering my voice, I nudge him. "Gail again? Mom thought she saw her at the store. I thought maybe... maybe that was why she was on edge, yesterday." The memory of our argument still burns.

He grunts. "Beck told me he's seen her around town, and Elaine mentioned she came by the deli." He pushes his glasses up his nose. "But it's not about Gail. It's your mother. I went to see her this morning."

I stop us, Calla pulling on her leash. "What for?" She didn't mention anything when I sent her my daily text, and I just assumed Noah was on a random errand.

He runs his hand through my hair, his gaze roaming my face like this is where he'll find the right words. "I just... wanted to clear the air."

Tough luck with that. Mom revels in drama. "How'd that work out for you?" I snort. Feeling my mood, Calla pulls forward, and I follow her.

Noah pulls me closer under his arm and kisses my temple. "I think she got the message."

Oh, Noah. Mom only hears her own tune. "What message?"

"That I love you." His words come out strangled.

I stop us again and wrap a hand behind my husband's neck. Calla sits on my foot, and even the puppies are quiet. A tear forms in the corner of my eye, surprising me. "I love you too, Noah. I don't care what she thinks. It's her loss." I deeply resent Marcy right this moment for putting Noah through this. He doesn't owe her anything. My breath shudders, anger threatening to spill out.

He kisses me softly on the lips. "You love me," he repeats, bringing his forehead to mine—our cocoon of privacy in the middle of town.

"Of course I do," I whisper. "Always have. Always will." Standing in the middle of The Green, stars above us, puppies at our feet, I savor this perfect moment with my husband.

He tightens his embrace and leans in for a deep kiss.

Calla exhales a loud sigh, making us giggle. Pulling away from my lips, Noah curls a strand of my hair around his finger. "She repeated that you swore you'd never get married. Made it sound like a serious rule you had for yourself. Is that true?"

Now why did she need to say that too? "Yes, it's true."

His Adam's apple bobs; a frown settles between his eyebrows. "Should I be... concerned?"

He's already worried, and something stirs deep inside me. "Well, clearly, rules are made to be broken."

He gives me his half-crooked smile, but it doesn't reach his eyes. "I really do love you, you know. I've been scared to tell you, but I do. I don't know when it happened but it's not going away. I need you to know that. I need you to know that everything that's happening between us, it's real to me. And it's deep. And if things had been any different, I'd be planning how to propose to you."

Tears of happiness blur my vision. He didn't shave this morning, and his rugged look tingles my insides. Suddenly I'm eager to be back home.

He takes me back under his arm, Calla leading, puppies in tow. "How would you propose?" I ask, a smile tugging at my lips. I make myself comfortable, burrowing deeper under his arm as we walk slowly.

His chuckle brings a smile to my lips. "Ah... pressure. Let's see. I'd want to make it low-key so you wouldn't see it coming. I'd take you on a hike, maybe to the top of Mount Mansfield, or down to Emerald Lake when the ice breaks, or when the foliage turns. Get us a nice picnic. Maybe a tent, make it a weekend thing. Build a bonfire just for the two of us and propose at sunset."

"Not sure you can build a bonfire on Mount Mansfield."

He pulls lightly on my hair. "See, in this scenario I'd have time to do my research—"

"—and you wouldn't have your know-it-all wife shoot down your ideas because she wouldn't be your wife yet."

"Wasn't going to go there, but... you said it." He ruffles my hair.

"Well aren't you glad I'm already your wife? No planning forbidden activities and getting in trouble with the park rangers."

"I'd get in trouble with way more than the park rangers for you. And yes, I'm glad you're my wife, though 'glad' doesn't even begin to cover it. We didn't get there the usual way, but I wouldn't have it any different."

My chest tightens with emotion—because he sees me as his real wife; because his feelings go way beyond friendship and gratitude; because he *loves me*—all I can manage to say is, "We got a Phish concert out of it." I was never meant to have the fairytale wedding anyway—I always knew that.

"Damn right we did."

Our footsteps bring us to the park, and the smell of freshly cut grass brings memories of careless ball games and lying under a tree reading all day. The simple pleasures of childhood, enjoyed only here, in Emerald Creek—my harbor, my home.

We naturally end up at the bench where we'd sat during Colton and Kiara's wedding. Calla ambles to the river, the more adventurous puppy tumbling out of the wagon to follow her.

I kick my shoes off, the grass soft and cool under my feet.

"So..." Noah leans back, his arm on the back of the bench, almost but not quite touching me. "You only agreed to marry me because it was fake," he states. "Which leaves me with only one option."

Before I can say anything, he's on one knee, holding my shoe. "Willow Fontaine, will you marry me for real, right here, right now, with Calla as our witness?" He takes my ankle in his hand, places my shoe at the tip of my toes.

I'm caught between laughter and tears of joy. My throat tightens and my heartbeat falters at the magnitude of what's happening: Noah's feelings are marriage-deep. He wants me as his wife. As in, forever. In sickness and health. Til death do us part. "Our witness is rolling herself on a sandbar," I drop, too choked up to say anything deep.

His gaze darkens. He slips the shoe on my foot, slides his hand up my calf, behind my knee, up my thigh. Straightening himself, he brings my foot to his shoulder and leans in for a kiss. "Is that a yes?" His voice is deep with raw emotion. He kisses me softly, his tongue gently parting my lips, his hand under my dress grasping my ass. "I promise to cherish you always and…" He huffs, his forehead gently touching mine, then continues in a whisper. "God, Willow… I don't know what else to say. I don't have the words. That should tell you something," he says, laughing softly, "but I can't imagine a life without you. I want this marriage to be real."

Chapter Thirty-Nine

Noah

I'm hanging by a thread here. She admitted that she swore she'd never get married. She's making a joke about Calla. And sure, I kind of had it coming, saying she's our witness. And right, I don't have a wedding band because one, I didn't plan this, and two, even if I had, she's already wearing the Callaway ring.

Hard to top that.

But I'm dead fucking serious about wanting to spend my life with Willow. Maybe she doesn't want to.

Although she did say she loved me. But what do I know? Maybe that doesn't mean marriage to her. She could love me but not want to remain married. Something about freedom, as if marrying me tied her down. I could see Willow explaining—

"Yes," she says, her voice firm.

She lunges herself at me, and I fall back on the grass, clasping her to me, my head on her chest.

Her heartbeat is a storm. Loud. Pounding.

I listen to every beat. Feel every tremor of her body. This. This is the magnitude of her love, and I want to seal it in my memory forever.

We stay embraced for moments that seem etched in eternity yet end too quickly when Calla nudges my arm aside. With a bump of her large snout, she turns this into a group hug. Soon she's licking us both profusely. "Is that her way of pronouncing us husband and wife?" Willow laughs, hugging Calla.

"She's certainly taking care of the *You may kiss the bride part*," I answer, pretending grouchiness.

Willow laughs harder and harder, wiping a tear from the corner of her eye. "What was that with the shoe?" she asks between two fits of laughter.

I shrug. "Something you said about Prince Charming, when you turned me down the first time?"

"Oh," Willow answers, her laughter subsiding. "Does that make me your Cinderella?"

She says it like it's a bad thing, and I wouldn't have a clue. "I dunno. Snow White? Little Red Riding Hood?" Don't they all have a Prince Charming? "Which one has the guy put her shoes on?"

"Cinderella?" She makes the question sound like a terrible answer. Like I did or said something wrong.

"Okay then, that one." I put her other shoe on while she's too busy trying to make a point I'm never going to get, and pull her up to me. "We have a missing puppy, Cinderella."

Chapter Forty

Willow

Two months later

Sun shines through the crimson foliage, warming the crisp fall air. Amy's roses are reblooming, the barn garden now bursts with the last sunflowers on a backdrop of violet-blue asters while the hydrangeas turned from baby blush to dusty mauve, their tips drying in places.

A raven croaks from the roof before flying gracefully to the barn, from where she watches me brushing Calla while the puppies, Muffin, Maple, and Myrtle, try to snatch the brush from me.

Lane sets two piping hot mugs of cinnamon apple cider on the garden table. "I missed this season so much. Fall at Lilyvale is just the best," she says in a monotone as she plops on a chair, her empty gaze betraying her words.

Since Noah real-proposed to me over two months ago, we've been absorbed in each other, making love in most every room of Lilyvale, going on overnight hiking trips, making a mini-honeymoon out of the Phish concert in Upstate New York, and spending our evenings into the night simply talking in the deep way that doesn't require spreadsheets.

I've neglected my sister-in-law, and I'm concerned about her. She spent several weeks in New York interviewing for jobs, but now she's back, helping Ms. Angela at the bed-and-breakfast. She even took some housekeeping shifts at Wendy and Todd's hotel. She hasn't said a word to Noah about where she stands workwise. I can't give her career advice, but I can listen.

"Thanks for the cider," I say as I pull a chair next to hers.

Today we took a day trip to Burlington to finish our shopping for Grace and Ethan's wedding a week from Saturday, and Noah's birthday after that. It wasn't the right time to ask the hard questions. *What's happening with the job search in New York? Why the gloomy face?*

And because Mom and Aunt Angela hitched a ride to the big city with us—it's been great to see that Noah was right, Marcy did get the message that he really loved me, and she's stopped bugging me about that—it didn't give me the opening for a heart-to-heart.

Now my gaze rests on the pumpkin patch Beck planted, vines gracefully climbing on wooden arches, heavy gourds dangling by some magic three-to-seven feet over the ground, and I hope for inspiration as I take a sip of the mulled apple cider.

Calla stands with a grunt and sets her big head on Lane's lap. "How did you know you were in love with Noah?" Lane asks, petting the dog mindlessly.

Oh. *Maybe an opening? I knew she was going through something. Heartbreak sounds about right.* But my heart skips a beat at her question. I never really thought about it that way. For so long I was convinced I could never have him, I give her the simple truth. "I could never see myself marrying anyone else."

"Wow. So if it hadn't been him...?"

I shrug. "Then no one else."

"That's... intense." She stops petting Calla. "Shit. How did you feel when he proposed to Anika?" Tears pool in her eyes.

I shrug. "Lucky girl." Somehow this conversation isn't really doing it for me. Rehashing the days when I was invisible to Noah isn't what I want. "Is there someone you want to talk about?" I ask Lane with a *you-can-talk-to-me-we're-sisters* smile. She'd been going on dates early in the summer, not coming back until morning—even leaving a few days with this Jake guy, who she even said she liked a little too much before she suddenly stopped mentioning him.

"I'm pregnant," she drops.

Shit.

Shit!

I was not expecting that. I set my mug down and let the silence drag on between us, giving her a chance to say more but also not knowing what to say at all. Whatever I ask (Do you want to keep it? When are you due? Who's the dad?) is probably going to be the wrong thing.

But she looks at me expectantly.

"Okay..." *Fuck. Am I supposed to say "Congratulations!!!" or "I'm sorry..."?* "Help me out here. I don't know what you need from me," I say, spreading my hands in a sign of utter helplessness.

She pulls me to her side, and I hug her back. "You're the best," she whispers in my neck.

"You got... pretty low standards. I didn't say or do anything."

Her shoulders shake.

"Hey, baby, I got you. We got you." I pull her away from me so I can look at her. "Are you crying or are you laughing?" I'm so confused by the state of her face.

"Both!" she says, hiccupping weirdly.

Hormones. And I mean, also, the whole freaking situation.

My heart swells and breaks for her at the same time. A baby!

I need to know where she stands with all this. To get her talking, I ask the safest question I can come up with. "How far along are you?"

"I'm due in six and a half months, and I'm not sure about the dad."

Holy shit!

She must read my facial expression, because she adds, "I *know* who the dad is. I... He's all sorts of wrong."

Lots to unpack there. "Didn't peg you for a bad boy kinda girl," I say with a smile in my voice.

"It's... complicated," she says with finality in her tone.

I raise my hands. "I'm sure. Now, what do you need from me?"

Her mouth sets the way Noah's does when he talks about the Callaway legacy, a mix of sadness and determination. And I hate that for her.

"A baby is happiness and only happiness," I urge her.

Her hands unconsciously move to her still-flat belly. "I don't know how to take care of a baby," she whispers, her eyes welling up. "But it's all I can think about! It's like... I'm a different person now. There's someone growing inside me. Counting on me." She's only twenty-two, but she has Noah's innate sense of responsibility, and in that moment I know she and her baby will be okay.

I move us to more practical questions. "What are you doing about work?" It's fair to assume that's why she hasn't moved to New York.

She looks away. "I already lined up some online writing gigs. I'm hoping to land something more permanent, but... I'd be working from here? If that's okay. I don't think I can do it alone." She seems uncertain and almost ashamed. "I'll pay rent and stuff."

I take her hand. In the space of a few months, she seems to have grown five years or more. The post-teenager who argued that this place was as much hers as her brother's is gone. As much as it's reassuring, it also makes me a little sad. "That's a great idea."

"I'm sorry," she whispers. "I know it's not fair to you guys, seeing as you just got married, but—"

"Oh shut up!" I scoff. "Are you kidding? A baby here is going to be the best thing ever. I can't wait!" I squeeze her hand harder, laughter bubbling inside me as I imagine midnight bottles and pitter-patters in the hallways.

"I'm scared to tell Noah," Lane confesses.

My heart clenches. She has no idea how much she's unconditionally loved in this family. "Oh, honey, Noah will feel the way you feel. If you're happy, he'll be happy. If you want him to punch the dad in the face, he will."

She ignores my attempt to know more about the father. "What should I tell him?" Her face is still scrunched with anxiety.

I let go of her hand to push a strand of hair behind her ear, then give her nape a reassuring stroke. "Let him know you already have a plan. That you need time to figure out what you're going to do about the dad. That you're staying here for the time being. Guys aren't always the best at dealing with something they can't fix. But ask them to install a nursery or attach a car seat, and all of a sudden they feel more in control, and it helps them."

"Gotcha." She nods a little sadly.

"Hey. Noah's going to be over-the-moon happy about having a niece or nephew. He'll just be worried about you for a while, until he sees everything's gonna be fine. It's... it's just how he is. He worries about you guys because he loves you so much."

She nods sadly again. "He sorta sacrificed his teenage years because of us and well, the rest of it too. I hate to be doing this to him."

"Honey. You're not doing *anything* to him." I wish I could tell her to let me worry about Noah, but this is her story to tell.

"Will you be there when I tell him? He's just so much... calmer when you're around."

A warmth akin to bliss lodges itself between my ribs. "Of course. Maybe after the wedding?" A night of fun at the King's family farm will put a lot of things into perspective. "He'll be more relaxed."

"So, Sunday?"

"I think so."

"That's a good idea." She worries her bottom lip. "D'you think he'll be happy I'm staying for now?"

I take her hand again. "Don't do it to make him happy. Do it because it's right for you."

She nods. "Okay. Yeah. That makes sense." She takes a deep breath, stands up, and looks around. "Willow?"

"Yeah?"

"You have your phone? We lost Muffin again." She stumbles around in the garden, but this time I don't panic.

Because since that unforgettable night at the river when Noah real-proposed to me with a shoe, after we spent a good two hours searching and finding the lost puppy, we had them all equipped with GPS sensors attached to their little collars.

Between the vacuum cleaners, which Zach installed a while back and have a tendency to stay stuck under furniture, and the puppies who actively search for the strangest places to get lost, my phone now looks like some kind of spy device. It opens directly on a 3D map of Lilyvale, with symbols and shapes slowly moving around.

Of the three sets of paws, Muffin's appears to be somewhere behind the barn. "Over here!" I call out to Lane, who comes rushing back up. I click on the icon, and a steady but faint beep sounds. "It seems to be coming from... the pile of leaves?" she says.

I laugh. "Yup, it's moving." We carefully move leaves around with our feet, until a furry tail wags. "Do you have terrier in you?" I ask the little guy as I bring him back to his mom. Calla barely gives him a lick.

"I think she's tired of her teenagers," I joke. I'm not, though. The puppies are a handful, but they bring more joy than I'd ever imagined. And yes, we named them. Because even if they end up leaving Lilyvale, they will still be ours, in a way.

"Oh yeah. Look at her. She couldn't care less." Lane gives Calla a head scratch, and the big dog plops down with a grunt. "Willow?" Lane asks.

"Yes sweetie?"

"Is it okay to be selfishly happy that Noah married you and not what's-her-face?" She takes me in a big hug. "You're just the best sister I could ever dream of."

Chapter Forty-One

Willow

"Did you book your spa day?" Noah asks me that evening from behind, wrapping his arms around me and kissing my neck.

His stubble tickles the sensitive part of my neck and I giggle. "I don't need a spa day," I say, tilting my head to give him better access.

He tightens his hold on me. "We've been through this," he grunts.

According to Noah, I work too much and need a rest day. Supposedly, the store is doing so well since I started "working my magic" that we're having a hard time keeping up with inventory. He says I need to step back and recharge.

I settle my hands on his arms, relishing his touch. "But I took the whole day off to go shopping!"

"I know," he grunts. "With Lane and Ms. Angela and your mom. That sounds even more exhausting than the store. You need some pampering."

"You pamper me plenty," I say, sliding a hand up his cheek. I wiggle inside his hold and turn to face him. "I don't need some fancy, expensive treatments. I have everything I need right here." I run my nails along his back the way that drives him over the edge.

He takes my hands in his, stopping my game. "What if I like the idea of you spending an afternoon at A Touch Of Grace to rest and relax? I don't know why you make such a fuss about it. If you won't do it for you, do it for me."

"I'll do it for you," Lane says as she barges into the kitchen, flashing a fake smile at her brother.

"Back me up, Laney," Noah growls. "Willow needs some time away from the store."

Lane nibbles on a grape and narrows her eyes on us. "I saw Cruella lurking around the store the other day. You might want to stay away for now and hide at Grace's. Who knows what she's capable of."

Noah tenses. "Gail was here again?! Are you sure?"

Lane nods. "The whole street stank of her perfume."

An uneasy feeling creeps in—the memory of the pungent fragrance floating at the store, the day Mom mentioned not being introduced to my "mother-in-law."

Noah steps away from me. Hands in his pockets, he stares out the window. "Beck said he saw her earlier this summer."

My mouth dries up. I can rationalize Gail snooping around town right after our wedding. But now that our marriage couldn't be more real, what is she up to?

I hate keeping secrets, but we can't talk about this in front of Lane. Any talk of Gail gets us dangerously close to discussing the estate—and our marriage.

Too much is at stake.

With a shrug, Noah paces to the fridge and pulls out some squash patties. "Babe, get us some plates?" he asks me. "Lane, why don't you pour us all a little wine, yeah?" he says as he coats a pan in olive oil. "I want to hear all about Burlington."

Lane's cheeks tint slightly as she pours some white wine for Noah and me, and apple cider for herself.

Noah's eyes narrow on his sister. "Early interview tomorrow morning?" he asks, making a false assumption about her choice of drink.

"Yup!" she squeals. "Not holding my breath, though. This one's for an online gossip magazine." Right then her phone alarm sets off with a meow, saving her from inventing more lies. "M&Ms! It's potty time!" she says cheerfully. Lane has appointed herself official potty-training schedule keeper. "They react to the sound of the alarm," she remarks with a chuckle. "Look at them!" Calla seems to be laughing at us while Muffin, Maple, and Myrtle trot to the kitchen door.

"I don't get why she has a cat sound for the dog alarm," Noah remarks as Lane goes out with the dogs.

"It's so they like cats!" Lane cries from outside.

Noah shrugs. "A'right then."

When the food is ready and Lane and the pups are back inside, Noah sits next to me at the island. "So? The spa? It's settled, right? You'll go?"

Not this again! "Care to explain your obsession with the spa?"

"No! No, I don't *care to explain*," he answers, bordering on exasperated. "I want my wife to go get some me time at the spa," he says, pulling his phone out.

I stay silent.

"Unless there's a good reason not to go."

Plenty of reasons. It feels too much. I've never been. It's superfluous. "Pretty sure Grace is closing in a couple of days because of her wedding."

"It's settled, then. Tomorrow." He pockets his phone, then gives me his slow smile, the one that goes straight from my heart to between my legs, always leaving me all sorts of confused. "You're all booked. Bring a swimsuit."

Grace's salon is a short walk from Lilyvale, on the other side of The Green. It's located in a Georgian mansion that she entirely decorated to turn into a beauty and wellness haven. There's even a hair salon in one room, and a nail specialist in another. She has two rooms for facials now, and a cute three-season deck to sip cucumber water after a treatment.

She recently expanded her second floor to add more massage and meditation rooms. Cinnamon- and orange-scented candles create a warm and energizing atmosphere, and I recognize a Noah Kahan tune softly drifting from the speakers.

My friend greets me with a hug and walks me upstairs. "You're booked for the whole Touch of Grace experience," she says as she hands me a plush robe and slippers with her salon's logo, then takes me to my own dressing room, that comes with a key on a velour rope. Inside the room I find a thick paper with my name on it.

Willow C.'S personalized menu of treatments.

Infrared sauna

Massage

Private meditation session

Wax (areas TBD)

Hair treatment with Fabrizio

Nails with Cheyenne

This is Grace's business. Grace is my friend. Surely there's nothing over-the-top about this. This is what people do. Right?

The swimsuit comes in handy for the sauna, which already deeply relaxes me. After a refreshing shower, I fall asleep under the expert touch of her new massage therapist. "Take your time," she whispers, startling me softly awake. "I'll take you next door for your meditation when you're ready."

I'm super mellow and feeling fantastic when I go downstairs, wrapped in the black and gold robe I'm to use for the whole afternoon. It says "VIP" on the front and back and I truly feel like one, especially when Grace pours me a pumpkin spice cocktail. "Created specially for us by Haley," she says.

Fabrizio brings me to the wash station, giving me the scalp massage to end all scalp massages. "You have *such* gorgeous hair," he fusses. "I'm thinking just a trim to give it umph, maybe a tiny bit of layering, and a glaze. I'm really working with gold here, just making it shine."

"And here I was thinking my hair was mousy."

"Whaaat? Sweetheart, don't ever say that. We're beautiful and we own it."

"If you say so."

He waves his comb at me. "Repeat after me. I'm beautiful and I own it."

I can't help but giggle at his enthusiasm. "I'm beautiful and I own it!"

He rolls his eyes. "Darling, say it like you mean it!"

"I'm beautiful!"

He leans toward me. "And I own it!"

"And I own it!" Whatever that means.

Their nail specialist, Cheyenne, starts on my manicure while Fabrizio works his magic. They must be used to working together like that, because they don't seem to get in each other's way.

Fabrizio leans into me, getting all conspiratorial. "We had the other Mrs. Callaway stop by this morning to make an appointment."

So it's true, then. My nape tingles.

Fabrizio continues. "Never heard so much venom come out of one's person mouth. I don't even know why she comes here, if she hates Emerald Creek so much."

Venom? "What do you mean?"

Fabrizio doesn't need more encouragement to get started. "Let's see. The store is flailing but it will be sold to a chain and we'll all be better for it. We'll have more people move into town once Lilyvale is turned into an apartment complex, and that will help the school." He keeps fussing with my hair while he continues talking. "Same music, different lyrics. This time things are going to happen that will be *wonderful* for the town."

"I don't know about before, but the store sure isn't *flailing* anymore," Cheyenne volunteers. "I saw the line of people on the sidewalk the other day."

I roll my eyes at the memory. "We've had to tell tour busses that it's only fifteen people at a time. And you saw our posting on ECHoes, right? During foliage season, locals should use the back entrance and go straight to Noah's office for check out if there are lines at the registers." The windows, lighting, and overall layout changes I've implemented were huge drivers of our new success. We're basically still selling the same local products and everyday necessities (with a few additions), but we've become *the* place to visit and shop—a town landmark.

If only Noah could pick a name for it, it would make marketing so much easier.

My hair done in lush, shiny waves, I move to the pedicure room. Once Cheyenne is almost done, Fabrizio comes in, followed by Grace nursing a tea in one of the mugs Ethan keeps giving her. This one has cat shapes on a pink backdrop.

"Back to the other Mrs. Callaway," Fabrizio says, "I never understood what Mac saw in her. It's so sad, the way she took him away from here." He crosses his arms, clearly upset by all that's happened.

"His kids missed him, for sure," Cheyenne says as she applies nail polish to my toes. "Noah is a rock. Always placed his family first." She shakes her head and her eyebrows narrow.

"That's why you were a perfect match for him," she says with genuine sweetness. "You always put your family first. You understand him. You understand each other. It's really that simple."

I think about Mom, and Lane, and even the pups—the M&Ms, like Lane likes to call them. And Beck and Griff in their own way. We do worry and care about them. Cheyenne is right. They are central to our lives.

"Any idea why Gail is here?" I ask, eager for more information.

"Someone said they saw her with developers, driving around."

What does she think she'll be doing? She has no say on this. It's a done deal. Noah is married, and he keeps control.

Grace stands from her seat while Cheyenne removes my toe splitters. "I wonder how long she's planning on staying," she sighs.

Wild guess? Until Noah's birthday, and a little longer.

My treatment done, I take care of tips and hand my card to Grace at reception. Her smile freezes as the front door chimes, cool air sweeping in a few dead leaves... and a beautiful blonde.

Pursing her lips, Gail steps inside.

"Mrs. Callaway, we didn't expect you so early," Grace says, her smile forced. "Fabrizio will get you settled in."

Fabrizio waltzes in. "Ah Gail, Gail, Gail, you are more beautiful each time!" He envelops her in air kisses. "Seriously—you have to tell me your secret," he adds as if she were the only person in the room. "What are we doing today?" he asks, coaxing her toward the dressing room.

Turning to me, Grace says, "You're all set, sweetheart. Noah already called to settle for you."

Gail sets her cold, assessing glare on me. "The apple never falls far from the tree, does it? Your mother must be proud of you. You leveled up."

The words hit me like a slap. Years suffering Marcy's lifestyle, rejecting my own mother so I could save myself? Still people look at me and see a price tag.

Behind her back, Fabrizio rolls his eyes and makes heart hands for me. But his clowning can't calm the tremor inside me.

Gail turns to Grace. "Definitely Pretty Woman vibes. You should choose your clientele more carefully."

My stomach twists. *Pretty Woman.* Does she even know what I had to go through to not be Pretty Woman? Or in my case, Pillow?

"Your mom got you all wrong. You're not Weeping." My new stepfather stands behind me as through the dirty window I watch Mom climb into a cab. His stench alone repulses me. "You're Pillow."

His hands land heavy on my shoulders. "You know what a pillow is?" His fingers dig into my bones. "It's something you sleep with."

The room spins, and I have to hold onto the register. I was smart and strong enough to escape him, back then. And while Mom later pretended I'd misunderstood, she sent me back to Emerald Creek and

Aunt Angela. Then why is this insult hurting so much that I'm left speechless?

Grace pales. "There's been a misunderstanding," she tells Gail, her voice cold as ice. "We can't fit you in."

All I can focus on are Gail's red nails digging into her crossed arms. My head pounds.

"Grace, it's okay," I whisper.

"No, it's not. We're the Bitch Brigade," she tells me, eyes shiny. "We don't just stand by when one of us is down."

My voice is thin as air. "But I'm not..."

Gail flicks her nails impatiently, and Grace turns to me. "You go on," she tells me softly, an apology she doesn't need to give in her eyes. "You don't need to be here for this."

Cheyenne breezes out with a grin. "I'll tell you how it goes," she teases, miming like she's eating popcorn.

But my feet are leaden.

Her face now cold as stone, Grace turns to Gail. "We don't tolerate this."

Gail hisses. "This *what*?"

"Grace, don't worry about it," I plead quietly. "It's fine. Really."

"It's my place of business and this is how I run it," she answers me firmly. "Like I said, the Bitch Brigade has got your back." Turning to Gail, she says, "Not your kind of B. Your patronage is no longer welcome here."

Gail's nostrils flare and her eyes throw daggers. "You'll regret this," she spits. "By next year this town will be *very* different. You'll be *begging* me to come back." She turns on her heel, slamming the door on her way out.

"The hell did she mean, *by next year*?" Cheyenne mutters, hugging me as Grace plants herself at the window.

I relax a bit in her embrace and shrug like I don't know what she's talking about.

Despite Grace's awesome support, my stomach is in knots.

The apple doesn't fall far from the tree... Pretty Woman vibes... You'll regret this.

After Grace assures me Gail is gone, I leave, feeling like shit. Ashamed. Unworthy.

"How was it?" Noah sneaks in on me in that adorable way of his, wrapping his flannel-clad arms around me and giving me the squeeze I need. I'm outside on the patio, adding logs to the firepit so we can eat al fresco while the dogs run around. My breath stupidly stutters. I shouldn't let this affect me, but I can't help it. "You okay, babe?" he asks, feeling my emotion.

"The spa was awesome." I let my head fall on his solid chest, already feeling rooted. Supported. Tilting my head up to him, I add, "Thank you for taking care of everything. That was very sweet of you."

"Thank you for taking care of me, sweet Willow. I don't say thank you enough to you."

"You don't have to—"

"Oh enough with the niceties," he growls, clasping me tighter against him. "What's wrong?"

I let out a huff. How does he know? "Honestly, nothing's wrong anymore. Don't mean to be all lovey-dovey gooey, but it's true." I turn to face him and wrap my arms around his neck. I do feel much lighter. Stronger. I kiss him softly, then take his glasses off and massage the bridge of his nose. "How was your afternoon?" I ask.

"Nuh-huh. You're not getting off so easy." He boops me, then trails a kiss down my neck.

I tilt my head back, breathing in the crisp fall air. Maple and elm leaves fall softly to the ground. Chipmunks and squirrels rustle loudly around, burying acorns in places they'll forget. "I'll tell you what happened, but first—this is what I love about fall. It's the season of letting go. Of forgetting certain things. Of letting other things die so they can be reborn differently."

"O-kay?"

I take a cleansing breath and tell him what happened with Gail, feeling him tense against me. By the time I'm done, he's vibrating with anger. "Season of letting go, babe," I remind him.

"I don't know if I want to let *that* go."

"And yet you have to. The only real problem we have, is why is Gail here?"

"We can get to that later." His gaze is stubborn, looking at something beyond me.

A raven croaks, giving me the nudge I need. "There's something you should know," I tell him, and this brings his gaze back on me. Funny how I was ashamed, but now I'm almost eager to tell Noah. He'll understand me better once I'm over with it.

"What?"

"It's true. My mother *was* a sex worker."

He barely flinches and wraps me tighter against him.

"I should have told you. I just didn't think it was—" *important*. I'm about to slip this under the carpet, as always.

Am I going to keep lying?

"I was ashamed to tell you."

He kisses my forehead. "It's your life, Willow. You shouldn't be ashamed of it." And god I love him even more for not saying how sorry he is and how awful it must have been. I don't need his pity. Only his acceptance.

"It's a part of my life I'd rather forget," I admit. "It wasn't easy."

He holds my chin and searches my gaze. "It made you who you are. It was shitty, and painful, and I can see how it created a distance with your mom. But it's over now."

My breath stutters, but I want him to know more. I want him to know everything about me. "When Gail was... insulting me..." I look at the gardens and find the courage to continue talking "...this memory came back to me out of the blue." In as few words as possible, I tell Noah the danger I'd been in with my stepfather, what I narrowly escaped.

His eyes are full of danger, sadness, and revolt. He's struggling to keep it together.

"I used to feel dirty for it," I say. "But I don't anymore. Fuck that. Right?"

Noah leans his forehead against mine. "I'm gonna need... a lot of time to process that. And I never want to be okay with it. But all I'll say is... let me kill your pain with my love."

Chapter Forty-Two

Noah

Willow says she's fine, but she's not. It's in the faint tremor of her voice. In her forced smile. In her brief intakes of air as she squares her shoulders against the world.

At least her body's shaking is reduced to a base buzz as she relaxes against me. I wrap her tighter in my arms, willing all the hurt to leave her. Her childhood scars might make her who she is, but I won't let these wounds rip back open.

The kitchen screen door clangs as Lane steps onto the patio, and I let go of Willow with the excuse of adding a couple of logs to the firepit and starting the barbecue. I'm livid at how Gail treated my wife, but I don't want to discuss this with my siblings. It's too close to what I've kept from them.

Hopefully the grapevine isn't as bad as I imagine, and—

"So much for hiding from Gail at the spa!" Lane exclaims. She sets a dish on the table then wraps Willow in a quick hug. "Are you going to have PTSD for the rest of your life?" *Grapevine fully functional.* "I heard Grace was so badass!"

Willow's distress from seconds ago is gone, and instead there's pure glee. "Ohmygod she was the best." Her voice rings warm and free, releasing part of my anxiety.

Whatever Grace did, I owe her.

The moment is cut short by the barn door slapping shut. Beck stomps toward us, brow furrowed, Muffin yapping and lolloping to meet him. Becks scratches the pup's head, then strides my way and drops a six-pack on the table. "I'll get the meat," he grunts.

We grill together, Beck's unusual silence welcome as I try to come to terms with Willow's confession, while mapping out the possible reasons and outcomes for Gail's presence in Emerald Creek.

Throughout dinner, Willow and Lane are the only ones talking. Shadows of the bonfire play on my wife's soft features as she sweetly encourages my sister in her puzzling job search. I want to push Lane to be more logical in her life choices, but for whatever reason she's stressed, and the couple of times I've tried to broach the topic of her next steps, she broke down crying.

Willow, however, manages to have a whole conversation that actually seems to make Lane feel better about herself.

"Everything okay?" I finally ask Beck. It's not like him to not have anything to say.

He narrows his gaze on me. "I dunno. You tell me."

The women stop talking, eyes on us. "Beck," Lane whispers. The evening shifts from lighthearted to loaded in that one word from one Irish twin to the other. These two have something going on and are having a quiet argument about whether to keep it from me or not.

"What?" Beck snaps. "Did you wonder to ask why Gail is here? Why she's stirring shit?" He's asking Lane but looking at me. "Maybe Noah wants to explain what's going on."

Lane's eyes widen. "That's not necessary."

"I'll clear the table," Willow mumbles as she stands.

"I think you should stay," Beck barks, his gaze locked on me. "This concerns you, Willow."

Lane sets a comforting hand on my wife's forearm. "Of course! Anything in the family concerns Willow."

"Beck," I warn. If he's figured it out, surely he understands it can't come out. Not now, and probably not ever.

Beck clenches his jaw. "I tried to understand. Tried to put myself in your shoes. And sure, I get everything you did for us, back in the day. But this is too far. You shouldn't have kept us in the dark."

Cold runs down my back as I scramble to say something.

Beck uncaps a beer—his second. "Griff says you can't help yourself." He pulls on his beer.

"Griff? What does Griff have to do with... anything?"

"That's all you got?" Beck smirks. "You're worried about what Griff thinks?"

"Beck!" Lane hisses.

Beck burps and waves his beer bottle my way. "Are you gonna tell our sister?"

"Tell me what?"

Willow's cutlery clinks against her plate. "Nothing... nothing major. We uh—"

My heart hammers in my chest. "Willow," I warn her.

"It's okay, Noah. You—*we* can't keep this to ourselves forever."

She's right, and the idea of sharing this burden feels close to relief. Yet the familiar panic takes over; It's simply too big. "It can wait," I plead, knowing it's way too late for that.

"Can it, though? What are you gonna do when it comes out?" Beck sneers.

"What are you talking about?" Lane asks. "There's nothing to be done."

"Your family—" Willow starts.

"It's yours too," Lane interrupts.

"The *Callaway* family has a trust—"

"Jesus, yes, I *know*. Why does everyone always treat me like a baby?" Lane looks at each of us in turn.

Beck rolls his eyes. "That is *so not* the point."

"The *point* is, they're *married*. So what is Cruella's fucking *problem*?" A stunned silence falls around the table, until Lane continues, "I mean we all know *why* they did it, but they did it, right? Not only did they do the getting married part but they're also doing the *doing it* part so… for all intents and purposes the trustee has met the condition and Gail can go fuck herself."

Beck's jaw clenches. Vaguely aware that the loud pounding inside my chest is just my heart, I feel my mouth hang open. Willow seems to have stopped breathing.

"Or did I miss something else?" Lane asks.

"When did you find out?" Beck grits out.

She grabs a beer, then sets it back on the table. "I always knew."

I glance at Willow, her wide eyes and paleness mirroring my thoughts. If Beck and Lane know, there's bound to be other people—less scrupulous people—who could come forward or be convinced by Gail to share what they know. How will this affect us legally?

The more I think about it, the more I can see how this whole running to Vegas to get married a few months before my birthday only threw a mask on the problem and created many more.

After a few charged moments, Beck rubs his face. "How did you find out?"

Throughout the million thoughts crossing my mind right now, the one that tops them and seems to bother me the most is the realization that Beck is hurting from feeling left out. But what was I supposed to do?

Lane scoffs. "Oh, come on. It's all in the office safe." I'm not going to ask her how she knows the combination. If she'd asked me, I would have given it to her. If Griff, Beck, or Lane had asked to see the trust or any of the Callaway papers, I'd have shared.

But they never did.

The shadow of a smile plays on Lane's face when she taunts Beck. "You never looked?" Resisting the temptation to mock him, she sets her gaze on me. "You didn't need to carry all this on your own. But I understand." With a pointed glance at Beck she adds, "And *I'm* grateful you did."

Beck stands, his chair rattling on the flagstone. "It's messed up," he says, looking uneasily between Willow and me.

I take Willow's hand, the feeling of her fingers closing on mine all I need.

Lane leans back in her chair. "Arranged marriages are common in other cultures. There's nothing inherently messed up about it."

Beck runs a hand in his hair. "But this was *fake*."

"Was it, though?" Lane asks.

A small smile plays on my wife's face. "Didn't feel like it," she whispers.

I pull her to me, kissing her lips lightly.

"Aw please!" Beck all but yells, and Muffin yaps and jumps on Beck. Beck crouches and ruffles Muffin, jaw still set.

"Come and finish your beer," I tell him.

I want to ask Lane how long she's known, but then I might have to answer questions about why I kept this to myself. *Maybe another time.*

"Beck, seriously, Noah and Willow were always meant to be together," Lane says.

My heart thumps. As if she hadn't dropped enough bombs yet. What is she even talking about?

"Oh, come on!" she cries, looking between Beck and me. "Like you don't know Mom always had a soft spot for her. Always said she loved Willow's drawings because she captured the soul of Lilyvale." Beck snorts, but Lane ignores him. "No one else ever spent hours in the garden, drawing and painting. I remember Mom telling me I shouldn't bother her. That she needed this time to herself. That Lilyvale was a refuge for her, but that one day, Willow would be Lilyvale's refuge."

Willow's hand is spasmodically clenching mine, tears falling down her cheeks.

"No one else?!" Lane looks, astonished, between Beck and me.

"I just thought she meant Willow had enough shit in her life, we needed to let her be when she was here," Beck says.

Same, brother. What the hell?

"You never said anything," Willow says in a voice so raw I barely recognize it. She bites her lip to stop the trembling.

Lane smiles softly at her. "It all made sense to me at Colt and Kiara's wedding. Except this idiot was supposed to fall in love *before* proposing."

Idiot sums it up, and it's not the first time I've felt like one.

Willow's grip on my hand has loosened, replaced by a soft stroke. "He was too worried about the estate, and what it would do to you guys if he lost it, to think about himself. Or to worry about falling in love."

Beck clears his throat. His gaze is still fixed on mine, but the animosity is replaced by an eagerness to help. "So what are we gonna do? About Gail."

The hell if I know. "We don't know what she wants."

"So what—we just wait?"

Pretty much. "A while back she filed some paperwork about our marriage not holding water. But she hasn't continued that—at least not in court. Your guess is as good as mine as to why she's in Emerald Creek."

Beck stands and stretches with a grunt. "We can ask around at Ethan and Grace's wedding. See if anyone knows anything. If she's been asking questions about you guys."

"No one at Game Nights believes there's anything weird about your marriage," Lane says. "I did some recon when you were gone for the Phish concert."

"Oh yeah, the *second one* we couldn't come to." Beck pretends to complain, but his smirk belies his words.

I shrug, warmth spreading inside me at my brother's change of attitude. "It was our honeymoon."

"You asked about us at Game Nights?" Willow asks, clearly shocked.

"Don't worry. I'm skilled at getting people to talk without asking obvious questions."

"And?" I ask.

"And everyone thinks it was about time you got your head out of your ass and saw what was right in front of you."

That evening in bed, Willow cuddled on my chest while we catch our breath, the sweet scent of sex in the air, I start chuckling stupidly.

"What?" she asks.

"Remember how we used to "study" each other? Did you ever answer all those questions we came up with?" The idea seems so silly now.

She sits up in bed, pulls the sheet up to cover her breasts. "Yeah. I put it in an online document folder so we could add to it from our phones. Remember? *I* did my homework."

I pull the sheet down to her waist, watching as her nipples pebble under my light touch. "Maybe?" I don't remember that at all. But now I'm curious what she put there, so I grab my phone and open the spreadsheet I'd all but forgotten about. A line catches my eye, under *Heartbreaks*—something Willow must have added herself.

Mom lied to me because she didn't think I could handle the truth.

I scoop her so she's straddling me. I want her full attention. "I don't care about your politics or how you talk to God or even your first kiss, though I'm mildly jealous of the fucker. I already know you don't care for blueberries but you'd get in a fight for the last blackberry. That the way you take your coffee depends on the weather, but you got to have almond milk because soy gives you inflammation and oat milk bellyaches and real milk the shits. I know the sound you make when you're about to come, but I'd kill anyone who'd even go there and ask. I'll never admit knowing your clothes size, and I love that you buy cruelty-free shit for your face."

There's so much more I want to tell Willow. How she's permeated every aspect of my life. How she's part of me. How sometimes I'm scared this is all a dream and I'll wake up alone, terrorized not about losing the estate, but about going through life without my dream girl.

But there's one thing I need to do for her.

"What really, really makes me sad is that you're carrying into this beautiful life of yours a pain that your mother gave you—her lie—but really she just wanted you to be shielded from the ugliness of the world. And I almost think I should thank her for that. Because all the shit that was going on in her life and yours, you didn't deserve it and she knew it. So kudos to her for lying to you if she thought that would make it less painful."

She cups my face in her hands. "I was always right about you. You're the best there is. The only one for me." The tenderness in her gaze is so deep it brings tears to my eyes.

Chapter Forty-Three

Noah

Standing next to Ethan as his best man, I'm having déjà vu. Same group of friends, different lineup. This time I'm the best man, Grace is the bride with Alex her maid of honor, and one of the bridesmaids is my wife.

We're at the King's farm, in the midst of acres and acres of green pastures and fiery woods. The Vermont sky is huge above us, brimming with pinks and gold in this witching hour.

And this time my wife is looking at me with adoring eyes instead of... *shit*... stealing glances at me. She *was* looking at me all those years. I just never saw it. Never saw her *truly*. What is wrong with me?

This should be us, standing at the altar with all our friends around us, exchanging vows. Willow should have had the wedding of her dreams. I shut my eyes briefly. How blind was I, that I didn't see her? Didn't sense what she felt for me?

Speaking of which, I need to get to the bottom of how and when this all started for her. I see some tender confessions in our future, a hint of sorrow soothed by an orgasm or three.

Shit. Wrong time to get a hard-on. My eyes open on instinct on Willow, her gorgeous body molded by a brand-new dress the color of sunset, *no tag,* her gaze on Grace and Ethan, and... tears in her eyes.

Is she thinking the same?

She deserved a wedding like this, something no one would ever forget, with pictures for generations to come in the hallways of Lilyvale.

She smiles feebly now, something Ethan said. What was it? Oh yeah. The man on my right is going on about the years being apart, when they should have been together. Some stuff about mistakes and making up for lost time. Smooth talker, my friend.

I won't get public declarations of love and she won't get a lavish wedding. But I'll make damn sure that 'til death do us part, she has the sweetest life she could ever dream of. I'll love her fiercely, entirely, and with devotion. She deserves nothing less.

When Grace and Ethan walk past us, I'm faced with Alex, Grace's maid of honor. "You owe me a swap," I say with a smile as I take Willow's arm. Alex slides behind me. "Hey handsome," she whispers to Chris.

I lean toward my wife as we follow the bride and groom and give her arm a squeeze. "You're getting better at this."

She smiles at me. "No tag to bother me."

"Oh, that's the only difference?"

She gives me a coquettish shoulder raise. "Pretty much."

"Really," I growl. By now we've reached the end of the aisle. I pull her aside, but still there's too many people. So I grab her hand and rush her behind the farmhouse.

"Where are we going?" she pretends to wonder, laughing.

Away from prying eyes, I lean her against the wall, needing to feel the length of her body against mine. Her heartbeat flutters like a bird against a window, her lips part, her eyelids close.

That's my wife.

I run my hands up and down her sides until I feel the bare skin at her thighs, then slide one hand under her dress and find... nothing but more bare skin. I cup her ass.

Not a single thread of fabric. "Fuck..." I growl.

"It's not what you think," she starts.

Not what I think? It's a bare pussy. There's no other way to put it. I plunge two fingers inside her to make my point.

"It's because..." a sigh as I pump in and out of her "the dress is so... oh Noah... so clingy you could see the... ahhh... the underwear so I... I..." She clenches her thighs around my hand. "Baby, *stop*. Anyone could see us."

"But you were doing so good."

She humors me with a chuckle. "There's kids. Kids tend to run around houses."

Good point. "Let go of my hand?" She has me in the iron clutch of her thighs and *damn*... I could use some of that around my head as I eat her, around my hips as I take her, around—

"Promise you'll stop," she breathes.

"Scout's honor."

She giggles and clenches harder.

"Open your thighs for me, woman," I order.

"You're so dirty," she whisper-moans in my ear. "I can't wait for you to fuck me." Then she opens her thighs, and I reluctantly remove my hand, sucking her juices off my fingers.

She pats the front of her dress as she pushes herself off the wall. "Do I look okay?"

"You look like someone who almost got fucked against a wall."

Her eyes widen, her mouth gapes. "What's that supposed to mean? You make it sound like a good thing."

I hold my laughter and reach to fix the strands of hair escaping from the fancy pile at the back of her head. "It means you have that hungry look on you and..." I'm not sure how to put the next thing... "these little guys are still calling for attention."

She looks down her dress and yelps at her pebbled nipples. "Ohmygod." Lifting the draped fabric, she looks inside. "I had those little thingies," she says, producing with widening eyes what looks like a petal-shaped Band-Aid, then another, "but I guess... I guess... the sweat?"

"Babe, you don't sweat. Not that much," I say with utter confidence. "Like I said. You look ripe for a good fuck."

She gapes. "That's not what you said!"

Shit. Now her cheeks are turning rosy, her nipples are begging for more attention, and why is her dress clinging halfway up her ass? ...maybe there is a sweat effect, the kind that would make me fuck my wife against that wall if there weren't any kids around.

"Almost fucked... primed... what's the difference?" My erection is getting painful as I get into the specifics of the different stages of making love to Willow. Judging by her bodily reaction, she feels the same.

We need to stop acting like horny teenagers. Getting a grip on myself, I take her hand and pull her to a side door leading inside the house.

"Noah Callaway, we are not having sex in here," she hisses, trying to resist my pull.

"Just showing you to the bathroom." Now she follows. "I think they might be waiting for us for photos," I add.

"Oh god," she says as she darts into the powder room and takes in the full extent of her appearance. From her small clutch she produces more things that I thought could ever fit. She swiftly places another pair of those sticky things on her nipples, plucks hairpins on what she calls her updo, dabs makeup on her forehead. She checks her ass in the mirror, then smooths her dress, takes a deep breath, and says, "You owe me a serious fuck session tonight."

I'm going to have to think about... nails on a chalkboard to get rid of the hard-on she gave me again with just her words.

A couple of hours later Willow nudges me. "You're up."

Alex is going back to her place at one of the dinner tables, having given a speech about how true love just finds you, and there's no fighting it or trying to forget it. She's talking about her own story as well as Ethan's and Grace's, and I can't help but wonder again... is there something wrong with me that I didn't see what was right there, in front of me, several times a week? Am I that broken that I couldn't see, couldn't find, couldn't recognize true love?

I always felt awed and amazed and a little bit scared by Willow. Shouldn't I have been able to see who she really was?

"Where's the best man?" Cassandra calls in the mic.

Shit, that's me. I head to the spot next to Grace and Ethan and recount the expected story about how Ethan fell head-over-heels for Grace. I skip the part where he messed up and disappeared for ten years, because no one wants to hear how a groom fucked up. I manage to make a tasteful joke about them seeing each other for the first time again in a massage tent. "Don't worry, Ms. Angela was right outside, and I checked with her. *Nothing* happened." The audience is falling over themselves laughing, but Grace and Ethan are just... blushing. A lot.

"Oh... so she lied," I state in the mic, my attention on them. "Good to know."

More laughter.

"Cassandra is typically credited for a lot of love stories in this town..." I tip the mic to her and get Cass a round of applause, "but I think Ms. Angela, who I'm actually proud to now call family, deserves a lot of credit as well." This time the round of applause is for Ms. Angela, who makes all sorts of faces and waves her hands no, then finally gives up and makes a heart sign with her hands like she's a millennial.

"Speaking of family, we want a redo of the wedding, No-no!" Beck bellows from across the party tent.

"Beck, this is Grace and Ethan's wedding."

Beck stands and bellows, "He shorted us a party!"

Is this guy for real? I glance at Grace and Ethan. At least they're laughing. "No one wants a Callaway family argument."

There's a Larsen effect from a mic, then Ethan's voice comes out. "We'd love to see that, actually. Free entertainment," he jokes, and Grace laughs.

I shake my head. "I'll only say this. Can't blame me for wanting to shield my bride from this little brother. Let her have one day of peace."

Beck places his hands on his heart as if he were mortally wounded but sits down, getting the message that this really isn't okay. These kids are going to be the death of me... especially considering they're absolutely not kids.

I wrap up my interrupted speech with a couple of heartfelt and lightly funny remarks, and am almost at my seat when Grace says in the mic, "Willow?"

Willow turns her head to look beyond me.

"We're expecting a vow renewal for your first anniversary, honey."

Willow glances at me like a deer in the headlights.

Kiara's voice sounds from god knows where, "Yeah, I'm calling in my one chance to be a maid of honor."

Willow is crimson, but nods at her friends.

"That's actually a great idea," I whisper in her ear.

She doesn't answer, just timidly dips her head down, and I'm not quite sure what to make of that.

Chapter Forty-Four

Willow

Forget my friends' idea for an anniversary vow renewal—which caught me totally by surprise—this wedding is just massive foreplay. When we're not glued to each other on the dance floor, Noah's hands are on my thigh. On my bare shoulder. Lightly squeezing my nape. Down my bare back.

When we're finally in our bedroom, he locks the door and growls, "Where were we," as he firmly presses me against the wall and drives his hand up between my thighs. I know exactly what part of the evening he's talking about. The one where he had me half-naked against the farm wall.

Wetness pools between my legs as my mind insists on holding on to the suggestion Kiara made that we have a renewal of vows. Any lingering doubts I may have had of Noah's true love for me disappeared at his murmured *"that's a great idea"* and it's not impossible I've been planning—

"Spread for me," Noah orders, throwing his glasses on the couch. His white shirt is open at the collar, sleeves rolled up, hair messed up from our heavy kissing in the car, a walking sex symbol.

"Show me how wet you are." His gaze dark with desire, he dips down and suckles my neck while his fingers plunge into me.

All thoughts of any conversation gone, I hike one leg over his hips, straddling his thigh to ease my need. I might come just looking at his corded nape flexing as he dips deeper, giving my nipple a bite through the fabric.

"Surprised that little dress of yours isn't soaked through."

It's been a concern of mine, too, but not anymore. "You like that dress?" I whisper in his ear, wanting him to talk dirty to me.

He grunts as he lifts his head back up, lust hotter than I've ever seen. "Such a fucking tease." With anxious hands he pulls on my updo, hairpins flying out, then kneads my head, combs through my hair with strong fingers, inhaling it with a touch of mad obsession.

My fingers fumble with his leather belt, my pussy clenching at the sound of the pant zipper I pull down, freeing his bobbing cock. Finally holding him in my hand, I stroke him, my thumb pad wiping precum. I give him a last stroke, then lock eyes with him as I lick my thumb.

He jerks my hand out of my mouth and gathers my wrists above my head. "Spread for me." I hike my leg higher on him. His jaw grazes my forehead, shivers from his stubble running down my spine. His breath is labored. "That's my good little wife. Take it," he says as he enters me, his heat and friction making my knees weak. "Take your husband deep."

"Harder, Noah, harder."

Something dangerous passes through his gaze. "Careful what you wish for." Something I could get addicted to.

"P-please."

He cups my throat in a careful hand. "Yeah, beg for me, little wife. Beg." His thumb rakes my ear, his palm clenching for an answer.

"Please fuck me harder," I whisper, straining to keep my eyes open to watch his desire, his *need* for me.

He rams into me, neck tense, jaw set, beads of sweat pearling on his forehead. "Such a sweet, sweet, cunt." With his free hand he unzips my dress. "*Greedy* little cunt." Then he cups my ass, the fabric of the dress messing with our connection.

The tear of fabric.

He pulls himself back an inch or two, looks down at my naked body wrapped around his, shreds of my dress on the floor. "That's better."

He's still fully clothed, dress pants straining at his hips, formal shirt clinging to his sweaty torso as he fists my hair, pulling my mouth to his. "God I love how you taste," he murmurs. "I love everything about you."

"Babe," I blabber. My orgasm is so strong it strikes me like lightning, arches my back, stretches my legs, interminable seconds of high-strung pleasure followed by the softest mellowing.

Limbs like cotton, mind checked out, I feel Noah carrying me to the bed.

"Fuck, that was beautiful." He fans my hair around my face on the pillow.

With weak hands, I start to unbutton his shirt. He sits up. "Let me," I say, sitting up to face him. "Let me undress my husband." Making quick work of the rest of the buttons, I run my hands on his torso, from his pecs down to the dusting of hair. I press one finger on him and he lets himself fall back, hands behind his head, a small smile on his face. He toes his shoes off while I get him quickly entirely naked, then kiss my way up his thighs.

My mouth closes on his dick, and he hisses. "I'm not gonna last long," he says.

I lock eyes with him. "Then let's make it count. I heard someone liked my ass," I say as I straddle him reverse cowgirl.

"Ah fuck, babe." He grabs my butt cheeks in his hands, then sits up to grope my breasts. His mouth comes down. "On your knees," he orders.

That's fast becoming my favorite three words.

The mattress dips beside me as the aroma of coffee dispels my dreams. I open an eye and see Noah in pajama pants, the Mrs. Callaway mug of coffee in his hand, lid off, that dusting of hair on his stomach teasing me awake. "Hey," I say, smiling.

"Hey yourself." He places the coffee on the nightstand and kisses me softly, then brings me against his chest, stroking my hair on my bare back. "You okay?" he asks, his voice unsteady.

I look up at him. "Why wouldn't I be?"

His eyes seem to search something in my gaze. "I don't know—I... the wedding... yesterday..." He blinks sadness away. "I wish I'd given you that."

I cup his face, stroking his stubble, the pad of my thumb on his lower lip. "Noah... You've given me so much more. Do you know how much it means to me that you let me hold you at night? That you're trusting me with the family store?" I'm so absurdly happy that he has a tight prenup which gives me absolutely no right in the estate. I love Noah for who he is, not what he has. I don't care about things. More often than not, they come between people. "You gave me a whole family, and your heart. I never dared dream of that."

He leans in for a deep kiss.

Before too long we're interrupted by a series of soft knocks at the door. "That'll be Lucius," he says with a chuckle.

Lucius is the second-floor robot vacuum cleaner. Edward is in charge of the first floor, and Rosalie the upstairs.

"Did I tell you Zach is working on a staircase model?" Noah asks as he dips his kisses from my neck to my breasts.

"I'm sure he is," I breathe. "Adapting his stair-climbing wheelchair contraption to the little guys?"

"Something like that."

After a quick shower, we come downstairs late and walk up to brunch set up on the patio. Calla and the pups greet us with wagging tails. Across the garden, Beck comes out of the barn, scratching his belly as he stretches.

Lane is at the table, reading a book. She smiles feebly at us. *This must mean she's going through with sharing her personal news this morning.* I want to tell her it'll be alright, because I know it will. But I can understand her apprehension.

"What happened to you, Lanie?" Noah asks as we take in the basket of fresh croissants, the apple cider donuts, the steaming coffee pot. He leans over her to kiss the top of her head. "Didn't party hard enough last night? Or are you too used to hangovers now?"

She shrugs. "I was up early, so I took Myrtle to see her future house, and Chris sent me back with all this. One thing led to another..." She glances at me nervously, a small smile on her face. No hangover for her, but her brothers don't know why yet.

"Myrtle?" Beck asks, ruffling Muffin's hair as the pup jumps to greet him. "I thought Muffin was called Muffin because he was going to live at the bakery."

I laugh. "Nope. Skye said Muffin was a great name but it couldn't be her dog's name." I count on my fingers all the reasons she came up with. "It's too obvious for a bakery. The dog would be confused every time they talked about muffins. And finally, she decided Muffin was a boy name, and she bonded with our little girl pup from the beginning."

"Myrtle sure liked the smells there," Lane says, petting the dog. "They already have a system to keep her out of the bakery."

Noah strokes my forearm. "Whenever you're ready, then," Noah says.

I take a deep inhale, trying to organize my thoughts. It's hard for me to accept that Myrtle should move to her new home. Yet I know it's time.

"You're going to be uncles," Lane blurts, interrupting my train of thoughts.

Beck, eyes bloodshot, high-fives his brother. "Dude, good job." Then he turns to his sister. "Wait. How d'you know?"

Noah, his hand still up from the surprise high-five, glances at me with a frown, then moves his gaze to his sister, his forehead smoothing as understanding dawns on him.

I place my hand on his thigh and give him a squeeze. Shock and a thousand questions are painted on his face. As he clears his throat to talk, Lane shoots him a warning look.

Before he can say anything, I stand, round the table, and pull her into a hug. "That's wonderful news, honey." I lock eyes with Noah over her shoulder, watching him as he rubs the spot where his glasses normally rest, then relaxes as he realizes it's really not the end of the world. It's actually the beginning of a new one.

"How the fuck did that happen?" Beck blurts as he catches up.

"You missed the lesson on the birds and the bees?" I tease him as I release Lane.

"Fuck," Beck says. "I did *not* see that coming." He leans over the table. "Are you okay?" His gaze searches his sister's.

She gives him nothing for a beat or two, until her eyes brighten and she bites her trembling lip. "I'm fine," she whispers.

He stands abruptly, Muffin scurrying from under his chair with a soft yelp, and rounds the table to take Lane in his arms. "Who's the fu—the father?" he asks as he nearly smothers her.

I'm not surprised by Beck's reaction. He's always acting a little goofy and immature, but he loves fiercely. I'm convinced his mostly irreverent attitude is a front to hide how big his heart is.

"I don't wanna talk about him," Lane says, her voice muffled from Beck's embrace. "Not yet."

Beck takes a long inhale, clearly struggling to keep his opinions to himself—and mostly succeeding. Finally, he pulls back from her. "You need me to talk to him, just say the word."

Lane wipes a tear. "I'm fine, really. I don't know why I got all emotional all of a sudden." She smiles brightly at Beck, then turns a hesitant gaze to Noah.

Noah stands to hug her while Beck sits back down. "Congratulations, Laney." He strokes her back. "What do you need from me?"

Noah, always the caretaker.

"Just maybe more of your hugs," she murmurs, nestling deeper in her older brother's comforting embrace. I know everything that's going on in my husband's mind right now, how worried he must be for her. I'm so proud of how he's handling it.

Noah rocks her gently. "I'll always be there for you."

"I know," she whispers back. "Thank you."

I refill everyone's hot drinks while Noah sits back down, and we all take a deep breath. Lane glances at me, mouthing *thank you* and giving me a small but genuine smile. I smile back at her. Is it crazy that I can't wait to hold her baby in my arms? I held Ivy at Alex and Chris's, and it was just the most overwhelmingly loving experience ever.

"So, what's the plan?" Beck asks.

As Lane explains how she'll be working from home for a while, Beck goes into builder mode, verbally drawing a sketch of where he could install a nursery and a home office in the other aisle of Lilyvale.

"How about health care?" Noah asks. "And an ob-gyn. You need to get on that tomorrow. Maybe this place in South Burlington where Alex went. Chris said they were great. We can ask about doulas and midwives around here. You need to get your team together."

Lane glances at me, and I smile back at her, blowing her a kiss. She's getting everything she needs from her family right now, and I couldn't be happier that I'm part of it.

"Lane will be alright," I say to Noah that afternoon. We're on a long walk up Hunger Path with the dogs while Beck and Lane are taking measurements and discussing the ideal orientation for the nursery.

He barely reciprocates my tug when I slide my hand in his. "Yeah. Eventually."

"Oh, honey. It's not the end of the world."

"Isn't it, though? For her? God knows I was hoping she'd stay in Emerald Creek. Do something here. But not like that. Not as a fall back." A small animal rustles in the fallen leaves, and Muffin barks, looking at his mother.

I take a deep breath. "She'll be fine." *In the end.*

A cloud obscures the sky, and I wrap my shawl tighter around my shoulders.

"And who's the father? And what's that shit about not wanting to talk about him?!" Noah continues.

Good question. "She'll come around." *I hope.* "Give her a little time. It's a shock to you, so imagine how she feels."

"You're right." He wraps his warm arm around my shoulders and kisses the top of my head. "Why would she have unprotected sex with someone who's not fit to be a father?"

"No birth control is one hundred percent fail-proof," I answer, feeling the need to defend her. We keep walking in silence, watching the dogs sniff around, hearing only the sound of fallen leaves cracking under our hiking boots.

"How long have you known?" Noah asks, glancing at me.

Does he feel left out? I never want to come between him and Lane. "Just for a few days. She needed to talk and—"

"It's fine." Noah's gaze is intense on me. "It's *great,* actually. I'm... Without a mother, or another sister, you're all she has, babe."

His emotion seeps into me. "She has you, too, and Beck. Maternity is not only a woman's thing." His reaction about putting her birth team together alone proves that Noah gets it.

"I know. It's just... you're so easy to talk to. I can be a bit stiff, and Beck is always looking either for a prank or a fight. I see how you are with her when you guys talk about her job search. She needs someone who will just listen."

"Now that you have the whole picture, it'll be easier for you to understand her."

We reach the high point of our trek and stop on the flat top of the hill. As we catch our breaths, we take in the scenery at our feet. Emerald Creek, nestled in a bend of the eponymous river, plumes of smoke billowing from a few chimneys, the delicate peals of the church chiming the top of the hour wafting to us.

Even Calla and the pups are taken by the serenity of the moment. They're quiet and almost still.

Calla turns her big head to me, and I swear... she's smiling.

Chapter Forty-Five

Noah

Minutes after Willow and I make it to the store the next morning, the doorbell chimes. "Well, that was an interesting start to my day," Ms. Angela says as she trots inside and straightens a few things. "Lovely display, my dear," she tells Willow, her pursed lips saying something's definitely wrong. "I need to talk to you two," she tells us, gesturing to the office. "Actually," she says as she switches the Open sign to Closed, "There's no one in here yet, right?"

"Only Elaine in the prep room and Dean at the unloading dock," I say while Willow looks at her with wide eyes.

Ms. Angela engages the lock.

"Coffee?" I offer.

"Sure. And let's maybe crack a bottle of the cheap stuff and pour a splash in it."

Willow frowns. "It's barely eight."

Ms. Angela nods eagerly. "Uh-huh. It's going to be a long day."

"You want to at least tell us what this is about?" I ask over my shoulder while I get the coffees and Willow goes to the liquor aisle.

"This requires a seat," Ms. Angela says. "Where is she going?"

"Getting the booze and running it through our house account."

She quirks an eyebrow. "Boy oh boy. Everything's above board now. I remember the good ol—"

Willow glances at me from across the store. "Aunt Angela," she calls out, sharing my growing aggravation. "Not even an inkling of a direction? You're killing us here."

"Fine," Ms. Angela says, taking the cup I hand her. She waits until Willow returns, twists off the cap, tops off her cup, then says, "One word. *Gail.*" Then she turns on her heel and marches to the office.

"She always knew how to manage suspense," Willow says as I fill our matching cups with piping hot coffee, almond milk and a splash of maple syrup for Willow, black for me.

Willow extends her mug with a wink. "Mr. Callaway."

Smiling, I clink with her. I don't care what Gail has up her sleeve, just looking at the travel mug my wife got me—the same as hers, with the words Noah Callaway in Millie's handwriting—makes me happy. Willow had her add *Mr.* and *Mrs.* on the other side, so the two mugs look like those bridal gifts I always thought were silly but now seem intrinsic to my happiness as a newly married man.

"Let's do this," Willow says with a small sigh, her chin pointing to the office.

"Sit down," Ms. Angela gestures to us. "You ready?"

I have a shit ton of work to do. I take a sip of the steaming coffee. Had this been the only change my wife made to the store, I'd still be thanking her for the rest of my days. "As ready as I'll ever be."

"Famous last words, young man." She takes a long sip, smacks her lips, then sets the cup down. "As of yesterday, the select board is in possession of a request from Mrs. Gail Callaway to schedule a special public meeting." The select board is our governing body. I've been a Selectperson for years, alongside Owen, Cassandra, Lynn, and Colton. Colton is our chairperson, and Ms. Angela our secretary. "As soon as I'm done here, I'm emailing the whole board."

Ms. Angela's tendency to sit on information is a little irritating, but I know better than to address this now. "Why would she do that? I expected her to take us to court."

"The only thing I can think of is that she doesn't want to pay lawyers."

Right. "She'd rather have the town do it, and she'll use the outcome to her advantage if it turns out the way she wants."

Ms. Angela makes a face. "She always had a way with money. Specifically, how to get some without working—by using others."

Gail is going to use the fact that the store would go to the town if the marriage was ruled as fake—whatever lawyers might call that. She's thinking that for some reason the town will want to own the store, and that they'll do what's needed to establish I didn't meet the conditions of the trust. Then she'll piggyback on that to get her hands on the rest of the estate. She's trying to get the town to do the heavy lifting of the lawsuit. "People will see right through it," I state.

"Some will. Others can be jealous or downright mean. I wouldn't take the threat too lightly," Ms. Angela says. "For all we know, they could be meeting with people behind our backs, promising who knows what if things changed here."

She takes a sip of her coffee, then resumes. "She made an official request, and she has a petition going. You'll be getting a phone call from Colton at any moment." She pulls out a manila envelope from her canvas bag and hands it to me. "I just spoke with him. I asked him to give me half an hour before he calls you."

I set my mug on my table, rip the envelope open, and pull my phone out. "I'll call him right now, get this over with."

Ms. Angela tut-tuts me. "There's more."

What could be worse than our personal affairs aired out at town hall?

She folds her arms, her gaze going between the two of us. "Gail Callaway will be staying at Lilyvale."

I choke on my coffee, my glasses instantly steaming up.

Willow laughs. "Over my dead body."

"It was my idea," Ms. Angela says, instantly sobering us, "and it's genius." She raises a hand to silence us. "Just listen. A week ago, Gail checked into the resort. Since then, she's been badgering everyone in town to give them information corroborating the fact that your marriage is fake. You have to say, circumstantial evidence is very much against you. For years, Willow has been pining after you, Noah, but you barely even noticed—"

"That's not true!" How can she say such a thing in front of Willow? It's so insensitive. I place my hand on Willow's nape, but she tilts her chin to Ms. Angela, indicating to let her continue.

"The point is, no one can even testify having seen you grab a cup of coffee together at Millie's or even just a drink at Lazy's before you came back from Vegas." She looks at me pointedly, and I have nothing to say to that. It's true. She turns her attention to Willow. "Remember that time at Game Nights, right after Kiara's wedding? It's not like I didn't try to get you to say something was up—"

Willow nearly chokes on her coffee. "Oh *that's* what you were doing? 'Cause it seemed to me you were just—" Ms. Angela's glare shuts her up. "Never mind," Willow whispers.

"I was giving you an opportunity to share the news. Course, I didn't know there was nothing to share. Sheesh. You really made it look like there was absolutely nothing going on between you two, and next thing you know, you're eloping! That doesn't look too good.

"What's worse, there's got to be someone who saw you go to the mansion after you dropped me off at home, and we don't know if this person will speak up or not. It's easy to put two and two together for someone who doesn't know you. Willow went to Lilyvale to offer Noah a deal, which he took."

"Or she just came to cuddle with me," I offer.

"Nope, that won't stand. She looked too uninterested in you at Game Nights."

"Is that so?" I ask, faintly bruised.

"Turns out your wife is an excellent comedian," Ms. Angela says. "Problem is, this wasn't the time to hide her true feelings."

I take Willow's hand in mine. I should have seen who she was, and how she felt about me, but feeling guilty about my blindness isn't going to do anything. Instead, I'm grateful she's who I'm sharing my life with.

"What does Gail staying at Lilyvale have anything to do with all this?" Willow asks.

"Right," Ms. Angela says. "So, Gail has been staying at the resort with some gentleman and his son—developers. She's been showing them around, asking questions about you, digging through documents at town hall. Now, last night, her suite at the resort experienced a spider infestation. They moved her during the night, but less than an hour after she was settled into her new suite? Spiders again crawling on the walls, on her bed. A real horror story."

I resume sipping my coffee, actually reveling in the woes of my stepmother. "Seems like good company for her."

"It gets better. She calls Wendy and Todd at the hotel, but they're sold out. So she calls me, begging for any room at the bed-and-breakfast."

"I hope you're charging her double," I say.

"You haven't been paying attention. I told her I was full as well, but that as the widow Callaway, she should sleep at Lilyvale, as was her right."

There goes my coffee again, down the wrong pipe. "Why would you do that?" I croak.

"Oh, I love it," Willow coos. "You're such a devil."

Ms. Angela points at Willow. "She's got it," she says with a big smile. She leans over to pat my wife's leg. "Good girl."

Chapter Forty-Six

Willow

Ms. Angela, or *Aunt* Angela—I've never been so proud to be related to her—really *is* a genius. We hammer out a rough plan, praying it works, then Noah calls Colton to figure out a timeline. "She has enough signatures on her petition to warrant an emergency meeting," Noah confirms when he ends the call. "Colton believes the sooner we have the meeting, the better. I tend to agree with him. We don't know what these people are up to."

"What's the meeting about?"

He takes a deep breath. "Just like we suspected. She wants to convince the town to challenge our marriage in court, so *she* doesn't have to spend money on it."

I interrupt him, appalled by what he's saying. "The *whole town* will know about the trust?"

Noah shrugs. "To be honest, I'm surprised we could keep it a secret that long around here." Adjusting his glasses, he resumes his explanation. "If the marriage were to be declared null and void, it would serve her interests—she'll be appointed trustee. But if that claim is dismissed, she'll have saved herself a lot of money. There's also the fact that a judge might be more favorable to a claim coming from a town in the Northeast Kingdom, where life is notoriously rough, rather than from a young widow living the life in the Caiman islands."

"I think it's Turks and Caicos," Ms. Angela counters. "Or somewhere in the Bahamas?"

I reach for Noah's hand. "But our marriage is real. What could she possibly prove?"

"It might be real now, but was it in Vegas?" Ms. Angela asks under her breath.

I shrug. "It'll be real when he turns thirty-two." *It already is.*

Ms. Angela raises her eyebrows. "Well, something good came out of this," she says, beaming, making Noah blush. "As for the problem at hand, none of us are lawyers. Could be that it would be considered fraud. It's not like we're going to ask a professional opinion on that."

Noah and I nod in silence.

"I say we stick to my plan." She sets her coffee mug on Noah's desk. "Now, I believe I have some town hall business to tend to."

I walk her to the door and turn the sign to *Open*, then stand on the doorstep for a minute. It's a crisp morning, the sky still blushing from the sunrise, birds chirping, golden leaves gently falling to a crimson carpet. It's the kind of day full of gorgeous promises, and somehow I can't bring myself to believe that Emerald Creek, the way we know it, could be living its last weeks, maybe less. I won't let it happen.

Turning back inside, I putter around the store, straightening the jars of jam so all the labels are front-facing, and dusting the shelves of custom-made wooden utensils until Dean comes back inside.

Shortly after, Haley arrives, followed by Chloe, Kiara, and Alex carrying baby Ivy in a pouch sling.

Puzzled, I return their side hugs with a tease. "D'you guys need Old Man Cal's Day After potion?" The herbal infusion is rumored to cure hangovers. "I heard the wedding party ended in the wee hours Sunday." Noah and I were long gone.

"Your husband was on the phone with my husband and it didn't look like fun," Kiara explains. It still makes my heart feel funny in a good way that we're both married now.

"We heard about Gail," Haley confirms.

A warm feeling fills me. "Aww, that's so sweet of you. We don't know when the meeting will be yet, but... d'you want supplies for signs or something?" I'm moved that the Bitch Brigade is coming together for me this time.

The front door chimes again with the arrival of Sophie, Autumn, and Cassandra. "We're here!" they huff, then let someone else in.

"Lane?"

"Hey, I'm a permanent resident now." She locks the front door and turns the sign back to *Closed*. "We Callaway women stick together, and most of all, we show up for our town."

A series of "whoop whoop" sounds throughout the store. Dean, who'd been in the back, appears and claps his approval while Lane shows everyone upstairs. "You settle on the floor sofas, we'll bring coffee." Sofas? Coffee? What's going on?

"Ms. Angela posted a call to the Bitch Brigade on ECHoes," Lane explains, cheeks bright with excitement.

"I'll bring up a whole pot of coffee and mugs," Elaine says, shooing me upstairs.

"I brought muffins!" Alex calls out.

Once we're situated, Sophie takes over. "The point of this meeting is to show the town what the store and the Callaways mean to Emerald Creek, in anticipation of the town hall meeting. We're going to channel Willow's vision for the windows," she says, making large gestures. "The back of the windows will have a whole backdrop papered with photos of the Callaway generations throughout the ages. The inside of the windows will display everything they sell that is local. Maple syrups, beeswax candles, local jewelry, art, pottery, wine and spirits, you name it."

Chloe's face lights up. "For the deli, we could make little chalkboard signs of the local produce and fresh meat and cheeses."

"Yes! I'm putting you in charge of that," Sophie says. "Who's with me and the history part? I'll be going through library archives, but I need you to call your grandmas and aunties and everyone you can think of, bring out those dusty photo albums and find some pictures of the Callaways. Bring them to the library and we'll blow them up to poster size."

"Love that," Cassandra says. "Willow already has a lot of pictures, don't you?"

I nod while Lane says, "We have tons at home."

Alex rocks her baby gently. "Literally, the store will be the window on Emerald Creek and the larger area. I love it," she says.

"People will walk by and see their own honey, or their cousins' leather gloves, or their neighbor's quilts, or their sisters' wreaths," Autumn marvels.

"Once we explain to them that a chain store won't be doing that, they'll have a literal vision of what could change," Kiara puts in. "Genius."

Tears prickle my eyes. "That's such a great idea."

Cassandra leans closer to me. "This is your vision, Willow. You started this. Like Sophie said earlier, we're only channeling you." She wraps an arm around my shoulders. "I'm so proud of you. But also,

I'm not surprised. You've always been Emerald Creek's little sweetheart."

My heart flutters.

"There's a reason for everything. Noah and you needed a gentle push from the Universe, but you were always meant to be together. You just didn't see it."

I open my mouth to answer that yes, I saw it, I totally saw it, but I think better of it. Not only would this mean going into the specifics of this marriage in public—not advised—but also....

Did I *really* see it, at the time?

Or was I just so convinced I wasn't good enough for Noah, that in his presence I made myself invisible?

"Thanks, Cass," I say, finally closing my mouth.

She takes me in a side hug. "Why don't you go get Lilyvale ready for the home invasion while this town helps you?"

Chapter Forty-Seven

Willow

Before leaving the store, I touch base with Dean and Elaine about the Bitch Brigade's plan.

"Wouldn't dream of interfering with the ladies," Dean says.

Elaine gives me a wide smile. "It's about time my department gets some recognition."

Lane leaves with me. "I can't wait to open up all these dusty photo albums," she says. "But what's this home invasion thing?"

Speaking in hushed tones because we're on the street, I fill her in on Ms. Angela's idea, then lay out the role she needs to play to make it work. I can feel her hesitation, but I know this will be good for Lane. Her coming to the store this morning shows a shift is happening inside her. Taking her mind off her own problems will help further.

And I also don't believe Gail will move into Lilyvale based only on Ms. Angela's word. She'll need some serious coaxing.

Enter Lane.

"I've never hidden the fact that I hate her," Lane tells me when I lay out my idea.

"Frame it differently. You haven't seen her in a while. You've matured. The death of your father brought you and Gail closer, and now you're set to unite with her against me—the intruder. The gold-digger. You could even play on the next generation, and how this whole…" I gesture toward her belly "situation, is making you see things differently."

She pulls a face. "And then what?"

"Then, the fun begins. There's a reason she hated Lilyvale and Emerald Creek." I don't want to say it out loud, in case I jinx it.

The mansion looks at me kindly as we walk up the path to the front door. It's been nothing but warm vibes since I've lived here. For whatever reason, Lilyvale has always been welcoming to me. That doesn't mean she can't feel differently about someone else.

As we brush against the cornstalks Beck attached to the pillars, Lane reads my mind. "That doesn't sound like a safe situation." The front door creaks ominously as we enter.

A small smile spreads on my lips. "How do you mean?"

"Gail is vicious. She's gonna snoop around."

"Let her. We've got nothing to hide." *Well, I might tell Noah to hide the prenup. She could draw conclusions. And that fake-marriage contract we signed too. We can't risk her finding that.*

While Lane goes on her search for photographs, I give Mom a call instead of sending my customary text message. "I heard there's some hoopla going on with that woman," she tells me. "Be careful."

"I'll be fine, Mom. But thank you." It means a lot to me that Mom is finally taking my side.

"Let me know if you need help," she adds before ending the call.

For the next hour, I work from the kitchen on my laptop, following up on our Christmas orders. Our pumpkin-scented garlands of dried leaves are so popular this season we're almost sold out, so I'm ordering double quantity of pinecone-cinnamon-orange rind-evergreen garlands for the holidays. Then I open my Ideas document and type, *Talk to Autumn about offering a Christmas decoration service through the store.*

With a happy sigh, I walk to the office. I've gotten rid of all the heavy, dark-colored drapes—which for the most part, literally fell apart when we pulled them down. In their place, gauze curtains and organdy panels filter the autumn light. Large bouquets of hydrangeas grace each room. Instead of changing the drab looking sofas, I've opted to have them reupholstered in warm neutral colors. Throw pillows in bold patterns uplift the tone of each room.

Noah surprised me by having some of my nature watercolors professionally framed, and although my art is amateurish, it's now adorning several rooms.

Walking down the hallway, I'm filled with joy.

Lilyvale has become my home.

I'm back in the kitchen, making apple cinnamon tea, when Lane comes in, her bottle-green sweater smeared with grayish dust. She places a stack of old photos carefully on the counter.

"I'll do it under one condition," she says. I realize I was almost hoping she'd say no. I'm becoming intensely conflicted about this plan. I instinctively feel how it might work. At the same time, having Gail here feels like a violation.

"Okay?"

"Beck and Griff have to be here. At all times."

That sounds reasonable. "I'll work on it."

"Good luck tying Beck down, and Griff won't come," Noah says, surprising us as he comes into the kitchen. He seems relaxed, looking devastatingly handsome with his three-day stubble, a lock of hair falling on his glasses, flannel open on a T-shirt. "Wanna go for a walk?" he asks me, standing behind me and placing his hands on my shoulders. "You're so tight."

He starts kneading my knots. "We don't have to have her here," he offers. I shake my head, but he continues. "I don't believe it'll make a difference in the end."

"It will," I assure him. Especially if it goes the way I think it will. "We just have to get through this and she'll be gone. Aagh..." I moan as he works a knot where my shoulder meets my back.

"Better? Come on, lets go."

I don't need to change. These days I'm always dressed for a walk. Jeans and hiking boots are my go-to, seeing as I'm on my feet all day at the store. Today I threw on a rust-colored Henley with cute little flowers embroidered down the opening, and a Fair Isle cardigan. You could put me on the cover of a fall magazine.

"I'll go drop these pictures off at the library so Sophie can blow them up," Lane says. "You should go. Enjoy this day."

I follow Noah out the kitchen door, Calla, Maple, Muffin, and Myrtle nearly toppling me over as they rush out. I take a deep breath, enjoying the warm sun on my face. Noah and Lane are right. I needed this, and we should enjoy every day while we can. Even if we get to keep Lilyvale and Emerald Creek intact for the next generations, this particular day will never come back: The swathes of white against the pure blue sky. The deep purple of the asters. The pile of pinecones on the side of the driveway, accumulated by some organized chipmunk.

"I think it's time for Myrtle to move to Alex and Chris's," I say as we reach the curve up the trail leading to the entrance of Emerald Creek.

"Alex seemed to be doing well today. She looked rested. Myrtle is pretty independent from the pack, and gentle. What do you think?"

Calla ambles in front of us, oblivious to the fact we're discussing her daughter. I can rationalize that she's a dog, and that in all likelihood they'll still see each other, but it still makes me emotional.

Noah wraps his arm closer around me. "Let's wait until all this mess is behind us. Just a few more days until we're back to normal."

"How worried are you about Gail?" I ask my husband, squeezing his hand.

He stops and wraps me tightly in his arms. His heart beats loudly in his chest when he talks. "There's more to life than a legacy. There's more than passing things on to the next generation. There's baring your soul to another. There's feeling like you're jumping off a cliff and you're not sure the water is deep enough where you're landing, but what the hell, if I'm jumping I'm holding your hand. There's realizing the best part of the day is seeing my wife's lovely eyes open when I bring her coffee in bed. There's adopting stray dogs, and making love on a staircase, and a million little things that will be forgotten when we return to ashes, but that will have made my life meaningful. This time with you is giving my life meaning."

He loosens his hold on me so he can look me in the eye. "I've never felt so alive than since I've been with you. So yeah, sure, I hope we don't lose *the things*. But as long as I have my people, I'm a happy man. And no one can take my people from me, least of all my wife."

I run a hand on his jaw, cupping his face. "Damn right they can't." A gust of wind twirls leaves around us, the air suddenly cooling. "So, you *are* worried," I say.

He thinks on it, then kisses me lightly. "I'm worried I'll lose my temper. I'm worried I'll use foul language at town hall. I'm worried Gail will try to insult you again. That's all I'm worried about."

The smile that fills me is contagious, and soon we're both beaming like idiots. "It feels like rain," he says as sudden clouds form above us.

"Let's go home."

When Lilyvale appears, Lane is outside, hands on her hips. We unleash the dogs, and they make a dash for her, leaving us behind. As we get closer, we can make out the frown on Lane's face even as she pets Maple.

Chapter Forty-Eight

Willow

"She said yes," Lane calls out to us when we're close enough.

"You look worried," Noah states.

"Somebody has to be! This woman is pure evil. I hate her." Sensing her distress, Maple stands on his hind legs and gives her a lick.

I take Lane in a side hug as we walk toward the house, the dogs tripping over each other as they clamber home. "Not anymore. Remember that for the next few days, you're her ally. She needs to trust you, believe she can use you." The walk and Noah's beautiful words settled my worries. Now I need to make sure Lane doesn't carry the emotions I let go of. "You've got this, Lane. You're not alone."

"Thanks. I know," she says on a deep sigh. "I made a fire in the parlor. Thought you guys might be getting cold," she adds right as fat raindrops plop-plop on the crisp leaves.

"I'll make sandwiches," Noah offers.

Once we're settled in front of the fireplace with our ham-cheddar-apple sandwiches on sourdough, I take my phone out. "I'm gonna text Beck and Griff. Give me Griff's phone number?"

Noah hands me his phone. "Your birthday," he mutters as I stare at the digits locking his screen.

I'm hit with a deep and fuzzy feeling right below my ribcage as he seems to think nothing of the trust and intimacy he just demonstrated. My fingers tingling slightly, I unlock his phone with a smile and send myself their contact cards. Then I create a group text.

Me to: Family

> Hey guys, Willow here. Emergency family dinner tonight, 7pm sharp.

Lane:

> You forgot to mention Cruella will be there

I glance up to smile at her, and get back to the chat.

Me:

> Thank you for this. We will be welcoming your lovely stepmother. Should I call her Mother? I'm not sure about the etiquette.

Griff:

> Sorry, hard pass. I'd have to leave in 3 hours to make it.

Noah grunts.

Noah:

> Perfect, this gives you time to pack your sunny personality and bring it along.

> **Beck:**
> Since when do we want to have dinner with her? And why the fuck at Lilyvale?

> **Noah:**
> Because my wife said so.

I glance up at Noah, and he takes my hand in his and squeezes it gently while Lane smiles at us.

> **Lane:**
> Willow is getting the hang of the Callaway household. I think you're gonna like it.

> **Beck:**
> Are you saying what you think I'm saying?

> **Lane:**
> I'm just saying.

Lane sighs. "Where's Beck anyway?" she asks as she types.

> **Lane:**
> I wouldn't want to miss it

"He's doing some landscaping for the resort," Noah answers.

> **Griff:**
> WHAT THE HELL

"Really?" I ask. I thought we hated the resort.

> **Lane:**
> @Griff at least you weren't asked to convince Cruella she should come and claim what's "rightfully" hers.

"It's a tactic," Noah answers me, his gaze on his phone, talking about Beck and the resort.

Noah: Get your ass here. Time to stop hiding.

Griff: WTF?

Beck: You kinda walked into that one

Lane liked a message

Noah lifts his gaze from his phone. "Well, I think it worked. Let's order from Chloe."

"On it," I say as I text my friend.

"Ugh," Lane says, slapping her phone onto the table. "Gail wants me to go have a *chat* with her." Frowning, she squints at the phone. "She said 'Cocktails at the resort on them' with a bunch of spiders and glass emojis. Uuuuugggggh."

"Cocktails for lunch?" Noah grunts. "She must be in a state."

I succeed only moderately in stifling my laughter. "That sucks, given you can't even have a cocktail."

She rolls her eyes. "My point exactly." Then she looks down to her belly. "Come on, little pea, let's go take down the evil stepmother."

"That's the spirit," Noah says, reaching out to squeeze her hand. "You can do this."

"I know," she answers, tears in her eyes. "I take after you."

Noah pauses for a beat, nods quickly, and says, "Take my car."

My throat a little tight from the subtle family bonding that just happened through our texting, I answer the call coming in from Chloe.

"Do you want family style service?" she asks. "We could do a stuffed turkey breast with a side of morels and fingerling potatoes."

"I just had lunch, but you're making me hungry. Make that two. Or three. The boys will be here."

"Even Griff?" she asks on an inhale.

"Looks like it."

"I'll tell Justin. He was hoping to see him at the wedding, but..."

Yeah, not sure what's going on with Griff. Any other time, I'd definitely bring it up to the Bitch Brigade, see what we know and if there's anything we can do, but one thing at a time.

"I'll bring the food around five. You're on your own for dessert though. Hope that's okay," Chloe says before hanging up.

"We're all set for tonight," I tell Noah. "Just need to know how long Gail will be here for."

"Colton just notified me the meeting is set for tomorrow," Noah says, pocketing his phone.

That's a relief. "No advance notice needed?"

"It's just an informational meeting, so no." He fidgets with his phone. "I should get back to the store for a bit. Dean's knee is acting up with the rain."

I nod. "Before you go," I say, suddenly remembering. "Lane said Gail might be snooping around. Did you put the prenup and the... *other* contract somewhere she won't find them?"

Noah narrows his eyes on me. "Completely forgot about that."

"It would put us in an awkward position if she found them. Especially the *other* contract." The one Noah insisted on drafting, explaining his financial support in exchange for us getting married.

He pushes his glasses on his nose and goes to the desk. Opening the top drawer, he pulls out a sealed manila envelope. "Prenup," he says, waving it in front of me. "Never sent it back to the lawyer." He walks to the fireplace and drops it in.

"Noah!" My heart clenches as the paper hits the embers. "No!" I say. But the paper curls, hesitating, then bursts in flames, throwing a bright light into the room. "Why?"

Noah pulls another envelope and hands it to me. "The contract looking over your interests. I'll put it in the safe. Where's your copy?"

My gaze fixed on Noah, I snatch the contract from him and step to the fireplace.

"Willow!" Noah starts, but one look from me and he quiets as I drop the two-pager in the fire, where flames engulf it.

"I burned mine a long time ago."

Noah pulls me into him for a kiss. His body is vibrating with tension but as I melt into him, he calms down. Then his heartbeat increases as I deepen our kiss, his stubble chafing my lips in a way I can't get enough of.

"I love you more than life itself," I confess when we break the kiss, my lips still skimming his mouth. "You giving me your heart is more than I could ever dream of."

"My little Cinderella," he teases.

His words ignite light laughter mixed with an extra burst of love. I used to take exception to this reference. But I don't anymore. This is my story, and I'm proud of it now.

Ironically, once Noah goes back to the store on account of Dean's arthritis, I ditch the pretty sweater and Henley for an old sweatshirt and arm myself with a rag, wood cleaner, and a cobweb duster. "Come on, Calla. We got stuff to do."

After taking the puppies out for their business, we lock them in the kitchen for the time being, ignoring their cries as we go do grown-up stuff like airing out bedrooms and dusting furniture. "We can't risk having dog poop everywhere. Not right now with Cruella on her way," I say to Calla, needing to justify myself.

I set up Rosalie (the upstairs vacuum robot) and open up the room Gail will be using, per Lane's instructions. Calla raises her hackles and refuses to come in. "Seriously, baby, they can't hurt you," I coo to the dog. But she stays stubbornly rooted at the entrance, sitting on her haunches, whining. "Lot of help you are," I pretend to complain.

The room smells stale, dusty, and downright old. I'll start with the cobwebs and make my way down. "Seems like no one's been in here in years," I say, opening the windows wide, letting fresh air in.

Located at the back of the main house, the large bedroom is equipped with its own fireplace. It has a four-poster bed, period furniture, bronze sconces, and oriental area rugs. I ditch my shoes and climb on an upholstered side chair to dust the crystal chandelier. Luckily the room has no chachkas, which adds to its austerity but also makes dusting a quick task.

Wiping the antique mirror, I'm pleased to notice that we'll be getting the support we need from the other residents in the house. Because my face is not the only one looking back.

"Anybody home?" Kiara's voice sounds from outside, right as the door to the bedroom slams shut. I should have used a doorstop to prevent the draft of air from shutting the door. I grab a chair to prop the door open, and turn around—only to see Elsbeth in all her gore hanging from the ceiling, in the corner between the bed and the bathroom. "Oh man, you scared me. Dude, *yes,* that's perfect."

Elsbeth graces me with a smile, curtsies, and vanishes right as the door opens. "You talking to a chair?" Kiara asks.

"Hey you! What's up?"

"Chloe said you'll need dessert, so I brought some things and figured we could bake together like the good old days? Ooh... nasty," she adds, looking up at the ceiling. "Let me get that." She grabs the cobweb duster from my hands and gets to work right where Elsbeth was. I look at Kiara attentively. She's not seeing her, right? Was I hallucinating? Yet she must be seeing *something*, because I just got rid of all the cobwebs.

"There, that should do it," Kiara says, moving onto the next angle. "What the fuck?" she cries.

I look at where she's staring—on the floor, next to the bed, expecting to see Elsbeth wriggling on the carpet. "Oh, that's Rosalie," I say as I shake the bedspread out the window.

"I almost tripped over that mother fucker. You gave it a name?" She says as she tackles another cobweb-free angle. *Elsbeth better not scare her away. This is a Callaway secret, dammit!*

"We have to, for the apps. We have one per floor. This one's the silent model. You should try it for your store."

Calla starts barking and runs downstairs, seeming content to have a reason to leave the dreaded bedroom. We barely have time to hear Beck's voice in the hallway, when the bedroom door slams again. "Let's make the bed, then we can move onto the next room."

"You guys need cute little aprons and short skirts," Beck jokes as he barges in, holding Muffin in his arms. The pup's legs dangle as he sets his head on Beck's forearm. "Why are these little guys locked up?"

The little guys are now as tall as a Border Collie and close to the weight of a Lab, but I get where he's coming from. They'll always be babies to us.

"They still have accidents," I say as Kiara and I adjust the fitted sheet. "Here," I tell Beck, handing him the pillow covers. "Make yourself useful."

"Yes, ma'am." He sets Muffin down, then punches the pillows inside the pillow covers. "I'll get Griff's room," he tells us once we're done in Gail's. "You guys go do your thing."

"You look happy," Kiara says as she carefully folds the ingredients for a genoise. "Like, *really* happy." We decided on a pear and almond cake—simple enough to make yet impressive to look at and always delicious.

I look at my friend. "I am. Truly am. Sorry to say, but you were wrong," I tease.

"And so fucking glad about it." She pours the batter into a baking dish. "Though I will say, I deserve some credit."

I open the oven for her. "Pff..." She all but made me swear I wouldn't fall in love with Noah. Might have called me an idiot when I confessed it was too late. "Excuse me?"

"Remember that argument we had, when we moved you out?"

Ah. So they were *arguing.* "What about it?" I never clarified that with Noah.

"I may have told him to tell you how he felt about you."

Wait. Backtrack. This was before we slept together. My palms moist, I ask, "And how did he feel about me?"

"Oh, he flat out told me he loved you and to fuck off."

"That's a lie. Noah wouldn't have told you to fuck off."

"True. But he did say, and I quote, 'I'm in love with her.' Also admitted he didn't see it coming. That's how I knew it was true. The kind of love he has for you, it's bigger than anything."

Chapter Forty-Nine

Lilyvale

The girls are the first to assemble, but they gather in the kitchen, where they spent most of their physical lives. It amuses them to see how much easier things are now, yet how louder people complain.

They compare their outfits, the quality of lace in their respective lifetimes, then move onto petty arguing—their way to gauge each other's state of mind. Finally the oldest one acknowledges the live women in the room and says, "I like this one."

"The pastry chef? She uses foul language," the more coquettish of the girls says.

"She has a good heart," her elder by fifty years says—although by her perfect figure and lineless face, no one can tell.

"I like her for our Willow," the one who spoke first explains. "She's a reliable friend. One needs friends like these, especially with what the world has come to."

A faint chorus agrees with her.

"I'm worried about Lane. What can we do to help?"

"I'll be on baby duty!"

A cackle echoes through my hallways. Different opinions on nursing, diaper changes, nap times, lullabies, until someone raises their voice. "What does The First want with us? We can't be having meetings every ten years now. It's disruptive!"

Noah Callaway The First runs the household of spirits the way he did the living. With an iron fist and a vision.

When the grandfather clock strikes four o'clock, he expects everyone to gather. Such a large meeting will go unnoticed in broad daylight, the form of the spirits easily confused with dust mites by unsuspecting living beings. And although time has no significance in this world, The First likes to sharpen his flock's attention to the world of the living. Without his constant care, who knows where Lilyvale and Emerald Creek would be now?

"Call to order!" The First croaks, making the girls jump and glide to the staircase, where the main meetings are held. The crowd of spirits is three rows high and extends as far as their glassy eyes can see, spilling into adjacent rooms, hanging off candelabras. The brownnosers are floating horizontally at the ceiling, hoping The First will notice them.

It's not every day a full meeting is called. In fact, such an attendance has never been seen at Lilyvale.

The cacophony struggles to die down.

"Welp, we've been summoned."

"Nobody says welp."

"Keep up with the times!"

"I'm pleased by the measure of your affection for our beloved Lilyvale," The First starts, his voice like distant thunder hushing everyone. "Times are dire and you are called to fulfil your duties."

"I told Amy what she needed to do!" Elsbeth pleads. "I promise I did!"

"I did like you said!" a distraught Amy answers. "I scared her! And look where we are now!"

"I'd like to have a word with The Sixth," someone in the back whispers.

"Tickling feet is not enough!" Elsbeth snaps at Amy.

"Now, now," The First says in a surprisingly understanding tone. "Sixth is on time-out for this one, and Amy is still learning the ropes." Elsbeth chuckles at his unintended pun. "Everyone else is hereby summoned to do your best. Think about the skills you had in the material world. How can they be useful now? We've let things slip, and it is our duty to amend this."

As The First vanishes from his flock's perception, conversations resume, louder. "I've an idea," The Fourth, who had a long career in engineering, says.

"Amy, you're coming with me this time," Elsbeth orders. "It's time you learned the ropes," she repeats. "Got it?"

"But what are we going to do about Lane?" Amy whines. She's been having a hard time letting go of the living, and she acts as if she were still around.

They all do. It's the way of humans.

Chapter Fifty

Noah

One good thing comes out of all this: Griff is finally back home. "Happy birthday, dude," he says as he steps out of his sports car and takes me in a hug.

"You remembered?" I ask as he lets go of me on a back slap.

He beeps his trunk open, grabs a leather duffel bag and a gift bag. "Isn't that why we're here?"

In a way, I suppose. "Let me show you to your room."

His smile is tight when he answers, "I'm sure I can still find it."

Taken aback, I let him go first.

"If you just tell me which one," he adds over his shoulder.

I grit my teeth. "Beck set you up in the yellow room."

"No shit."

I have no idea what he's talking about, and he doesn't elaborate, so I just let him be. Things were always hard with Griff. He was colicky as a baby, crying for what seemed like hours. As a child, he'd always try to pick a fight with me, and he'd ignore Beck to a point that made Beck insanely mad. But he'd dote on Lane like we all did.

I wonder if he knows she's pregnant.

"Hey, Griff," I hear Willow's voice upstairs.

His low timbre answers. There's a back-and-forth I can't make out, then Willow comes downstairs, her facial expression strained. "Lane just texted," she explains. "They're on their way." She stays in the foyer, wringing her hands, and suddenly I realize this might be too much for my wife. All this pressure.

Getting the house ready—I should have known she'd feel this was her burden to carry.

But mainly, facing Gail again. Why did she go ahead with this? Why did I not see she was placing us first again, instead of focusing on what was right for her?

Griff's footsteps sound in the distance, accompanied by some muffled shouting. Soon Beck and Lane will be here, and I wonder if we'll have a moment, just us, without Gail, before Griff takes off again.

The last time we were together was for Colton and Kiara's wedding. I was too preoccupied to really care about what was going on with either of them, and Griff left that evening.

Before that, was for Dad's memorial at Lilyvale. We were all dealing with our emotions in our own way, and connecting wasn't easy.

"Hey, where d'you go?" Willow asks, bringing me back to the present.

I shrug. "Just thinking how this house was meant for a big family, and how empty it feels most days."

She wraps her arm around my middle and leans her head against mine. "Lane and her baby will solve that for a while. And maybe we could think of another usage for Lilyvale."

"Like what?"

She shrugs. "A history center. An animal rescue. An artists' retreat—"

Before she can continue, the front door opens on Chloe carrying tonight's food. Moose passes her and rushes to the kitchen, and he and Calla start horsing around. Maple, Muffin, and Myrtle follow them in a flurry of wagging tails and sharp yaps, skidding awkwardly on the hardwood floors.

"I think Lane might need help," Chloe says as all five dogs rush out the front door.

A high-pitched shriek sounds. I can tell Willow is biting the inside of her cheeks so as not to laugh, but before I can confirm that Gail just met the dogs, Griff comes stomping down the stairs.

"Where the hell is Beck?" he barks. "I'm too fucking old for his fucking pranks."

"Awww, little sweetheart!" Beck says, coming from the garden through the kitchen to hug his brother. "I missed you too."

Real barking and more human shrieking come from outside, but my attention stays on my brothers. Are they really going to argue this soon?

Griff's gaze stops on Willow. He hesitates, then slaps his brother's back. "You're still a little shit," he grumbles affectionately.

"Someone's got to be."

"Little help here?" Lane says in a small voice as she hoists a huge suitcase up the front steps, while Gail, smartly dressed in a bright pink skirt suit and heels, follows rolling a tiny golden carry-on.

"Ooops, right this way," Beck says as he grabs the suitcase from Lane. "Mama!" he exclaims, momentarily leaving the suitcase aside to take Gail in a bear hug. He swings her around, and we all hold our laughter at the set of muddy paw prints on her back. As if that wasn't enough, Beck ruffles her severe bob before letting her go. "Long time no see!" He singsongs then picks up the suitcase, turns around, and winks at us before going up the stairs.

Griff and I exchange a look, taking a beat too long to figure out our next steps.

Willow and Gail are face to face.

"Welcome to Lilyvale," Willow says, extending her hand. "Make yourself at home here."

Bang! Nailed it. I wrap my arm around my wife's shoulders. "We're delighted to have you," I add, staring at Gail. Pretty sure that long white-ish streak across the front of her skirt is a sling of drool.

Reluctantly, she takes Willow's hand, then quickly releases it, averts her gaze, and follows Lane up the stairs.

"Well look who made it!" We all whip our heads back to the front door, where Ms. Angela just materialized, closely followed by Marcy who looks extremely uncertain.

What the hell?

"Gail! Didn't I tell ya it would go easy peasy?" Ms. Angela pulls on Marcy's long sleeve T-shirt to bring her inside the house. "You didn't meet Marcy yet, did you? Come here and say hello, darlin'," she says, still talking to Gail.

Gail is now unsteadily on the third step, holding onto the railing, her skinny legs wobbly on her spiky heels.

"Don't move!" Marcy says. "I'll come to you. You're quite the little trooper, braving 'em stairs with..." she frowns and bends slightly... "five-inch heels?" She hoists herself to Gail's level, places both her hands on Gail's shoulders, and declares, "We're family now! Come and say a proper hello." Then promptly places a loud kiss on Gail's cheek, takes a step back, looks at her daughter, and says, "What's for dinner?"

Willow seems to be teetering between horror and hilarity. "Stuffed turkey breast with morels and fingerling potatoes," she recites robotically as her mother comes down the steps.

"Welp, you sound tense. I brought some gummies. It's for my pain, but it works for lots of things." She pats the bulge in the pocket of her too-large pants. "Got my stash right here, you just let me know."

"I might need one," Griff mutters.

"What did I miss?" Beck says, returning empty-handed from Gail's bedroom. "What happened to your skirt?" he finds smart to ask Gail.

Ms. Angela claps her hands. "Lane, dear, I think Gail will want to freshen up?"

Lane and Gail seem to unfreeze as they promptly resume the trek that will take them up the stairs, down a hallway, and up another set of stairs.

"Well, I'm gonna leave you to your awkward family reunion," Chloe says, chuckling once Gail is out of earshot. "Moose, come here, boy. We've got lots to tell Daddy."

Ms. Angela snickers. "ECHoes is gonna be warming up tonight!"

Chapter Fifty-One

Willow

"Mother, a little more gravy?" Lane says, taking Gail's plate and loading it with food. She's been playing the part of the doting stepdaughter to a T, and one of the side effects is that Mom is literally and figuratively sticking by my side.

"No carbs, Delaney, no carbs. Carbs are a woman's worst enemy," Gail declares for the third time.

"I'll have just the gravy," Mom states, handing her plate across the table. "The bird is too dry for me. Pour it on that piece of bread, will you, sweetheart?"

Noah smiles at me over the length of the table. We're each at one end, with Gail, Griff and Mom on Noah's right, Lane then Beck and Angela on my right, which frames me with Aunt Angela and Mom as my private security guards.

Gail sniffs nervously, "That's quite a jump in stations for you, Willow, isn't it?"

This again?

My stomach clenches so hard I'm about to throw up. This whole evening has been the most bizarre and stressful and even comical at times but *this*? And in front of *Mom*? How dare she?

Gaze fixed on her, I hold her stare. "I'm sorry—what do you mean?"

"Although," Gail continues, "I suppose you're just continuing the family tradition, right?"

Don't look at Mom. Don't look at Noah. You *brought this mess here. Squeaky wheel. This is* your *battle.*

Droplet of grease.

"What tradition?" Beck asks in the deadly silence. I don't know if he's not reading the room, or if he, like me, wants to push Gail. Have her say it out loud. "Mother?" he insists sarcastically. "Care to elaborate?" He takes a long draw straight from his beer bottle then sits back in his chair. I half expect him to burp loudly, but he spares us.

Noah clears his throat, takes his glasses off.

Not his battle to fight. "Working to pay for your expenses," I say before Noah tries to rescue me. "It can be jarring when you're not used to it."

"So you admit it?" she says, one thin eyebrow raised.

She has the gall to look at Mom, who sits up straight and looks at me with a small smile that nearly undoes me.

I've never been so ashamed of myself. Not of Mom. Not of my childhood. But of myself, for being upset at Mom, for resenting those years with her, for sometimes wanting her gone from my life, for hoping she'd forget me in Emerald Creek while she was living her shitty life god knows where.

For not being able to find it in myself to forgive her for being... who she is. A woman with her struggles, her weaknesses, her lack of support system, trying to cope with whatever shit put her in the situation she was in.

Why does this woman think she can attack her? "Who the fuck are you to speak to my mother this way?" Rage has me clasping my cutlery in iron fists.

My mother's hand finds mine. She taps it softly, forcing me to look at her.

She has a soft smile on her face. "She's just scared of the future. Doesn't think she can handle it on her own. Or maybe she thinks she's past her prime, and she won't catch a man. The things she says about you? They're just what she believes about herself." Turning to Gail, she continues, "Twelve years in the business, I could teach you a trick or two, woman to woman, if that's what you think you need. Men are idiots, you know—no offense," she says to the men at the table "they think women over thirty are old, but did you know that your gag reflex diminishes with age and practice?"

"Mooom!" I cry out while Beck laughs out loud, Griff tilts his head with interest, Lane hides half her face in her napkin, and I don't know what Noah thinks because I am absolutely not looking at my husband in this moment.

"She's right," Ms. Angela confirms, which has Beck nearly toppling over his chair and Griff snorting happily. "And that whole thing about being less tight—absolute nonsense. You have wonderful years ahead of you, dear," she says to Gail. "If you just focus on giving instead of taking, you'll rebound faster than I can say 'Hold my beer.' And I hope the boys at the table won't forget these little tidbits of information."

This time everyone is laughing except Gail and me. "Aunt Angela, we should start a topic in ECHoes," Mom says in between hiccups. "Ms. Angela's wisdom for men."

"Oh—I'll ask Cheryl. She has lots to say on the topic," Ms. Angela answers.

The scene is so surreal I finally find the strength to look at Noah. "Looking forward to our twenty-year anniversary, darling," he says out loud.

"Ewww!" "Gross!" "Get a room!" His siblings shout.

"Welp, I think that's our cue to go," Ms. Angela says, nodding toward Mom.

"But... dessert?" I ask stupidly.

Gail pushes her chair back, nose pinched as she glances coldly at Noah before leaving the room.

We clear the table in no time, send Ms. Angela and Mom home with pear and almond cake, and let the next part of the plan unfold.

Chapter Fifty-Two

Noah

During the night, I stir briefly when the clock strikes midnight, pulling Willow's naked body close to mine. She slides her cold feet between my calves, lets out a contented sigh, and sinks deeper in her sleep.

I'm so proud of my wife.

I had to tame my inner caveman at dinner. He just wanted to throw Gail out of Lilyvale, make her feel sorry for hurting Willow. But who was I to deny my wife her moment?

She was simply spectacular. She used to be ashamed of her mother's past—but not anymore.

At first I was hurting for her. So. Damn. Much. To be insulted in her own house? In front of her own family?

But she awed me, as she always does. As she always has. She stood proud and strong. As she should. And even if no one said anything while she dressed Gail down, she had her whole family's support. You could feel it around the table, the circle of energy, of love.

She truly has become Lilyvale's main... *human*.

When Marcy and Ms. Angela took care of lightening the moment while embarrassing Gail, showing her true colors without being openly mean, I was this close to clapping.

It was the stuff of family legends, stories we'll recount through the decades after the children are in bed, just to relive the moment.

Children. I'm thinking about children with Willow.

She stirs in my arms. "Try and get some sleep," she murmurs. "Everything'll be alright."

I caress her hair off her forehead. Her eyelids flutter, the shadow of a smile plays on her lips, then she's lost in sleep again.

She thinks I'm worried about tomorrow, but I'm not.

I'm not that man anymore. Everything I told her during our walk is true. Although I do care about Lilyvale, about the store, about all that the Callaways have been passing down generations, only the people I love are truly important to me. It may sound obvious, but I'd lost sight of that.

And tonight, with the exception of Gail, they were all around the family table. My wife, my siblings, and the unexpected and colorful addition of *Aunt* Angela and Marcy.

A loud noise coming from upstairs pulls me from my sleepy thoughts.

Then there's a sharp cry.

I tense. Is this what I think it is? Should I check or—

Willow's arm tightens around my chest. "Wait," she whispers.

"Did you hear that?" I grunt.

"Sshh. Yes."

Another loud bang, followed by a longer cry. Willow grabs her phone.

My phone dings. "What are you doing?" I ask, but she doesn't answer.

My phone dings again.

Another bang, another cry, then an agonizingly long silence.

Another ding.

Willow's face is lit by her phone screen, and she starts shaking with silent laughter.

I lean over to read from her screen.

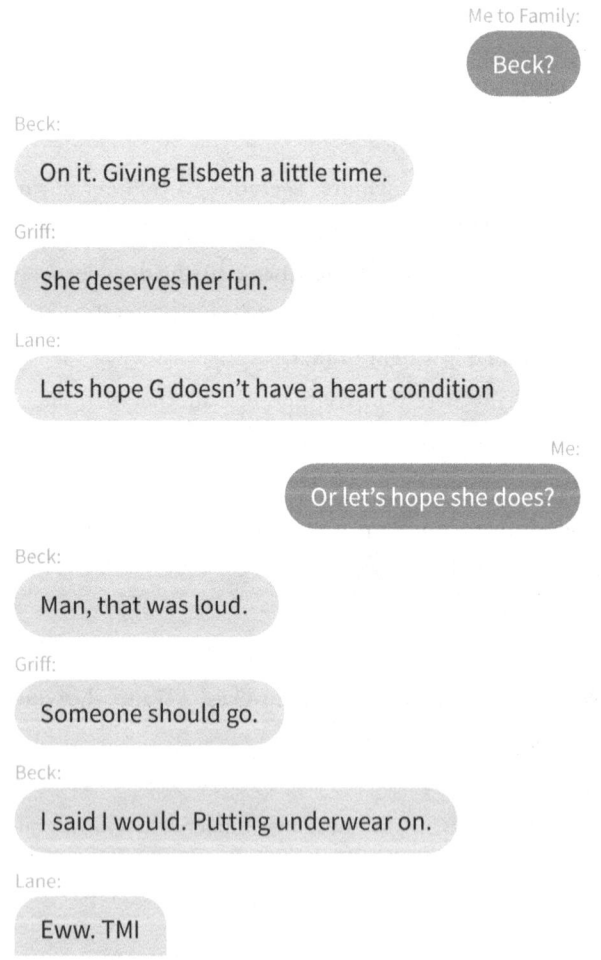

Me to Family:

> Beck?

Beck:

> On it. Giving Elsbeth a little time.

Griff:

> She deserves her fun.

Lane:

> Lets hope G doesn't have a heart condition

Me:

> Or let's hope she does?

Beck:

> Man, that was loud.

Griff:

> Someone should go.

Beck:

> I said I would. Putting underwear on.

Lane:

> Eww. TMI

I rub my eyes. *Only here.*

Maybe I'm wrong. Maybe I can't let this place go and be reduced to a pile of bricks. Because where would *they* go? This place is not just a house.

I dismissed them as the freaky part of our family, and Willow unknowingly showed me the way back to them. "Did I tell you how proud of you I am?"

She snaps her head up at me. "Ssshhh," she says, her eyes all soft on me, her mouth going in for a kiss. The sound of voices coming from upstairs distracts her. She perks up, gets out of bed, and tiptoes to the door, stepping over the nightie she wore for less than two minutes last night. Cracking the door open, she tilts slightly forward, her naked body glowing in the semi darkness.

I put my arms behind my head to admire her as she tugs a strand of hair behind her ear. She looks over her shoulder at me, a big smile on her face.

"It was just a nightmare," Beck's voice sounds in the hallway.

"I don't think so," Gail's shaky voice answers.

"There was no one there, I promise."

"I'm not stupid, Beck," Gail snaps back right as they pass our bedroom. "I saw you standing there in your underwear—"

"Swimsuit."

"Whatever. I *saw* you, just like I *saw* her, up in a corner, with a rope around her neck, and that *fucking* smile."

"That's just not possible, you know," Beck answers.

"It's not funny!" she hisses. "How can you be laughing at me for-for-for seeing a-a-a..."

"A ghost?" he suggests, laughter in his voice. "Come on," he adds, "you're just confused. Let's get you a cup of hot milk and honey."

Willow snorts and gets back in bed with me. "Beck going all soft on Gail." She snuggles on my chest, stroking my shoulder.

A ruckus of loud barking and sharp yaps echo through the mansion. "I guess they made it to the kitchen," Willow whispers.

"What do you have planned there?"

She lifts herself off my chest, looking at me with mock offense. "I didn't *plan* anything. I just... let the household know what was at stake. Dogs are very perceptive, you know."

"Get them off me!" Gail shrieks.

Beck's voice rumbles in the distance.

"Is that poo?"

"Jesus, woman," Willow mumbles, trying to get back to sleep. "Get a grip."

"Ah shit!" Beck yells right as Gail shrieks again.

I muffle my laughter in Willow's neck. "What do you think is happening?"

"Pretty sure Edward encountered dog poop."

"I thought Zach wrote code for them to avoid it." He actually said picking up poop was below a robot's paygrade.

"Stop!!" Beck bellows. "How do you stop that fucking thing?!"

"Sounds like Edward decided it was time for—"

"—shit to hit the fan," Willow continues.

"Sounds like it." With a deep sigh, I pull Willow closer to me, laughing softly at what my brother is dealing with in the kitchen. For a while we hear angry voices, doors being slammed, rummaging in the kitchen that I hope is the sound of Beck cleaning up.

I fall asleep holding my wife close to me, not worried about what tomorrow will bring.

The next morning, Willow and I get up early. We find Griff sitting on the floor of a clean kitchen, cuddling a puppy. "I let them out," he says. "They're pretty well trained. Did their business and came right back in, but they're whiny."

"They're just hungry," Willow says as she pulls out their bowls and I get their kibble.

While we take care of feeding the dogs, Griff makes coffee. "What's this one's name?" he asks.

"That's Maple," Willow answers. "He's our little troublemaker. I'm surprised he let you hold him."

"So, are you keeping them?" Griff asks.

"No! No-no-no."

"But aren't they getting a bit... big?"

"They're still young," Willow declares. "We're not sure about Muffin and Maple yet. There's no rush."

Griff raises his eyebrows and glances at me. I shrug back. If Willow wants to keep the dogs, we'll keep the dogs.

"Myrtle over there will move to Chris's at some point. Skye pretty much claimed her right away," Willow adds.

"Skye... that's Chris's daughter, right?" Griff says.

"That's right. His fiancée, Alex, adopted her, and they had a baby last spring. Ivy."

Griff has missed so much since he moved away. I'm a little sad for him about it, but if that's what he wants for his life, who am I to judge? I used to resent him, be angry even. I'm past that. It's time I rebuild our connection. Time I stop acting like the older sibling slash substitute parent. We're all too old for this shit. I've kept it going for too long, and all it's done was create a wedge between us.

The front door slams shut, the whole mansion shaking. "I'm gonna take a wild guess that your lovely stepmother chose to have breakfast elsewhere," Willow says.

Good riddance. My stomach suddenly growls, and I realize I barely ate last night. I open the fridge. "Who wants scrambled eggs?"

Just then, the kitchen door opens and Lane pads in. "I'll have some, thank you. Hey, I just saw Gail from my bedroom window, hauling her suitcase to her car. Mission accomplished?" She crouches and pets Myrtle. "Come here, you. I bet she scared you last night. Awwww." With a sigh, she adds, "They grew too fast. I can hardly carry them now." Myrtle plops on her back with a goofy grin, and Lane gives her a belly rub.

With a grunt, Calla stands up and goes to sit on Willow's feet.

"We should repurpose the puppy carriage for Calla to pull the babies around town," Willow says.

"What babies?" Griff asks.

"Alex's," I say quickly.

"And mine," Lane says.

Griff frowns. "You... you're *expecting*?"

Right then, Beck barges into the kitchen, hair a mess, shirt open on his bare chest.

Lane turns her attention back on Myrtle. "I was waiting for the right time to tell you."

Griff looks at Willow and me in turn, and we just shrug and smile.

Beck gives Griff a healthy back slap. "Isn't that cool? We're gonna be uncles."

Griff's mouth hangs open for a beat, then he goes to sit cross-legged next to Lane. "That's... that's awesome, Lanie. How long have you known?"

Ah. There's that hint of jealousy, and I get it. I totally do. But he chose to leave. He didn't have to. Yet, as in the past where I'd feel a mix of anger and frustration, today all I feel is empathy for my brother.

Something Beck said a while back plays in my head, about the reason why Griff may have left. Something about it being my fault, more or less. I'll need to address that just between the two of us, before Griff leaves.

Loud screeches sound outside. Calla jumps and barks, a rare occurrence for her. Her hair is standing on her back, her teeth are bared.

"Easy, sweetie. It's only Gail," Willow coos, petting Calla.

I rub my face. "Let me check what's going on," I say.

I step out into the chilly morning, pulling the door shut behind me. Gail is kicking a red Mercedes coupe, her luggage at her feet. Did she lose her key?

"Everything okay?" I ask.

She turns a lethal gaze at me. "Does it *look* okay to you?"

I close the distance between us. "Need a hand loading the car?" At this point I'm not asking why she's leaving.

She points the fob at the car and clicks it repeatedly, but nothing happens. "Who did this?" She's seething, gaze pointed at the car.

"Your fob battery is dead. There should be a manual key lodged inside it."

"I'm talking about *that*," she spits, chin pointing to the car itself.

I take a closer look, my mouth gaping. Through the tinted windows, it's not hard to tell the seats are mounted… facing the back. Like an automotive version of The Exorcist. "Uh…" *Could Beck have done this? Nah. Kids in town? Hard to pull off.* "You locked your car last night?" We don't usually lock anything around here.

"Really? That's your question?"

"Yeah, that's my question, lady." I pull my phone out. "Colt? Any chance you could tow a car from down here and do some... inside rearranging at your place?" He starts telling me about his whole schedule. "It's an emergency," I interrupt him. Turning away from Gail, I mutter, "a mental emergency."

Ten minutes later, Colton pulls up, backing his flatbed to Gail's car. He nods at the both of us, then hooks Gail's car and wrenches it up. Gail is shivering, so I haul her suitcase inside the cabin while she takes the passenger seat. After the car is secured, Colton peaks inside it. With a small smile, he slaps me on the back. "Wicked shit." In a lower tone, he adds, "you'll have to tell me how you pulled it off."

I start protesting, but he cuts me off. "Yeah, right." He laughs and glances in Gail's direction. "See you later."

"You alright?" Willow asks me when we're back in our bedroom, getting ready for the day. The meeting isn't until tonight, and we'll both be heading to the store as usual. "Worried about the meeting?"

"It's Griff. I wish I could get across to him. Know what he's thinking."

"He showed up when the family needed him. That's huge, right?" She places her hand on my chest, in the way that made me lose my composure in the beginning and now makes me feel invincible.

I skim her lips with mine. Running a hand down her back, I bunch up the fabric of her dress and reach between her legs.

"Baaabe," she whines.

"Mmm?" I wrap her tighter as our kiss deepens, our mouths seeming to meld to each other. "Remember how I feel about begging now." With Gail definitely out of here, we have a minute or sixty before the day starts.

"Please," she whispers in my neck, raking her nails against my back.

"Yo! You guys in there?" Griff's voice sounds outside our door.

"Great timing," I mutter for Willow's benefit.

"I love you too," Willow whispers in my ear, her hand still on my chest as if she's cradling my heart.

The room spins around me, the world stops turning, and my dick maintains it's go time. I get lost in Willow's big brown eyes, going down for another kiss.

"I think they left," Griff says as his footsteps recede down the hallway.

"How is it that this thing you do with your hand on my chest turned me on even when we were faking it?" I whisper, kissing her forehead.

Willow's eyes widen. "It's never been fake for me."

She says it under her breath, like a confession, an admission of guilt. And maybe it is, to her. I can see that.

Slowly, the implications of what she's saying become clearer.

Holy fuck.

Willow married me for real when I was just... using her. Respectfully so, but still using her. Every time I'd jokingly suggest a reason for our future divorce and she brushed it off? That was why.

Her strangled "yes" at the river when I proposed with a stupid shoe? The way her voice betrayed her emotions? The beating inside her ribcage when she threw herself at me?

This was not a crush that had turned into something more.

This was *everything*, and again I hadn't seen it.

Pulling my wife close to me, I bury her face in my chest so she doesn't see the tears threatening to spill from my soul. For years she's loved me, and I didn't know. She married me out of love, and I didn't know.

She says it was a crush, but it wasn't.

It was love, and it was given to me without hope, yet without restraint.

Now I understand why she turned me down at first. And why she changed her mind, and how much that must have cost her. And I've seen her with me: honest, brave, kind. Not trying to be more to me than what we had agreed upon.

She made the sacrifice of her heart to help me.

This woman is so much more than I deserve. I'd give up everything to keep her mine.

Chapter Fifty-Three

Willow

Noah twines our hands together as we walk the short distance to the store. Elm street is decorated in full fall glory now, with cornstalks on lampposts, autumn wreaths on front doors, porches overflowing with pumpkins, and window boxes brightened by mums.

"Busses already?" I mutter as I notice a group in front of the store.

"Nuh-huh," Noah says. "That's Nathaniel, and Cheryl, and Sophie, and even Louise. These are people from Emerald Creek."

They're talking among themselves and pointing at... "Ohmygod it's the windows!" My heart flutters as we quicken our pace, emotion seizing me just by the looks on people's faces.

We stand in the back of the small group, but they part ways to let us stand in front. "Ohmygod, Noah, look what they did!"

"That's my momma when she worked here before she got married," someone says, pointing at a photo.

For a moment I get lost in the contemplation of these long-gone times, the people in the pictures becoming alive to me. I recognize family names and buildings that have hardly changed over time. Here, men are cutting chunks of frozen ice at the lake. There, skinny children pose in ill-fitting one-piece bathing suits, girls and boys alike. I imagine this is what looking through a family album must feel like. A sense of familiarity yet difference, that awkward clash between past and present, the measure of time passing, yet so much being the same—emotions, hopes, dreams. All painted in the children's timid smiles, the men and women's stares as the camera captures their everyday lives. And all intertwined with newspaper articles about the store's expansion and yellowed advertisements with prices in the cents.

"Oh that's me!" I can't help but shriek. At the very bottom right, a picture that's been edited to old-timey sepia tones shows me opening the store, looking back on the street with a huge grin on my face.

In front of the pictures, as planned, local pottery, quilts, leather bags, mittens and more are artfully arranged on haystacks and apple crates. The names of the makers are inked on a hand-drawn map of Vermont pinned at the center of the photo display.

"I didn't know Freya sold her candles here!" someone says. "She's my second cousin."

Noah kisses the top of my head and pulls me to the other window. There, meats and produce are advertised in chalk on slate signs, while Dutch ovens, table linen, and locally made plates and mugs yield an invitation for a laid back, comfortable dinner scene. Mini jack-o-lanterns, a doll-size scarecrow, a row of locally made barbecue sauces, jams and chutney complete the homey feel.

But the star of the show is in the back. The theme of this photo display is the store. A historical timeline runs on three sides, from its creation at the end of the nineteenth century to today. Photos of staff and Callaways in work and formal attire make for a fun and varied collage.

The center? It's entirely occupied by a photo of Noah and us on our wedding day, laughing and looking each other in the eye. We look happy. Carefree. Triumphant.

But my silly heart thumps like crazy in my ribcage. Wiping a tear, I turn to Noah. We never talked about ordering wedding photos.

He wraps a strong arm across me, pulling my back to his front. "We look good, right? After this is over, we're hanging this photo at Lilyvale."

I nod, silenced by my emotions. "*We did it*," Noah reminds me in a whisper—the words we had said to each other when this picture was taken, in Vegas. "And so much more, my love."

That evening, town hall is packed when we arrive—and we thought we were early. Noah gives me a quick kiss and heads up to the stage, where the rest of the select board is assembling. I find Lane, Beck, and Griff near the front.

On the other side, standing next to a projector, Gail stares straight ahead. She's flanked by two men in suits. An older one and a younger one. The younger one turns slightly, and I recognize Jake.

Lane goes rigid beside me. Her color drains so fast, my stomach clenches.

I place a hand on her bunched fists and give her a gentle squeeze. "You okay?"

She blinks without looking at me. "Fine."

Beck's jaw tightens, eyes locked on the same man.

"Lanie," Griff says, "there's food back there if your sugar is low," he says, pointing to the back of the room where food is piling up—cakes made by Kiara, finger food by Lazy's and Chloe's Nook. Residents are loading paper plates and assembling for what, for them, might be the peak of the entertainment season. "Want me to get you som'thin'?"

"She's not hungry," Beck growls, his eyes locked on Jake, his fists balled up as well.

"Beck, please," Lane whispers.

Beck clenches his jaw. "It's him, right?"

"Not now," Lane says, pointing in front of us. As secretary of the board, Ms. Angela is taking her spot at the high end of the table where the select board assembles, shuffling papers and plugging in a laptop.

Owen, Cassandra, Lynn, Colton and Noah take their customary seats on the long side of the table, facing us. While Ms. Angela tells them something we can't hear, I struggle to return my attention back to the meeting about to start. Is Jake the father, and if he is and they're not talking, what does this mean?

But then Colton, as chair of the select board, raps his gavel and calls for silence, and my attention is back on this moment, crucial for the Callaways and Emerald Creek. "Alright, guys," he says in his casual manner that just puts everyone at ease, "just a reminder that this meeting is informational. No decisions will be made. There will be no vote as there's nothing to vote on. Let's—"

"Sorry," Owen interrupts, and a general sigh rises from the audience. Owen loves to interrupt Colton. "I just think Noah should recuse himself."

Noah locks eyes with me, smirks, and imperceptibly shakes his head. I roll my eyes at him in understanding. *Effing Owen.*

Colton clears his throat. "There's nothing for him to recuse himself from. We're not voting."

"Right, but-but-but he could be exercising an undue influence, given his position."

Colton shakes his head. "You wanna make a motion, Owen, please go ahead."

Owen puffs his torso at the easy win. "I move for Noah to be excluded from the debate."

That makes no sense at all.

"Who seconds that?" Colton asks.

He's met by silence. Lynn is picking at something on her sweater, Cass is shaking her head at Owen, Noah is just staring ahead at the audience.

"No one?" Colton looks around the table.

More silence.

"Motion dismissed. Alright, Mrs. Callaway?" He turns his attention to Gail. "Someone get her a mic. Great, thanks. Mrs. Callaway, please explain why you called this meeting, in a few words. I think everyone's read your arguments in ECHoes, but for the sake of this meeting, and in case anyone's missed your point," he says, and this is met by scattered laughter from the audience, "please recap the reason we're all here tonight—apart from the food, of course," he adds, his gaze softening as he pointedly looks at Kiara.

Clenching the mic, Gail turns to the audience. "Good evening," she says, a tight smile on her face. "Five years ago, I married a wonderful man—"

"Gail—ma'am, please?" Colton says. "Just the point of *this* meeting."

"Oh right, okay. Well, this person," she says, pointing her finger at me, "is trying to rob Emerald Creek from what's rightfully yours."

The room stays silent. "Hand me the pecan pie," someone mumbles in the back.

"Maybe backtrack a bit, sweetheart," Cassandra intervenes. "Give us some context."

Owen clears his throat. "I think what Mrs. Callaway is getting at, is that the Callaway estate is governed by rules that are currently being bent to the detriment of the town. You see," he says, addressing the audience, "it was the intention of the founders that the store and other assets be managed only if the executor was married, because of the burden of such an endeavor."

"By founders, you mean Noah Callaway The First," Noah interrupts him.

Owen nods quickly.

"My ancestor," Noah adds.

Owen ignores him. "The founders expressly stipulated that if that condition wasn't met, if the successor wasn't married by age thirty-two, then the store should go to the town. Because ultimately the store is essential to the town, and it can't be run by just one individual."

"That's boloney!" someone in the back shouts.

"What do you care, Owen?"

"Is it true you're working with a chain to take over the store?" someone else asks.

"Who are these people with the missus?"

Colton drops his gavel. "Guys, please. Let's do this in order. Gail, now would be a good time to bring up your particular point. I believe there's a presentation planned?"

"Thank you," Gail says and turns her face to a rectangle of light that materialized on the wall, above the select board.

"Someone please kill the lights," Colton says. "Alright, the room is yours."

Grabbing a clicker, Gail starts. The first slide shows Noah on the left, frowning slightly behind his glasses, his arms folded, standing in front of the general store, wearing a freshly pressed white button-down shirt, the creases of his khakis clearly visible. The image is split in half by a torn paper effect, and the right side of it is a picture of...

Is that me? That *is* me. Yup. I'm at karaoke at Lazy's, holding the mic right against my wide-open mouth like I'm about to give head, my eyes droopy by too many beers, runny mascara giving me the racoon look, big hair like I just got electrocuted, short skirt looking even shorter because of the angle of the picture. Pretty sure if Gail zoomed in you could see my panties.

"These two individuals would like you to believe that they are married, and we're here to prove that just because an Elvis impersonator signed a piece of paper doesn't mean they can take away what should be yours."

"There's a lot to unpack there," Kiara whispers my way.

Someone right behind me taps my shoulder. "Did you actually have an Elvis impersonator?"

"Ya forgot to say ya get a big piece of the cake if the marriage's not real!" the same person from before shouts in the back.

"That's right!" someone else bellows.

Gail ignores them and continues. "I have testimonials that neither Noah Callaway Junior—"

"You mean The Seventh," Noah interrupts her.

She looks at him, seeming at a loss.

"Not *Junior*. Noah Callaway The Seventh. My ancestor founded this town. He made the rules for the managing of our estate. And I'd like to think he would have approved of my wife." He leans into the mic and whispers into it as if he's speaking just to Gail. "Would love to have that picture of her, by the way." Then he adds in a normal voice, "But please, continue."

"I have testimonials that their relationship is totally fake." She clicks, but nothing happens. "It's uh... it's a recording of someone who wants to remain anonymous."

Murmurs ripple through the crowd, then the screen crackles and the picture is replaced by a black rectangle for a beat before shapes appear. A door opens, and... puppies bark. That sounds like our puppies, and... That's Lilyvale's front door, captured from the inside. From the staircase?

"That's not... that's not," Gail stammers, waving the clicker at the screen.

The door opens on Noah carrying me through the threshold. My voice comes out, totally sultry. "There's too much happening!" I'm licking my bottom lip, my hand on Noah's chest, looking totally turned on by my husband.

"There's not enough happening," on-screen Noah answers as he kicks the door shut.

I widen my eyes, wondering who took this and where this stops. It can't be the vacuum robots—we didn't have them at the time this was recorded. Thankfully, the shot doesn't follow us to the bedroom.

The screen crackles again and another shot appears. This time it's Noah carrying a piping hot cup of coffee to our bedroom. His voice comes out clear when he mumbles, "Never thought one of the best parts of married life would be to bring her coffee in bed every morning."

A few whistles sound through town hall. Meanwhile, I'm just... flabbergasted as to who took these videos and how.

Gail seems to be with me on this, because her voice gets louder and louder. "Stop it! Who's doing this?"

"Just take out the USB!" Owen shouts.

Gail waves a small object in the air. "I did! Stop that thing!" she yells at the high schoolers.

"We can't!" they say as they look at the screen, where a third clip is now playing.

I'm coming down the staircase, wrapped in a robe, sex hair and puffy lips. The shot is taken from above... Ohmygod. It's *them*. How is that even possible?

I don't have time to think on that because on the screen, Noah comes into view, holding a takeout bag from Chloe's Nook. He puts the bag down and... oh no they didn't. I put a hand on my mouth, my eyes glued to the screen as Noah wraps me in his arms.

Thank god the angle doesn't show my hand sliding down between us... but the shot is sensuous as hell, our kiss deepening as Noah bends to kiss my neck. Our speech comes out unclear this time, but there's no mistaking the heat between us.

Lights flicker in town hall, then get brutally bright for a second before settling on their normal intensity.

My gaze locks on Ms. Angela. She's beaming at Noah, then glances my way, and I blow her a kiss. This was so much better than I ever expected. I'm having trouble containing my nervous laughter.

"Thank you for your presentation, Mrs. Callaway," Colton says, poker-faced. "Are there any questions?"

Gail snaps, "Someone tampered with my presentation!"

Owen comes to her rescue. "Who did you give the flash drive to?"

She spreads her hands. "No one!"

"Must be the ghosts, right, Gail?" Noah teases her.

"Seeing no questions," Colton thunders, "meeting adjourned! Enjoy the food." His gavel rap is nearly drowned out by the sound of exploding conversations, unrestrained laughter, chairs being moved around. Noah leaps out of his chair and lifts me in his arms, placing a kiss on my lips, while Colton links his arm around Kiara, looking at us with a big smile.

Griff and Beck take advantage of the commotion to rush outside unnoticed, while Lane stays inside, arms wrapped around her.

"Free first round of drinks on me!" Justin says in the mic. "Let's bring this party to Lazy's."

Twenty people dutifully volunteer to straighten out the room. The rest grab the dishes, and a happy procession forms from Town Hall to Lazy's. We share food, drink a little too much, and then my husband shouts across the room, "Karaoke!"

Everyone cheers and claps, Justin takes out his karaoke machine, four big guys move the furniture around and set up the small stage, and before I know it Noah says, "My wife deserves to open!"

I take an ultimate gulp of liquid courage and grab the mic. "You asked for this, Callaway. I don't think there's a karaoke version of this, so this'll be a capella."

A few whistles sound. "Here we go."

And I start belting "More" by Phish. Whistles and friendly catcalls die down.

Halfway through the first verse, someone connects the instrumental to the sound system, and Noah joins me on stage.

We fumble some of the lyrics, but mostly we sound awesome, if my tipsy self may say so.

When we're done, Kiara yells, "Damn! My girl can *sing*!"

Chapter Fifty-Four

Noah

I wake up with a faint headache and the smell of coffee tickling my senses. Opening my gritty eyes, I see my wife leaning over me. "Rise and shine, handsome," she says. Why is she placing a coffee mug on my nightstand? Did I oversleep?

She pulls her sweater above her head, revealing her full breasts. "Happy birthday," she purrs, kicking her leggings off and sliding under the covers. Her mouth closes on my dick—the most alive part of my anatomy right now. I rest my hands on her head, not needing to guide her but just enjoying the feel of her silky hair.

My woman knows exactly how to please me.

I hold myself for her and sit up, sliding my hand between her thighs. "You're soaked. Come here." With how wet she is, she'll come in under two minutes.

Not that I'm in a hurry or anything.

She resists my pull, groaning against my dick. The vibration almost makes me come in her mouth. "Babe, I'm close."

She lets go of me with a pop and locks her gaze on mine. "And I said, happy birthday," she orders before going back down on me.

Ah fuck. Bossy Willow will be the death of me. "It's my birthday," I groan.

"Mm-hm."

I hiss, trying to contain myself. "I'd like to come with my wife's tits in my face."

She pauses, looks up at me, my precum pearling on her full lips. "You will," she whispers. "Later." With a smile, she goes back down on me.

Much later, after she keeps her promise to me, we're lying in bed. I'm filling in on the serene and powerful after-sex energy that Willow never fails to give me. It's late, but who cares? The shop can wait.

"Griff is leaving tomorrow," Willow says, running her hand on my chest in that way that I absolutely love, "so I thought we could make it just the five of us for your birthday. That's okay, right? I thought you'd want some quality time. It's so rare to have him."

The way she gets me is absolute perfection. "Couldn't have wished for anything else." I kiss her head, bringing her close to me.

She sighs deeply and adds, "I just need to take Mom shopping. She insisted."

I kiss her forehead, smiling inwardly. *I* insisted that Marcy find an excuse to get Willow outside of Emerald Creek for an hour or two. "That's fine. I have stuff to do at the shop, and then we can all hang out when you come back."

"Then let's get our yoga session in now," she exclaims like that's the best idea ever. "With all the tension from the past few days, we need it."

I want to counter that I just had two orgasms, but I don't.

Thirty minutes later we're in the parlor on our brightly colored mats, and I'm working up more of a sweat than during this morning's sex.

"Downward facing dog," the woman on YouTube calls out. Her dog moves across the camera and settles with a grunt next to her. Calla echoes the sigh while the puppies lick my face, wondering what's wrong with me.

I glance at my wife, looking graceful in her upside-down V figure. The puppies aren't worried about her, and that should be my sign. But she roped me into agreeing to thirty days of daily yoga, and dammit, I'm gonna keep my word.

"Try to extend your legs if you can," Willow says.

The puppies yap and jump. They're *big* now, and their puppy enthusiasm matched with their Saint Bernard size make them a lot to handle. "Almost there, babe. Almost there," I croak, ignoring the pups.

I struggle for a few more beats, until finally the instructor calls for *Child's pose* and I collapse to the floor. "That's my favorite," I mumble. Willow needs to believe I'm getting something out of this. She did put up quite a fight to convince me. Her tenacity should be rewarded.

The pups crawl on top of me, lick my neck, climb up the slope of my back, all the way to my protruding bum. Willow says it's okay that I look nothing like her when doing the positions. Something about men's hips.

Finally the end-of-session music sounds, and Willow switches the soundtracks from the instructor's parting words to Phish's latest live upload while we rest on our backs—a position named after a dude called Sebastian.

More puppy paws, more licking.

"Maple, leave Daddy alone," Willow laughs.

"What the fuck?" Beck snorts, barging in on us. "Dude, I thought yoga was supposed to be hard."

I haul myself up on one elbow. "Wait 'til you try it."

"Not gonna happen. You need help getting up, old fart?" He extends his hand, but I'm not falling for that trap again.

I roll onto my knees and stand up, feeling—I hate to admit—marginally better each day. "I'll be right there," I say.

Griff is waiting for us outside, and we don't have far to go. Everything is ready on the store's loading dock. We just need to make sure Willow won't walk in on us, so we sit outside on the dock, sipping coffee and eating fresh apple cider doughnuts delivered by Kiara an hour ago.

"Good shit," Griff comments, raising his cup of coffee.

"Willow's idea," I say proudly.

"You don't say," he teases.

"Fuck off," I answer with a chuckle.

"Dude, what if she doesn't like it?" Beck asks.

"Shut up," I say. "She's gonna love it." *Right?*

"Yeah, she'll get used to it," Griff says.

I chuckle. "Is that supposed to make me feel better?" I can't believe my brothers are throwing this shit at me now, but at the same time, I've missed that kind of ribbing.

Though to be honest, did we really ever have that?

A comfortable silence stretches between us, one that I want to commit to memory. The fact that they're here for me right now means so much to me, and I need to tell them. "I need to put this out there,"

I say. They both look at me. "I've been sort of a dick to you guys, more often than not."

Griff shrugs and takes a sip of coffee, looking in the distance.

"Dude, come on," Beck says uneasily.

I turn to my youngest brother and don't see the troubled kid who kept me up at night. I don't see the shouting matches or the shameful trips to the police station. I don't see his face bloodied by some fight he decided to pick at The Growler. Instead I see a man who fought his pain the only way he knew.

"I should have been more understanding. Yelling at you didn't help."

Griff huffs. "Course it did. The little shit would have ended up in jail for more than one night if you hadn't done anything. It's not like Dad cared."

"Dad cared," I snap at Griff. I want to tell him he doesn't know how much pain our father was in—he didn't see it. I want to tell him it was the second time Dad lost a wife, but I don't want to lord over him that I was there the first time and he wasn't, or that the second time he was too young to understand. I'm trying to get us to the other side of that.

I need to break the caretaker role.

I need them to be my *brothers*.

"He cared," I repeat, softer. "He... he was just too messed up for the day-to-day." And that's why I had to step in. "That's all it ever was."

Griff sniffs and Beck clears his throat, but neither say anything.

"I took my role as the oldest too seriously, and..." I take a deep breath. Why is it so hard to say the simplest things? "It came between us. And no one is sorrier than I am. Griff, I'm sorry you no longer felt like you had a place here in Emerald Creek. And Beck, I'm sorry you feel like you always need to run things by me. You don't. We're equals."

Beck slaps my back. "Yeah, you're the only one who still thinks I need to run things by you, Noah. Glad you're seeing the light."

I shove him playfully. I've reached the limit of what Beck can handle in terms of an emotional moment, and I get it. "I'll get a call in with Tamberly to talk about restructuring all this. Legally. So nobody feels they need to ask for my permission."

After a few beats of silence settle between us, Griff rubs his beard. "Speaking of, we talked to—what's the shithead's name again?"

My stomach bottoms. If Griff and Beck bonded over something, it has to do with Lane.

"Jake," Beck growls. "He's who got her pregnant."

Fuck. I'd noticed him next to Gail at the meeting. "He used her to get to us." Bitterness fills my mouth. "Gonna be hard to forgive that, but we'll have to—"

"The fucker doesn't want anything to do with her," Griff interrupts. "He'll be signing away his parental rights once the baby is born."

"Say what?" A part of me is relieved, another part is downright outraged.

Beck kicks a pebble off the loading dock. "Said it right to our faces last night."

My heart goes to my sister. "It never ends, does it? Shit way for her to start her adult life."

"She's better off without him," Beck says.

"She just wants peace," Griff adds.

"Then we'll make sure that's what she gets," I say. I'll start by keeping today gentle—no questions, no plans. Just family. Turning to Beck, I add, "How did you manage not to punch him?"

Beck smiles. "Who said I didn't?"

I have to chuckle at that. For the first time in my life, a part of me hopes he did.

We finish the last dregs of our coffees in silence, then Dean pokes his head outside. "Just saw Willow and Marcy drive away!"

No time for second thoughts. We grab the ladders, the large slab of wood, the toolbox, and get to work.

After an hour, we're done measuring and pre-drilling. Lane joins us with a large swath of fabric and the disposition of a field commander. If what happened last night between Griff, Beck, and that asshole Jake affected her, she's not showing it. But I still give her a quick hug before we tackle the fine-tuning of our project.

"A little more to the left!" she cries out. "Now to the right! This right! Beckettttt! To here!" she yells, pointing up. "Not so much!"

Griff grunts under the effort.

"Lanie! Are you sure?" I ask, my shoulders tensing under the effort.

Lane walks to me and shows me the last picture she took.

"Beck, up two inches," I confirm.

"Perfect!" she cries out.

"Fucking building is totally out of whack," Griff says.

"Yup."

We finish our drilling and fastening, get down our respective ladders, and cross the street to admire the handiwork.

"She's gonna love it," Lane states, and I breathe easier. "Now you guys need to go back up there and help me with the draping."

"Holy fuck, seriously?" Beck growls.

"Is that really necessary?" Griff adds.

"D'you want a surprise or not?" she asks me.

I glance at my brothers, seeing the exasperation in their gazes. But this is Willow we're talking about. My wife. If this is the last time I'm going to be a pain in my brothers' neck, I'm gonna make it count.

"It's non-negotiable," I say, repressing a smile. "Sorry, guys."

Chapter Fifty-Five

Willow

Mom keeps going on and on about what a nice man Noah is and how lucky I am and am I sure I'm doing everything I can to make him happy?

Her constant yapping would have gotten on my nerves in the past, but now I get it. She's worried about me. She thinks I'm going to do something to ruin it all and lose everything. This is her way of showing me her love.

"Do you think he'll like it?" she asks of the knit scarf she bought for his birthday. "It's just to show I care and sort of... to say I'm sorry."

I place my hand on her lap, my eyes on the road. "Mom, it's fine. He'll love it. And you two are good. Okay?"

"Yeah, okay. I'll leave it at Lilyvale. You'll give it to him, right?"

"Of course I will," I say as I pull in from the back alley and park next to her car.

"Do you want some apple cider before going home?"

"Home?" she asks, suddenly looking a little lost. "No, but I'd love to walk to the store with you."

I'm impressed by Mom's stamina. "Let's go!"

As we turn onto Elm Street, the crowd in front of the store worries me. "What's going on?" There are even more people than yesterday, when the new window displays were up. Could it be because of last night's meeting? Did they come to show support?

"Oh, they're probably just looking at your beautiful windows. Wonderful friends you have there."

"No, they're not looking at the windows. They're... they're looking at us!" Self-consciously, I look down at me, then Mom. "What's going on?"

Right then Noah detaches himself from the crowd, walking toward me with a huge grin. "Close your eyes," he says, covering my eyes with his hand as he takes me in his embrace and walks me closer to the crowd.

Murmurs die down.

"What seems like a long time ago," he says loud enough for everyone to hear, "a woman whose wonder I was about to discover told me a lot of things about love and life and entering the Callaway family. I've memorized them all." He takes his hands from before my eyes, and I meet the expectant gazes of all my friends, and the entire town assembled behind them. "One of the things she said seemed... whimsical." Scattered laughter sounds through the silent street. "She said," and he points to the top of the store, where a flannel sheet is spread across the whole length of the building, "that the store should have a name."

Beck and Griff are each holding a corner of the flannel, looking at us with huge grins.

He named the store? *Finally.* I jump with excitement, wondering what Noah came up with, even if a part of me wishes I'd been part of this conversation.

He glances at me with a dreamy smile. "Specifically, she said the store should have my wife's name."

I gasp as he continues, "Ladies and gentlemen, I present to you..."

The flannel drops, "...Willow's Whimsy!"

My hands fly to my mouth, my heart pounding in my ribcage. The sign is a beautiful bottle green, with the name in gold cursive brushstrokes. Looking closer, I even notice a paintbrush dangling from the last letter, with a... a young girl holding the brush as if she had just finished painting the name!

I jump into Noah's arms, laughing loud with more happiness than I've ever known. As he twirls me around, I get lost in his eyes, then focus on the people of Emerald Creek—our family and friends—clapping for us.

"I need you up there, now," Noah says, taking my hand and walking through the crowd to the entrance of the store.

A red and black plaid ribbon closes the entrance. Cass hands me giant scissors. "You're opening the new store, Willow!" she tells me with a huge smile.

"Pause and look at me!" Alex cries out, her phone in her hand.

Noah, Griff, Beck, and Lane are lined up right in front of me, with Mom and Ms. Angela by Noah's side. Tears prickle my eyes, and my lip trembles as I take in the immense honor they're bestowing on me.

But I'm not going to pretend I don't want this or that I don't deserve it. The store feels right for me. Lilyvale feels right for me.

I found my home and my home found me.

With a big smile and tears of joy, I cut the ribbon.

Epilogue

NOAH

The following spring

I set a mug of coffee on my wife's nightstand, kiss her temple, and walk to our bedroom window.

It's already open on our gardens and the village beyond—Willow likes to sleep to the sounds of nature. As the sky turns from mauve to baby pink, mist rises from the river, shrouding the morning beauty in mystery. Calla trots through the gardens, now dashing to the barn as it opens on Maple and Beck. The dogs horse around while my brother admires his work.

He truly outdid himself, turning Lilyvale into a fantasy that would put any botanical garden to shame. He's been planning this since last fall, when he moved shrubs and planted hundreds of bulbs. Then he resumed his work after the thaw, adding perennials and annuals in strategic places.

Now Willow is getting her fairytale wedding (or vow renewal, to be exact) in the spectacular setting of Lilyvale.

Meanwhile I worked with our friends to plan a party for the whole town where Willow wouldn't have to worry about anything. She kept saying she didn't need that, but she's a Callaway, dammit, and she's getting her fairytale "wedding" at Lilyvale.

Even the ghosts are excited. Last night the women were in their best attire, giggling amongst themselves. And some of the men appeared to me—a first—nodding with respect. I felt a burst of pride.

And peace.

Willow wraps her arm around my middle and leans against me. "Hey you."

I pull her closer to me as she takes a sip of her coffee.

"I don't know what to say," she says, emotion raw in her voice. "Look, even the roses are blooming."

"'Course they are." It's as if I can sense Mom's presence today, and I know she's here with us.

"It's even more beautiful than in my wildest dreams," she whispers. "See, it's perfect. We'll be saying our vows looking at the river and the mountains and with Lilyvale at our back."

"Lilyvale will always have our back," I say, smiling into her hair.

We're having the ceremony on the patio, with guests overflowing in the garden, and the party will spill down onto our riverbanks. Tents are already up, tables set. An archway of flowers intermingled with fairy lights leads from the house to the water.

Throughout the garden, Beck built out small garden nooks that we're using for beer and cider stands, creemee stations, s'mores nooks, and even a tiny cheese-and-charcuterie cabin.

"We should get ready, Mr. Callaway. The ceremony's at three, but you know how it is…"

"Yup." Half the town is already trickling in to help, and the pre-party is already started.

Beck's voice wafts up to us. "What are these little burlap bags?"

"Don't touch!" Ms. Angela answers him. "They're maple candy favors, and you'll ruin your appetite."

"Yo! I'm making breakfast," Griff barks, his voice sounding through the garden and inside the house.

Lane's baby, Wren, lets out a piercing shriek. "Better get used to it," Lane says from somewhere down the hall. "No sleeping with the uncles around."

I hold Willow's hand in mine as we walk up the aisle to our spot next to Ms. Angela and turn to face our assembled friends and family. "We weren't sure how a vow renewal is supposed to work," I say, "so we're going to do this our way." I look at Willow, and she encourages me with a smile. We discussed what we were going to say, and she wanted me to be the one to deliver the message.

"It didn't feel right for us to have Willow walk down the aisle. Or for me to be waiting for her up here. After all, this isn't a wedding. This is just an excuse you all wanted to throw us a party."

Laughter ripples through the garden. "And thank you for that. Thank you to all of you for making this happen." Willow smiles and nods, and Ms. Angela straightens, ready to take over with her part of the ceremony.

But I signal for her to wait, and with a tightening throat, deliver a part of the message that Willow isn't aware of. "But as we all know, Willow is who made us happen. It wouldn't be right for me to be waiting for her up here. She's who loved me all along. Silently. Quietly." I slide a finger under my glasses to wipe a tear. "Too quietly."

The assembly has gone eerily silent, and it feels like even nature is holding her breath.

"Luckily for me, she decided to claim what was meant to be hers—my heart. And Lilyvale."

A chorus of awws echo throughout the crowd. "Hey, that's my part," Ms. Angela jokes, taking our hands in hers. "Look at them," she says to the audience. "Aren't they just perfect for each other?"

"Woot! Woot!"

"We know these two were meant for each other. We just want to hear it from them." She turns to Willow.

My wife's deep brown eyes set on mine, and she's all I can see now. "Noah, ever since I can remember, you've been my rock and my protector, even when you didn't know it. I think I've always loved you, as long as I've known you." She pauses, and I can hear my heart pounding. "I didn't think I'd ever..." her voice breaks a little, and she takes a beat. "I didn't think I'd ever become your wife, but..." Now her chin is wobbly, and I can't stand to see her like that.

I caress the tremble away. "But?" I whisper to encourage her.

She takes a deep breath. "But it's..." Tilting her head, she says just for me, tears in her voice, "it's been the best year of my life." She shakes with nervous laughter and joy, and I wrap her in my embrace.

"She said he's on probation, and if he makes it, we'll have another party next year," Ms. Angela shouts to the audience.

While everyone's laughing, Willow whips her head toward Ms. Angela, her mouth rounded in a shocked O.

I lift our joined hands in the air. "Challenge accepted!" I boom.

"You're supposed to renew your vows," Ms. Angela quips from behind us. Then in a lower voice, she snaps. "This isn't a joke, you know."

It doesn't matter that *she* just made a joke at my expense—she's right. Turning to face Willow, I take both her hands in mine. "It's been the best year of my life too," I start, then forget the words I was supposed to say.

"This is when you reaffirm your wedding vows," Ms. Angela whispers.

Right. "Since we became husband and wife a year ago, my feelings for you have grown immensely. I couldn't be a happier man, and it would be my honor to cherish you for years to come, be by your side through the seasons of our lives, and help you through whatever trials might come our way. I truly don't deserve you, and every morning I have to pinch myself." I take a deep breath. "So, this is me. What do you say?"

Willow jumps into my arms, and I swirl her around. "I think we're good for another year!" I shout to the audience. Half of them are laughing, half seem to be wiping away tears.

"And this concludes the feud between the Callaways and the Fontaines!" Ms. Angela declares.

I set Willow down carefully and turn to her. "The what now?"

She spreads her hands. "The Feud! which started when a Fontaine set fire to the house that used to stand here, then continued when the Callaways stole—"

"Enough!" Willow and I both shout at her.

Ms. Angela rears back at the power of our words. "It's just like I said. It's over," she says quietly, her eyes rounded at us like we're a pair of lunatics.

And although this is not a wedding, all our friends cheer and clap as we walk between them to get the party started.

Willow stops us on the way to give Beck a long hug. "Thanks so, so much for all your hard work. You're the best gardener ever. I can't wait to see what you do with your landscaping business." She looks him in the eye, and he smiles briefly before letting her go. "Something wrong?" she asks.

"Nothin'."

He takes me in a bear hug and slaps my back. "Happy for you."

"You do realize we've been married a year, right?"

Another shrug. "But were you really?" he teases before leaving.

"What's up with him?" Willow asks once he's out of earshot. "He's been acting weird all day."

"You haven't heard?"

"No!?"

I take my time savoring this little piece of gossip that has my brother's panties in a tizzy. "You know how the resort heard about the décor he did here for us today?"

"Yeah, their events person was even touring our gardens this morning. Can you believe it?"

I nod. "They want Beck to work on some of their high-end weddings. And guess what?"

Willow smiles at me with amusement. "You're turning into Ms. Angela, you know that. Keeping all your gossip close to your heart, dripping information in episodes." Her smile turns into full-on laughter, a sound I will never tire of. It's the sound of life.

I pretend to ignore how stupidly happy she makes me just by laughing, and focus on delivering the payoff. "He's been asked to do a winter wedding—think Christmas and wedding all rolled into one—for.... drum roll...other drum roll...oth—"

"Oh come on! I'm growing old here."

I smile at her words and cup her cheek. "You'll be a lovely old Willow."

She rolls her eyes. "And you'll be sorry if you don't tell me—"

"Jules," I say under my breath.

Willow gasps. "No... Jules is getting *married*?" Her eyes round. "And *here*? But... *why*?"

I glance at my brother. "You're missing the point."

She gasps. "I haven't *gotten* to the point yet." She looks at Beck and stifles her laughter. "She does know he's going to ruin it, right? He can't help himself."

I look down at my feet, shaking my head.

"Wait. Does *Jules* not know he's involved?"

"I doubt it. There's no way she's getting anywhere near him after what he... well, after what happened."

It was back in Beck's inglorious days. The town had been divided into two unequal parts after what happened: Callaways one side; everyone else: other side. It was the only time the whole town was against us.

And it was all because of Beck and what he did to Jules. You'd think he had hurt her or something.

Not at all.

Ironically, for once he was just trying to help.

And now he'll be staging her wedding? I lock eyes with Willow, and we start laughing hysterically.

Didn't get enough of Noah and Willow? As a thank-you for signing up to my newsletter, I'll send you an extra chapter! Click here or scan below:

Acknowledgments

As the Emerald Creek series illustrates (I hope), I'm a firm believer that we are nothing without a village to support us. My village is the indie writing community at large. You are simply the best. From simply being there for encouragement, to sharing your knowledge freely or supporting each other come pub day, you rule.

I'll be eternally grateful to Angela James for sticking with me through the writing of How to Fake a Husband. For no reason that I can explain, this book took a while to shape up. I can picture her puzzled look as I sent her a glob of chapters that made sense only to me. But as I was climbing the steep mountain leading to The End, I just needed Angela to hold the manuscript for me while I caught my breath, and her expert guidance to stay on the right trail. I'm truly sorry for the work this one was—but also, we did have a few good laughs, so there's always that.

Thanks to Grace Wynter for polishing my prose and to Teresa Beeman for her scrutiny right before release day! These ladies are amazing at their craft. Any remaining awkwardness is a result either of my own stubbornness or oversight.

All you advance readers—you rock! Thank you so, so much for helping spread the word about How to Fake a Husband in advance of its publication!

And to my husband who believes in me more than I believe in myself: thank you for putting up with all my doubts and weird hours, for being my biggest cheerleader, and for joining the team of proofreaders!

About the author

Bella Rivers writes steamy small town romances with a guaranteed happily ever after, and themes of found family and forgiveness. Expect hot scenes, fierce love, and strong language!

A hopeless romantic, Bella is living her own second chance romance in the rolling hills of Vermont. When she's not telling the stories of the characters populating her dreams, you can find her baking, hiking, skiing, or just hanging around her small town to soak in the happiness.

Her newsletter is where Bella shares progress on her writing as well as sneak peeks into upcoming books, the occasional recipe from her characters, and books from other writers she thinks her readers might like. You can also find her and interact with her on social media. To subscribe, browse her books, follow along on social, or get in touch, visit www.bellarivers.com

Made in United States
Cleveland, OH
16 February 2026